Secret of the
NORTHERN LIGHTS

Secret of the
NORTHERN LIGHTS

Eugenia Nick

gatekeeper press™

Columbus, Ohio

The views and opinions expressed in this book are solely those of the author and do not reflect the views or opinions of Gatekeeper Press. Gatekeeper Press is not to be held responsible for and expressly disclaims responsibility of the content herein.

Secret of the Northern Lights

Published by Gatekeeper Press
2167 Stringtown Rd, Suite 109
Columbus, OH 43123-2989
www.GatekeeperPress.com

The cover design, interior formatting, typesetting, and editorial work for this book are entirely the product of the author. Gatekeeper Press did not participate in and is not responsible for any aspect of these elements.

Library of Congress Control Number: 2021936929

ISBN (paperback): 9781662912023

PART I
THE BEGINNING

Chapter 1   October 18, 1887

The soft white snowflakes that fell outside the window of my log cabin created a beautiful winter scene. It was October, yet the snow had already started to fall. I experienced a sudden urge to be a part of this beauty. To merge in with the white. To be invisible. My long legs took me outdoors, and I turned and swirled in the descending snow. I stuck out my tongue to unsuccessfully catch a few snowflakes. The crisp scent of a first snowfall filled my nostrils. The scent in the air was that of logs kindling in the hearth. A stiff wind tore at my black skirt. I caught at it with my reddened, chapped hands. I should have put on some gloves.

The first snowfall of the year was a time of splendor and hope. I stopped in my reverie and peered into the morning shadows of the dark forest in front of me. Did I hear a lonesome wolf howling? Perhaps those were just the trees moving to the new winter breeze. I turned to head back into my small one-room home. It looked like a photo from one of the magazines I had brought in from town, perfectly nestled in between two gigantic pine trees with a small half-dried, half-flowing brook to the right of the dark green front door. My home, as some would call it, with its perfection on the outside, barely mirrored the loneliness and emptiness I often felt upon entering.

Sighing, I trudged back into my cabin. Bobick, my faithful dog, jumped around my feet. Mary-Louise had given me Bobick as a gift before she had left. He was a relatively young dog. My future lay like a blank slate before me. I wondered many times if I should have gone West with Mary-Louise and her husband. She had offered it, but they had just married, and I did not feel like troubling her. She had done enough for me.

She had found me on the Maine Harbor when I was five years old, all alone, with nothing but some food and a travel pack. In the travel pack, she had discovered a black and white photo. The photograph's back read: *Mark, Lubov', and Anna: Fort Yukon, Alaska, 1874.* I was the little girl in the photograph. My eyes looked back at me from the photo, two large black wandering pools. What was the cause behind our separation?

It is unknown how I became detached from my parents; I do not remember the day that Mary-Louise had found me. I wondered much about this unanswered question, and I dreamed of going to Alaska and finding my family. Mary-Louise had found me in southern Maine, and I had never returned to Alaska. Mary-Louise, after a fruitless search for my parents, had moved north with me. She had been on holiday in southern Maine on the harbor when she discovered me.

The whereabouts of my parents remained a mystery. They had likely given up their search for me. Twelve years had passed since that time. Mary-Louise had made inquiries year after year but never found a trace of my family. I frequently wondered what my parents had been like and what their reasons were for leaving me on the seaport. I could not believe that their actions had been intentional, as some people had suggested.

Yet here I was, in the year 1887, all alone. Perhaps I should have gone with Mary-Louise? I had no future here. I wanted to go to Alaska. That is what had stopped me from leaving Maine. I saw no way of getting to Alaska from Kansas. The elusive truth haunted me.

I loved them, even though my only connection was a photograph. My mother was beautiful. My father was tall and looked strong. In the photograph, I sat between my parents. My mother's name was

Lubov', which I had discovered stood for 'Love' in Russian. What a beautiful name. I liked my name also, Anna. It was such a soft name. I wondered if it genuinely fit my appearance or my personality. My father was a handsome native man, and my mother a beautiful white woman. Marriages such as these were not looked upon favorably. How had the union come about? I had black hair and eyes that were the color of charcoal. My skin was olive-colored. Many people thought I was an American Indian.

Bobick bounded around my legs as I sat down on my pinewood stool. I leaned over to pet him. At the moment, there was not much I could do to improve my situation. I was alone with my dog, almost penniless. I could not afford transportation in any way. I had to keep alive by trapping animals for fur. Two years alone had made me withdrawn. Sometimes I enjoyed the isolation. Seclusion had become my ally, my solace. I was not sure if this was healthy. Mary-Louise had homeschooled me since the local school did not accept natives. Now I lived in the Maine wilderness, five miles from the nearest town.

"I have to save money, Bobick," I told my dog, who had calmed down and lay at my feet. "Perhaps we can go next year." Bobick pushed his wet nose up against my hand.

I had not gone to town for a while. Most of the time, I traveled to town once a week. The summer months kept me in full stock, and I did not relish traveling to town. All of those staring faces, wondering who I was and what I wanted, made me uncomfortable. However, I was getting low on food supplies, and I needed to bring my summer stock of furs in for a profit.

Later that afternoon, I put on my heavy winter boots and my coat. The weather had not turned too cold, yet I knew how uncomfortable it would be to get my shoes wet. My traps awaited. I doubted that I had caught much; traps were better off in the winter. I wondered what the exchange rate would be this year; the rate needed to be fair to buy anything in town.

Darkness was settling in around me as I came home from collecting animals from my snares. The unsuccessful day created exhaustion and hopelessness within me. I had only several furs stored up. I owned my trapping trail; no one shared it with me. I skinned the animals and cleaned the furs. I would have to take what little I had from my cellar the next day to town.

Weary from the long day, I readied for bed. I said prayers and lay down. In the twilight of sleep, I dreamt up ideas of how to get to Alaska. I decided I needed to save money and put it away for safekeeping. If I gathered enough, my journey could start. I longed to travel by train. However, I needed money for the train fares and for the hotels along the way. Would I ever be able to set aside a sufficient sum? I was impatient. I desired to reach Alaska right then and not have to wait a year, two, or even three. I could be twenty by the time I achieved my goal. I turned over on my side and snuffed out my candle.

Early on the following day, as the sun displayed its light beams along the crystal earth that now lay covered with light snow, I made preparations. I tied my furs to my one-person dogsled. My furs would not be enough to get me what I needed for the winter. I would need to travel to town quite a lot this winter if I wanted to have sufficient supplies and save money to find my parents.

In about an hour, I arrived in the town. It had grown over the last two months, and I was surprised at the many new buildings that seemed to have popped up overnight. Townspeople, even though it was early, surrounded the trading post. Many inhabitants of the town traded furs for money. Early mornings gave them the opportunity of purchasing different items at the small posts or shops set up along the busy street. I looked at the tough, burly men who stood in line. I never liked trading furs. It appeared to me that I was invariably the lone woman at the trading station. There were many children there, but no women. I stepped into the shorter line.

After what seemed like an eternity, I found myself in front of the tradesman. "How much per fur?"

The man who stood there gave me a strange look; he was new. "Ten cents."

I looked at my little pile of furs. Ten cents a fur would not be enough to buy what I desired. I traded my furs and only got two dollars for them. I thanked the man and walked down the street toward the general store. Some people would allege that that amount was a good deal, but this type of money only covered minimal living expenses. How would I ever lay aside enough money to move to Alaska? I dragged my feet as I made my way towards the store.

I tied Bobick to a railing outside and stepped towards the entrance. A small bell rang, signaling my entry. The sound reverberated through my mind. Fortunately, only one person stood in the store at this time, and he stood behind the counter. I removed my hood and let my long black hair fall about my shoulders. I pushed wisps of hair out of my eyes.

The young man behind the counter was tall and had wide-set muscular shoulders. He had dark skin, dark brown hair, and blue eyes. He appeared to be an American Indian. However, I remained unsure of his ethnicity due to his blue eyes. I shrugged. I was about to ask him if he had any of the items that I needed when the bell rang again.

I turned to inspect the person that had entered. A pretty young woman with bluish eyes and short curly brown hair walked through the doorway. She had on a shiny white fur coat. She was thin and walked as if she owned the town.

The young man smiled. "Hello, Mary."

She was beautiful. I wondered if I heard a hint of annoyance in the man's voice or if I just imagined this because I had an instant dislike of the girl.

"Hello, Alexander, how are you? I'm just fine, I just needed a few things for myself, and then I'll be running along." She plowed through the conversation without giving Alexander a chance to answer.

"All right, what would you like?" He seemed relieved that she needed just a few things.

The young woman glanced back at me. "Oh, it's so warm in here, Alex. Have you paid heed to her?" The girl regarded me as if I had simply come through the ceiling.

The young man looked at me and then turned to her. "No, but what do you want?" I was hurt, and I felt left out. The young woman was beautiful, but I had arrived first.

"Oh, I need some sugar and, oh, some peppermints." Peppermints! How I yearned for them. However, after surviving two years in the wilderness, I recognized that I did not need the candy to pull through.

"How much sugar?"

She tipped her head to one side. "How about two pounds?" I had the urge to ask her what she needed with two pounds of sugar, but I kept silent.

"What do you need it for?" Alexander asked as if reading my thoughts

She smiled up at him. "Oh, how silly of me, I forgot to tell you, I'm baking a cake." Had she been planning to tell him that she had wanted to bake a cake? I was confused about the girl's train of thought. I just shrugged to myself and wondered how she managed to stay so thin.

"Oh, well, have fun baking it," Alexander responded with a smile. It did not look genuine.

She laughed. Her laugh grated on my nerves. "It is great fun. I love it. Joseph says that my cake is probably the best in this whole county." There are not that many people in this county, I thought.

"I didn't know it was so much fun to bake cakes," Alexander replied. He sounded rather bored. Nonetheless, he grinned and added, "I'll have to try it sometime if Joe likes it."

She giggled. "All right, come over any time."

I was about to depart this ridiculous scene and find another store when the girl turned to Alex. "Do you suppose she speaks English?" She fluttered her eyelashes at him and then nodded towards me.

Alexander gave a slight wave of his hand. "I don't know."

I felt the heat in my cheeks.

The *wonderful* girl continued to speak. "She looks so foreign and not at all gentle."

I felt as if I wanted to throw all the peppermints in the store at her. Now, who did she think I was, a barbarian from the untamed wilderness? I wondered if the young man felt the same as me.

Alexander gave the girl a secretive smile. "Well, if she does speak our tongue, perhaps we shouldn't say anything mean about her." I was counting in my head to keep calm. It was clear Alexander preferred her to me. They both then looked away from me.

"How many peppermints would you like?" Alexander asked.

"Five bags should be enough."

Alexander gave her a shaded look before reaching for a shelf to get the peppermints. "Definitely."

The girl just laughed once more. "Don't look at me with such strange eyes, Alexander. Obviously, I'm going to need candy while I'm painting. Art makes me so hungry." Oh, obviously, I thought. I knew that I would never leave the store if this meaningless conversation between this girl and the young man continued.

"Excuse me," I said in a loud voice and stepped between Alexander and Mary.

"I am a customer, and I do need to get going, even if I look quite barbaric and can't speak English."

"Of all the rude... oh Alex, how can you let her say that?" the girl crooned. I glared at her in response.

Alexander turned toward her and gave her an apologetic look. "Well, she was here first. I'm sorry, Mary, but I'm at work now."

Mary looked exasperated. "Well then, I shall tell my father about this. I'll see you tomorrow Alex, and not before that!" she exclaimed and walked out, shutting the door none too gently.

The young man looked at me with remorse. "I'm sorry about the delay. I apologize if we embarrassed you."

"It's quite all right, really. I just have to purchase a few things and then head home."

"Well, what would you like?" His voice sounded kind, but he seemed to have a certain abruptness about him.

I worried that I did not have a sufficient amount of money. "How much are the dried vegetables?"

"Twenty-five cents a bag." He looked up at the clock as he answered. Irritation filled my mind. He did not have to be so open about his impatience.

The price made the room swirl and turn about me, twenty-five cents a bag! "The prices have gone up, haven't they?"

"I can drop the price if it is too expensive."

I tried to laugh. "No, no, it's quite all right; maybe I can be like that girl who was just here and leave without paying."

He managed a wry smile. "Her father owns this store."

"Oh, I see. I'll take two bags then. I also need a new trap for small animals and some fresh meat."

He turned to the shelf behind him and pulled out the items. With a smile, he turned to face me again. "Here you go."

I took my purchases from him and balanced them in my hand. "Thank you, how much is it?"

Alexander raised his eyebrows at me. "Well, how much do you have?"

"Two dollars." The amount would not be enough to obtain the materials I wanted.

"Good, you're in luck. The purchase is two dollars," Alexander replied. His voice sounded a bit too enthusiastic. I suddenly figured out his trick.

Anger boiled up inside of me. "No, it is not two dollars. You're lying. I know your trick. It's more, isn't it?" I was not a candidate for charity yet.

He grinned. "Take it; it's a good offer." I had a feeling that he was laughing at me.

"Well, all right, just make sure not to get in trouble for selling goods at a lower price." I left the two dollars on the counter, took my purchases, and walked towards the door.

"Aren't you going to say goodbye?" he asked.

I turned to look at him. "I wasn't going to, but I'll say goodbye if you insist."

He laughed. "I insist, goodbye!"

"Goodbye," I muttered.

"What's your name?" he called after me. He was making fun of me, but I did not like him. He had treated me rudely. I felt as if he had made a deliberate attempt to make me feel underprivileged.

I paused at the door and turned back to Alexander. "There is no reason for you to know my name." The bell rang behind me as I stepped out of the store.

Out on the street, I wondered why he had wanted to know such a useless fact. I walked along the cobblestones, and I peered into the small shops. Many women walked by dressed in pretty dresses and wrapped in decorative shawls. They reminded me of the Christmas ornaments Mary-Louise used to hang from the tree. For the first time in my life, I longed to look like these women. Indeed, I looked grubby in comparison. The experience at the store had left me flustered.

All the town girls had an air of grandeur about them. Some girls even had fur necklines on their coats. I wore my oversized fur jacket, a plain warm shirt, and a large gray skirt Mary-Louise had given me. I carried my snow boots and bag on my back. I realized that I did not possess the qualities that one would consider attractive.

Perhaps this was the first time I had ever felt this. Now I became painfully aware of the gun tied to the jacket that I wore. No wonder the brown-haired girl had thought me wild! All of the girls in town had hair that stood pinned high upon their heads. I let my dark hair hang loose about my shoulders. Longing for change seemed to press upon me more than ever.

My cheeks burned when the wind hit them as I rounded the corner. After looking around for shelter, I decided the shop down the street would be just the place to find a warm stove. As I entered, I felt the walls close in on me. Rows of shelves lined with yards and yards of soft, vibrant material seemed to encompass the space. Great barrels of gunpowder hogged the aisles, and the scent of roses permeated the air.

"Excuse me," I whispered as I pushed past two men who stood by the stove. One of them leaned upon a stack of magazines, and the other had his back against a pile of firewood. I tried to push as close as possible to the warmth of the black iron. While doing so, I accidentally knocked over a can of soup on the shelf behind me. The stout lady behind the counter looked up from her customer as the soup rolled down the aisle. I ducked behind the stove. As I ducked, my eye caught a colorful poster on the wall. Its bright colors made it stand out among its black and white companions.

The poster read:

EXPERIENCE GREAT ADVENTURE!!!!
Dogsled to Fort Yukon, Alaska
HELP GET SUPPLIES TO ALASKA
At No Cost to You
Just Show Up and You Can Help!
Come to Owell's General Store to Sign Up!
Sign Up by October Twentieth!
Only men allowed

While no one was looking, I tore the poster off the wall and thrust it into my pouch. Alaska! This was where I longed to be. I could at least pin up the poster in my cabin. The poster had a stunning picture on it of a dogsled and a map of the Alaskan territory. This poster would keep me motivated to save money for the next two years. I said goodbye to the lady, smiled at the men, and walked out of the store. Another bell rang behind me.

With relief, I returned to Bobick, whom I had left tied up at Owell's General Store. After placing the harness on him, I loaded my pack and my gun onto the sled. I rode off, leaving the awkwardness of town behind me. The sun's rays sent brilliant mosaics across the snow-covered earth. I needed to double it back to my cabin, or I would get caught in the woods after dark; darkness created fear within me.

*****

My worries dissipated as I neared the cabin; the journey back to my place proved uneventful. As I entered, I realized that the cabin's small room seemed to be a vast black hole without emotions. I questioned whether or not I should move to town. What was the cause? I knew no one there, and I got along fine on my own with Bobick. I never actually needed assistance. I took out my pack, my new trap, and the vegetables I had bought. I loosened the brown paper tied around the meat and began to prepare it for supper. I took a match to the wood in the fireplace, set the skillet on the table, and placed the meat in it.

"Oh Bobick, I forgot to show you," I said as I took out the poster from my bag. "Here, what do you think? We can put it on the wall." I smiled at my dog as he wagged his tail.

Bobick probably did not understand me. I took the poster and hung it up over the bed in the corner of my one-room cabin.

I moved over to the skillet and placed it on the flames. Fumes from the good meat filled the cabin. I took the pan off the fire and put it on the table. I prayed and sat down to eat. I looked at my small room and shrugged my shoulders. I did not even know how to speak to people. Why had I not told the young man at the shop my name? Three years would be unbearable. Suddenly, an idea dawned upon me that sent a shiver down my spine. I looked up at the poster; Sign Up by October Twentieth! Only men were allowed. My thoughts spun in my mind as the flames threw foreboding shadows on the wall.

My idea was unfathomable, and yet I was thinking about undertaking this impossible task. I knew it would be dangerous, but I saw no other way that I could reach Alaska. I could manage it. I was strong, and I had lived by myself for two years. I could dogsled and skin animals. There was only one problem, how could I disguise myself? I shook my head. No, this irrational idea was not possible. This train of thought remained pointless. Suppose any of the men found out the truth? The threat of jail hung over me. No, no, I thought and put away my dishes. I gave the rest of my food to Bobick and started preparing for bed.

The idea, however, planted itself in my head. I could not stop thinking of ways to disguise myself. The Trojans and the Greeks kept fighting in my mind. I became increasingly worried that I would not rest unless I gave this foolish thought a try; Achilles was winning.

If I followed through, I would be able to search for my parents, and I would leave this cabin. Even if someone did find out I was a girl in the middle of the trip, the caravan would never go back, and they would have to take me with them. I hoped this would not be the case. All that awaited for me then in Alaska would be a jailhouse. My thoughts stopped, this was impractical, but I knew that I had agreed with myself to go. I already lived in a jail of my own creation.

I could perhaps pass as a man if I cut my hair and acted like a man, although I was not sure how men behaved. Oh dear, this must work,

I thought to myself. If it does not, I will be stuck here forever. I was tall, and I could dress in different clothing. Yes, I convinced myself one more time, tomorrow I am going to Owell's to sign up. Time was of the essence, for tomorrow was the nineteenth.

I lay down after saying prayers. I was thrilled at the prospect of this trip, but I did not believe that I had made the best decision. It was then that I remembered that Owell's General Store was the same general store where I had encountered Alexander. What if he recognized me? Perhaps I could tell him my secret, and he would help me. No, I decided against that plan. He would probably never agree and think I had flown off my moon. Doubts ate at my mind. I tossed and turned as I considered this new plan. At last, I prayed for assistance and went to sleep.

In the morning, I awoke with unwavering confidence. The sun's rays came through the window, and the light made a colorful pattern on my sewn rug. The clock displayed a later time than I hoped, so I jumped out of bed and started preparing for the day. I had to make myself look different and make sure that none of the items I carried were the same as any of my previous trips to town. I found some slacks in my trunk; I did not remember where I had gotten them. Then I looked for a shirt that only a boy would wear. Later, I found another coat. It was just as heavy as the one I had yesterday, but the garment was a different color. Then I took my rifle instead of my gun and found a new bag to take along. None of my clothes looked the same.

I realized the need to change my appearance, but I did not want to cut my hair. I looked at it. Its length fell past my waist; black, dark, and sleek. I questioned how I ever would part with it. With sheer determination, I put my hand to the scissors I had laid out on the table. Then I grabbed them, gathered my hair into my hand, and cut it off. I continued to snap at the hair a while longer. Now all I had was a crop of hair not even reaching my eyes.

A small hand mirror lay on the table. I reached my hand over to the mirror and held it at eye level. Devastated, I lay the decorated mirror on the table. My hair was ugly. I was quite surprised I looked nothing like the girl from yesterday. The strands of my shorn hair lay around my feet. I tousled my cropped hair. I put on the slacks and made sure that I wore the loose shirt I had chosen. Once more, I gazed into the mirror. I doubted that Alexander would recognize me, even after our encounter yesterday. Anyway, why should I worry? The chance that he had also signed up to go on this journey was slim.

Another problem occurred to me. I had left Bobick and my sled outside of the store the whole time I had been in town the previous day. To avoid any suspicion, I decided to walk to town. The long road wound through the forest. The sun was high in the sky. My feet dragged, and a shudder went through my bones. The sun was a pale, cold color that filtered through the woods, and the pine trees hung heavy with snow.

When I reached the town, my boots felt heavy and wet. I walked up the street to Owell's General Store. It seemed strange to be in town and to be wearing pants. No one looked at me oddly now since I was not a girl carrying a gun but a man carrying a rifle. I just had to remember that I was supposed to be a young man. I came up to the store and looked through the window. There stood Alexander, counting money. He looked as if he would rather be outside riding a sled through the streets.

After taking a deep breath, I pushed the door open and stepped inside. I decided to disguise my voice. I nervously took off my fur cap. I wore it instead of the hood I had worn the previous day.

Alexander looked up, and he appeared surprised. "Would you like anything?"

"Hello," I said in my deepest voice as I walked up to the counter. I tried to appear as confident as possible. "I would like to sign up for that trip to Alaska. We are supposed to sign up here, right?"

"Yes, of course, let me bring out that paper. Tomorrow Mr. Shubert is coming to see who signed up. You arrived just in time. It would have been too late if you had not come today." He grinned as he handed over a paper with a list of names and a pencil. "Simply write your name after the last person; you are over eighteen, aren't you? You know you have to be that old to go." He gave me a look that told me he had doubts about my age.

I hoped he did not observe the faint blush I felt creeping into my cheeks. Even if I looked like a boy, I probably looked young. I was seventeen; I had lied about everything else. What was one more lie?

I lifted the pencil and surveyed the names on the paper. The top line read, *Alexander Milichkov, age 22,* I wanted to ask Alexander if the name was his, but then I remembered that I was not supposed to know him. The following line read, *Seraphim Smirnov, age 21.* Under that name, there was a whole list of men. The list read: *Matthew Davis; 30, Andrew Redlock; 40, Joseph Shubert; 21, Joseph Smith; 22, Timothy Howell; 30, Red Fern; 29, Fur Hunter; 37, Steven Lake; 33, and Rideon Smith; 27.* I put my pencil to the paper and wrote down: *Andrei Strelov, age 18.*

Alexander looked at me with a curious glance. "Are you Russian?"

"Part Russian and part Alaskan Native," I responded, wishing I had never decided upon this hair-brained scheme.

"Ah, I see." He nodded his understanding. "Do you know what tribe you're from?"

A warm feeling crept over me. "I'm not sure."

"Oh." He looked down at the list. "That means we have something in common; I'm part Russian too."

"Oh, really? That is wonderful."

"My mother is from the Tlingit tribe. My father came to Sitka from Russia when he was very young. He later met and married my mother."

I had no idea where Sitka was, but I nodded. "Are your parents still in Alaska?"

"Yes, that's why I'm going on this trip. My name is Alexander Milichkov. My name is first on the list."

I had figured out that he was on the list, but I made no mention of it. "I'm coming along to look for my parents."

Confusion darkened Alexander's facial features. "Don't you know where they are?"

I shrugged. "No, I don't even know if they are in Alaska."

"That's an odd arrangement, wouldn't they tell you?" he asked.

"No, I mean, let me explain." I went on to tell him my whole story. I left out any parts that would include that I was not eighteen and not a boy. I felt awful for lying so much. Finally, I finished with the story.

"You know, your search might not turn up anything. Do you remember anything from when you were in Alaska? It's a vast wild land. Most people dwell in the coastal areas or close to the Canadian boundary line. You'd have to search for a long time to find your parents."

"I'd like to try anyway."

Alexander nodded his head. "Suit yourself, but I'll help you out. You can stay with my family when we arrive; then you can stay until you are ready to go to your family."

"That's awfully kind of you, but I would hate to impose," I protested.

"No, my parents wouldn't mind, at least I don't think so. I haven't seen them in twelve years, but a friend of mine will be staying with us when we arrive. What possible damage could another friend do?"

I did not realize we were friends. Our friendship could do a lot of damage if he ever found out I was a girl and not a boy. I had an impulse to tell him the truth and to tell him to forget the whole plan. However, the thought that I might find my parents in Alaska propelled me forward.

I grimaced. "Well, thank you for the kind offer; I really must go now." I hoped I sounded convincing. I did not have good knowledge of how men spoke to each other.

"There's going to be a meeting about this trip in a day. Mr. Shubert, the head of the company, will be addressing all the men. The meeting will be in the room behind this store."

"Thank you. I'll be there."

"Goodbye! See you soon."

"Goodbye." I walked out, and the bell rang yet again. The tingling of the bell now sounded like the ringing of a death knell. Even so, a small hope arose inside of me. I thought that perhaps I could trust Alexander, even if he were to find out my secret. I hoped Alexander did not suspect anything unusual. I sighed. I had to prevent myself from making mistakes. When I had been telling Alexander the story of my family, I almost made several errors.

I arrived at my cabin as the sun's rays barely touched the leaves' edges on the trees. Thoughts of regret ate at the edge of my mind. However, I also felt a tingling in my arms and toes. A new adventure lay ahead of me. Thoughts of escape from my dull reality had often been with me, and now I found a way out.

*****

In a day, Bobick and I traveled to town. It was difficult to describe the emotions that tumbled inside of me. It seemed as if the entire earth shifted and moved as I tried to focus my thoughts on the upcoming meeting. Upon my arrival, I parked my sled and walked into the room behind the store. Several men were already there. My nerves felt raw. I removed my cap; it revealed my short messy hair. I deliberately walked up the aisle and sat down next to Alexander, who sat in the third row.

"Arrived here early, huh?" Alexander grinned. I nodded and clasped my hands together in my lap to keep them from shaking.

"Sima's coming later," Alexander told me.

"Sima?" I questioned.

"My friend I told you about, you know, the one who is staying with us. Anyway, we're both employed by Jason Shubert. We finished school here in America, and we were waiting for Mr. Shubert to take this trip to get back home."

"I see." I nodded and looked ahead of me. I didn't know what to say. I felt as if I was on trial and that at any moment, a judge would appear and yell, "Guilty!" I fingered at a thread that was coming off of my sweater. I noticed Alexander giving me an odd look, but he refrained from speaking. More men started to appear. Two men came in and sat down in the seats just in front of me.

One of them turned and looked straight into my eyes. "What's your name?" he asked in a rude tone.

"Andrei," I replied in a trembling voice.

The man threw me an arrogant expression. "Another Russian Native?"

I lifted my chin and replied slowly, "Yes."

The man gave me a glare that spoke of superiority. "Hmm... Russians."

I blinked. My mouth seemed to be frozen shut; my brain felt like a void empty of thoughts.

Thankfully, at that moment, Alexander stood up and interjected, "Andrei is my friend, Steven. He has done nothing to offend you. If you have a problem with him, feel free to leave."

All of a sudden, I heard a booming voice behind me, "Alex, I'll tell who to leave, but point well taken. Gentlemen, I don't want any arguing." The man came up to Alex and put his hand on his shoulder. "Sit down, Alex."

Alex sat down. The massive man came forward. He had a large black beard, and his dark brown coat looked like a tent. The tent coat made him appear larger than life.

"Who's that?" I asked, nodding toward the man that had just walked in.

"Mr. Shubert, he's in charge."

Every nerve seemed to be ready to jump out of my body as I stared at the giant man. "Yes, is he nice?"

"Rather nice, but very strict as far as rules are concerned," Alex answered.

How lucky for me, I thought. If Mr. Shubert ever found out that I was a girl, would I also be welcome to leave? I let out a few slow breaths to steady myself.

Jason Shubert stood in front of the room now. Everyone came to attention. He turned his massive head towards us and asked, "Alex, where's Sima?"

Alex moved his hands in a questioning gesture and shrugged. "I don't know, sir." Jason Shubert gave a deep sigh and shook his head.

"Sima better get here," Alex whispered to me. I nodded in agreement.

"Well," Mr. Shubert started speaking. His voice filled the entire room. "This trip is a great task to undertake, and I'm happy that all of you can join me." He surveyed the room. I shuddered as his eyes rested upon me and then kept going.

Jason Shubert kept talking in a voice that sounded like trees falling at the lumber mill. "I know this trip is hard and dangerous, but taking supplies to Alaska is important since Alaska is now American soil. As many of you likely know, disease and famine have struck Fort Yukon. Since there is great difficulty with trains and pack horses, we are taking dogsleds instead. I trust that you are all able-bodied men."

He stopped, and his gaze swept the room again. "Now, I know some of you are going to your homes, and some are just going for an adventure. This is going to be a long grueling trip, and dangerous. None of you are obliged to go, even if you signed the paper. Now, we're starting a week and a half from today, and I'm telling you, we will leave without you if you do not show up. Tomorrow we are starting to make preparations. Every man has to come since there's a lot we must do."

He stopped, let out a deep sigh, and then boomed on, "So, I suggest that you go home tonight, get your belongings and all the supplies that you need, and then come stay in town. You can board at my place if you want…" Jason Shubert was interrupted mid-sentence by the sound of the creaking door at the entrance.

Everyone turned to look at the intruder. There stood a tall, thin young man who looked to be about the same age as Alex. This man, I gathered, was Sima. He had a thin face, a sharp nose, and blonde hair that hung loosely just below his ears. His gait was arrogant as he strode forward. He was rather handsome. As he approached, I realized he had brown eyes. I considered this to be strange because he had blonde hair. I had expected him to have blue eyes.

Jason Shubert looked at him in disappointment and asked in a sharp tone, "Seraphim! Where were you?"

"I'm sorry, sir," Sima started, "I…." He looked back at the door as if looking for some excuse.

"Sima, sit down!" Jason Shubert ordered.

"Yes, sir." Sima hopped over the seat next to Alex and plopped down. Mr. Shubert shook his head and continued his long-drawn-out explanation of the upcoming journey.

"You're in for it," Alex said under his breath to Sima.

"I'll talk the man off any day," Sima replied.

"Sima, listen," Alex whispered, "you won't be able to go if you act like this."

Sima looked annoyed. "Alex, calm down. You always pretend that you are so much older than I am and that you're like Mr. Shubert." Alex just gave him a glance that spoke of impatience. Mr. Shubert cleared his throat at Sima and Alex and then continued to open a map of the route to Alaska. Alex turned to face the front.

Meanwhile, Sima pulled a piece of wood out of his pocket and a small knife. He then began to whittle away at the wood. My interest in the carving grew as more wood chips fell to the ground. However, Mr. Shubert's loud voice made it impossible to focus on anyone else but him.

"Here are our checkpoints. I have duplicated this map, so you men will know where to go if we get separated. In that instance, you will have to go on by yourself. The supplies here are important, but so is everybody's life. If a group gets lost, everybody will keep going. Hopefully, if you reach the checkpoint, others will be there. The groups will wait if one is missing. I am assigning the groups the day before we leave. That way, I'll know who's going for sure. If you do decide to go, be here tomorrow."

Jason Shubert kept on talking about the trip and how many miles we would cover each day. I discovered that we were going to Montreal in Canada. Montreal would be our last break before the long haul to Alaska. The distance seemed unmanageable. The task began to feel impossible. How would this trip turn out? Would I be discovered? Would I ever find my parents? The thoughts of uncertainty toppled about in my mind. I hoped no one would recognize I was a girl. My mind whirled. I turned my attention back to the map as Jason Shubert slammed down a stick against it. I almost jumped out of my skin.

"And that, my friends, will be the last checkpoint before Alaska. It is a small trading post. It is only about fifty miles from the Alaskan border, and then we'll be in Alaska. From there, Fort Yukon is not too far. Well, men, for those of you who are still planning on joining me, meet me here tomorrow morning at about seven. Thank you for coming today."

The men started to stand up. Some of the men came up to Jason and spoke with him before leaving. As I began to walk outside with Sima and Alex, Jason called to us in his booming voice, "Sima!"

Sima turned around and questioned, "Yes?" He pushed his blonde hair out of his eyes. No sense of fear seemed to affect his appearance.

"You will stay behind, please," Jason Shubert ordered.

"Yes, sir." Sima exchanged a look with Alex and returned to the room that we had just left. I walked outside with Alex. Bobick was still tied up outside. I came over to him and began to unhitch him from the post.

"This is your dog?" Alex asked, pointing to Bobick, who pulled my sled.

"Yes," I answered.

"How recently have you been in town?" Alex inquired. I thought I heard a note of suspicion in his voice.

"Why?" I asked him.

"Well, I've seen your dog before."

I stopped short. How stupid of me. I had brought Bobick when I had traded for furs and then had left him in front of the store where Alex worked. I thought about what I should say. I had taken precautions to guard myself against suspicion before, but I had somehow forgotten about the details in the case of Bobick this time.

"Well... I haven't been in town for a while, you see, only to sign up for the trip, and I didn't take my dog with me." I hoped Alex did not remember that Bobick belonged to a certain girl who had walked into the store with a mere two dollars. "Perhaps he comes from a large litter." I shrugged my shoulders. Deep down, I felt as if I was gasping for breath like a fish cast out of the sea.

"Well, I suppose it does not matter." Alex brushed off the subject.

"I wanted to ask a question," I began; my voice sounded timid. I cleared my throat.

"What about?"

"I know that Jason Shubert is supplying us with dogs, but do you think I could take Bobick? Do you suppose he'd be able to lead?"

"Bring him around tomorrow. I'm sure Mr. Shubert will look at him."

"Yes, well, I will," I told him as I looked at the door of the room we had exited. I could hear loud voices in the building. One voice was Jason Shubert's, and the other was Sima's voice.

"Is Sima in trouble?" I asked, biting my lip.

Alex laughed. "Yes, he always is. Nothing to worry about."

I was scared for Sima. I'd be frightened to have such a big man yell at me. What if Jason Shubert found out I was a girl? I swallowed hard.

"You all right?" Alex asked.

"Yes, I better go home. It's growing late. The meeting was longer than I had expected."

"Right, see you tomorrow then." He lifted one hand in goodbye as I drove away.

That night I barely slept. Terrified, I thought that perhaps I should not return to town the next day.

The thought of my parents kept me from caving. I kept telling myself that the train fare was too expensive. I would never sell enough furs to pay for a passage to Alaska, and I would not know anybody. At the moment, at least I had Alex as a friend. Sima, I supposed, could also be a friend. Sima seemed peculiar to me. He had appeared to take pleasure in disobeying Jason Shubert. I did not understand why.

The next morning, after a fitful night of sleep, I awoke at five o'clock and pushed all my fears deep inside of me. I packed my supplies and loaded them onto my small sled. The open trail lay ahead. My sled moved in the direction of the sun. Hope filled me from my toes to my newly shorn hair. A determination that loneliness would not be my fate propelled me forward. With one last look back and a prayer, I left my shell of a Maine cabin forever.

Chapter 2   November 3, 1887

Ten days flew by. We were leaving during the first week of November. The list of preparations that Mr. Shubert handed to us made my head whirl. Dog teams were to be assigned, sleds packed, tents checked for tears and then patched, food purchased, guns loaded, shoes repaired, and teams chosen. I spent most of my days chasing around after Alexander and Sima. Alex had insisted that I come with them. Sima did not look at me more than twice and busied himself with the task of talking Alex's ear off. By the end of the ten days, my list from Mr. Shubert looked old and ragged.

Mr. Shubert had approved Bobick, and I practiced running with him hitched up to the rest of the team. Several men brought their own dogs and had extra dogs on their sleds. These dogs were not a burden since the sleds were heavy with supplies.

The day when we had to depart came too soon. I was tying the rest of the supplies to my sled with a length of rope when Alex came up and slapped me on the shoulder. I jumped back and looked down again in haste so he would not see how embarrassed I felt.

"Ready to leave?" he asked.

"Yes, I am just tying up my final supplies. Do you think that we'll be traveling the whole day today?"

Alex leaned over to pet Eagle, his lead dog. "Yes, Jason Shubert wants to reach Canada in a week or two. Today we're stopping at a small town south of here. You know, in two weeks we might get to see Montreal. I've never seen it."

"I haven't either. I mean, I don't think so," I added.

"You don't remember anything about your parents or what they did, strange."

I shrugged. "That's why I want to find my parents. I mean, I don't know much, but they're somewhere in Alaska."

"Well, you certainly narrowed the area down," Alex said with a laugh.

"I'll do my best." I laughed too, but my laugh sounded shaky to me. What if I never found my parents? What would I do? Would this whole trip be worth the bother? It was dangerous. I put away my reservations for now. I did not want my day to continue with endless panic and despair.

Sima came up to Alex and me. "Good morning, men."

"Good morning," Alex greeted him with a grim smile.

"Alex, what's wrong with you? I was early today." Sima again pulled out a piece of wood from his pocket and continued to work away at it with a knife.

Alex pointed to the sled. "Very early; mostly everything is packed."

Sima stuck the knife and the wood in his pocket and started walking towards his sled. "I'll pack my sled quickly. I can do anything at top-notch speed if I put my mind to it."

"When you stop being lazy and decide to do something, that is," Alex said with a smile.

"Sure thing," Sima replied and started packing his sled. I was surprised by the rate at which he finished the task. As soon as Sima finished packing his sled, Jason Shubert walked out of his store.

Jason Shubert surveyed the long line of sleds. "Excellent, everything is almost ready to go. I will now be announcing teams. Remember, you are to always stay with your team."

When Mr. Shubert announced that Alex and I would be in one group with Matthew Davis, I was surprised and thrilled. While Sima appeared to be good friends with Alex, I had not wanted him in our tent. He did not seem to care much about this journey or anything else for that matter. He was assigned to the tent with the two Josephs. One of them was Jason Shubert's son. When Mr. Shubert announced that Sima would not be in a tent with Alex, Sima and Alex exchanged a look of shock. Sima had then leaned over and whispered something to Alex. Alex had responded with a frown. I did not care. Matthew Davis appeared to be hardworking and talked much less than Sima.

I breathed a sigh of relief. I had worried that I would get stuck with Steven Lake, the arrogant man from the first meeting. The absence of Steven Lake or Sima in our tent would not be detrimental. Groups had to stay together and share a tent. I was in luck; Alex had pulled a few strings with Mr. Shubert and had acquired an enormous tent. Matthew had the most room in his sled, so we placed the tent inside. Jason Shubert had said we would be leaving shortly, and all of us sat down to eat breakfast before we left. Alex, Sima, and I sat together.

"Who names the dogs?" I asked after we had sat down and started to dig into our breakfast of eggs and pancakes.

"Mary Shubert, since they're mostly Mr. Shubert's," Alex answered.

Sima leaned back against a sled that stood next to where we sat. "Mary is Shubert's daughter, beautiful, but not very nice. Why do you ask who names the dogs?"

"Well, the names were just not something a man would usually name a dog. For instance, some of my dogs have names such as; Birdie, Star, Princess, and Spot." Precisely what I would name a dog, I thought to myself, but I had to play along.

"Sounds like Mary Shubert, only she would think of silly names like that," Sima said with a laugh. I was offended, but I pretended to laugh too.

Alex turned to Sima. "By the way, about three weeks ago, I saw Mary in the store; she was buying peppermints."

Sima cut him off. "Again? How does she stay so thin?" He turned to me. "This girl-"

"Let me finish," Alex cut in. I now realized who Mary Shubert was, and I remembered this encounter quite well. Alex continued the story. "Well, Mary Shubert was there, and suddenly this beautiful girl came in. I don't know who she was. I'd never seen her before. She had such pretty long black hair, and..." as he continued to describe the girl, I realized he was referring to me. I felt the heat radiating from my cheeks.

Sima directed his gaze at me. "Alex, the poor boy is blushing."

"Ha!" Alex exclaimed. "Seems that Andrei is ahead of the game." The tips of my ears now turned warm.

"Do you know her?" Alex asked.

"Yes, I do," I answered.

"What's her name?" Alex asked. I did not know what to say, I opened my mouth to speak, but Jason Shubert's voice interrupted me.

"Leaving in ten minutes!" Mr. Shubert yelled out to all of the men. Everyone began to scurry. We washed our food tins and grabbed the rest of our belongings. The whole field seemed to be a maze of tents, bags, dogs, and sleds. I navigated my way through this mess and checked over my sled. I looked in the small wallet tied to my belt. All of my papers lay inside. I leaned over and hugged Bobick while my heart raced. My dreams were coming true as Alaska did not seem so far now.

Impossible as the task had seemed, we were lined up in ten minutes and ready to leave, all twelve men. Jason Shubert spoke for a moment, and then we all lowered our heads in silent prayer. I prayed for a safe journey and that my journey would not be fruitless. Most of all, I prayed to find my family. In those moments, I thought of all that lay ahead. I wondered what Canada was like. I was excited because I wanted to see Montreal, and then we would be in Alaska, my homeland. My family was out there somewhere in the vast unknown. I had to locate them somehow. After five minutes of prayer, Jason Shubert gave the call for the men to ready to leave. All the men started whooping and yelling and calling out to their dogs.

Sima let out a loud yell, "Hah, Caesar, let's go, hah!" The obnoxious screams made me feel like closing my ears. Alex also let out a loud whoop. I felt ridiculous, but I followed suit.

*****

We stopped after the sun had set. We had paused in a small village earlier for lunch. Even though I had practice with a dogsled, I realized I would never be able to keep up with the rest of the men. I could keep up only if I pushed myself to the brink of exhaustion every day. Matthew, Alex, and I lagged behind a bit since our group was supposed to keep together at all times. I became aware that my lack of physical strength and size created this delay. Sima ignored the rules and lagged behind with us. He would lean on the sled and whittle away at his ever-melting piece of wood. I wondered how he managed to stay on the sled. My hands felt cramped from holding on so tight.

After lunch, I moved along quite well. However, by the time evening came, my body lacked energy. I wondered if I had made a dreadful mistake in deciding to make this trip. We came to a stop as the darkness closed in around us. I guessed the time was nearing seven o'clock. We stopped in a clearing not far from a small town. Sima said that we were already near the Canadian border. I wondered how many miles we had traveled. The miles had seemed endless. After taking care of our dogs and settling them near our camping ground for the night, Alex, Matthew, and I set up the tent.

All I wanted to do was go to sleep. However, Alex asked both of us if we wanted to go to the nearby town tavern and get a drink.

I decided that perhaps I would seem strange to him if I disagreed, so I complied. I walked over with Alex and Matthew to where Sima stood talking to two other men: Joseph Smith and Joseph Shubert. Joseph Smith seemed to be a pleasant sort of man. I had my doubts about Joseph Shubert.

"Come on, Andrei and Alex," Sima spoke, impatience laced his voice. "How long does it take to set up a tent?"

"You could have helped," Alex said, glaring at Sima.

"I was helping my team," Sima answered and leaned back against the wooden pole that held up one side of his tent.

Joseph Shubert stopped talking to Joseph Smith and said, "Much help you are."

Sima laughed. "I was going to help, but I got side-tracked."

Alex shook his head while he laughed. "Side-tracked talking; next time, you should help."

Sima grinned. "All right, I agree to be of the utmost help next time. Shall we go?" Sima turned back to the two Josephs. "Coming with us?"

Joseph Smith stepped forward. "I'll come with you."

Sima looked over to Joseph Shubert. "You?"

Joseph Shubert shook his head. "No, thank you. Be sure to come back early."

"Don't worry," Sima replied and led the way to town.

We walked about half a mile before arriving at our destination. We could see the entire town from about two hundred feet away. Three inches of snow on the ground made for easy walking. I breathed in the cool night air and let it calm my burning lungs. I felt relieved that I could breathe after a long day of running. We spotted the tavern without a problem.

Alex, always the leader, now walked ahead confidently, and the rest of us followed. My heartbeat increased as we neared the door. I had never been in a tavern before, and I did not want to venture inside. The place was smoky, crowded, and noisy. Rough men sat at the tables with large cigars that emitted a rancid smell. I had the feeling that I should turn around and tell everybody that I wanted to return to camp and sleep, but I stepped in line behind Sima, Matthew, Alex, and Joseph. We all pushed up to the counter. The chill from the air outside made me crave a hot tea.

The man standing behind the counter turned to us. "What would you like, boys?"

"I'll have a brandy," Sima told him.

"Me too," Alex, Matthew, and Joe replied in unison.

The man turned his gaze towards me. "And you?"

"I'll have some hot tea, please."

The man stared at me, and Sima came over to me and put his hand on my shoulder. "No, he wants a brandy. You know, he's kind of young."

"Sima, I don't want brandy," I protested.

"There's nothing like some alcohol to warm you up, not hot tea," Sima said to me in a tone that did not invite argument.

Joseph Smith chuckled under his breath. "Where did you come from? Nobody goes to a pub to order tea."

"Sima, Joe, that's enough," Alex cut in.

I sent him a silent, grateful look of thanks. Sima, Matthew, and Joe did not say anything more to me. They turned their attention to a discussion about the impending miles we still had to travel. I remained silent and listened. The man at the bar gave us our drinks about two minutes into the conversation. Sima gulped his down. Joe, Matthew, and Alex followed suit, then they all turned to me. I did not know what to do. I wondered if there was a way in which I could pour out the brandy and still pretend to drink it. Sweat trickled down my back. Everyone in the room seemed to be watching me. I saw no escape. The warmth of the room closed in on me. I grabbed the drink and poured it down my throat. Alex, Sima, Matthew, and Joe cheered, and I started coughing.

Alex laughed and said, "You've been in that cabin of yours too long."

"Another drink?" Sima asked. I was about to say no, but he bellowed to the bartender, "Five more brandies!"

I thought I was going to pass out. My whole throat burned, but I had to keep my cover. Doubtless, I already seemed odd to Sima and Alex. I did not want anyone to get too suspicious. The man behind the bar pushed our drinks towards us. I gulped it down without hesitation and resisted the desire to run outside and spit out the vile liquid.

"Not bad?" Sima asked.

I pretended to laugh. "Not bad at all."

"Some more?" Sima questioned.

This time Alex interrupted, "No, we have to get back."

I breathed a sigh of relief.

"I want some more," Joseph Smith said.

Matthew nodded as well. "I'll stay with Sima if you don't mind."

I forced a smile. "I'll go back with Alex. I think that for the first time, I've had enough." My head was swimming. The whole place made me feel sick. The smell of the pub clogged my nose and choked up my throat.

Alex nodded. "All right." He then turned to Sima with a look of warning. "Watch out, Sima. You better get back before Jason Shubert discovers you've been gone too long."

"I'll do my best." Sima rolled his eyes and then turned to the bartender and ordered drinks again.

"Let's go," Alex said to me. He then looked at Joe and Matthew with admonition and whispered, "Watch him, will you?"

"Don't worry, Alex," Matthew answered and then turned back to Sima.

With a sigh of relief, I walked out of the bar with Alex behind me. He seemed to be the only levelheaded person in the group. As we walked down the road away from the town, I felt one foot slide out from under me, and I came crashing to the icy ground. Humiliated, I lay unmoving on the ground.

Alex gave me a hand to help me up. "The alcohol hitting you or what?"

"No, there's just some ice here," I answered, feeling rather dim-witted.

"You must have been kidding about the hot tea," Alex said with a snort.

"Well, I just never drank before, and..." I stopped mid-sentence. All excuses escaped me.

"Now you have. Good for you." Alex looked at me as I brushed the snow off my coat. I noticed he was not just looking at me. He had a strange glint in his eye- as if he knew something.

I did not like the expression on his face, so I decided to change the subject. "Do you think Sima will come back in time?"

The strange expression disappeared from Alex's eyes as he answered, "I don't know. With Sima, one never knows."

"That's not too bad. Nothing ever gets too dull then," I observed. Alex and I were already in sight of the camp.

Alex kicked some snow that lay on the ground in front of him. "Yes, nothing gets too dull. I don't mind him being like that. It's just that Mr. Shubert is involved, and I don't want to make him angry."

"Well, it's Sima's skin, not yours," I stated.

Alex strode ahead. "Yes, and I always get blamed for something that Sima did."

I was silent. I had no idea what to say. What did men talk about? How did they answer each other? We were already near the tent, and Alex stepped in first. I climbed in behind him. I wanted to tell him my secret. I knew I had a good chance. Perhaps I still could return home if he told someone else. My courage disappeared. I went ahead and sat down on the blankets that I had arranged as my bed. Alex put some sticks in the middle of the tent and began making a small fire.

My bed was on the left side of the fire, Matthew's on the right, and Alex was at the far end of the tent opposite the entranceway.

"Well, I'm tired from today. I thought we traveled too fast," I told Alex.

He looked at the flames and nodded. "I heard that Jason doesn't like to slow down. We might reach our destination earlier that way. Still, the thought of traveling at such a rate makes me nervous."

"Me too," I answered. I lay down and placed my hand under my head.

Alex also lay down on his quilted blanket. "I suppose this trip is worth it. Anyway, we get to see Montreal in two weeks."

"I presume so. I could not think of any other way to reach Alaska. If I had another way, I would use it," I said and added to myself, without a doubt.

"Jason Shubert helped to pay for my schooling and Sima's education too. He's looked out for us since we were ten. We couldn't just leave and not offer him our assistance." Alex let out a loud sigh and turned over to face the tent wall. "I hope Sima returns soon. It's getting late," Alex said into the air.

I could not help thinking that Alex worried too much. Sima seemed as if he could talk anybody out of a bad situation. "Don't worry about it," I answered and closed my eyes.

Chapter 3   November 4, 1887

When I awoke the next morning, Matthew was sleeping on the opposite side of the tent. I had not heard Matthew return in the night. I guessed I had been more exhausted than I thought. I regarded the tent's gray sloping roof in the early morning light as I heard some talking outside. The constant bustle felt uncomfortable. I studied Alex for a while as he and Matthew slept. His stern face had softened; instead, he looked kind and gentle. Matthew, curled up in his blankets, looked like a little boy still asleep at home. I wondered if I needed to awaken them. I had not heard a call yet.

A shrill whistle broke the silence, and Mr. Shubert's voice cut through the morning air. "Leaving in an hour!" I sat up as if a bolt of lightning had struck me.

Alex awoke. He yawned. "Was that the call?"

"Yes," I answered. Alex rolled over and looked at Matthew, who was still asleep.

"Should I wake him?" I questioned in a hesitant manner.

"I'll wake him up, don't worry," Alex answered and reached over and shook Matthew by the shoulder.

Matthew turned over and rubbed his eyes. "Remind me never to drink with Sima again. My head is buzzing as if a harmonica player is sitting inside of it."

Alex made a face. "That's what I was afraid of; your one consolation is that Sima probably does not feel much better."

Matthew gave a half-hearted chuckle and sat up. "Are you joking? You know as well as I do that Sima can drink any man from this camp under the table with the exclusion of Jason Shubert perhaps."

Alex started to roll up his blankets. "Unfortunately, I have to agree with you, and unfortunately, we don't have time for his antics or much conversation right now. Let's go." Alex stood up and carried his blankets out of the tent. He was so confident and sure of himself.

I turned back to Matthew, who rolled his eyes. "Do me a favor and don't always listen to Alex. Just because he finished medical school in Boston doesn't make him an expert about everything in life."

I turned in surprise. "He's a doctor?"

Matthew stood up and started to put utensils in his travel pack. "Yes, we need one for this trip, and they need doctors up at Fort Yukon. Alex used his doctoring skills to get Sima to come on this trip. He said if Sima were not allowed to come, he would not go, and Shubert needed him."

I began to tie my boots. "Alex never said anything to me."

Matthew also reached for his boots. "Alex thinks he's humble."

"What do you mean?" I stood up and got ready to exit the tent.

Matthew pulled his laces tight. "Never mind, you are young. Watch yourself, all right?"

I nodded and then walked out of the tent. Matthew's words made me feel uneasy. Try as I might, I could not shake the sense of foreboding that now hung around me.

We started packing and putting away all of our meager supplies into our bags. I grabbed the meat from my sled and threw it to the dogs, who jumped about me and licked my hands.

I neared Bobick and leaned down to hug him. I whispered in his ear, "Another day, Bobick, I'm all right so far." His soft fur gave me comfort. He knew my secret.

"Andrei? What are you doing?" a voice asked from behind me. I stood up in an instant and turned on my heel. Sima stood watching me.

"I am just giving my dog some encouragement."

"I see," Sima said with a smirk and then sauntered off. He then yelled something to Joe Smith and kept walking. I looked after him, hoping that I had not blown my cover. As Matthew had said, I had to be careful.

Alex came up to me. "Stop sleeping, will you? You have to help me get the tent down."

I looked at him. "Yes, sure." I knew I appeared distracted.

Alex looked over at Joseph Smith and Joseph Shubert as they rolled up their tent. "Where's Sima?" he asked me.

"I'm not sure. He just walked by, but then after that, I do not know where he went."

"Again? He's neglecting his duty."

"Alex, this is not the army," I told him.

"I know, but Mr. Shubert thinks it is." Alex looked at me and then added, "Come on, you get that side."

I went to the tent and grabbed the pole. I could not grasp it, and my hand slipped. The wood splintered and cut into my palm. "Ow!" I stumbled backward.

Alex came over. "What?"

My hand was bleeding; fresh red blood was falling on the snow. "It's nothing. I just cut my hand against the pole, that's all."

"That's all?" Alex sounded suspicious. "There's blood on the snow. Let me see your hand."

I was about to give him my hand, but then I realized how feminine my hands were, despite my years of laborious trapping.

"No, it's all right, really," I protested.

"If you say so, let's get going." Alex went back to his work with an odd glance in my direction.

I realized that I was not getting anywhere with my actions and that it would be wise to give myself up, yet I plodded on with my work. Matthew came and sent a grin in my direction. He seemed to be the kindest person here. At least I had some hope.

As we rolled up the tent, Mr. Shubert came up to us. "Good morning, boys."

"Good morning," we answered in unison.

"Alex?"

"Yes, sir?"

"Where is Sima?"

"He is with your son, helping him," Alex answered.

"Alex, do not lie to me. I was just with my son, and he is not there."

"I am sorry, sir, I do not know where he went," Alex replied. He regarded Mr. Shubert with a proud defensive look in his eyes.

"Listen, Alex, you know that I trust you to keep him under control. Now, if you cannot do that, I will have to ask Sima to return home."

"But sir, he does not mean to be neglectful," Alex argued.

"You make sure that he isn't neglectful. We are leaving in ten minutes. You better find him," Jason ordered.

"Yes, sir." Alex turned back to his work. Jason Shubert walked away, and the snow made a small cloud around his feet as he walked. I thought that Mr. Shubert was unfair. Sima's actions had nothing to do with Alex. When Jason had plowed off, Alex stuffed the tent into Matthew's sled with impatience.

I helped him tie it down. "Alex, why is Jason so annoyed with you? It is not your responsibility."

Alex turned to me. "I suppose it is. I talked Jason into taking Sima along. He was not going to take him. Sima doesn't care anyway. No matter what you tell him, he doesn't listen." Alex tugged on the rope and tied a final knot to hold the tent in place.

I wanted to comfort Alex, but I had no way of knowing how. "Maybe he does, Alex."

Alex appeared irritated. "You have a kind outlook."

"Well, I suppose I could talk to him." I shrugged.

"What are you going to say? No Andrei, only something drastic could change Sima's outlook on life."

"What are you suggesting?" I asked.

"I do not know," Alex replied and walked off to find Sima.

*****

That evening, we made camp about fifty miles south of the Canadian border. Mr. Shubert had wanted us to reach Montreal in several days. That day's travels had sapped all of my energy. We had traveled almost without rest since morning, and I had tried to do my best to keep up. I was doing better, but I was already looking forward to a break. I had no idea how I was planning to get through the rest of the trip after Montreal. I retired early, and I was thankful that we were not near a town. At least I could avoid being forced to go to another tavern. I was spreading out all of my blankets on the ground when Alex and Matthew walked in. Sima, as always, trailed along behind them. Alex and Matthew had already spread out their bedding, but they did not lie down when they walked in. I had started up a fire earlier and now was melting snow on it for tea. Sima opened his pack and got out a pipe, and packed it with tobacco.

He then put the pipe between his teeth and struck a match. "Do you smoke?"

I shook my head. "No." The thought of smoking made my stomach turn.

"You'll have to if you want to keep up appearances," Alex said. I looked at him. I hoped that my face did not reveal my complete disgust.

"Don't worry. We won't make you smoke." Sima lit his pipe and leaned back on his elbows, his pipe still between his teeth.

"Thank you," I replied in a sarcastic tone.

"I don't like it much either," Matthew said in a comforting voice.

I swallowed and sent him a grateful look. "I see." Smoking was worse than drinking. I hoped I would be able to escape this appearance. I decided to change the subject before Sima chose to change his mind.

"Tell me a little more about yourselves." I took the water pot off the fire and began to pour tea for Alex and Sima.

"What do you want to know?" Alex seemed to be wary.

"Well, how did you end up in Alaska? What are your parents like? I mean, you told me a little bit Alex, but I am just wondering."

Alex shrugged. "I guess there's nothing much to tell. My parents at first lived in Sitka. It was only later that they moved up to the north near Fort Yukon. That was when they had me." Alex stopped for a second to take a mug of tea I handed to him and then continued his story. "My father was part of the Russian American Fur Trading Company. He quit later and moved to where he said it was quieter. He did not like noise."

"It seems like my parents are the other way around," Sima interjected. "They lived in southern Alaska and then moved up north. That's where they met Alex's parents and decided to send us to school in America when we were nine and ten."

"They sent us by train and by pack horses," Alex said as he also lit his pipe. "That was easier than the route we are taking now."

"Do you have any brothers or sisters?" I asked. I thought that Sima and Alex must have had a lonely childhood. How could their parents have sent them off to America? How could they have known what would happen to them?

"I don't have any brothers or sisters," Sima answered, looking into the fire. "Although, I have spent so much time with Alex that at times it feels as if he is my brother."

"Yes," Alex added while he nodded in agreement. "I don't have any brothers or sisters. When I was five, my parents took in a girl named Katya. Her parents had died of disease. They had lived in Fort Yukon. My parents were smart enough to stay away as much as possible. As you know, Fort Yukon is still suffering."

"How far away do your parents live from the fort?" I asked.

"About twenty miles, there is a small town about ten miles away from where they live, but it is minuscule. My parents enjoy life away from the crowd."

"How are you going to be a doctor then if you live so far away?" I asked.

Alex shot me a look and then looked at Matthew, who said, "I apologize, Alex. I told him. I did not think this was a camp secret."

"Good thing your parents live so far away. Hopefully, the disease and famine will never reach them," Sima stated. "My parents thought it was too secluded up north, so they moved to Harrisburg, which is now named Juneau."

"So, when you reach Alaska, you'll be heading home to Juneau?" I asked.

"Who knows?" Sima said with a casual shrug. "I think I will stay with Alex's family for a while."

I was about to ask why when I noticed Alex give me a look of warning. I felt as if his gaze held some type of caution. I decided not to ask Sima more about his parents.

"Well, men, I am getting tired," Sima said with a yawn. "I think I will rest. There is another day of running tomorrow and riding. I think I should tell Jason to slow down. We are not pack horses. Our dogs are strong, yet we could wear them out as well."

"I would love to back you up with that statement," I told him.

Matthew laughed. "Me too."

I took Alex's empty mug from him and poured some more tea into it. "How about you, Alex?"

"No, you know that I wouldn't say anything to Jason Shubert. Anyway, we are in enough trouble as it is. It's all because of you, Sima. I did not tell you, but Jason was livid this morning. I am serious. I am tired of standing up for you."

Sima stood up and stretched. "Don't stand up for me then."

"Sima, please, you know that I had to beg Mr. Shubert to bring you along."

"Perhaps you did, but I would have gone along anyway."

"Maybe, but Sima..." Alex started to say something else in a demanding tone of voice.

Sima looked straight at Alex. "Alex, stop worrying. There is no use in you lecturing me all the time. I understand. You need my help to keep you out of a mess with Mr. Shubert. All right, I will help."

"Sima, you are not being fair," I interrupted. Both Sima and Alex turned to me. I swallowed as an uncomfortable feeling came over me.

"Fair?" Sima sounded as if I had taken leave of my senses.

"Well, Alex keeps getting the blame for everything. Jason could make you leave, and I am sure Alex would not want to be without you."

"I am sure he would not want to be stuck with you either," Sima answered. I was hurt. Alex gave me an irritated glance.

Matthew shook his head. "Listen, arguing will get us nowhere, and if you plan to act like children, please do not waste my time. I need some sleep."

"Never mind," I answered.

"Of course," Alex agreed. I could sense the annoyance in his voice.

Sima chuckled as he went and stood at the tent entrance. "Go to sleep, all of you. I am just joking, in case you did not realize. Anyway, all of you need to relax. What is the worry? Enjoy life." He then left the tent.

Alex finished off his tea and threw his mug in the snow. "If he gets eaten by a bear on this trip, I do not think I will care."

About two minutes later, I could tell that Alex had fallen asleep. I looked over to where Matthew lay. He also slept. I pulled the blankets around me and tried to get comfortable. I could not understand how they could fall asleep without a worry. I had plenty of fears. I dug through my bag and pulled out the photograph that lay on the bottom. I drew a line with my finger around my mother's face. I could not believe that I would meet her someday; if I ever found her. This trip was a wild, insane chase. There was no reason for me to go, but I had a chance, and at least I was doing something and not sitting in one spot back in Maine.

*****

The next day, I awoke to the sound of the morning whistle. Alex and Matthew were both awake. Alex had already left the tent.

"Hello," Matthew said as I sat up. He had begun to pack our supplies.

I rubbed the sleep out of my eyes. "Where is Alex?"

Matthew chuckled. "Where do you think? Already feeding the dogs."

"I better hurry." I busied myself with my blankets and the mugs we had not packed away the night before. We both finished our task at a headlong speed and ran out of the tent.

We found Alex feeding the dogs. He grinned at us as we came near him. "I have to challenge the both of you to move a little faster in the morning."

I had to stop myself from admiring his grin and his confidence. I did not have much time to do so anyway. Jason's yell that we would be leaving in five minutes interrupted my thoughts, and we ran to take down the tent. I looked over to Sima's tent and saw him helping the two Josephs. At least for this morning, he kept his side of the bargain.

Soon enough, we were off. The dizzying speed at which the dogs ran gave me a rush of energy that I adored. I lacked professionalism; my steps and my dogs were slow. Although I managed not to fall behind as on the previous day, our group remained in the back throughout our journey.

I suppose our dog train would have been an incredible sight to those who saw us from a distance. Thirteen sleds in a row, moving at a quick pace across the brilliant snow. The ground and the snow were hard and slick. The sled runners made a crisp sound as they cut through the ice.

That day we did get a chance to break for lunch. Alex, Matthew, and I sat on the top of Matthew's sled. Sima came and plopped himself right next to me. He pulled out his pipe and lit it. He then pulled out his knife and that infernal piece of wood. He looked as if he were carving some kind of animal out of it.

Sima turned his attention away from his carving for a second. "Listen, I want to make it to Montreal today."

I put down my fork. "So do I."

Alex stopped chewing for a second. "That does not seem to be Mr. Shubert's plan."

Sima stuffed his piece of wood in his pocket and hopped up from the sled. "Alex, how do you always know Jason's plan? Matthew, do you know how Alex always knows the plan?"

Matthew laughed. "I'm sure, Sima, that as the company doctor, Alex needs to know the plans that Mr. Shubert has."

Sima narrowed his eyes. "Oh, I'm sure he does. Anyway, I'm going back to my group since the company doctor is so important." He then added, "Andrei, hurry up. You eat slowly."

At that moment, I had a momentary lapse of memory and asked, "Who is Andrei?"

Sima gave me a suspicious glance and smirked. "I hope you're joking."

I gave a fake laugh and said in a voice that sounded as unconvincing as I felt, "I am."

Sima looked at me again, laughed, and strode off. My cheeks flushed with heat. I knew that my disguise was not remarkable, but so far, I felt as if I had been pretty believable. Yet if I continued to make mistakes, I would be thrown out. Which at the moment, I was not sure if I would mind so much. I shoved the rest of the food into my mouth.

Matthew watched Sima leave. "He is an odd man."

Alex took his plate and put some snow on it to rinse it off. "I would have to agree."

*****

We did not even reach Canada that day. Needless to say, Sima and I were a bit disappointed. We had gotten into a regular routine of unpacking and packing. Feeding dogs and unloading tents had become an automatic task. As soon as the dogs were removed from the sleds and tethered, Alex, Matthew, and I fed them. I carried a lot of meat in my sled.

Much to our chagrin, we reached the Canadian border only three days later. As we pulled up to the border, we saw officers dressed in red uniforms standing at the border, ready to greet us. I felt terrified. I had my papers on me when I left home, and I hoped they would not check them. My documents clearly stated that I was a girl. Of course, the officers would never let me pass if they found out the truth. One woman traveling with twelve men was unheard of. I fingered the paper in the pocket of my jacket.

"Alex," I whispered as we all pulled our sleds to a stop.

"Yes?"

"Will they check papers?"

"I don't know," he answered. "You have them, right?"

"Yes... yes, I do have them, but I hope they don't take the documents or look at them."

Sima, who stood nearby, said, "Who cares? Let them check. They don't mind. They only look at them for a second anyway."

"All right," I said as a note of doubt crept into my voice. I noticed Alex studying me again. Jason was speaking to the officers. What would they do to me if they found out that I was a girl after all? They could just look and pass by. Nevertheless, I stood in between Sima and Alex with bullets of sweat running down my back. I attempted to listen to the conversation between the officers and Mr. Shubert.

"Yes, we are going to Alaska, gentlemen. No matter how strange that sounds to you, we are all carrying supplies to Fort Yukon," Mr. Shubert was telling them.

"I see," replied the commanding officer.

"Yes, we all have our papers in order, if that is what you need or what you want," Mr. Shubert continued without hesitation. I wondered what would happen if they did not let us pass.

The leading officer took the papers from Mr. Shubert and looked through them. "We must check all papers before letting you cross our border. It is protocol. Then you may proceed. Anyone's papers that are not in order or are incorrect will need to stay behind."

The leading officer glanced over at one of the younger officers. "Charles, you check that half of the men."

"Yes, sir." The young man marched over to Joseph Smith, who stood in the middle of the row of sleds. Some of Joe's dogs barked at the young officer. My heart beat harder and harder, sweat began to form on my hands. The man moved at an efficient pace through the papers, and he did not seem to be perusing them thoroughly. I was almost sure that I would not pass. The word female stood right on the top, and my name stood on the top of the page as well.

The young officer was now looking at Alex's papers. I began to pull out my documents from the pocket of my jacket. In an instant, the officer stood in front of me. I noticed how young he was. He could not have been older than eighteen. He looked at me, and I handed him the paper with hesitation. He opened it and stopped. I could almost see his green eyes bulge out of his head. He looked at me. I was happy that there was a commotion at the other end of the line because the senior officer had wanted to look through some contents on Andrew Redlock's sled. The young officer stared at me and then looked at the paper and then stared at me again. I saw his brain turning, questioning his next move. He looked down the line and then looked at me one more time. I formed with my mouth the word, *please*. The young man anxiously folded the paper and handed it to me with uncertainty.

"What's the problem?" Sima asked. "He's not a baboon."

"Nothing," the poor young man answered and turned to take Sima's papers.

"Sima," Alex said with a warning in his voice.

"Sorry."

"It's quite all right," the young officer replied and hurried through Sima's papers. He handed them to Sima in a matter of five seconds.

The officer curiously glanced at me as he passed by me on his way back to the front of the line. I mouthed, *thank you*. He hurried forward. I hoped that Alex, Matthew, and Sima did not think anything to be odd. Alex did not say anything. He carefully watched the officer and appeared to be deep in thought. Alex, I was sure, would figure out my secret before Sima did. I did not know if Matthew would think anything of it. He seemed to be the least nosy and did not seem to like Mr. Shubert. I hoped that, at least for now, I could keep things quiet for as long as possible.

"What was wrong with him?" Sima asked.

"I don't know," I answered. "There's nothing wrong with my papers," I lied.

Sima started to reach for the papers in my hand. "Let me see them. Maybe I could find something wrong with them."

I shoved the papers deep in my jacket pocket. "No, I assure you there is nothing wrong."

"Oh, come on," Sima pleaded.

"No, please, we're going now anyway," I protested.

Sima looked at me. "Andrei."

"Sima!" Matthew gave Sima a stern glare. Sima pretended to be hurt and looked away from me.

"Everything seems to be in order. You may go along now. Have a safe journey," the lead officer was saying to Mr. Shubert. I let out a sigh of relief as we all moved over the Canadian border.

Much to our chagrin, we did not reach Montreal that day. Mr. Shubert assured all of us that we would reach it the next day. I needed a day or two of rest and no dogsleds.

That evening after a quick supper, Sima, Matthew, Alex, and I spoke outside our tent. "Listen, Fur Hunter is having a bonfire in front of his tent. Why don't we go over?" Sima asked.

"No, thank you, Sima. I am tired, and Fur Hunter bothers me," I told him.

"Everything bothers you," Alex commented.

"Well, I suppose maybe it does."

Matthew put his hand on my shoulder. "It's all right, Andrei, rest, and we'll go without you."

"All right," Sima said with an impatient sigh. "Alex, Matthew, you are coming, right?"

"Yes, I am," Alex answered. "Nobody bothers me, well maybe Joseph Shubert and Steven Lake."

"I am not surprised." Sima walked ahead. Then he added without looking back at me, "Good night, Andrei. Get some rest. You need it."

"Thank you," I said as I watched the three of them walk away.

In the tent, I was relieved to be alone. I wanted to have some privacy. My thoughts lingered for a while on Matthew, Sima, and Alex; they did not seem so terrible. I just hoped that they would never know the truth. I wondered if Sima would care at all. I knew Alex would. He seemed to be honorable and as if he would never lie.

On the other hand, I did not think Sima would think it strange if I told him I had lived with a pack of wolves. Matthew seemed to be the one person I could trust. I washed with some melted snow and then fell asleep.

I awoke to strange sounds. I half-opened my eyes, expecting to see the gray morning light filtering through the cracks in the tent. It was not morning, though. It was just Alex and Sima coming in from Fur Hunter's bonfire. I shut my eyes and pretended to be asleep.

"He's asleep," Sima observed as I heard him walk in.

"Good, don't wake him up," Alex replied as I heard footsteps behind Sima. I heard Alex sit down on his blankets. I thought I heard Sima sit down too.

"Alex, do you like him?" I heard Sima ask.

"Yes, he's not bad, strange, but tolerable."

"Tolerable? Where did you get a word like that?" Sima laughed a bit.

"Don't you think he's odd?" Alex continued while ignoring Sima's question.

"No, why? He's just quiet, that's all. He's young, Alex," Sima retorted.

"I sometimes wonder if he is too young," Alex mentioned.

"I do not think so. Mr. Shubert let him come, didn't he?" Sima sounded like he could care less.

"Yes, of course, but he has such a young face, almost like a pixy," Alex observed. My cheeks were flaming. I knew that Alex was not stupid; if he had not figured out the truth yet, he would pretty soon. Sima laughed again. "Like a pixy, Alex? You are too tired."

"Too tired?" Alex asked. I could hear that his voice sounded uncertain. "Then explain to me what that was at the border? There was something wrong with his papers. That officer was not just staring at him for fun."

"Alex, I don't know, that officer was young too, and who cares anyway? Andrei's here, and he isn't bothering anyone, so leave him alone. You always get so worked up about things. This is not a big deal." Sima gave a loud yawn.

"Not a big deal? That officer was young, so he let him go," Alex argued.

"Well, so there's something wrong with him, just leave it, Alex," Sima said, sounding like he was ready to drop the subject and go to sleep.

"All right, but I'm telling you, he acts suspiciously too," Alex added.

"So, he acts suspiciously? Alex, stop worrying, please." I heard Sima stand up. "Anyway, I have to go back to my tent before Mr. Shubert has a heart conniption."

"Matthew's not back yet," Alex replied.

"Yes, he's also not on Mr. Shubert's horrible person list." I heard Sima snicker and get up to leave.

"Good night."

"Good night." I felt the air coming in through the tent that Sima must have lifted to leave.

Alex spoke again. "Sima?"

"What?" Sima asked in an annoyed whisper.

"You know, I thought I heard Andrei say 'thank you' to the officer."

"You always hear things," Sima replied. "We have a big day tomorrow, and I do want to sleep tonight."

"I am telling you something is wrong," Alex kept talking.

"Alex, all right, I agree, something is wrong. Go to sleep!" Sima did not sound as if Alex had convinced him of anything. I began to realize that Alex made observations like a hawk.

"Sima, you never pay attention. Watch him some time," Alex was still talking. My cheeks were burning like hot coals as I heard those words.

"Alex, once again, there is nothing wrong with him, and if there is, I have better things to do with my time. Stop thinking."

"That's something you never do," Alex told him.

"Yes, and I have more fun." Sima laughed. "Now, if you say one more thing, I will honestly punch you in the face." There was silence in the tent then, and I heard a light snore coming from Alex a few minutes later. I put my pillow over my head, and I tried to sleep.

Chapter 4   November 9, 1887

The next morning, every man in the camp appeared to have a smile on his face. We packed our bags and sleds in record time. The dogs ate their food in a flash. Even they seemed to feel the energy of the day. Montreal lay ahead of us. We could even reach it by midday. The pace of our sleds was quick as we moved through the fields towards the big city.

Alex pointed to the tall structures on the horizon. "Look over there, Andrei."

My heart lifted in joy. I had never seen such tall buildings before, and they made quite an impression as we drove through the outskirts of the city. People ran out of their houses to look at us passing by.

"Four days' rest, men, and a whole lot of interesting things to do!" Sima called back to us. He and Joseph Smith were just ahead of us.

Alex grinned. "Thank you, Sima. We were briefed by Jason Shubert ahead of time."

I just loved the thought of staying in one place at a hotel. Four delightful days lay ahead of us, no blankets, no unpacking, and no snow. We were pulling up to the city of tall edifices that looked gray and green in the midmorning sun. I could see the rooftops glimmering. I could not wait to go and explore all the different sites.

"You've never been here before?" I asked Alex and Sima. They shook their heads no.

Sima seemed impatient. "Let's hurry up! I want to get there faster. We're getting a bit behind. Who's going to be first?" Sima asked in a challenging voice. He then called to his dogs to quicken the pace.

"It's not a fair race, Sima, if you have a head start," Alex called and chased after him.

"Wait for me!" I yelled. I struggled to catch up with them.

"Tough luck Andrei!" Sima shouted back at me. I ran faster. Joseph Smith also sped up, and he kept pace with Sima. Matthew did not seem to want to change his speed and stayed behind.

"Come on, Bobick!" I hollered with all my might and ran too fast. I had difficulty breathing, but I was catching up with Sima, Joseph, and Alex.

"Come on, Bobick!" I kept yelling. A cold wind blew in my face, but the breakneck speed propelled me to keep going. Our sleds seemed to fly through the air. We passed Jason Shubert and Steven Lake.

"Where are you boys going?" Mr. Shubert called.

"To Montreal!" Sima yelled out the obvious answer.

I kept running and yelling to my dogs, "Let's go, ha!" I had forgotten myself.

I was soon in front of Sima. I reached the city's outskirts ahead of Sima and Joseph, although Alex was ahead of me and waited for us to catch up.

"Who lost now, Sima?" he called to Sima as he drove up.

Sima laughed. "I did not think Andrei could go so fast. He keeps to the end of the train most times. At least it did not take all of my yelling might to get my dogs moving like Andrei."

I shook my head and laughed. I did not care. The feeling of speed and freedom had been worth the effort.

Jason Shubert rode up to us. "Why did you think you could go so fast? You could've lost us."

"On such a short distance?" Sima asked with a smirk. I saw Alex kick Sima from behind.

Jason Shubert furrowed his bushy black eyebrows. "Well, you better not go ahead like that again."

Sima did not stop. "Why? You go ahead." I was standing next to Sima, so I hit him in the arm. He just hit me back.

"Listen, Sima," Jason said as he came up to him with a menacing glare. "You are pushing your luck. You better keep quiet."

Sima grinned at him and said, "Yes, sir." I then saw Sima swallow hard after Jason walked towards his sled. Sima looked brash, but I wondered if he worried about Jason Shubert's threats.

"Stay behind me," Jason said to us as he drove by. We followed at the back of the group. Matthew stayed with us.

Alex turned to Sima. "Listen, Sima, why don't you keep quiet? You know he could leave you in Montreal."

"You know, I was not the only one racing," Sima retorted.

"Well, you keep your mouth shut!" Alex ordered.

"Alex, I do not have to listen to this from you. You are not Mr. Shubert. Anyway, if I stay in Montreal, that is better."

"Sima, I am telling you for your own good, you should not act this way."

"Alex, I do not think that there is a reason for this argument." Sima sped up a bit and pulled in front of Alex.

Matthew, who had kept silent until now, spoke up, "Alex, he's right. Leave him alone." Silence hung around us.

I decided to lighten the mood. "Well, Alex, you know at least we will be sleeping in warm surroundings tonight."

"I agree, at least for a few days." After that, Alex's disposition seemed to improve, and we arrived in the city without argument.

What I noticed first was the size of the buildings. The gray stones formed impressive brick houses that lined the wide streets. I wanted to be alone to explore. I worried that I would not have much respite with Alex, Sima, Matthew, and Joseph.

The streets of the city overflowed with stands where people were selling clothing and food. Smells of fresh-baked bread, chestnuts and coffee filled the air. Yelling and conversation clouded my mind.

Jason Shubert drove in front of our train of men and dogs with determination and pride. We produced great delight in the city. Some children ran up to the sleds trying to touch our dogs. One little boy ran up to me and asked if he could pet Bobick. I smiled at him and allowed him to do so. During my exchange with the boy, I noticed that Alex was giving me that odd look again.

Jason Shubert led us to a hotel not far from the edge of the city. The hotel had been nice enough to lend us their back storage house for the sleds and the dogs.

After situating the dogs in the storage house, Mr. Shubert gathered all of us together. "Men, please remain calm for five minutes more." Sima rolled his eyes in my direction in response.

"He sounds like a teacher," Matthew whispered to me. I smirked and scuffed my feet against the floor.

"Men, I want you to be careful. Otherwise, I want you to enjoy yourselves. The hotel has offered each man his own room. They will even give us free food. I have paid for the rooms in advance. Please make sure that you thank them for their generosity, especially you boys." He looked straight at Sima, Joseph Smith, and me.

"Us?" Sima raised his voice.

"Listen, sir," Joseph Smith started saying, "we might be young...."

Steven Lake turned towards us and cut Joseph off in the middle of his sentence. "He just means that you boys should behave." Sima made a face when Steven turned around.

"We will discuss more at the hotel. We will be leaving four days from now. Pretty much you will be on your own." Jason Shubert was dismissing us. I was eager to explore. I had never been to a big city such as this.

"Would you like to do anything?" Joseph Smith asked as Joseph Shubert also joined us. The group began to break up as soon as Jason finished his uninspiring speech.

"I am going to get a shave," Sima announced to us. "Anyone coming with me?" Both of the Josephs agreed to go. Matthew shook his head and told Sima that he and Rideon Smith had already made plans to look at the Cathedral. I watched Matthew walk off with Rideon; my heart sank. Matthew had become my rock.

"I can shave by myself," I announced.

"You don't need to," Sima chided.

"I do not need a shave," Alex said. "I'll go with Andrei." I had a feeling that he just wanted to keep an eye on me. At the same time, I felt relieved that at least Alex stayed behind. I did not want to look too ridiculous.

"All right," Sima said in a decisive tone and turned toward the door. "See you at supper, six o'clock then."

Alex nodded. "Yes, have a good time." Alex then turned to me. "So, is there anything you would like to do?"

"Just see the city. I wanted to shop, I mean buy some necessities, but otherwise, it is up to you."

"Well, they, I mean Steven Lake said there are some ice sculptures created every year. Perhaps you would like to see them?"

I gave a slight shrug with my shoulders. "Sure."

Hesitation filled me as I followed him down the street. Men were splitting off and walking in different directions. I was left alone with Alex. In reality, Alex was a stranger to me. Could I trust him at all? The gray walls rose around us. The sun peeked through the spaces between the buildings and warmed my skin. There was no need to worry now. The streets bustled with people who were all muffled up against the cold. I noticed how ragged Alex and I looked compared next to them. Girls my age went by in long skirts, warm muffs on their hands, and caps of fur on their heads.

"You must be rich to buy furs like that," I observed.

"Furs like what?" Alex asked. We were now walking down a wide street crowded with food vendors.

I pointed down the street. "Like those girls, standing around the vendor who's selling chestnuts."

"Oh yes, although those who hunt for those furs do not get all that money," he said, sounding bitter.

"Yes, I know, why just recently before we left, I had gone to town to sell furs, although the season had not been so good and then in town they gave me strange looks because," I stopped mid-sentence.

Alex turned to me. "Because what?"

"Oh, never mind." I had almost said: because a girl like me would never trade furs.

"Because you look too young?" Alex suggested.

I let a sigh of relief escape my lips. Perhaps he did not suspect anything. "Yes."

"It's all right. You are at least full height. I mean, you are tall, and that is not bad." If he had known I was a girl, I would have taken that as an insult.

He turned to look at the girls as we passed by them. "Well, anyway, those girls, I don't care much for those furs. I mean, I'd want a girl who would like the wilderness. She would hunt furs with me, and she would have to be just like me." He laughed. "Maybe it is just asking too much."

I agreed in silence. Where did he expect to find such a tremendous outdoors girl? But, if he knew that I was a girl, I might just be the one he was looking for. That thought made me self-conscious, so I decided to change the subject. "Where were those ice sculptures?"

Alex waved towards the street on the corner. "Well, Mr. Shubert said that they were somewhere on this road." He led the way with confidence. "Let's go."

I took off my gloves. "It's warm, and I do not see any ice sculptures."
I stopped to look around.

He hit me in the arm and walked forward. "I do, you idiot, up there."

I laughed and trailed behind him. We reached the frozen figures
in three minutes. They were larger than I had imagined they would
be. One of them was about the size of a one-story building.

"Do you think we can climb on it?" Alex asked.

"Why not?" I asked. "There is no sign that says we cannot do so."

Alex walked up the pathway towards the ice sculpture. "Come on."

I touched the smooth side of one of the structures. "Look, it is
built like a house."

Alex grabbed the side of the roof and pulled himself up. "Yes, it is.
I will try to get up to the top."

He tried to steady himself. "It's slippery."

Laughing, I squinted up at him. "It's ice, Alex."

"Come on, Andrei, climb up!"

"All right, I am coming." I could not help thinking that I would
never do such a thing before coming on this journey. I had my qualms
about climbing ice sculptures. I grabbed on to the side of the ice
window. Without warning, a rough hand pulled me down. I turned
around, and I was face to face with a tall, husky man. I was frightened,
but I kept my composure.

"What's wrong?" I asked in an innocent voice. The man yelled
something at me in a language I did not comprehend. I shook my head
in response. Without another word, the man stormed off.

I stepped away from the ice sculpture. "Alex, where are you?"

Alex slid down the roof. "I am right here. Why did you not come up?"

"Some man just came up to me and pulled me off the sculpture."

Alex looked around. "What man?"

I rubbed my shoulder. "I don't know. He just stormed off. So much
for looking at ice sculptures. He also spoke some language I did not
understand."

"Was it French?"

"No, I have heard French before from French trappers, and that was not French." I snickered. "Let's get out of here before he comes back."

Alex nodded. "I wanted to get some rest before supper anyway. Let's get back to the hotel."

Both of us ambled down the cobblestone street—an older man with a rickety cart passed by us. The smell of warm potatoes drifted up from the cart. The scent made my stomach rumble.

Alex stopped by the older man with the potato cart. He turned to me. "Would you like one? Jason gave me some Canadian money earlier this morning."

"Of course," I replied. I felt a bit envious of Alex and his high standing with Mr. Shubert. I understood he had known him for a long time, but Mr. Shubert seemed to prefer him to many other men and sometimes even to his son.

After we purchased the potatoes, we both attacked them as if we had never seen food before. Alex bit into his potato. "This is first-rate food."

"Yes," I agreed. I studied Alex at that moment. He had a handsome face. In the past few days, I realized I took notice of him more often. I even liked the way he ate. There seemed no use in entertaining such thoughts. He did not realize I was a girl.

*****

When we arrived at the hotel, I was delighted that we had neighboring rooms. "This is good," I told Alex as we neared our rooms. "It will be much easier to plan out our next course of action."

"Yes, however, I do want to rest before supper. Jason said to head to the pub next to the hotel and not to the main dining room. He will buy us supper. This hotel is high class, and I do not think we are allowed in the main dining areas.

I nodded my agreement. "It is strange that the management is even allowing natives to stay here. I'll go rest before supper as well."

Alex looked towards his room and then back at me. "Jason Shubert has good connections. Anyway, I'm going to rest." He then turned to open his door.

I placed the key from my room in the doorknob. "Knock on my door when you are ready, will you?"

Alex took a step into his room. "I will. See you later." He then walked into the room and shut the door.

Relieved to be alone, I walked through the door of my room. The richness of the room overwhelmed me. Never in my dreams could I have imagined that a bed could be so vast or look so soft. I just wanted to lie down and sleep on it for years. A door near the entrance of the room led to a water closet. I looked inside. The white marble tub sparkled under the gas lights. The copper pipes that carried the water also glowed. I had never used a civilized tub before, and the sheer thought of using one made me excited. I looked back at the room and the ornate wood-carved ceiling. My body longed to lie down. I took off my boots and jumped onto the bed. I felt like a young girl. I pressed my head against the cool pillow.

Sleep pulled at my body. My mind, however, did not rest for a second. I started thinking, what if I hid in Montreal? Then there would be no need for me to go on. I could become like those beautiful girls who wore fancy furs. Mr. Shubert had said he would pursue us if we left the train without proper notice. However, if I dressed like a girl, he would never know it was me. All the men on the trip thought that I was a boy. I was stupid to have said I was a boy to go along. Danger lurked at every corner. I feared that my disguise would not last long. What if I did run off? My flow of thoughts stopped. If I ran off, I would not reach Alaska. I had to remember why I had come. My ultimate goal needed to remain at the forefront of my mind. Money also remained an issue. If I stayed in Montreal, I would be homeless.

Only one option remained; I had to press on. There was not much to unpack. I reached for the travel pack that stood next to my bed and pulled out the photograph of my parents. I lay back and studied their faces. A knock sounded on my door.

I knew who it was, so I shoved the photograph back into my bag. "Come in."

Alex opened the door. "You ready?"

"Yes," I said, picking up my hat that I had placed on the bed. "Have Sima or Matthew returned yet?"

Alex shook his head. "No, Sima will probably not come back for supper."

We walked down the rich green-carpeted hall. Crystal lanterns hung from the vaulted ceilings. "Jason Shubert has some pretty influential friends," I observed out loud. "Just walking through here makes me feel rich."

"Yes, I know," Alex agreed. We continued to make our way through the hotel.

"I have never thought of riches such as these," I told him.

"My thoughts never lingered much on wealth. I saw Shubert's place back in Maine. It is very nice but not as beautiful as this."

"I never saw Mr. Shubert's place," I said, hoping to make Alex laugh.

Alex grinned. "Of course not." Montreal seemed to make a good impression on Alex. His face had lost the stern expression he often carried. He stopped unexpectedly in his tracks. "I forgot the name of the place we are supposed to go to. I'll go back to my room and get the address. Wait for me in the lobby."

*****

My steps were swift and light as I skipped down the grand staircase. The large lobby appeared vacant. A huge vase of vibrant red roses stood on a table near the entrance to the hall. I skipped over to them and leaned over to breathe the smell of their magical aroma. Their sweet fragrance filled my nose, and I pulled off a petal from one of the roses in sheer delight.

It was at that moment that I felt someone's eyes watching me. I turned, and my blood ran cold. Fur Hunter stood in a deep corner of the lobby. His gaze did not leave mine for a second. He had the most captivating quality to his eyes. How could I calmly exit this situation? I needed to make a quick escape. I could not confront Fur Hunter. Even if I did, what would I say? By facing him, I would only give myself away. Out of the corner of my eye, I spotted Alex's reflection in one of the lobby's mirrors. I turned on my heel and hurried over to meet him. I looked back over my shoulder as we headed towards the door. Fur Hunter's eyes were still on me.

We walked outside, the streets were getting darker, and the street lamps sparkled. I took a deep breath. "This is wonderful. I never imagined Montreal like this."

Both of us continued our short journey in silence. When we reached the restaurant, I realized it was for those of the lower class. My eyes had to adjust to the dim lighting upon entering. At the far table sat Jason Shubert, Steven Lake, Andrew Redlock, and Fur Hunter. I wondered how he had gotten there at such a fast rate. He had just been at the hotel.

There was a bar near the door. Alex turned to me. "Beer?"

"Of course," I answered. I never had drunk beer before, but what could I do?

He turned back to the bartender. "Two beers." Soon we were walking toward the table.

I sipped my beer. "Nothing like a good beer, huh?" I turned to Alex. I hoped I sounded convincing.

"It's great, but I have had better."

"Don't you think Fur Hunter is odd?" I asked in a whisper as we neared the table.

"No, he seems normal. I like him," Alex said as we came up to the table. Maybe he liked him, but Fur Hunter made me uncomfortable. I wished Red Fern was there. He seemed gentler than his cousin.

"Jason, do you have room for us?" Alex asked.

"Sure, boys, sit down." The men shifted their seats to make space for us. A claustrophobic feeling pressed on me as I sat down. This place seemed worse than the tavern we had visited back in Maine. The room was dim and musty. Men smoked pipes and cigars.

"Alex, have you seen my boy and Sima? I believe Joseph was with them too, wasn't he?" Jason Shubert asked.

"Yes, Joseph was with them," Alex answered. "I have not seen them."

Mr. Shubert furrowed his eyebrows. "I hope they do not run into trouble."

"They can take care of themselves," Mr. Redlock stated. "Let them have fun; they are still young."

"It seems that the young ones tend to get into the most trouble," Mr. Shubert responded. He gave Alex and me a hard stare as if we were planning to get into some kind of mischief.

Alex did not reply, but he glared at Jason over the rim of his glass as he drank. Fur Hunter pulled out his pipe, and I was glad that I sat on the other side of the table. His pipe had a terrible smell to it. I wondered if anybody else noticed the caustic quality that his pipe seemed to contain. Jason Shubert continued to stare at Alex and me. His gaze made my throat tighten.

I rose from the table. "I'll go get some food. Where is it?" I had only just realized that most of the men had their suppers in front of them.

Jason pointed to the spot. "On the side table in the next room."

Relief flooded through me as I left the room. I could not understand why Jason Shubert decided to stare at us. I heard footsteps behind me, and I turned. Alex was close at my heels.

I glanced back at the table. "What was that all about?"

"Jason Shubert constantly tries to intimidate people for some unknown reason," Alex replied. "You just have to show him that you are not scared of him. You will get used to it as time goes on."

I shook my head. Mr. Shubert intimidated me enough as it was. He had no reason to try to frighten me further. What if Fur Hunter had mentioned my odd behavior at the hotel to him?

"Mr. Shubert was gnawing on my nerves, as was Fur Hunter's pipe. I could not stand the smell anymore," Alex said as we both came upon the buffet of food lined up against the wall in the next room.

"You too?" I asked, laughing as I picked up a plate from the end of the table.

Alex grinned. "It is a good thing that I am not the only one that is bothered by his pipe."

I felt my knees go weak. I felt a strange magnetic feeling when I stood near Alex. I chided myself for being silly. "I am starving. Well, at least the food looks edible." Changing the subject did not seem to help my feelings disappear.

"It looks more than edible." Alex leaned over to pick up a plate, then he added, "I wonder where Sima is."

I laughed. "Probably in a jailhouse somewhere."

"Hmm? Yes, I know, no joke. Joe Shubert is no good. Don't tell anybody I said that. However, he is just a bad influence. He's been spoiled all his life by his father, just like his sister. I mean, if they get in trouble, Sima will get yelled at, or better yet, I will. Joe, on the other hand, won't even hear one cross word from him. Jason's son is terrible. That is why I did not go with them today."

"Oh, I didn't know. Why does Sima like him?"

Alex shrugged. "I don't know. It sometimes is difficult to explain why Sima acts the way he does." Alex piled three spoons of mashed turnips on his plate.

I got to the end of the buffet. I loaded my plate with food. "Are you done?"

Alex looked down at his full plate. "Yes."

"Let's hurry up and eat."

Alex and I returned to the dim room. I looked at the dull room ahead of us. "Do we have to eat there?" I asked as I made a face.

"Yes, look, Fur Hunter isn't there anymore, so don't worry."

I followed Alex into the next room. We finished our food with the rest of the men, talking about our plans and where else we would stop. To me, it seemed that Jason's plans seemed far-fetched. He wanted to travel for four more hard weeks after we left Montreal. After that, he said we would stop to rest at a cabin of his friends. I listened only with half interest. I could scarcely suppress the feelings that had sprung up on me. Alex sat right next to me, and my insides bounced and turned like stones in a fast-paced current. I shifted my full attention to my food in an attempt to push away these ludicrous emotions. I could not imagine what he would say if he knew the truth. I felt that if anybody discovered my secret, he would be the first to find out.

Some of the men left soon, and Alex and I were quickly left alone with only Andrew Redlock. He appeared to be a kind man. "Did you boys not see Sima at all?" asked Mr. Redlock. His voice sounded gentle and caring.

Alex spread his arms in question. "We have not seen him since we broke off into groups this morning. Matthew and Rideon are also absent."

"I trust Matthew and Rideon," Andrew said as he stood from the table. "I cannot say the same for the two Josephs and Sima. It is now nine o'clock. Perhaps I should go look for them."

"Will you?" asked Alex. "I do not believe it to be necessary, I mean, this is Sima, but I think he is fine."

"I just do not want Mr. Shubert to be angry at Sima again. He already overdoes it when he takes his rants out on Sima." He let out a heavy sigh. "I better go find Sima, but mark my words, if Sima is in trouble, it will be Joseph Shubert's fault. I'll tell you if and where I find him. Good night." Andrew Redlock walked away.

"I do not know why everybody is so worried," I said as I tried to finish drinking my beer. The liquid left a bitter taste in my mouth. "I mean Sima is always somewhere, and no one is asking where Joseph Smith is."

Alex placed his glass on the table after downing the rest of his drink. "No, no one is asking about Joseph. Look at Sima; at the academy, he was known as the biggest troublemaker. He left medical school one year before graduating and squandered the rest of his parents' money. Jason Shubert promised his parents he would look out for him. Sima has been quite unsuccessful in making a good impression thus far."

"I'm sorry, I had not meant to pry." I wondered why Alex had told me all this information. It was apparent that he cared for Sima a great deal. Yet, I did not need to know Sima's entire history.

Alex looked at me for a second and then said, "I'm exhausted. How about we turn in?"

I nodded my agreement, much pleased to be away from the darkness and the uncomfortable turn in the conversation. "I hope to sleep as long as possible. I need to muster up as much energy as I can for the rest of the journey."

Upon entering the hotel, I again admired the entryway. Red carpets covered the floors, and the spiraled staircase added flair to the already bright room. Two girls passed by me with huge skirts and big diamond necklaces as I followed Alex upstairs. I longed to be like them. My heart ached for a change. The girls sailed down the steps. I looked at my beaten jacket and pants. We arrived at our rooms. How many more months of Jason Shubert, Fur Hunter, Sima, and Alex? Could I endure such an ordeal? Alaska seemed to be a far-off reality.

In my room, I stared at myself in the mirror. My hair was a mess on top of my head. The once long beautiful locks of hair did not even reach my ears. I put a ribbon around my head. There, I looked a little prettier and a bit less wild. Again I wondered if Alex would ever discover my deception. I did not have a boy's face. I sighed, and after changing into a pair of boy's pajamas that I had brought but had not used since the trip had started, I said my prayers and fell asleep in a matter of seconds.

In the middle of the night, I woke to what sounded like yelling in the next room. Half asleep, I stumbled out of bed and listened. The yelling seemed to be coming from Alex's room. Curiosity got the better of me, and I decided to investigate. I quickly put on my jacket and socks. Then I remembered I had a ribbon on my head. I ripped it off and messed up my hair. I went and knocked on Alex's door. It was torn open by Alex. He had a murderous look in his eyes. I took a step back.

"Oh Andrei, it's you. What do you want?" he asked in a rather loud voice.

"I am sorry to disturb you, but I thought I heard some yelling. What's going on?" As I was asking this question, I noticed Sima standing inside Alex's room.

"Come in," Alex said, opening the door to let me in.

I realized he was still in his clothing. "Haven't you slept?"

"No," Alex answered. I stepped into the room; Sima stood to the side, ablaze with anger. His chin had a bruise on it. I decided to take a seat in one of the chairs.

There was a short silence, and then Sima burst out, "What is wrong with Fur Hunter anyway?"

Alex sat down on another chair. "I was unaware that he was out looking for you. I did not know he would tell Jason. Redlock was going to go look for you as well...."

"Why does everybody worry so much anyway? What was the search for? They know that we'd be back. Shubert said we were on our own. What does it matter to him anyway?"

Alex glared at him. "Sima, you can't take care of yourself. You were in jail when Fur Hunter found you, and somehow he knew that was the first place he should look."

Sima stood up. "Well, Alex, since you are so smart, why did Joseph Shubert not get told that he was going to be left in Montreal? Jason knows it was his son who started it." Sima lost any composure that he had left. Before this night, I had not imagined that a single person could emit so much negative emotion.

"You got into a fight?' I asked. I almost laughed and would have done so if Sima had not been so furious. I then noticed that Sima had bloodstains on his shirt.

Sima turned his face to me. "Well, what is it to you? What business is this of yours?"

I stood up and took a step towards the door. "Sima, calm down. Anyway, you should talk to Jason. You know this is not fair!" I exclaimed.

"Oh, just talk to him? Just like that." Sima looked like he wanted to hit me. I inched closer to the door.

"Sima, calm down," Alex said in a soothing voice.

Sima shoved Alex in the chest. "You stop telling me what to do. You are not my father."

"Sima, don't start," I pleaded.

"Sima, I'll tie your hands if you don't stop!" Alex shouted. Sima glowered at us. I had the unsettling feeling that I needed to make a quick escape.

Sima looked around and sat down on the bed. "Well?" he asked in an irritated tone.

Alex sat down too. I moved behind the safety of a chair that stood nearest to the door. I saw Sima's pride was hurt. Alex's eyebrows furrowed and an intense fire burned in his blue eyes.

Alex looked through his bag, pulled out a clean shirt, and shoved it at Sima. "I'm still going to talk to Jason," Alex stated. "Sima, take care of yourself if you can."

Alex turned to me and commanded, "Andrei, you better go to sleep!" I wanted to leave, yet I waited. I wanted to see how these events would play out. Sima sat unmoving on the bed.

"Sima! Go get cleaned up; you look terrible!" Alex ordered.

"Yes, good night, I suppose." Sima looked dreadful as he stepped past me. I again saw the blood on his shirt and turned away. Alex looked at me with expectation.

"Will Sima be all right?" I asked.

"Yes, he asked for it. I tried to explain to him that telling Mr. Shubert to mind his own business is never a good idea."

I gave a half-hearted laugh. "I see your point."

Alex began to unlace his boots. "It still isn't fair. I still want to ask Mr. Shubert why he thinks that his son should get away with everything."

I felt torn by what had happened, and I felt the need to talk more about these events with Alex. However, Alex sounded like he was in no mood to talk. I decided it would be best to return to my room and process all the day's events.

"Good night." I walked out and went to my room. My energy faded. The reality of this expedition was hitting me full force. Also, fear began to grip me. I had seen what Jason Shubert was like when he was angry. What if he found out I was a girl? I did not want to spend any part of my life in jail. Jason Shubert did not seem to be a fair man. If I explained the truth to him, it could well be that he would not understand. I had the desire to pack my bags and sneak out.

Thoughts whirled about in my head as I sat on the bed and removed my jacket. Something was exciting about hiding and living on the verge of an undiscovered secret. Also, how would I find my parents if I ran away now? I might never get another chance to find them. I also pushed away from the thought that perhaps there was another reason why I stayed.

The following day I awoke late. For a second, I thought that I was in my cabin back in Maine. A few moments passed before I sat up in my bed and realized that I was in Montreal. Jason Shubert slept in a room down the hall, and Sima slept in a room across the hall. I had never felt so alone in all my life. After dressing, I headed downstairs. I had knocked on Alex's door, but he had not been there. I bounded off the lower step in the lobby.

"Sleep late enough?" asked a voice next to the staircase. There stood Sima, leaning against the wall with his arms crossed across his chest.

"Good morning. How are you?" I greeted him.

He came toward me. "I am all right, I suppose. It is the afternoon anyway. Haven't you slept in the past few days?"

"Yes, I was tired," I told him.

"Really?" He pretended to be surprised. He then tossed his hair out of his eyes. "Would you like some lunch?"

"I would not mind. What were you doing hiding below the stairs?" I asked him suspiciously.

"I am waiting for Alex. He is talking with Mr. Shubert. Let's go, he's taking a long time, and I'm hungry. I did see about ten pretty girls from my hiding place." He smiled again, and I wondered if I had dreamed up the occurrences from the previous night.

"Only ten?" I asked. "I thought I saw more girls here yesterday," I told him as he strode ahead of me.

He turned to face me and walked backward. "But you see, you need to know which ones are pretty." As he spoke, he stumbled upon a young woman standing in a group of young ladies. All of their dresses were quite exquisite. They had been talking to each other and laughing, but they stopped as Sima had approached them.

"Pardon me," he said as he fixed one of the girl's feathered hats that he had tilted. The girl just nodded at him and turned away.

"It was worth a try," he said to me, pretending as though he had walked into the girl on purpose.

I laughed. "Let's get some food." I walked towards the door. "I can tell that you feel better than you did last night."

"Not really," he said, then smiled and added, "I am a good actor."

"How could I forget?" I jested. I wondered if he had perhaps had too much to drink, but then I decided that Sima always seemed to act strange. There would be no harm in eating with him. Sima and I walked to a small café just a block away from the hotel.

"We need to find a table with one chair for Alex," Sima said as he pointed to a table near the window. "I wonder how he is faring." Sima sat down. He looked solemn for a moment. "If Alex is lucky, he will not get told that he is staying behind as well."

"He didn't do anything," I said. A thought then came to me. "Fur Hunter told Mr. Shubert, why?"

"He didn't tell him. It was Joe Shubert that told his father where we were," Sima said with a slight lift of his shoulders.

"Why did he tell? There seems to be no sense in that."

"He would never get in trouble, but...." Sima paused.

"You got worse," I told him. I did not understand men. Maybe there was not much to understand. I had no idea why they fought so much. I also found it hard to believe they still thought I was a man.

"Well," Sima said and gave me a dark look, "I guess I was asking for it, or that's what Alex said." Sima then grinned at me, and we both laughed.

"We both know Alex, huh?" I asked.

Sima grinned. "I suppose he just acts that way. I've known him forever. After a while, you just get used to him." Sima finished the sentence and began eating his food. Then I saw Alex approaching our table. My heart flew up into my throat. I had to give myself a mental shake before he noticed my general discomfort at his presence. I smiled in greeting and pretended that nothing was wrong with me.

"So, how is your meal?" Alex asked as he slapped Sima and me both on the back.

Sima straightened out and said, "Alex, do not dare do that again."

"Oh, I'm sorry, I forgot," Alex said as he sat down.

"How could you forget?" Sima asked. "You just spoke with Mr. Shubert, didn't you?"

Alex nodded. "Yes, he wants to talk to you too."

"It took you about two hours to come to that conclusion?" Sima asked, and he laughed a bit.

Alex looked hesitant. "No, he said that he is seriously considering leaving you here in Montreal."

"Did he say that?" Sima asked, his voice ablaze with new anger. "What about his son?"

"Well, his son is his son. You know what Jason is like," Alex answered Sima's question with bitterness.

Sima leaned forward. "That's it! I don't care if I have to stay here. There are much prettier girls here anyway. I highly doubt that there will even be any girls in Alaska." He stood up and threw his napkin on the table. "I'm going to go settle some questions right now." Sima stormed off.

"Goodbye," I said while I suppressed a laugh. Then I turned to Alex. "I can't believe that Mr. Shubert would do that. Just because... I mean, isn't he friends with your father?"

"Yes, but Sima has been enough trouble as it is. Jason can't help it."

As I listened to him speak, Alex took Sima's plate. "Now that Sima is gone, I hope he will not mind if I eat his food."

I put some pancakes into my mouth and regarded Alex. "But Alex, maybe you're wrong. Maybe Sima just got to Mr. Shubert in the wrong way. I thought that Mr. Shubert was pretty kind to you,"

I protested. In truth, part of me did not want Sima to stay behind. "Suppose Sima is left behind here in Canada? What will he do?"

"Andrei, calm down. Sima's a grown man. He will have to figure everything out."

I picked up another forkful of pancakes. "I certainly hope he will be able to do so."

Alex and I were drinking some coffee when Sima returned. "Alex, I think you were wrong," Sima stated as he came up to the table. "Anyway, I apologized and everything should be good now. I am allowed to continue on this *wonderful* expedition to Alaska," Sima said with the correct measure of sarcasm. He then glanced at the empty table. "Where's my food?"

"I thought you weren't coming back, so I decided to eat your food," Alex answered.

"Thank you for deciding for me that I didn't want it. For that, you have to go get some more food." Sima sat down next to me. Alex nodded and stood up. He then walked to the café counter.

Sima then looked at me and whispered, "Don't tell Alex, but I argued with Mr. Shubert for a while. I still do not understand why he did not punish his son..." Sima's voice trailed off. Sima's voice turned mischievous, and he laughed under his breath. "Look, Andrei, it is those girls from the hallway, you remember."

"How could I forget?" I asked with an edge of disdain in my voice. Sima did not notice. He waved to them. They gave us a strange fleeting look and walked at a brisk pace in a different direction. I could understand their looks of disgust. They probably thought that both of us were insane.

Sima leaned back in his chair. "Can't blame me for trying. Anyway, those girls are not worth a dime. They are all the same. All they care about is their hair. I want a girl who would throw snowballs once in a while and loves dogs and me, of course."

Excellent, I thought to myself, another man from the wilderness. No wonder Sima and Alex were friends. I began to realize that despite their outward appearances, the differences between them perhaps were not so significant.

Then I snickered as a funny thought dawned on me. "Enjoying your stupidity was not on your list."

Sima gave a loud snort. "You have a high opinion of yourself. I have to have a smart wife to balance out all my shortcomings." We both started laughing. I was beginning to enjoy Sima's company. I smiled at him. I could use as many friends as I could get.

*****

The rest of the days in Montreal passed without much event. I rested a great deal. Also, Alex, Sima, and I explored Montreal and avoided getting into fights. On the last night of our stay, I felt an empty feeling come over me. I did not want to go into the untamed wilderness again. I enjoyed Montreal so much that I promised myself that I would return.

I left the hotel that evening and walked alone into the city. Treading carefully so as not to slip on the road, I strolled in no particular direction. The gas lights inside some of the large houses burned bright, and they threw shadows onto the cobblestone street. I looked with longing into the windows and wondered what it would be like to live in such a wealthy home. They seemed so comforting and secure. The people in those homes belonged to a place, to a family, to a city.

I turned and walked to the hotel at a slow pace. I looked over my shoulder several times because I had a feeling I was being followed. The wind blew at my cap, and it fell off my head. I ran to get it. The air had a definite chill to it. As I bent down, I heard soft music carried on the wind. It was coming from a corner café. I hoped they allowed natives to eat there. My stomach grumbled. My decision was final. Matthew had given me some money that morning, and I had not yet spent it. I entered and sat down. A young woman came up to me and asked me what I would like to eat.

"Please, anything that is warm. How about some mushroom soup? Would you have that?" I asked.

She nodded and walked away. I admired the large room. A violinist played a soft melody at the side of the room. I looked out the window into the windy street. I dreaded the thought of the next day. Suddenly, Alex walked into view. Now I knew who had been following me. He turned in my direction. When he saw me in the window, he waved. His guilty expression gave him away. He walked in and strolled over to where I sat.

I was so angry that my heart squeezed hard together as he approached. "What are you doing here?" I asked suspiciously.

"Same as you, going to order some food."

"I already ordered."

"All right, I'll order for myself." He snapped his fingers at the waitress. "Waitress." The same girl that had approached me came up to our table. The air of confidence about him unnerved me. I wondered if he ever had any fears. "Please, may I have some crepes wrapped around some mushrooms?"

"Yes, sir." She nodded and walked away.

"Pretty girl, huh?" he asked as he nodded at the waitress that now walked towards the back of the restaurant.

My cheeks became warm. "Yes." I decided to change the topic of the conversation. "Did you enjoy it here?" I asked, steering away from the subject of pretty girls.

"Yes, except that whole fight at the beginning."

"That's all right, I suppose, the rest of the time made up for it," I told him.

"Really?"

"Yes, the time spent here was pleasant. I did enjoy the ice sculptures, even though we did not get to spend a lot of time looking at them." I gave a small giggle. Then I stopped myself when I realized how feminine I sounded.

He did not seem to notice. "I know. I enjoyed the sculptures immensely."

"It would be interesting to learn such a craft," I responded. Our conversation was interrupted by the young woman who brought out our food. She set down my soup and gave Alex his crepes.

"Thank you," Alex said and winked at her.

She blushed. "You're most welcome." She did not seem to mind at all that we were natives. Her eyes lingered on Alex's face just a second too long. I was astounded at Alex's boldness. If he had winked at me in such a manner, I would have been somewhat offended.

When she left, Alex turned back to me. "Are you looking forward to tomorrow?"

I was surprised by his question. Was anyone looking forward to the next day? "Not particularly."

"Why not? I feel a bit restless just sitting here."

"It is comforting to stay in one spot and know what the next day will bring. I am a bit afraid of going out into the wilderness."

"I think it is pretty exciting. Why did you come if you were afraid? Anyway, what is there to be scared of?" Alex looked like he was challenging me.

I looked straight back into Alex's deep blue eyes. "You know how dangerous this trip is. I had no other means of reaching Alaska. If I had, I would certainly take them. Did you want to go on this trip?"

Alex regarded me with a guarded expression. "I went on this adventure, if you can call it that, because I had a debt to Mr. Shubert. He practically raised me. I could not let him down."

"That is kind of a silly reason to risk your life," I told him. As soon as the words left my mouth, I regretted them.

His eyes turned steely. "Is your reason any better?" Alex asked, his words crisp.

I felt defensive. "I am looking for my parents."

"And I am going to meet mine," Alex said, with his voice full of anger. "Anyway, what chance do you have of actually finding your family? Alaska is the wildest and biggest place left on the North American continent."

I slowly moved the soup with my spoon. "I apologize, Alex, for saying what I did. I had not meant to attack what you thought was right."

His look softened a bit, and he added, "I suppose we are both a bit worried about what the coming months will bring. Let's enjoy our dinner."

We finished our food in silence. The soup was delicious, although I had lost my appetite. I started to become apprehensive about the coming days, weeks, and months. I began to worry that I would disappear and never return after I entered the Canadian wilderness.

As we walked to the hotel, even with Alex at my side, I knew I was entirely alone. I was the only girl. If anyone were to find out the truth, I had no idea what would happen. I felt as if I had to tell someone. I felt the closest to Alex. Perhaps he would understand. I did not know if I could risk the truth, though, not yet at least. At that moment, we reached a hill where we could see a good part of the city. It was beautiful. The lights burned bright against the dark sky. The city created a gorgeous silhouette against the black of the night. Alex turned to look at the sight. I stopped and wished that moment would go on forever.

Alex ruined it. He turned to me then and said, "You know, there is something strange about you."

His statement caught me off guard. I tried to remain as calm as possible. "What do you mean?"

"Don't you know?" he asked, tilting his head back to look down at me.

"No, I don't have any idea of what you are talking about," I answered him. I told myself that I had to remain composed. I did not know if the truth would be adequate at the moment.

"Listen, there is something different about you. I can help you if you need help. You know you can trust me." His deep voice echoed in the cold air. Perhaps, I could trust him, but not with the kind of secret that I held.

"There is nothing that I need to tell you," I assured him.

"Suit yourself." He looked into the distance, and his eyes rested on the bright lights of the city. Then he turned on me again. "Know this; if you are hiding something, I will find out." There was a definite threat in his voice, and a chill ran down my spine.

I decided that I needed to divert his attention. "Alex, you know you are too imaginative. I have no idea where you came up with this idea. Anyway, I am getting cold. I think we should return. I would like to get an ample amount of rest before starting tomorrow." I laughed and walked on towards the hotel.

Alex and I spoke little upon our return. I went right away to my room as soon as we entered the hotel and did not linger. I fell on my bed and pulled my blanket around me. I was shivering with apprehension. I knew that the truth would need to come out sometime, but I wanted to hold on to it for as long as possible.

Chapter 5   November 20, 1887

Gray dusk filtered through the streets as we pulled out of the city the next day. I was well-rested, and I hoped the coming day would turn out fine. Our band of men, dogs, and supplies made slow progress through the streets. Even though I was nervous about the coming months, a certain feeling of exhilaration did sneak up on me. Alex had told me he wanted to get moving. I began to feel restless when I awoke. Sima was quiet that morning, and so was Alex. I did feel uneasy around Alex, but he acted as though nothing had occurred the night before, and I began to wonder if I had imagined last night's episode.

Nevertheless, I knew that I had not conjured up Alex's doubts in my imagination, and he had reasons for his suspicions. I decided to try not to give him any more reason to doubt anything about me. Still, I knew that this task would be quite tricky.

We drove for several hours before resting, and my refreshed muscles began to ache again. I had forgotten the painful feeling of overused muscles, but now that it returned, I remembered my muscles reaction quite well. After a quick lunch of salted meat and rolls from the hotel, we kept moving. After lunch, we traveled another five miles. At least the weather was not too cold. We had reached a vast stretch of land that glistened in the setting sun.

"We'll rest here, men!" Jason called. I worried that it was too windy to stop there, but all of the men pulled up their dogs, and soon we were all setting up camp. Our tents were placed in a circle to protect our camp from the wind on the open plain. We built a large campfire in the middle of the tents. We all ate. Some men spoke of the magnificence of Montreal. I sat in silence, wishing that I could somehow fly back there. I also realized that I was about only ten days of hard travel from my home.

Running away now seemed ridiculous. I would not get far before someone would catch up to me. Anyway, most of the dogs on my sled were Jason Shubert's. My actions could amount to stealing. I excused myself and returned to our tent. Matthew and Alex had just been talking to Mr. Howell when I left. My bag was lying on top of my blankets. The photograph was inside. I sat down on my blankets and pulled out the photograph. I noticed how old and faded it looked. I brushed my hand over my mother's face. There was not much for me to go on. How could I find my parents from a simple photograph? What if they had stayed behind in Maine and had never found their daughter? Doubts refused to keep away from my troubled mind. I held the photograph close to my heart. At that moment, I heard footsteps, and I replaced my picture to its previous location. I glanced anxiously towards the entrance.

Alex lifted the flap of the tent and walked in. He glanced at me. "Are you all right?"

"Yes," I answered.

Alex looked down at me. "I was worried you did not feel well."

"Just tired," I explained. "Is it necessary for us to travel so many miles during the day?"

"Well, it certainly would do no good to travel during the night," Alex answered with a laugh.

"You know what I mean," I said this statement in an exasperated tone. "The dogs may tire rather quickly if we keep moving in this fashion, not to mention the men."

Alex lay down on his blankets. "Don't tell Mr. Shubert that. As you well know, he thinks he is doing the right thing. Anyway, we will have a chance to rest eventually."

"We do have to save some rest for the dogs. They are the ones pulling our sleds. If Mr. Shubert wants them to travel for the rest of the trip, he needs to give them an ample amount of rest."

"Listen, Andrei. I suggest you stop worrying about the dogs. They are strong, and they just received a good amount of rest in Montreal. They are just as anxious to get moving as we are. I think you are more worried about yourself than your dogs." Alex closed his eyes, and he looked as if he were lying in a ray of bright sunshine with green grass blowing in the wind around him.

"I don't think so. I hope Mr. Shubert does not believe that losing a couple of dogs and men is just part of the whole process." I sighed. I wondered if he ever thought that his men had any emotions.

"Losing men, I hope not, but losing dogs, Andrei, it could happen. That's part of most excursions that involve dogs, especially such long excursions. Now, how about you rest? I would not want to lose you tomorrow." I could hear a hint of sarcasm in his voice. I wondered if his legs ached. I did not dare ask.

I turned over on my side. This conversation seemed useless. "Good night."

"Good night," Alex answered from where he lay.

Again I wondered if I should tell Alex the truth. I wondered if telling Matthew would be safer. He might not convey the truth to anyone. I shrugged and decided not to mull over all of these questions at the moment. I felt the time to reveal secrets would come soon enough.

Every day of the following week began and ended similarly. There were loud whistles and calls. Also, the dogs had to be fed and cared for regularly. I would check their paws for scratches and put oils on them. Even though I was tired, my body began to adjust to the constant movement. Jason Shubert seemed to believe that alternating hard and easy days was the best way to travel. I agreed with him on that point, though I dreaded the days that I had named "hard." Every night one of the men would hold a bonfire in front of their tent. I avoided these bonfires like the plague. I rather hoped that I could avoid speaking to most men; I did not want to join the conversation.

On Friday of that week, I turned down Sima's offer to have supper at his tent and went back to our humble quarters. After Sima's misadventures in Montreal, he seemed a bit less spirited. When I reached our tent, I found Matthew building a small fire inside. I nodded a greeting and sat down on the blankets I had placed on the ground earlier. I took out my gray traveling bag and pulled out two tins of soup. I opened them with a careful hand and poured the soup into the black pot Matthew had just placed over the dancing flames. We sat in silence. I preferred this calm to the constant ruckus and conversation in the camp. Matthew appeared to favor it as well.

As I poured some soup for Matthew into his traveling cup, he cleared his throat and broke the silence. "Andrei, I have meant to ask you a question for about a week now."

I tore my concentration from the soup to look up at him. "Yes?"

Matthew took a big gulp of soup as if he needed his strength. "What do you think you're doing?"

I stared at him. "What do you mean?"

Matthew gave me a harsh glare. "I've been married for ten years now. You would think that I would recognize a woman when I see one."

I felt the color drain from my face. The pot of soup in my hand seemed frozen. "What are you talking about?" I tried to sound nonchalant.

Matthew placed his soup on the ground. "Don't play games with me. Who are you, and how long do you think you can keep up this charade?"

I swallowed a big gulp of air and calculated my next move. It seemed impossible to avoid the truth. "If I tell you the truth, you must promise me not to tell anyone."

Matthew gave a quick nod of his head. After letting out a deep breath, I told Matthew my name and my purpose. Matthew listened with attention. When I finished my story, he studied me for a few seconds. "Did you think you could hide the truth for long?"

I lifted my shoulders and avoided his gaze. Shame spread through me like a dangerous infection. "The further we travel, the more difficult my secret becomes," I admitted. "I'm afraid that Alex suspects, and I am almost positive that Fur Hunter knows the truth as well."

Matthew studied the flames in front of him and then put his hand over mine. "I understand you need to find your parents, and I will protect you as much as possible. Fur Hunter will do the same. Alex, on the other hand, I'm not sure what he would do. He has more loyalty to Mr. Shubert than he does to you, so you should be careful."

I placed my hand on Matthew's. "Thank you; you cannot imagine what comfort your presence has been to me."

Matthew grinned. "My wife must never find out I shared a tent with a girl this whole trip. She'd skin me alive."

I laughed at that, and the tension around my heart released. "I would tell her that it was with the most honorable intentions."

Matthew handed me his cup. "I'll drink some soup to that."

"Why have you never mentioned your wife?" I asked as I poured the remaining food into the cup.

"It never came up, really, and it makes me miss her more when I talk of her. I have a little daughter too."

"I am sure they are wonderful. Matthew, I appreciate the fact that you are so understanding." I wanted to say something else, but then I heard footsteps outside. Matthew made a quick motion with his hand for me to keep quiet.

Alex entered. "What have you two been up to?"

"You just missed some delicious soup," Matthew stated as if nothing had occurred. "I have some more in my bag. Would you like some?"

"No, I'm fine. I just shared some bread with Sima." Alex crossed the tent and lay down on his back. I watched him with caution. He had seemed to have forgotten about the conversation we had the last night we were in Montreal. I also tried to ignore the fact that my heart rate seemed to increase at least by one thousand beats per minute when Alex had entered the tent.

Matthew threw me a meaningful glance and said, "I know, I am tired. I am going to sleep."

"I agree." I took the eating utensils from Matthew, cleaned them, and put them away. I then lay down and covered my head with the thick blanket. "Good night."

Sleep escaped me. While I was grateful for Matthew's friendship, the fact that he had figured out my secret without much effort bothered me. Too many men, except for Sima, had taken notice of my peculiarities. I had to be more careful from now on.

*****

The next evening, Rideon and Joseph Smith jeered me into going to the bonfire. They caught me as I was walking to get my supper. Joseph Smith stopped me. "You're not skipping out on a bonfire again?"

"I was hoping to get some rest," I answered.

"This bonfire will cheer you up. You don't want the rest of the men thinking you are yellow," Rideon sounded amused.

"No, I wouldn't want that," I answered with less humor.

"You better come then. You know Steven Lake says you are strange," Joe Smith told me.

"Really?" I asked, and then I added, "Steven Lake talks too much."

Rideon grinned. "You better make him stop talking by coming."

"All right then, I'll be there." I went to my tent to prepare for the night. While every nerve in my body protested at the thought of the bonfire, I decided it would be best not to create more questions.

Alex appeared glad that I agreed to go. He walked outside. Matthew followed him, but he stopped and gave me a reassuring glance before leaving the tent.

Hoping to avoid the evening somehow, I sat on the blankets to retie my boots. Sima poked his head into the tent. "Come on, Andrei, you are one of the slowest men that I know."

"I'm coming." I sighed as I tightened the laces. I wanted to tell Sima that I desired to lie down and sleep. I wished that we could have stayed in Montreal for a bit longer. Four days had not been enough, and now, a week later, I wondered if I had dreamed up Montreal.

I trooped along behind Sima as we came up to the fire lit in front of the tents. All the men already gathered. They were laughing and talking. Sima sat down next to Alex; Alex whispered something into Sima's ear. I thought I heard him say, "Late as usual." I was a bit hurt by Alex's words. Would he ever really like me?

Someone handed a cup of hot tea to me. I drank slowly, allowing the warmth of the tea to seep through my veins. Alex gulped down his tea and set it down. Jason Shubert began to talk at that moment, and then he said, "I hope the snow keeps up or it will become a blanket."

Sima turned toward Alex and me and whispered, "He is trying to be funny again."

"Jason, come on, tell us a good joke!" Timothy Howell exclaimed.

Jason seemed a bit offended, but then he proceeded to tell a long and involved joke. Everyone laughed besides me. I had not understood what he had been saying at all. I then noticed that Alex was not laughing either. Alex looked at me and shrugged; I shrugged in response. I studied Sima in puzzlement. He seemed to have a hard time getting a hold of himself. Even when the rest of the men had calmed down, Sima would break out into short sporadic laughs. I noticed that no one was paying attention to him, and the rest of the men were busy talking about the trip.

"Yes, we are on schedule," Jason Shubert was saying and then added in a threatening tone, "and we better remain that way." Did Mr. Shubert's eyes land on me, or did I just imagine that they did? He kept talking.

"Jason, how many times did you make this trip?" Joseph Smith asked.

Mr. Shubert looked at him with pride. "Several."

"That narrows it down," Sima whispered to me. I laughed. Alex smirked, his amusement reflected in his deep blue eyes.

"Andrei, is there something funny about this?" Jason Shubert turned his scrutinizing gaze towards me.

I stared at him while the blood froze in my veins. "No, no sir," I stammered.

Sima hid his face in his teacup. All of a sudden, he spit his tea out on the snow. I felt disgusted. He started to laugh rather long and hard. "Andrei, can't you gather up even the slightest bit of courage?" Then he imitated me, "No, no... sir." He continued to laugh.

Humiliation spread throughout my body, and I wanted to disappear into the snow. Warmth crept into my face. While I was happy that Sima had not been left in Montreal, there were days when I could not stand him. The resolution to not let him bother me seemed to be failing.

Alex began to laugh as well. "Cheer up, Andrei. Why are you so serious all the time?"

Most of the men roared with laughter. Matthew sat silent. He could do nothing to stop the teasing. What would happen, I wondered, if I would tell them right there and then that I was a girl?

Andrew Redlock, one of the older members of our team, tried to interject by saying, "Let's leave the poor boy alone. He probably has never been out much." That statement did not help the laughter subside. Never had I been so mortified before in my life. How would they feel if they were singled out in such a manner? Probably they would laugh along. I lacked humor; perhaps I needed to figure out how to find it. My mind began to hurt. I wanted to tell them all that they were ridiculous, that I was a girl, and that I did not belong here. I kept silent. The consequences of the truth could be disastrous.

Finally, the laughter subsided, and Sima began to tell stories about him and Alex at school and the university. I tuned out the conversation and gazed into the dark sky. Smoke went up from the fire into the night sky like an old native signal. How far were we from anything? On a night like this, I believed that I could stay out under that sky forever. I drifted out of my thoughts as Sima reached the end of his story. Silence fell over the camp of men. Jason took out his pipe, and the rest of the men followed suit.

I had no pipe, but Sima handed me one behind my back. "Alex and I got it for you."

"You can't look too sissy," Alex whispered.

I hung my head as I realized there was no other option but to smoke. All of the men in the camp seemed to be staring in our direction. Matthew and I exchanged glances, but even his reassuring presence could not protect me at the moment. I lifted the pipe to my mouth and lit it. I suppressed the cough that came up in my throat. A heavy silence fell over the camp again. Nothing seemed to stir. All of us seemed to be the only people alive in the world. Even Sima looked as solemn as a statue of ice as his gaze became lost on the snow. Chills began to creep into my skin, and despite the large fire, I became cold. After a few puffs of the pipe, I felt like I had mastered smoking. I knew this was not a good habit, especially for a girl.

In a few minutes, Matthew stood and said, "I'm exhausted; good night." He gave me a meaningful look as he passed by me.

Fearing that it might seem odd if I left right away, I waited until Andrew Redlock departed as well.

My legs felt cramped as I stood. "I'm turning in. Good night."

Several men glanced up at me as I walked by. "Good night." The mood did not seem to lift from the camp, and I wondered whether I imagined a sense of fear in the men.

While walking back to the tent, I knelt near Bobick and hugged him. "Oh, Bobick," I whispered. "I am so alone."

Suddenly someone's voice interrupted me, "You're far from home."

I jumped to my feet. In the shadows stood Fur Hunter. He came into view like a deer emerging from the brush.

I shifted my weight from one foot to the other. "Fur Hunter, I thought you were still at the fire."

"I was tired, just like you."

I gave him a half-smile and said rather stupidly, "Yes."

His eyes revealed little kindness. "No."

"No?" I questioned while keeping my gaze steady. His presence chilled me to the bone.

"Do not leave the bonfire early anymore and come to every single one. Steven Lake is not the only one who asks questions."

I stared at him. Was he trying to tell me that he knew what I was hiding? I laughed a bit. "What questions?"

"Do I look foolish?" Fur Hunter's cold eyes stared straight at me. I could feel him critiquing every move I made. His nose was like an eagle's, and his black hair glistened in the moonlight. Fur Hunter certainly was no dolt.

"No, you do not look so," I answered him.

"Indians are wise people. You know this."

I observed his close stare. My uneasiness increased. "Perhaps."

"Then do not be a fool and do not lie. If the truth is asked of you, you should answer."

"What lies?" I asked, my voice quivering.

"Do not worry. I would not tell. You know this too."

"Fur Hunter, that smoke must have clouded your head," I said, trying to laugh.

He sneered at me, shook his head, and then disappeared again into the shadows. A shudder ran down my spine. I could not tell if he knew the truth or if he was just trying to trick me into telling him. At that moment, I heard Sima and Alex coming up to the tent. I had no time to hide from view.

"Andrei, why are you still out here?" Sima asked. "I thought you were tired."

"I was just making sure Bobick was all right," I answered as Fur Hunter's voice still rang in my head.

"He looks fine to me," Sima said, laughing. "Come on; we're tired."

Although sleep had been creeping up on me the whole evening, I now did not feel tired. That night, I did not close my eyes until I had heard all of the men go to their tents and silence fell over the camp.

*****

The next day proved to be complicated. It seemed to me as if we were driving through endless blank open spaces. Then, when we reached the wooded areas, we would have to fight trees and branches. Even if Jason urged us to stay at the edge of the woods, this situation did not help. Several times a branch would hit me in the face. I felt scrapes forming on my cheeks. Once a branch hit me right in the mouth because Alex forgot to hold it for me. I had to stop myself from crying out. I wondered if any other people lived in Canada besides the ones in Montreal. Near Montreal, we had passed a lot of homes, and then there seemed to be nothing. We were traveling northwest. I soon realized we were moving far from all civilization. I also began to wonder whether or not Mr. Shubert knew precisely where to go.

That day felt as if it was the worst day of the entire trip. Exhaustion took over me, and I could hardly help Matthew and Alex put up the tent in the evening. Many men were getting together at Rideon Smith's tent that night, but I refused to go. At that moment, I did not care what anybody said. I was too exhausted to even think about whether or not someone was suspicious of my actions. As soon as Alex and Matthew left, I sat down on my blankets.

My arms were shaking from exhaustion. I absentmindedly took out my pipe and started smoking it. I thought of Jason Shubert. He yelled all the time, it seemed. Most of the time, I felt as if his anger was towards me. I was a bit slower than the rest of the men, even though it seemed to me as if lately I was doing a much better job at keeping up. I did not hear footsteps approaching the tent. So when Alex opened the tent flap, I looked up, surprised. Alex was giving me a funny look.

"What is it?" I asked.

"Andrei, you're smoking by yourself? I thought you didn't smoke."

I looked at the pipe with embarrassment. I had hardly realized I had taken it out. "It calms my nerves, I suppose," I replied. "I just wasn't thinking."

"Hmm," Alex made the sound as he smirked and sat down on the bedding across from me. I realized I had wanted him to stay. I was relieved that he was not leaving. My eyes felt glued to him. I shook my head; I had to clear my thoughts.

"I'm tired," I told him.

"We're all tired, Andrei." He stared into our small fire.

"You see, Alex, I just don't think that I can keep going. Look, I'm shaking." I showed him my trembling hand.

Alex showed me his hand as well. "Yes, I'm shaking too." I looked at him in surprise. I had imagined he would be so strong.

He untied his boots. "Going on this trip was suicide."

"Yes, too bad I found that out after we left."

"Hmmm? Yes, I know, but let's talk about something cheerful for once. Jason Shubert, all he seems to think about is getting through at full speed. He could give us men a break at least once."

"Well, there was Montreal," I countered. I sighed then and added, "If only he would not yell at us so much. It seems as if we are not so slow anymore. I know I have improved. I feel bad because I seem to be the cause of a lot of trouble."

Alex then lit his pipe. "Jason can yell at us because we are younger than the rest of the men. He knows we can't put him in order. Anyway, he looked after Sima and me most of the time we were in America. He knows my parents. We can't disrespect him."

"I see," I said and then put out my pipe and lay down, resting my head on my arm.

"Alex, what's your father like?" I asked.

"You know, I don't know. I only remember a little bit about my father. He did not write much. Katya wrote a good deal, and she also penned letters for my mother. Part of the time, I suppose the mail never got through. Sometimes by the time I got the letters, it was six months later. I know my parents were trying to do what's best, but I never really wanted to leave Alaska. Then… well, I suppose it doesn't matter now. I can't wait to get back." He let out a long deep breath of smoke into the air.

I turned to look at him. "You're lucky to know at least where your parents are."

"Don't worry. I am sure things will work out fine for you in Alaska. For a boy your age, there is so much going on in Alaska, a new country, and so forth. It's a frontier just waiting for exploration. Now for a woman, it's different. It is a defenseless country. She would need to marry to survive. They may not like it, but that's the truth. That's why women hardly go there. That's why Alaska has a lot of bachelors." He closed his eyes.

I thought that if he knew that I was a girl, I would take his words to hint that I was plumb crazy to go up there. I studied him intently. At least, I thought, it might be easier for me to find a husband if that was the case.

I curled up on my blankets. I was too tired to think straight. "Do you plan on getting married, Alex?"

"I'd want to, but I suppose that most girls would think that I am too serious."

"Oh," I stated. What was I to say next? I was sorry that I had brought up the subject. Then without thinking, I said, "Mary Shubert certainly did not think so."

He sat up then and looked at me. "How would you know?"

I realized my mistake. The only time I had seen Mary was in the store when she was buying peppermints. I theoretically had never seen her. I bit my lip and then stammered, "I just gathered from what Sima said that she got on your nerves." I felt foolish and tried to avoid his intense gaze.

Alex put out his pipe and then lay down and turned to face the tent wall. "That's what I thought."

"Good night," I said quietly. My nerves were raw. I had to watch what I said. Even though I was becoming much better friends with Alex, I still did not know if he would betray my secret. He was a challenging character to figure out. I finally fell asleep.

The next morning I awoke and looked at the sloping tent ceiling. I shuddered; another day had come. I dreaded waking up every day. I wanted to go back to sleep, but I knew I could not. Cold air came through the tent cracks. I sat up and began to tie my boots. My fingers were stiff, and they hardly moved. I looked at Matthew and Alex. Both of them were still asleep. Sima unexpectedly popped his head into our tent. There were dark circles under his eyes, and he had a shade of a beard on his chin; he looked older.

He looked over at Alex. "He's still asleep?" he asked this question in a surprised tone of voice. "How does he usually always wake up first?"

"I'm not sure," I answered.

Sima walked over to Alex and shook him roughly by the shoulder. "Wake up!"

After rolling over on his side and giving Sima a dazed and confused look, Alex snapped, "What?"

"Are you ready for another robust day of sledding?"

"No," Alex answered and shook his head as he stood up. Sima gave him an annoyed all-knowing look. Alex walked out of the tent then, and Sima and I looked at each other and smiled.

"I don't feel a bit sorry for him," Sima told me.

I began to gather our blankets. "Neither do I."

The day proved to be a lighter travel day; the teams did not cover as much distance. Sima and I joked and laughed the entire day. Towards mid-afternoon, Alex's mood brightened slightly, and we enjoyed the rest of the daylight hours.

That evening, I went to the bonfire that Mr. Shubert held. None of the men made fun of me that evening. I began to feel accepted.

*****

The following day, I regretted I had been so content the night before. When I awoke, my entire body felt sore and tired. With my eyes still closed, I hoped that if I kept them closed long enough, all the men, the dogs, and the surrounding snow around me would disappear. The cold now seeped through my veins and into every single bone of my body.

Finally, I got up and shook Alex by the shoulder. I just smiled at him as he awoke. "Get up."

"Now you're starting," Alex said after he had opened his eyes. He was pretending to be upset, but I could tell he was joking. "I'll be right up. Just allow me to enjoy a few minutes of peace." All Alex got was a few moments of peace. A few seconds later, a shrill whistle sounded.

"Come on, men, get up, and time to start moving!" Jason Shubert bellowed. The familiar voices and bustle started rising in the camp.

I could hear Joseph Shubert yelling to Joe Smith, "Wake up, Joe. We've got to get this tent down!"

Matthew, Alex, and I started to gather our packs of food from the tent floor at a rapid speed. There were not that many items to gather after all. I buckled my boots up and then paused in my bent position.

Alex put his hand on my shoulder. "You all right?"

"Yes, I'm fine."

He looked concerned. "Are you sure?"

My temper got the better of me at that moment. "Would I say that I am all right if I wasn't?"

"You are not altogether well, but if you do not want me to continue questioning you, that's fine." Alex then followed Matthew out of the tent. I knew that something was not right with me. I needed to rest. I was not healthy, and the pain that had begun to form in the lower part of my legs over the past few days had not subsided. My strength would probably not hold out as long; I was only half as strong as Alex.

"Hey Andrei, help us out here!" Matthew called from outside. He and Alex had already begun to take the tent down. I quickly hurried outside. We took the cloth down first and then the wooden poles, they were not too tall, but the tent was nice and wide. Of course, the tent was heavy to carry in the sled.

"Why don't one of you carry this tent?" Matthew asked. He gave Alex and me a defiant glare. He had carried the tent in his sled every day of the trip so far.

"I'll take it," Alex offered. With Matthew's help, he put it in his sled. Then Alex took some bags from his sled and put them into Matthew's sled. "You don't get a free ride, though, and I hope you know that. Do you think these supplies are light?"

"Sure, Alex," Matthew replied with a sigh and then leaned over to pet one of his dogs.

After a hurried breakfast, we pushed off. My legs were rocks. Lifting them off the ground proved to be quite difficult. I will never get to Alaska, I thought, as I kept moving one leg after the other. Of course, since Alex and Matthew had to stay with me, we fell behind. The distance between the rest of the men and us seemed to be more than half a mile. Alex began to throw irritated glances in my direction. Also, the skin on my hands began to itch. Matthew and Alex kept moving forward, but they would have to stop and wait for me. My head pounded along with my heart. Stop, please, let's stop. My mind turned on the thought. Finally, I ended up just driving on the runners as I called out to Bobick to go faster. Of course, I did not end up going more quickly, even though Bobick pulled the sled along in a good-natured fashion. I began to wonder what it would be like to be a dog and have to pull a heavy sled with a girl standing on the runners. I needed to rest soon.

Noon came, and I was far behind the rest of the men. Even Alex and Matthew had seemed to have given up on me. They both traveled at least fifty feet ahead of me. Even so, they lagged behind the others. As we drove up to the rest of the men, they had all settled down to eat. I called my dogs to a stop. Matthew, Alex, and I took out our food packs and sat down with the rest of the group.

"What took you so long?" Jason Shubert barked at us. "We were all here nearly half an hour ago, and you're trudging along. You're holding everybody back, and it is impossible for us to move faster."

Alex swallowed the bread that he just placed in his mouth. "I'm sorry, sir, we'll try going a bit faster."

"You better go a lot faster!" Jason Shubert exclaimed. "I cannot keep up a good dog train if we are not going anywhere."

"Sir, we are going somewhere, and we covered as much ground as we usually do. We will catch up to you," Matthew said with an edge to his voice. I threw him a grateful glance.

"So you did," Mr. Shubert's voice was mean. "We'll just have to continue, and then you can catch up to us so that we will cover enough ground." Jason Shubert gave us a cold glare and then said, "All right, men, let's go! Since these young men won't keep up, we have to give them an early start." He stood up.

"Sir, that's not fair! We just got here!" Alex exclaimed as he stood up and faced Jason Shubert.

"Who says life is fair?" Mr. Shubert asked. Then, without a pause, he walked to his sled. "Let's go!" he bellowed.

I had not completed my meal, and neither had Alex or Matthew. Alex grabbed his bag and furiously shoved food in his mouth. With difficulty, I held back tears and plodded to my sled. Then I called for my dogs to go. As we moved on, I looked longingly at the snow. It looked like a soft cushion on which one could lie down and sleep. I felt terrible, of course. Matthew and Alex did not deserve punishment for my inability to keep pace with the rest of the men.

The air seemed to get colder as we moved forward. My lungs felt like ice cubes after we had traveled just another mile. I felt as if I were breathing fire. As we kept going, we fell behind worse than before.

Alex then drove up next to me and said, "You could have said something, stood up for us. It was stupid of me to talk back, but why do we have to stand up for you?"

I wanted to tell him the truth. I wanted the reality to be out in the open. Perhaps then the men would understand why I could not keep up. I kept silent, blinking to keep tears away from my eyes. I did not cry often, but now I was on the brink of pure exhaustion. Alex drove on ahead and ignored me. I was glad that Matthew and Alex were in front of me. They did not see the two hot tears that rolled down my cheeks.

I realized that most of the men were working too hard. How long would it be until, one by one, each man would begin to expire? My dogs followed behind Matthew's and Alex's sleds. They were far ahead, making it seem as if I was alone at times. Darkness began to settle in. Matthew and Alex waited for me now. I knew that they were aware that for one person to travel alone in darkness could spell death. We could not see the men in front of us. By this time, I had slowed to a walk.

Alex stood with hands across his chest. "Come on, Andrei. We'll be in big trouble for sure if we don't hurry up a bit."

"Alex, look, I have a feeling that Andrei would not act like this on purpose. He's not feeling well, you know," Matthew intervened. I was glad that he stood up for me. However, there was only so much he could do. I had begged him not to give me away.

Fifteen minutes later, we saw a fire burning, and we came upon the camp. The tents were all already set up. As we pulled up, we saw Joseph Shubert feeding his dogs.

"You're back," he observed unnecessarily. "Father was going to send out a search party for you soon."

"Really?" I asked.

"No, I am only joking, but seriously, where were you?"

"We're just tired, Joe," Matthew stated. "If we could just get some rest, I at least would feel better. Do you think that you could talk your father into moving slower?"

"We did move a lot faster today," Joe admitted. "I do not think I could tell him to slow down."

"I'll talk to him tomorrow then," I said. I felt that I had to shoulder some of this responsibility.

Alex began to unload the sled. "Come on, let's get settled."

"I'll tell father that you're here," Joseph Shubert said and walked away.

Alex gave me an ungrateful glare. "Now we're in for it. Listen, Andrei; please tell Jason Shubert that this trouble we're in is your fault."

"Alex, what's wrong with you?" Matthew asked.

"What's wrong with me?" Alex's voice sounded piqued. "Well, I'll tell you," he said as his bright blue eyes burned with an intense fire. "Why does Andrei think we have to stand up for him? Why does he want to talk to Jason tomorrow? He'll never speak to Jason Shubert because he is a big sissy, and he's going to get us all in trouble."

"Well, you finally came," Jason Shubert's voiced boomed from five feet away as he walked towards us.

"Yes, we did, sir," Alex answered.

"Go and rest then," Jason said. Matthew and I exchanged a surprised look.

"Except for Andrei, I want him to stay. Alex and Matthew, you may go."

"Good night, sir." Alex turned to leave. I gave him a pleading glance. Alex went.

Matthew followed but then turned to me behind Mr. Shubert's back and mouthed the words, "Don't worry."

Those words were not much comfort for me. I was the one left standing alone with this bear of a man. Jason waited until they were gone; then he turned to me and said, "You and I both know whose fault it is that you boys fell behind today."

I clasped my hands tightly together and then answered, "Sir, I was tired and did not feel well. The whole train did not fall behind as much. We are still on schedule."

"Yes, I suppose we are still on schedule, but you should know that a man who falls behind like you could easily become hurt. You also hold Matthew and Alex back."

I took a few steps back. "Sir, I do my best!"

"You're best?" Mr. Shubert's tone was callous. "Why did you come anyway? I thought you might have the strength to make this trip. That's why I brought you along. You lived by yourself. How come you're not strong? I never knew a man who was so weak."

Passionate anger grew inside of me. "Listen, sir, only because I do not feel well does not qualify me as weak. Maybe if you slowed down, allowed all the men some rest, then I would not be as tired."

Jason stared down at me from his great height. "Oh, so that's how you feel? You're acting like a woman, a silly-headed woman."

"Sir, I have gone from being weak to a silly-headed woman!" I was offended by his statement, even if it was true.

"You better learn, boy, you understand?" Jason Shubert turned away from me. "Good night. Get some rest; you need it."

"Yes, sir," I answered quietly.

As he walked away, I wondered how much he cared about his men. Did he care at all? The thought that I would not survive this trip kept entering my mind. I shut my eyes. I would not allow such thoughts to puncture my tired brain.

I walked towards our tent in a distressed state of mind. I had nowhere to go but Alaska. My whole future lay there. If someone else were to discover my secret, no, I thought, they could never find out. I would continue on my journey and try as hard as possible to keep up. Even Fur Hunter did not appear to know the real truth.

In our tent, I collapsed onto my blanket. The weather grew cold, and the frozen blankets below me did not provide any warmth. I removed my hat and leaned towards the small flames at the center of the tent. Snow crunched outside, and then Alex entered the tent. He stopped to look at me for a few moments.

"Hello." I had no other words to say.

"Hello," he said and walked in, closing the opening behind him. He picked up his bag and started to shuffle through it. The small fire in the tent now warmed my hands. I began to take off my mittens.

"You all right?" asked Alex looking down at me. I had not noticed earlier, but now that I took off my mittens, I noticed that my hands' skin was so dry that it had cracked open. Blood covered my hands.

"Do you have any bandages?" I asked.

He tossed me some rolled white bandages from his bag. "Here."

"Thank you." I looked up at him. At that moment, as his eyes rested on my face, he stared at me as if someone had just struck him. In haste, I looked away and began to wrap my hand in a bandage.

"Do you need any help?"

"I'll deal with the situation," I answered.

"Good, I'll go see Sima about some hot tea. I'll bring you some if you would like."

"That would be nice."

Alex walked out. I sat while wrapping my hand tightly. The itching intensified. When I had finished the task, I lay down and gazed at the tent ceiling a foot away from my face. I gathered from Alex's expression that Alex had understood what I had not wanted him to realize, that I, the boy Andrei, looked an awful lot like the beautiful girl he had seen in the store. At that moment, I did not care. I did not want to care. I rolled over to look at the tent wall. Unfortunately, it was white, the same as everything else I had seen in the past two months. I sighed to myself. Cold air came into the tent. After turning around, I noticed that Alex had re-entered the tent and held a mug of hot tea.

Alex handed me the mug. "Andrei, are you sure you're all right? You look sick." He sat down and started opening his pack.

"I don't want to go on anymore," I told him.

Alex gave me a concerned look. "Who does? Jason Shubert didn't scare you away, did he?"

"No," I said, pretending that what had happened with Mr. Shubert and had not affected me.

Alex pushed the fire around with a stick. The snow reflected the gleaming rays. I covered the snow with my blanket. Snow, I was so tired of it. Where was I going? To Alaska, some people called it the icebox. Why had I been so lured by it? Maybe, because it was my homeland. That's the truth, I told myself. My parents are there. Failure was not an option.

Alex looked at me from under his dark eyebrows. "You're quiet."

"I was just thinking."

"I see," Alex said and finished drinking his hot tea. His eyes and whole bearing began to make me uncomfortable. I suspected he knew the truth. Why did he not say anything?

At that moment, Sima entered the tent. "Hello, men." He plopped down on Matthew's blankets.

"You do have your own tent, you know," Alex told him with a laugh.

Sima's eyes traveled from Alex's face to mine. "What's the solemn occasion?"

Alex just handed Sima a mug with hot tea. "Here."

Sima began to sip his tea. "Is something wrong?"

"Just thinking," Alex and I replied at the same time. I looked at Alex, embarrassed; he did not seem to notice.

"Good," Sima said as he lay down on his back.

"What did Joseph Shubert say? Anything interesting?" Alex questioned.

"Oh yes, he said there might be a big storm tomorrow. Mr. Shubert might try going around it."

"Might try?" I asked with suspicion.

Sima sat up and threw his empty mug to Alex. "Yes, he said we might go through it."

"Through it? That's suicide!" Alex exclaimed.

"He said that to get ahead of the storm we will push off early tomorrow." Sima lay back down. I groaned inwardly. I then wrapped myself deep in my blankets. I was ill, and there was nothing I could do about it. The shadows of the flames danced on the tent wall.

"Let's go to sleep then if it's an early start tomorrow," Alex said as he made sure the flames of the fire died out.

"Yes," Sima agreed. "By the way, Andrei, what did Jason Shubert say to you?" Sima's voice lifted with curiosity.

"Nothing."

Alex settled into his blankets. "Don't worry about it, Sima, and go back to your tent."

Sima jumped up from his blankets and grinned. "I'll go bother somebody else then since the both of you are so dull. Good night!" He withdrew from the tent with a laugh.

"Good night," I replied.

Alex closed his eyes as silence fell in the tent. I heard some men still walking outside. An eerie feeling came upon me. The hope that we would not have to go through a large storm reeled in my tired mind. Perhaps Mr. Shubert had acted a bit ridiculous so far; I supposed I could have tried harder, but traveling through a winter storm would be sheer madness. The looks that Alex had given me earlier now returned to memory. Apprehension filled me. The fact that Alex might know my secret was disconcerting. Of course, he had not said anything. Maybe he did not say anything for a reason. What was he waiting for?

*****

The following day I awoke early. My whole body was stiff, and my hands hurt from being so dry, but I felt in much better health after a night's rest. After standing up and stretching my body, I felt refreshed. I sat back down on my blankets and started to change my bandages from the day before. The old bandages had blood on them, but parts of the blood had dried on my hands. I still decided to re-tie my hands.

As I finished, Alex awoke. "Awake already?"

I finished tying my bandage with a final knot. "Yes."

"Still worried about Jason Shubert?"

I shook my head in response.

Alex smirked as if he could see right through me. "Don't worry about him. He's always been like that, even when I met him ten years ago." Alex got up and stretched his arms above his head.

"Seems like I'm getting stiffer every day," he said and bent over and shook Matthew's shoulder.

"Time to get up, Matthew." Alex straightened out again.

Matthew sat up and rubbed his eyes. "I cannot wait to get to our next checkpoint. Even one day to sleep in would be wonderful."

Alex leaned over and began to roll up his blanket. "We are only about a week away from our next checkpoint." It appeared as if he wanted to say something else, but Jason's loud shrill whistle interrupted us. Matthew groaned and covered his head with his blanket. Alex and I both chuckled.

*****

The day turned out to be windy and cold. A silence hung over the entire crew of men. Even though I felt some renewed strength and I was able to keep up with the rest of the men, I found my legs buckling intermittently; seeing Jason Shubert made me want to go even faster. I did not want to get another lecture about being a man. We stopped for a rest and ate some lunch. I felt like I could not eat, but I scarfed down some food to make sure I would have enough strength. Mr. Shubert pulled us to a halt relatively early, which surprised me. The belief many men shared was that the storm had moved in a different direction. I hoped so.

We set up our tent. Red Fern and Fur Hunter were setting up their tent next to ours. I kept throwing wary glances at Fur Hunter. His hawk-like nose and shrewd eyes frightened me. Red Fern, on the other hand, I did not believe could scare anybody. As they worked, I wondered how two such different men could be related to each other.

Getting food for our dogs was always an adventure. They would all jump around me excitedly as I threw them the meat. I had grown to love my dogs. My favorite, of course, was Bobick. He led the other dogs with absolute resolve.

I had pulled out some meat and was throwing it to my dogs for supper when Alex came up to me and said, "We don't have much meat left."

"Oh, I have some in my bag," I replied, looking over my shoulder at him. "I can go get it."

"No, no, you wait here, I'll get it." Alex dismissed my idea and went for the meat. As I threw some meat to Star, I remembered the photograph. It lay at the bottom of the bag next to the meat that was in brown paper. Cold beads of sweat began to form on my lip. What if Alex discovered it? He did not return for a while, and my fears began to rise.

Sima came up to me just as I was about to head into the tent. "Listen, Andrei; I was wondering…" he did not finish because we were interrupted by Alex, who had just returned.

He handed the package to me. "Here's the meat."

I studied his face. He showed no change in his expression. I suspected that he already had known something of the matter. Still, it would be so much better not to confirm any of his doubts. Absentmindedly, I pet two of my dogs. Alex left before Sima or I spoke another word.

Sima turned to me again after Alex left. "Andrei, do you want to come over to our tent? We are having a bonfire."

I shook my head. "No, thank you, Sima. I'll turn in. I am a bit weary."

Sima nodded and walked back towards his tent. I smiled at Sima as I watched him go. If not for him, Matthew, and Alex, this journey would be unbearable. My footsteps crunched on the snow as I walked back to my sleeping quarters.

As I walked in, I stopped short. Alex was sitting on his blankets, and he held my photograph in his hands. His eyes seemed to have a storm of emotion as he glanced up at me. I stood without movement. Words escaped my mind. I waited for the storm to break and for Alex to speak. He stood up and started to come towards me. His gigantic frame towered above me; I took a step back. Alex needed to lean down because of the sloping tent; this made him seem even more frightening.

"Anna?" he started in a questioning, annoyed tone of voice. I took off my mittens and stared at the snow that was our tent floor in order to avoid looking into his eyes.

Alex leaned closer to me. "So, I suspected that there was something strange about you. I realized that you were pretending you are someone else. Especially when we had reached the Canadian border, all that deal with the papers. I knew you had whispered something that sounded like, thank you, to the guard. I could not quite place what was wrong, though."

Alex stopped, took a deep breath, and continued in a deep angry tone. "Then last night, I saw you look at me with those big brown eyes, and I realized you looked exactly like that girl I had seen at Owell's all that time ago. I thought it was the fire playing tricks with my eyes, but I began to have a mounting suspicion that I was right." He stopped as if he was waiting for me to speak. I said nothing at first and then looked straight into his blue eyes. All the warmth had disappeared. They looked like ice crystals.

"I...I had to find my parents," I stammered.

"And you thought no one would find out?" Alex had a tone of ill amusement in his voice.

I shrugged. I was not sure what I had thought. Even though I had suspected that Alex knew, I did not know that he would ever confront me in such a fashion. "I suppose I did not think out my plan completely," I began in a quiet voice.

"I should say not. Didn't you realize that you were putting yourself in a lot of danger? Don't you see that your reasoning is stupid? When Jason Shubert finds out, don't you know that you'll be fined and probably thrown in jail?"

I stared up at his angry face. Did he mean to tell Mr. Shubert the truth? "Well, the jail is quite far from here," I told him. "Anyway, I thought of all these things. I had my doubts and worries. Even so, I had to take action. For me to sit in my cabin hoping to earn enough money to travel west would be ridiculous. That day when I walked into Owell's, I realized how lonely and miserable I had become. I had to find my family. That thought has never left me."

Alex stared at me; his gaze did not soften. I felt like a young child that had done something wrong. How strange these occurrences must be for him. For him to find out I was a girl, and the same one he had thought to be so beautiful all that time ago must have sent him into a state of bewilderment.

Alex stood unmoving. I was not sure what he was waiting for; I tried to keep my gaze steady as I stared straight into his eyes that were now vacant of emotion. "Are you going to tell?"

"Tell?" Alex began in a questioning tone. He then narrowed his eyes as if in thought. "It seems as if I should. I'm not sure about what to do."

"Please don't," I begged.

"Why shouldn't I?" he asked in a sharp voice.

"Well, you see..." my voice trailed off. I had no reasons to give. All of my arguments died on my tongue.

"I don't see anything," Alex answered.

"What? Are you blind?" I asked, regaining my composure.

Alex grabbed me by the shoulders. "You listen to me, Miss."

The tent opened, and Matthew walked in. He looked from me to Alex. "What's happening here?" Silence ensued in the tent. Matthew threw Alex an angry glance. "Alex, stop arguing." Alex dropped his hands from my shoulders. He and I scowled at each other.

"Listen, Alex. I wanted to go to the bonfire at Joe's. Would you like to come?" Matthew regarded us suspiciously. He had no idea of what had just transpired.

"You go ahead," Alex said.

"All right," Matthew started to walk out, and then he turned back to us. "What is happening here?"

Alex responded with silence.

Tears threatened to spill down my cheeks. I pressed my teeth hard against my lip. "He found out, Matthew."

Matthew's shoulders fell, and Alex looked from me to Matthew in surprise. "You knew?"

Matthew sat down on his blankets. "I found out, the same as you."

Alex seemed to calm a bit. He also sat down. "And you said nothing?"

Matthew narrowed his eyes at Alex. "What good would come of us giving Anna away? She is alone and has no home. Not everyone in this camp is trustworthy enough to care enough about her."

I stood in silence and looked down at both of them.

Alex appeared to be deep in thought. He then turned to face me and said, "I'll keep your secret as long as I can, but don't trick yourself into thinking that no one else will find out." With one last glance in my direction he stood and left the tent.

When he left, I threw myself down on my makeshift bed and turned to Matthew. "I appreciate the fact that you stood up for me. I do not know what I would do without you."

Matthew smiled in return. "I do not mind standing up to Alex. I will warn you, however, if Mr. Shubert finds out, I will need some reinforcements."

The tears that threatened to roll down my face earlier now found their way down my cheeks. "I feel as if you are the only person I can trust. You have done so much for me already."

Matthew waved the praise away with his hand. "This is no time to start getting emotional. There will be plenty of time for that. Right now, you focus on getting to Alaska and staying safe. I will do the best I can to protect you, but you need to have some backbone as well."

I nodded. "I'll try."

Matthew lay down. "Trying is one thing. Succeeding is another subject. Anyway, I'm going to sleep. I have had enough drama for one night." He closed his eyes. I felt empty, and again, I was alone.

Obviously, I did not sleep well that night. I awoke early the following day and felt a need to escape the closeness of the tent. The campsite was so quiet, nothing moved. The stillness of the morning hung in the air. I let out a heavy sigh and sat down at the edge of the camp next to Bobick. I placed my hand on his head and rubbed behind his ear. Then I leaned my head back against him and closed my eyes. For some reason, there was a sinking feeling in my stomach, and I felt disoriented. There were footsteps behind me. I turned and found Matthew standing there. I was surprised to see him up already.

He sat down next to me. "I hope I didn't startle you."

I shook my head and gave him a sidelong glance. "No."

"You're up rather early," Matthew stated.

"Yes, I had trouble sleeping."

Matthew sighed. "Me too. For some reason I felt a need to go out and enjoy the morning. I don't know why."

"I was wondering why you were up," I told him. "This expedition is so long and tedious, and I am tired of traveling so much."

"We all are," Matthew said. He picked up some snow in his hand. "Do you ever feel as if we are never going to reach Alaska?"

I looked at him, and I saw the troubled look in his eyes. "Well, I sometimes feel that way, but I try to shake off those thoughts when they come to me."

Matthew leaned his back against one of the sleds. "I suppose I should not think that way either. Anyway, I think you have been doing just fine, for such a young girl. You know, when I first saw you, I did not think you would even reach Montreal. You're brave."

"Jason Shubert would not agree with you," I told him.

Matthew took some more snow into his hand and threw it at one of the tents. "He thinks that everybody is too slow. Do not worry. You might think that you and Sima are his only target, but you are not. He's a good man. He does care, even if it might not appear that way."

I grinned. "I suppose I am a bit ungrateful."

Matthew chuckled. "I haven't been grateful to him for a second. I have wished many times that I could turn around. The reason why I came seems silly now. I needed the money. This trip is torture. Why didn't I find another way to earn it instead?" He shook his head.

"You never mentioned this."

"I lost my job, and I was unable to find a new place for months. We have a daughter to take care of, and we were running short on funds. I saw Jason often in town, and he offered to pay me in advance. I left the money for my wife and came."

"I'm sorry to hear that."

"Don't be sorry." Matthew looked at me and then turned to stare straight ahead into the distant woods. "My wife and I have had many good years together."

I kicked at some snow with my heel. "And you will continue to have a wonderful life when you get back."

Matthew did not speak for a few seconds and then said, "I wanted to ask you a favor."

I did not like the sound of his voice. "Yes?"

Matthew pulled out a folded piece of paper from his jacket pocket. "If I do not make it back home, I want you to send this to my wife. The address is inside."

I stared at the paper and did not take it. "What are you talking about?"

"You know what I'm referring to; this trip is dangerous. I came because I wanted my wife and daughter to have financial security. I have done my job." His voice sounded impatient.

My fingers reached for the yellow paper. They shook as the paper came into my hands. I shoved it in my side coat pocket. "You shouldn't talk like this."

Matthew sighed. "Perhaps I shouldn't, or perhaps I am just tired. However, I feel as if it would be better to give this to you for some reason. You are the only one I can trust, Anna. So please do not challenge me on this."

My heart tightened. "Matthew, there is no guarantee that I will survive too."

"Then you pass it along to someone else."

"It's this stupid storm that everyone is talking about; I am sure it will pass, and I am sure that Jason Shubert will be wise enough to stay away."

Matthew smiled. "I certainly hope so. I apologize if I upset you. However, I want to make sure that if all of a sudden I do not survive, that my thoughts and parting words will not die with me."

A shudder ran down my back. "Matthew, please do not speak like this anymore."

Matthew's mood seemed to lighten. "All right, I won't. Anyway, I have to stay alive to help keep you out of any mischief."

"Do you have a photograph of your wife?"

Matthew grinned at this question. "Of course, I carry it with me always. Somebody took it some time ago at a fair. My daughter was just born." He pulled a tattered photograph out of his pant pocket and handed it to me.

I examined it. His wife was lovely. She sat straight and unsmiling, but her eyes added a glorious light to the photo. "She is beautiful." I handed the photo back to him.

He took it from me and placed it back in his pocket. "Thank you, that's why I married her."

I stood. "I think I should get back to the tent and start packing." Before I left, I said, "Matthew, please believe me when I say this, you are the most decent man I have ever met. If something does happen to you, I will certainly deliver your message to your wife. I will pray that you stay safe."

Matthew stood as well and brushed the snow off his pants. "Thank you, Anna. I appreciate your help. For now, let's enjoy today. I will be back soon to help pack up. Please tell Alex that I will be back, so he doesn't get his feathers too ruffled."

I laughed at that. "I think Alex's feathers have been ruffled enough. I will see you later." I turned and walked away a few feet. I then returned my gaze to Matthew. He stood leaning against his sled as if he were a man in pain. I shook my head to clear my befuddled mind. Matthew must be imagining things. Even so, the gloomy feeling returned to me. I reminded myself that we still had a long way to go. Living in fear would do nothing.

After giving myself another mental shake, I walked past the row of sleds to my tent. As I neared my tent, I saw Sima sprawled on his sled, the back of his head rested against the handlebar. He had his wooden pipe between his teeth, and he was carving something into a piece of wood with his knife. He was one person who never seemed to carry any sadness.

As I came closer to his sled, I waved to him. He nodded at me in greeting. Curiosity got the better of me. "What are you carving?"

He removed the pipe from his mouth. "I do not know yet. Carving helps me calm my nerves, so does drinking." He then pulled a flask from under the canvas covering his sled, opened it, and took a sip. He held it out to me. "Would you like some?"

I shook my head. "The sun has just started rising."

Sima took a swig out of the flask, closed it, and stuck it back in his sled. "Suit yourself. It does help to dull the sound of Jason's annoying whistle." He then put the pipe back in his mouth and resumed his carving.

Words escaped me. I agreed with Matthew; Sima was the strangest person that I had ever met. "I'll see you later."

Sima nodded to me again without taking his eyes off his work.

I walked past the rest of the sleds to the tent and entered. Alex was already awake and was sitting on his blankets. He gave me a dark look as I walked in.

"Good morning," I said. Alex just looked at me and then turned his eyes away.

"Is anything wrong?" I asked cheekily. I was annoyed with his cold disregard of me. He then stood up and walked out of the tent. So much for a good friend, I thought to myself.

"Where's Alex?" Sima popped his head into the tent. I wondered how he had managed to arrive at the tent so quickly.

"Sulking," I answered.

"He always is." Sima laughed. "Aren't the three of you awake early?"

"So are you."

"I just couldn't sleep during the night. Joseph Shubert snores."

I began to wonder if Sima had overheard my conversation with Matthew earlier. How long had he sat on his sled?

I wished he would leave. "I think most of the men will be up soon. I should start packing." Matthew had not returned yet, and I needed time alone to think.

"Sima, what are you doing?" Alex returned. "Please move from our tent entrance so I can get in."

Instead of moving, Sima came in and plopped onto Matthew's blankets. "Alex is there something bothering you?" he asked insolently.

Alex glared at me and then said, "Not really."

"I see." Sima looked from me to Alex and then shrugged. "Whatever it is that the two of you argued over, forget about it; it can't be that important. There's only a bunch of dogs and snow around here anyway."

Alex picked up his rolled blankets and his black travel bag. "You'd be surprised." He then left without another word.

Sima turned to me and said, "You probably have figured out that going to school with him was no picnic."

I grinned and replied, "Yes, I have."

Sima smirked and then stood and walked out without warning. I looked after him for a moment. He did not seem to have any concerns other than about himself. I let out a deep breath. At least he did not know the truth.

Slowly I packed my belongings. My thoughts all ran into each other. Too many thoughts and emotions had crossed my mind. I was in no hurry to begin the day. I needed to keep my thoughts clear. My only choice was to survive. I could not live in fear, loneliness, and insecurity. I also decided that I could not leave this world feeling as if I belonged to no one.

With my mind made up, I went out to the sleds. Alex was tying his supplies down with a rope. He gave the rope one final pull and then looked up at me with a cold stare. I wished that he would stop being angry. His anger felt exaggerated. He had already figured out the truth before; why was he so angry now? I shrugged and went on with my task.

Chapter 7   December 1, 1887

That morning we moved at a quick speed through the extensive plains that surrounded us. Towards the afternoon, we came upon a dense forest. I looked at the thick foliage with a sinking heart; that was the last place where I desired to go. At that moment, Jason Shubert pulled us to a stop. All the men gathered around him with their sleds. For some reason, Bobick, and Sima's dog, Caesar, started snapping at each other. I pulled Bobick away.

"Listen, men, in a few days we will make it to our next checkpoint," Mr. Shubert said. "That is, we will stop and rest for a few days at Richard and Ellen's cabin. They are my friends. According to my map, the city of Ontario is only fifty miles south of here. Ellen and Richard travel north during the winter for trapping. We will rest here today and continue tomorrow. We'll push hard tomorrow so we can reach them by nighttime. There is no use trying to push through the forest today." Sima and I exchanged glances. No one wanted to push through the forest the next day either.

Alex, Matthew, and I set up our tent. Alex still did not speak to me, and Matthew kept throwing him irritated glances. Matthew walked away to talk to Rideon after setting up the tent, and I found myself alone with Alex. I wondered if Matthew had left us alone on purpose.

I sat down on my blankets in the tent and looked up at Alex. He was pretending to be busy filling his pipe with tobacco. I stopped to take a deep calming breath. "Alex, look, I apologize."

"There is no reason why you should apologize to me," Alex answered without a glance up from his pipe.

"Then why are you not speaking to me?" I asked.

Alex looked up at me. "Listen, what difference does it make to you? I have nothing in common with you."

"That doesn't mean you have to act like you are a young schoolboy," I answered.

Alex sighed irritably and gave me a cross look. "There are many things that you do not understand." He rose and departed the tent.

I watched him leave. He frustrated me so. At the same time, I began to realize how agitated I became around him. Sometimes I found myself longing to be in his presence even when he displayed fits of anger. I shook my head. These feelings were new to me, and I was not sure if I enjoyed these new emotions.

Sima came in at that moment and asked, "Did Alex disappear again?"

I nodded in response.

"He certainly is mad this time. What did you do to make him so angry?"

"I'd rather not talk about it," I answered.

"Suit yourself, but if you told me, I could talk him into speaking with you again."

I looked into his deep brown eyes and smiled. "I don't think that is necessary. I am sure that Alex will soon give way. I know him. He cannot stay angry for too long."

I wondered if I had to tell Sima the truth. Sima did not seem as if he would care at all. Perhaps he could help me. As I watched him, I decided against it. It could come as a bit of a shock to him.

Sima sat down on the blankets on the other side of the tent. "Listen, do you remember Mr. Shubert ever mentioning his friends Ellen and Richard?"

"I don't remember. When we had that first meeting, we did discuss checkpoints, and Mr. Shubert might have said something. Do you have the map that he gave us?"

Sima stared at me as if I had fallen off the moon. "What map, Andrei?'

"The map that Mr. Shubert gave us, never mind, I think I have it." I sorted through my bag and found the crumpled map at the bottom of it.

"Here," I said with triumph showing it to Sima.

Sima laughed. "Now, if we can read beyond the wrinkled paper, perhaps we will be able to make out Mr. Shubert's plans."

"At least I have my map," I retorted.

"Maybe we should ask Alex for his map. I am sure there is not even a crease in it."

"He probably won't need to look for it," I added.

"I'll ask him when he returns," Sima said.

Of course, Alex had his map folded neatly in his bag. Sima and I could not help laughing when he pulled it out. "I forgot all about the different checkpoints until after we left Montreal," Alex told us. "I had thought I would check the map more often."

"Yes, well, I don't have a map anymore, and Andrei's is all wrinkled," Sima told him. "Anyway, Jason Shubert would show us the way regardless."

I laughed. "Well, if Jason Shubert ever gets lost, I have a feeling that we would not last too long."

"Mr. Shubert would never get lost, at least I don't think so." Sima grinned. "But in case he does, as long as Alex is with us, we will stay alive."

"Let's not talk about getting separated or lost, please," Alex said. "Trying to find everybody again would be a nightmare."

A chill ran down my spine. Matthew's words from the morning still lay fresh on my mind. What if the men were to become separated? I did not think that there would be a way that all of us could locate each other.

Our conversation was interrupted by Steven Lake. He stuck his head into our tent without ceremony. "Why don't you boys come to my tent tonight? We're building a large fire in front of it. Fur Hunter got some fresh venison this morning, so we can have a fine feast if you like."

"We'll be right there," I answered. Steven Lake nodded and left.

"You actually agreed to go without being hassled into coming?" Sima asked.

"Yes," I answered with a laugh, "fresh food never sounds bad."

Sima and Alex laughed; I was pleased that Alex approved of something I said. We left without hesitation and went over to Steven Lake's tent. The rest of the men had gathered there already. Fur Hunter and Red Fern had even brought over some logs for men to sit on. I sat next to Sima and Matthew. I had placed myself strategically far away from Alex.

That night I felt as if all of the men had become a family. I felt that even Steven Lake, despite his mean comments, was becoming more amiable. Rideon Smith, one of the men that rarely even spoke, started telling about his life at home. He said he was going to Alaska for adventure. I wondered if he felt the same way now as Matthew did, that there was no adventure in this trip, just pain.

Sima then whispered to me, "Rideon's wife died a year ago. He came on this journey to get away from Maine."

"How do you know this?" I asked.

"I found this out from Joe Smith. They became friends shortly after the tragedy last year."

"I see." I watched Rideon Smith, who was still talking about his home in Maine. I could understand his need to get away. He probably felt that going on this 'adventure' was the only way for him to escape his pain. My heart went out to him. Eventually, he stopped talking. An eerie silence fell on the group.

Unexpectedly, Jason Shubert began to sing, "Sweet wind, sweeter than the roses, blowing through the trees, creating a beautiful breeze." I knew the song and joined in. The song seemed to be popular with all the rest of the men. We sang it loudly and not at all in tune. I had to make sure my voice did not sound too much like a girl's. I loved the refrain of the song. I had heard it sung by Mary-Louise several times.

We finished the song, and then Sima and Alex began to sing, "My true love is waiting for me, by the banks of the river near the willow tree." The rest of the men began to join in, and one by one, more voices gathered in song. I did not know the song, but I started to join in with the rest of the men once they had repeated the song two times. I thought it sounded rather sad, and I saw Alex catch my eye several times throughout the song. I sang the last few lines, and I felt my heart turn cold. The music was not supposed to be sad, but the last words put agony into my heart; "I'll wait for you my love, I'll wait for you, I'll never say goodbye."

We sang the song repeatedly, and the words in the middle of the song also began to give me an ache in my heart. "The time comes when we must part, but I will never forget thee." Still, the men sang away with cheer. Sima sang out of tune in a loud tone. After we sang several more songs, the men began breaking away and heading to their tents.

Matthew was singing to himself as we got ready to go to sleep. Alex sat brooding. I glanced over at him several times. I wondered if his mood was similar to mine. The words of the song contributed to a melancholy feeling that I was trying to shake off. Alex caught my gaze at the moment, and he gave me a quick smile. I smiled back and then looked away. I fell asleep in the deep night while Alex and Matthew snored peacefully.

The following day when Jason Shubert gave the signal to wake up, we were all still sleeping. Alex jumped up rather hastily. It took me a few minutes to focus my attention.

Matthew woke after Alex repeated his name several times. "Please let me sleep."

"Unfortunately, the whistle blows." Alex laughed a bit and threw a glance in my direction. I smiled back at him. He shared my smile and then went about getting ready for the day. Relief washed through me. Perhaps we could be civil towards one another.

That morning we were slow to move our train of dogs through the dark forest. All of the men traveled far apart because of the thick woods. Alex, Matthew, and I were far behind the others; I could scarcely see Andrew Redlock's sled, and he was in front of us. Some of the branches whipped my face as I traveled. Alex was traveling ahead of me, and Matthew was behind me. I was excited to be staying at someone's cabin for a few days, although I wondered how twelve men would fit into one cabin. My thoughts kept me occupied, and the hope of resting soon drove me to continue through the thick woods. I stopped several times to walk at the head of my sled and pull Bobick behind me. I was relieved to be in the back. Jason Shubert broke the trail for us.

As I traveled, the air seemed to be getting colder, and the woods seemed to be getting darker and darker. I could not see any of the men ahead of us.

"Alex! Do you see anybody?" I called.

"No," he answered from the front. I looked back, and Matthew was far behind me.

"Let's try to move faster," Alex called. I nodded in agreement. A strange and uncomfortable feeling came over me. Tiny snowflakes were beginning to filter through the trees.

"Let's get out of these woods!" Matthew yelled. I also felt the urgent need to get out of there. Alex began to move swiftly, and I pulled Bobick's harness with all my might. The dogs seemed reluctant to move. Matthew was still far behind. Soon, I saw a clearing. Alex was already traveling out of the woods. The sky now appeared murky and foreboding. I looked ahead. There were no men on the clearing; I had no idea how far along they had traveled.

"Alex! Do you see their trail?"

He continued tall and strong. "Yes, keep following me."

The snow outside of the woods was coming down much harder, and the wind had picked up. I looked back. I could not see Matthew; he was still in the woods. The wind ripped at my clothing. I thought that perhaps I should stop and wait for him. I tried to call Alex again, but he did not seem to hear me. The wind hurt my eyes, and I could not breathe. I thought perhaps that I should turn back and seek protection in the woods, but I was afraid of losing sight of Alex. I turned my head again; Matthew had just reached the clearing. I could scarcely make him out in the snow. As I looked ahead, I was unable to see Alex. Fear began to creep into my heart. The wind was howling, and the snow was flying around me like a whip. Matthew was nowhere to be found. A tunnel of snow surrounded me. Blinded, I pushed on. I had to find Alex and Matthew. I had not expected the snow to turn so ferocious without warning.

"Ha!" I yelled at my dogs as I jumped on my runners. They stood still. I ran up to the sled's anterior, holding the gangline in fear of losing my sled in the blizzard. I pulled at Bobick's harness with all my might. His steps were reluctant, but he began to move. I had no idea what to do. Where had Alex gone? The blizzard had taken me by complete surprise; I hoped Matthew would catch up. I stopped for a moment in hopes that I would see Matthew. As I stood, cold fear began to sink deep into my veins, and my clothes became wet and heavy. My teeth began to chatter. I had to move to keep warm; I would freeze and get buried in the snow if I did not travel. I yelled with all my might at my dogs. Finally, they sped up. I had never lived through such horror, but I kept running.

My feet kept pumping against the ground, but I knew that I could not go on forever. Hours seemed to pass. Time and space did not matter. The darkness enveloped me as I stared out into the white curtain. I had no idea if I was traveling in circles or a straight line. My only hope now was to find someone. I did not understand how so much snow could fall so suddenly and swiftly.

The hope of finding anyone in the storm faded with every second that I moved forward. Yelling into the storm did not seem to help at all. The wind picked up and blew my voice in a thousand directions. I was praying hard now without a pause. The fear of certain death now hung like a cloud around me. Desperately I yelled to Bobick. All of a sudden, the dogs sprang forward and then lurched to a stop. I flew against the bar of my sled. I shouted at the dogs to keep moving. I could hear Bobick's muffled bark at the end of the sled. Then a sound came from the same direction. I thought I had become delirious.

"Anna! Is that you?" a muffled voice called out the question. I realized that the voice was Alex's.

"Yes!" I shrieked. Bobick and my dogs still stood rooted to the ground. I held the gangline as I moved in the direction of Alex's voice. Finally, when I reached the front of my sled, I felt another dog, and then I moved up again. My relief was great as I felt the next sled. Again I cried out to Alex. He answered in the same tone, only this time his voice sounded loud and clear. Then there was his hand outstretched to catch mine. I almost fell into his arms.

"Alex, I thought I would never find anyone." I straightened out when I realized that I was embracing him. I still held his arms; I was afraid to lose him.

"Listen, Anna, now that we have found each other, we must make some shelter and make a fire." Alex released my fingers from his arm. I realized that I had been holding him with an iron grip. He remained close.

"How, Alex?" I asked. Even if we had found each other, there was no guarantee that we would not freeze to death.

"You have blankets in your sled, do you not?" he asked.

"Yes," I answered.

"Now listen very carefully. Take the blankets out of your sled. We'll make a tent with them by tying them to our sleds." I was about to move towards my sled and released his hand.

He grabbed my arm. "Wait, I would not want to lose you again."

Still holding hands, we moved slowly through the whipping wind. The snow made it hard to see Alex, even at such a close range. He rummaged through his sled and pulled out a rope. Then he tied my arm to his. He left enough rope so we could move apart. "We won't get lost this way."

I fumbled my way back to my sled. After much digging, I found some dry blankets at the bottom of my sled. Then, while I listened to Alex yell instructions, I helped to create a tent. Soon we were under the blankets that we tied to the back of our sleds. There was hardly enough space for both of us to sit down. Alex lit a match and put fire to some papers and a blanket that he had found in his sled. We were out of the blasting wind, but the storm raged on outside. At least I could see Alex's face. The wind blew so harshly that speaking was impossible. I already had a terrible ache in my throat from yelling so much into the wind. I sat huddled close to the burning blanket. Burning an extra blanket for warmth seemed to be a waste of a good blanket, but at the same time, I only cared about surviving the night. Eventually, the howling wind subsided. Alex peered out from behind our makeshift tent.

"What is it?" I asked.

"Ice."

"What about the dogs?" I asked.

"I'll walk out and make sure that they are breathing every half hour."

I looked over at Alex with concern. There was not much we could do. We sat in silence.

Then Alex crawled out from under the tent and returned five minutes later. "The storm is letting up."

"The dogs?" I asked.

"They're all right. The dogs have huddled close together and are keeping warm." Alex put in some more supplies from his sled to feed the fire.

"Do you not think we should try to save those?"

"At the moment, no."

I looked at him uncomfortably. "Oh."

"I see no way that we will even reach Alaska. Who knows who else is alive at the moment, and if they are, our only hope is to keep alive ourselves and try to find them."

I nodded in agreement. I shivered. My top coat was still wet from the storm, and the cold had begun to seep through my clothing.

"Are you cold?" Alex asked.

I nodded.

"Here, take my coat. I don't need it at the moment. The most dangerous act you can commit is to sit in wet clothing. My coat is at least insulated from the inside."

I removed my coat, and Alex handed me his oversized, heavy jacket. Grateful as I was, I worried that he would freeze to death instead of me. "Thank you," I said as I put the warm coat over my shoulders. "Will you not get cold?"

He shook his head. "The fire is warm enough, and I have a light coat on, as you can see."

I nodded slightly. Alex stared grimly into the fire. It was hard to tell what truly worried him, but I had a few guesses.

"Are you worried about Sima and Matthew?" I asked.

"Yes. When we came out of those woods, I could only see you. When the storm started, I realized that Matthew had been far away. Jason Shubert was a fool to let all the men travel through the woods so far away from each other. Of course, I do not think that he was expecting such a blizzard."

"I hope not. Matthew was only coming out of the woods when the blizzard started. With any luck, he was able to turn back in time and seek shelter." I tightened the coat around my shoulders. A certain sense of doom and frustration hung over us.

"I hope that Sima stayed close to Joseph."

"I hope so. Anyway, Sima had their group's tent in his sled. Perhaps he had enough strength to set it up."

Alex did not seem to be too sure of this idea. "With all that wind howling around him, I am not sure that action would be possible."

We sat in silence. It was at that moment that I realized that the silence had become deafening. "Alex, did it stop snowing?"

Alex peered out from behind our makeshift tent. He gave a grim shake of his head. "It seems as if the storm has gotten worse again." Our fire of blankets was beginning to dwindle, and Alex again climbed out of the tent. This time he brought a pile of blankets and some boxes with supplies. "We'll have to burn this if we want to keep warm."

I nodded. I felt awful burning supplies that were so significant, but I wanted to live and saw no other alternative. The wind picked up outside again, and I felt the cold fingers of the wind coming through our blanket tent. My body began to shake. We had not come up with the best shelter imaginable, and the fire sometimes had to burn low so we would at least have a bit of warmth and not waste all of our blankets at one time. Alex glanced over at me. He then moved nearer and put his arms around me.

"I apologize for the inconvenience." He looked down at me and continued, "I would rather keep you alive." While I did feel awkward, I was now too cold to speak and did not care at the moment if I was ensconced in Alex's arms. I closed my eyes. The howling wind outside of the tent made me fear the worst for every man outside in the storm. I wondered if Alex and I would be found frozen together with our arms wrapped around each other for warmth in the morning.

*****

Many times throughout the long hours of feeding the fire with extra blankets and beating the gathering snow off the roof of our blanket tent and our sleds, I felt as if the entire world had become one giant blanket of snow. My hands became so numb that I had to hold them almost in the fire to make them warm again. The gloves on my hands had become soaked, and Alex's coat, as well insulated as it was, began to feel icy and wet against my shoulders. Soon I sat with no coat on, relieved to have several sweaters and my warm pants on, but those also began to feel stiff and frozen.

As the hours stretched on, I felt that we had no chance for survival. Supplies to keep the fire going were dwindling. The morning was dawning upon us. The blizzard had continued through the entire day and night. Several hours into the morning Alex looked out from under our blanket tent. "It stopped."

I ventured to peek out from under our makeshift tent for the first time. The snow had built up in drifts around us, and the sky had become light gray. The world looked as peaceful as ever underneath the new white crystals that lay upon it.

"What do we do now?" I asked.

"I suppose we should get moving and see if we can get back to the woods and build a decent shelter. I am not sure if it will snow anymore, but I do not want to take a chance of being unprotected again. Also, I hope that if we travel in the same direction, we might find Sima or someone else."

Alex started to gather all of our meager supplies. I helped. We worked in silence; conversation was not necessary at this time. Nerves and lack of sleep worked me into a great ball of fear. Sima and Matthew were nowhere near us, and I knew that Alex would not rest until we found them.

Wet clothing and exhaustion rapidly became our enemies as we traveled through the early morning. We had no idea in which direction we were supposed to travel. We had not voyaged for more than one mile when I saw the woods. Alex pulled up to me on his sled. "Never would I have guessed that the woods were so close to us."

I peered at the long foreboding branches of the tall trees. "I believe I traveled in circles."

Alex nodded, and we moved towards the imposing darkness of the forest. As we got nearer, I heard a faint bark of a dog. At first, I believed the bark to be my imagination playing tricks on me. Alex did not react, as if the sound did not reach his ears. Then I was sure that I heard it again. After calling Bobick to a halt, I said, "Alex did you hear that?"

He paused beside me. "Hear what?"

"A dog just barked, to our left, I think."

Alex stopped and listened. "I did not hear it…" as he said this, we distinctly heard a dog yapping.

Alex yelled to his dogs. I raced after him. The cold and fear had seemed to melt away, and a new hope built up inside of me. Alex was far ahead of me when I heard him call his dogs to a stop.

"Anna!" he yelled back at me. I hurried to reach him. I stopped cold when I saw what lay in front of us.

Under the boughs of a large maple tree lay Joseph Smith, face down in the snow. We found his dogs tangled up in their gangline, and the sled lay smashed to pieces all over the ground. My heart thudded as I looked at the dreadful scene.

Alex put a brake on his sled and walked forward. One of Joseph's dogs growled as Alex got nearer. Alex put a calming hand on top of the dog's head and pet it. He then leaned down and turned Joseph over. My heart sank. Joseph did not move. After checking for a pulse and examining him, Alex let him go slowly. I watched, frozen and terrified. Alex looked up at me with intense pain on his face and shook his head. He did not have to say the words. I knew that Joseph was no longer with us.

Alex stood while still looking down at his friend. "Anna, can you start to help untangle the dogs?"

I nodded and walked over to the pieces of the broken sled. My impulse was to run to Joseph and to try to breathe life back into him. Yet, I knew that my efforts would be futile. I worked without speed. Some of the dogs had knots of rope around their feet. They seemed hungry and irritable. I kept throwing uncertain glances at Alex, who did not move from his position.

He looked over at me with indecision. "I think we should bury him here under the tree."

"Do you think perhaps there are other men near here?"

Alex thought for a moment. "Perhaps we should search for them first." He walked over to me without haste. "Listen, you take the rifle and travel about half a mile in each direction. If you find someone, fire your rifle. I will finish untangling the dogs and dig …" He did not seem to be able to finish his sentence, and I understood why. The reality of the situation did not seem to catalog itself in our minds. Who knew how many more friends we would find just like this?

The rifle lay on my sled, and I started to load it. "I'll be back as soon as I can."

Alex did not respond for a second, and then he seemed to come out of his stupor. "If another snowstorm starts, keep firing your rifle, and I will find you."

I agreed to do so and got on my sled. I threw a look back at Joseph. Life seemed to be so unfair. How could this teasing carefree young man just die without warning? I called for my dogs to move. Part of me was relieved to get away from it all. However, another part of my heart ached so much that I did not think that I could ever move again. My sled had not traveled more than a quarter of a mile when I saw Matthew's sled.

As I neared, I noticed that his sled and dogs appeared to be intact. However, Matthew seemed to be missing. "Matthew!" I screamed.

Never had I experienced such an intense terror as I did at that moment. The memory of the conversation that I had just had with Matthew the other morning was still fresh in my mind. No response came to my calls. I parked my sled and ran to where Matthew's dogs jumped for joy at seeing a familiar face. Matthew, again, was nowhere to be seen. I grabbed the rifle and walked away from the sled.

When I saw Matthew lying in the snow, I did not even react. The horror of seeing Joseph frozen had barely registered in my brain. I came over to Matthew and touched his arm. It lay lifeless on the ground. I then turned him over and took his face in my hands.

I kissed his forehead. "Matthew, I failed you. You are the best person I ever knew." There was no response from him. In complete astonishment, I placed my head on Matthew's chest, hoping to hear a heartbeat. His heart did not beat. His chest was as hollow and empty as an arctic plain. He was gone. I do not know how long I sat with my head pressed against his chest, hoping to hear a sound.

"Please, Matthew, do not leave me in the cold," I whispered.

When the shock began to wear off, I felt unchecked tears rolling down my cheeks. I wrapped my arms around Matthew. I hoped for a miracle. The warmth from my arms did not transfer to him. He remained frozen. The miracle did not come; Matthew was gone. I noticed the photo of his wife lying on the ground next to him. I picked it up and placed it in his pocket. "Now you can watch your family from heaven."

I sat on the ground as tears poured out of my eyes until Alex found me. Together we buried the bodies of the two men. Terrified and completely drained of any emotion, we stood looking at the graves in silence. We then stood with arms wrapped around each other while the feeling of shock and fear overwhelmed us. Finally, we gathered the strength to read several prayers.

Alex turned to me. "We really should move on, in case anyone else is around here and still alive."

I shook my head. "I can't just leave them here."

"Anna, we have to. We can't stay here. Unfortunately, in this instance, we don't have time to grieve. Staying here will do nothing for them. All their suffering is behind them."

I nodded. With one final look at the graves, we turned and headed west. After about a mile of aimless traveling, we heard another dog barking. Alex and I looked at each other. A small fire of optimism lit in my chest. Although I knew well enough that it could be another poor man who had frozen to death in the storm. Alex and I took off in the direction of the barking. We caught a fresh trail cut by the runners of a sled. Hope grew within me. If these tracks were not covered, it meant that someone had just passed by recently. The volume of the barking increased.

A small frozen brook ran in between the clearing and the woods. Next to it lay Sima. He lay on the ground, and blood ran in a river from his forehead. My blood coursed like the water in the ice-covered brook through my veins.

Chapter **8**

December 3, 1887

Time and air seemed to remain paralyzed as we stood staring at Sima, then Alex sprang into action. He put the brake from his sled into the snow and ran forward. Sima's dogs had surrounded him and his lead dog, Caesar, barked at Alex in a menacing tone.

"Quiet boy, it's all right." Alex took him by his harness and led him away from Sima towards me. "Here, hold him."

I moved over to Caesar rapidly. Caesar tried to protest and pulled away from me. I held on fast, even though I thought I might lose my arm.

Alex leaned over Sima and felt his pulse, and checked to see if he was breathing. "He's breathing, at least." His voice reflected some hope.

Relief washed over my body. The previous experiences of the day had led me to expect the worst. Alex stood up. "Get some bandages from Sima's sled. He should have some in there. We'll set up camp here."

I hurried to follow Alex's directions. Fatigue was taking a toll on me. I wondered how long Sima's condition would last. While Alex bandaged Sima's head, I struggled with the supplies. We pulled the tent out of Sima's sled and set it up together. To our chagrin, Sima did not come out of his unconscious state.

"I certainly hope that he did not injure anything but his head," Alex said as he dragged Sima through the snow into our tent.

"I hope not."

129

When we had gotten Sima comfortably situated on several blankets in the tent, Alex glanced at me and then started to head out of the tent. "Anna, come outside with me for a moment." Bewildered, I followed him. Once outside, he continued to speak, "I don't know if this will work, but you and I both know that Richard and Ellen's cabin should be somewhere near this area. That was our next checkpoint. Perhaps some of the other men have gathered there. We might be able to give Sima more aide if he is not out in the cold."

"Alex, do you think that you'll find the cabin?"

"We've got to try, but I do not want to haul Sima around, especially not if he's hurt."

"I understand."

Alex began to walk towards his sled, and I followed him. "If I find anything, I will return for you and Sima. I'll try to mark the trail."

"Shouldn't you rest first? You are probably exhausted, cold and hungry."

Alex picked up the brake from his sled. "I'd rather get to safety first and then worry about being warm and fed."

"Alex, wait. Take some biscuits. They should be in Sima's sled. He always keeps them there for a snack on the trail." I walked over to the sled and searched Sima's knapsack that hung off his sled handles.

"I'm not sure that you'll find anything. Sima probably ate them all," Alex said with a small smile.

"For once, you're in the wrong, Alex, here they are." I handed the biscuits to Alex.

He bit into one of the biscuits. "Thank you. You make sure to eat too."

I took a step back from Alex's sled. "I will. Good luck. I'll be waiting."

"Make sure that Sima's all right and clean his head properly."

"Yes, I'll do my best."

Alex got on the runners of his sled. "Goodbye, then." Our eyes locked for a moment. Alex then yelled to his dogs, and they were off.

I waved and then ran back into the tent to make sure that Sima was still alive.

While I did try to clean Sima's wound to the best of my ability, I felt a bit sick every time I looked at the large gash. I applied a new bandage to his head. I hoped that Alex would return soon and with good news. We were running short on supplies. In my sled, I carried many medicines and food, yet we were short on bandages.

Dizziness forced me to get up and look for food in Sima's sled. After some nourishment and rest, I felt much improved. Still, the hours seemed to slog by. I watched Sima's chest move with every breath he took. I wondered if he was unconscious or sleeping.

Suddenly Sima sat up and asked, "Alex, where are you?"

"Sima?" I questioned.

He did not appear to notice me, but he lay down again. I moved closer to him. He still seemed to be unconscious. I hoped Alex would return soon. Sima began to turn his head back and forth and murmur. I could not understand what he was saying. I put my hand on his forehead and tried to calm him.

Time seemed to have come to a grinding halt. I heard strange howling in the distance. The howling animals sounded like wolves. I hoped that they were not howling at Alex and that they would not discover the tent. I knew that wolves did not usually attack humans, but distress was beginning to play tricks with my mind.

I was beginning to contemplate the danger of the situation and what I would do if Alex did not return when I heard a sled outside. I jumped out of the tent like a woman running from danger. There stood Alex- like a beacon of light and hope in front of our tent. I had an urge to run and hug him.

"I found the cabin," Alex stated. "I am not sure though if it is occupied. I decided to get back here as soon as possible. How's Sima?"

"Acting strange as usual," I told him.

"Well, at least he's breathing. He's not come back to consciousness?"

I shook my head. "No, he keeps muttering something."

"I think we should move right now. The sooner we get into a more stable and safe environment, the faster we will be able to provide Sima with more substantial support."

"Alex, you need to rest first," I protested.

He indeed looked tired. Dark circles had begun to form under his eyes. "I do not need rest, Anna. I need Sima to stay alive." Alex said this so sharply that I was taken aback at his tone. "Now, let's get moving." I had failed to mention to Alex that I, too, was exhausted. Still, Alex seemed to be so determined that I followed his every order.

"Is the cabin far?" I asked.

"I would say about seven miles. It's hidden in the far woods. That is why it took me a while to find it."

"Will we reach the cabin before dark?" I questioned.

"If we move quickly, we'll reach it before dark." There was no arguing with him. Alex and I strapped Sima into Alex's sled, and we also packed Sima's tent into his sled. We had decided to attach Sima's dogs to both our teams and tie Sima's sled to mine so the dogs would drag both sleds. Of course, this was difficult to achieve, and we could not move as quickly as we had wanted to. Darkness began to fall upon us. Still, Alex urged the worn-out dogs on as we traveled. I was surprised that the dogs were able to keep going. They seemed to feel the need for urgency.

Alex's earlier sled marks in the snow had not yet disappeared. Finally, after three hours of hard travel, we reached the cabin, nestled in between several pine trees in a deep wood. Alex knocked. There was no answer. We tried the door handle and found it unlocked.

Alex and I looked at each other. "I think that no one would mind if we borrowed this place for a while."

I shrugged. We had no other option.

Alex untied Sima from the sled and picked him up. "You start to take the sleds and dogs to the barn, and I will get Sima inside. I'll come and help you as soon as I help Sima get settled."

I was certainly glad that Alex was so strong. I indeed would not have been able to carry Sima anywhere. I could get Alex's sled and dogs into the large barn that stood at the edge of the clearing. All the dogs felt overjoyed at the fact that they had finally landed in a warm place. Caesar, Sima's lead dog, still seemed to be unsettled. He seemed to sense that Sima was in danger. I hugged him and waited with him until he calmed down.

Alex came in only a short while later. "It does not seem like anyone is home. Perhaps they have gone somewhere trapping. They also could have gotten caught in the storm."

I nodded and then said, "I hope Sima will come to consciousness soon. It frightens me that he appears to be so sick."

Alex stood silent for a moment and kicked at the dirt floor with his foot. "Is there food here in the barn?"

"Yes, there is some food in the barrel over there. There is hay covering the barrel. It's not much for our dogs to go on." I knew I did not sound enthusiastic. I was hoping that soon someone would appear. Perhaps men from our train would begin to trickle in. I knew the chances of any men coming to the cabin were slim. However, if we had found the cabin, I was sure someone else would see it as well.

Alex reached into the barrel and started throwing the food to the dogs. "We'll do with what we have for now. When Sima is a little better, you and I can go hunting."

A fear that had been forming in my head ever since that morning came to me, and I felt that I had to speak my mind. "Alex, what if Sima does not get better?" My voice shook a bit as I posed this question.

Alex sighed heavily and shook his head. "I don't know." He stopped and then tossed some meat to the dogs. "From what I have assessed, I believe that he is not in such a bad situation. Some rest and medication will help." He fell silent, and I decided that perhaps it was better not to question him further. Anxiety and distress were playing with our lives at the moment, and no matter how many times I tried to shake myself from a stupor of doubt, I could not do so.

*****

That night I went to bed in a state of exhaustion. Both Alex and I had reserved two bedrooms that we found in the cabin. Sima lay sleeping in the main room. Strangely enough, the large main room had a bed. I was relieved to lay down in the privacy of a bedroom and sleep. While I did sleep soundly, as anyone would sleep when denied a whole night's rest, I awoke in the night. My nerves felt tight. I saw a light coming from the main room. I wondered perhaps if Richard and Ellen had returned. I tiptoed across the small hallway.

When I looked through the door, I was relieved and disappointed to find only Alex sitting at Sima's bedside. He had a look in his eyes that I wanted to understand. At that moment, Alex looked kind and gentle. I had a hard time believing that it was him. He looked up in the next second, and I wanted to hide. My reaction was not quick enough.

He saw me and motioned for me to come forward. "Did I wake you?"

"No, I saw the light in this room. I was not sure who it was."

"You'll be happy to know that Sima awoke from his unconscious state. He called out because he was not sure of where he was. I heard him because I was not asleep yet."

"So he's all right?" I asked with a tone of excitement in my whisper.

"I think he will be just fine. He fell asleep again. He spoke to me, and I told him where we are."

"Did you tell him about Joseph and Matthew?"

Alex shook his head. "I think it is best that he sleeps first and gets some food. It would do no good to go upsetting him now."

"I agree. Do you want me to be present when you break the news to Sima?"

Alex tilted his head back a bit. "I would rather talk to him by myself. He has been my closest friend for years. He may not want anyone else to witness his reaction."

I understood. "All right, but you need rest too, Alex. Perhaps I should sit up with Sima in case he wakes up again."

"No, you go on to the bed. I'll go to sleep soon. Sima should be well enough to sleep on his own."

"I don't believe that you will go to bed soon."

"Well, we will stay here for a while so that I can rest then. Go to sleep Anna." His tone was almost commanding.

"I will. Don't stay up too late, Alex. You'll never wake up tomorrow morning, and then I will have to take care of Sima all by myself."

Alex smiled. "Good night."

I left the room and returned to bed. Sleep evaded me. The loneliness of the dark Canadian night pushed against me. I could not focus. I wanted to release this tension, but tears did not come. I had not cried since we had left Matthew. I lit a candle and sat staring at it until it almost burned to a stub.

The following day dawned clear and beautiful. The sun peeked through the windows in brilliant rays of light. There was a sudden knock on my door, and I flew to open it. It was Alex.

"Good morning," I greeted him. "You're awake early, are you not?"

"No, I never went to sleep," he told me.

"You must be tired. You have not slept in two nights."

Alex leaned against the door frame and managed to shrug his shoulders at the same time. "Well, I was planning to go to sleep, but by the time I was ready to go to sleep, the sun began to rise, and I decided to go feed the dogs instead."

"Alex, you need rest. You could have woken me." I looked up at him. I wondered if he felt the same amount of despair as I did. The deep circles under his sleep-deprived eyes told me that he was not only tired but anxious as well. Unfortunately, none of the men had arrived. I thought of poor Rideon Smith, who had lost his wife and had come on this trip. He had looked so forlorn the day before the blizzard had occurred. Where were all the men? I did not want to believe that Sima, Alex, and I had been the only ones who had survived this terrible ordeal.

"Alex, go rest. I am sure you are exhausted," I said this even though I wanted to ask him a million questions.

"Sure, I will. Scrounge up some food for Sima and me. He's still sleeping like a princess. I am sure he will be hungry when he awakes." Alex turned and walked out of the room. My eyes followed his strong lean frame down the hall. A feeling that I had experienced before when he was near me began to form in my heart. Although before meeting Alex, I had never experienced this feeling, I had a suspicion that I knew what it meant. I shook myself from my daydream. At the moment, stranded in a cabin with hardly any food and a hurt friend, it did not seem the right time to have thoughts of anything but survival.

Scrounging up food, as Alex called it, was not the easiest of tasks. Yet, I was able to make some pancakes and find some salted meat in the small pantry. The kitchen and the main room were the same. So as I cooked, I watched Sima with a wary eye, waiting for him to wake up at any second.

Sima did not wake for a while, and I began to wonder if he was still breathing. I suppose I was just overly concerned. Still, I crept to his bedside and leaned over him to see if I could feel his breath on my hand. He looked so peaceful as he slept. Although he was always joking, I could see now that the strain that he carried during the long days of travel had disappeared from his face. A sudden wave of tenderness swept over me, and I kissed Sima on the cheek.

"Anna, is everything well?" Alex's voice came from the direction of the door.

I straightened up immediately. A wave of warmth swept over my face as I stared at Alex, who stood at the main room entrance.

"Yes, everything is well. You did not sleep long." I fingered my shirt nervously and tried to avoid his eyes. I was not sure what he thought of me.

Alex smirked as he came forward and sat at the table. "I was afraid I was going to miss the romantic scene."

"It was not romantic, I just," I said as my voice died on my lips. I had no reasonable explanation. I had no real reason for kissing Sima on the cheek.

"Perhaps you think he is handsome?" Alex asked.

"No!" I answered quickly.

Alex laughed a bit. "There must be a reason, but if you do not want to tell me, you do not have to."

I decided to change the subject. "I made food for you."

"Thank you, did you eat?" he asked. He seemed to forget the subject of Sima suddenly.

I was relieved he did not pursue the matter. "No, I forgot to eat."

"Sit down and eat then." He pulled out a chair next to him. I suddenly felt awkward and uncomfortable. I sat down next to Alex and took two pancakes for myself.

He sliced his pancakes in two and slowly chewed each piece. "These are not bad."

"Do not act so surprised. I do know how to cook," I said, offended.

"I never said you did not know how to cook. I said the pancakes are not bad." Alex took another bite of his pancakes. "Anyway, you know, before you decide to kiss Sima again, I suggest you tell him a certain fact about yourself that he should know in case he wakes up while you are kissing him."

"What fact?" I asked.

"That you're a girl." Alex's eyes held mine. "Do you not think that Sima should know?"

I stood with our now empty dishes and walked to the water pump. "No."

Alex stood up and came over to me. "Then I'll tell him." He turned serious. "Anna, it is very likely that no one else is going to show up, and if we are to continue traveling together, I do not think we should keep secrets from each other. Both of us would be lying to Sima if we concealed the truth."

"Lying about what?" the question came from Sima in the corner of the main room. Alex and I turned to face Sima, who had propped himself up in a sitting position on the bed. I looked up at Alex.

"Nothing of consequence," Alex answered, throwing me a meaningful glance.

I took a cautious step towards the door. "I am going to check on the dogs." I did not look back as I fled the room. I did not relish the thought of what would transpire between Alex and Sima. I feared Sima's reaction. I somehow felt that if I heard Alex's words, the reality of the situation would be too much to bear.

Alone in the barn, I sat with my head in between my hands. Bobick nestled up against me. "Oh Bobick, it would have been better to stay in Maine."

I sat motionless for a while until I felt a light touch on my shoulder. "Anna, are you well?"

I took a deep breath. "No, Alex, but time heals all wounds, doesn't it?"

Alex gave me a wry smile as he sat down next to me. "Sometimes, it just creates a big ugly scar."

*****

We finished the task of filling buckets with snow and then brought them into the house so they could melt. Alex had told me he would check on them later.

As we neared the house, Alex stopped me. "Listen, I want you to understand the seriousness of this situation. Since none of the men have come yet, I think we will have to continue alone. We are short on supplies, so we will have to find anything in the cabin that we can use. I know this seems almost like stealing, but I think that Ellen and Richard would not mind. We can leave a note for them that we were Jason Shubert's friends. I think that they would understand."

"Maybe Richard and Ellen will appear soon."

"There is no knowing where they are. They might have decided not to come up here this winter, or they got caught in the storm."

"I certainly hope not. Anyway, Alex, I understand that this is an awful state of affairs. You do not need to impress that upon me." I then walked ahead of him into the cabin. Sima was lying on the bed with his eyes closed. I decided not to bother him and went into my room. I heard Alex walk in a few seconds later. There was talking in the main room. I assumed Sima had not been asleep or that Alex woke him up. I crept to the door of the main room and listened to what they were saying. I knew that it was wrong to do so, but I desperately wanted to hear what they were talking about; I worried that Alex would tell Sima the truth about me.

"Do you think that no one else is alive?" I heard Sima ask. His voice sounded odd.

"I do not know. Tomorrow I was planning to go hunting with Andrei. Perhaps some men survived but were unable to find the cabin. Andrei and I might be able to pick up a trace of some of the men."

"I certainly hope so." Sima sounded depressed. "I wish I was not injured, Alex."

"Everything will get better, Sima, you'll see."

"How can it be better? Joseph Smith was one of my best friends." The tone in Sima's voice made me back away from the door. Guilt about listening in made me return to the bedroom. The last place where I wanted to get caught was at the door listening to Sima and Alex.

That night, as I lay in a restless daze, I prayed hard that we would be able to find some of our men. There was little hope. Even so, somehow, Alex, Sima, and I had survived. It was hard for me to believe that Jason Shubert might not have survived the storm. He seemed indomitable. I thought of some of the men, Steven Lake, Fur Hunter, and Andrew Redlock. Where could they be? After many troubled thoughts flew like birds through my mind, I fell asleep in the dark night.

As the early morning light began to come through the window, there was a knock on my door. I had woken up only a few moments before. The door opened after I called out that it was all right to come in. Alex stood at the doorway. Dressed in his oversized coat, he looked like a gigantic bear.

"I think we should get moving. I want to get a good amount of our hunting done before Sima awakens."

"Let me get dressed. I'll be ready in a few minutes." Alex nodded and walked out, closing the door behind him.

Cold air came under my blankets as I lifted them from the bed. Why could Alex not go hunting just a few minutes later? My fingers shook as I put on my heavy boots. While I was not excited about getting up early and hunting food, I was thrilled about the fact that Alex had decided that I should come with him. Then again, after the blizzard had occurred, I realized how foolish it was to go into the wilderness without a companion.

He was waiting for me in the barn. Two rifles leaned against the wall. One was mine, and one was his. Silence consumed the cold air as we moved through the high snow. The game certainly did not seem to be plentiful. I knew that if we wanted to keep moving, we would have to find some big animals to last us a little while. When we were about a mile from the cabin, I spotted a deer.

"Alex, look." I pointed to the spot where the deer stood.

"There might be more than one," he said and began to load his rifle. I did the same. Alex looked over at me, and I saw that he had an amused expression on his face.

"What?" I asked.

"Nothing," he answered and picked up his rifle. "Quiet now. We don't want to frighten it away."

"Thank you, Alex. You know I have hunted before." Perhaps I sounded a bit piqued, but I thought that Alex should realize that I could accomplish different tasks.

"Let's see how well you can shoot." Alex seemed to be almost challenging me.

"All right," I said and turned away. I crept up to the deer slowly. The deer continued to eat the bark of the tree in silence. The snow made my quiet approach easier to accomplish. I aimed. I knew that I could not miss or Alex would never forgive me. The shot of the rifle rang out through the woods. I looked up. On the ground lay the unmoving deer. My heart quenched inside of me. No matter how many times I hunted, killing an animal never rested well with my conscience.

"Well done," said Alex, running up from behind me. "We'll take the deer back with us to the cabin and skin it." Alex did not seem to have any qualms about shooting the deer.

I gave Alex a smug look. "I told you that I had hunted before."

"Don't get too confident. I'll prove to you that I can hunt too."

"I am sure that you, of course, will be able to get the deer in less than one shot," I joked.

While we tied the deer to a large branch to carry it back with us to the cabin, I thought I heard a far-off barking of dogs. I looked up. Alex also noticed the sound. Automatically both of us ran in that direction.

"It must be one of the men," I said as I ran after Alex, trying to keep up with his bounding steps.

"I'll fire my rifle. They might hear the shot." Alex fired the rifle into the air. The loud echo of the shot rang through the woods.

"Careful!" a voice shouted from the trees in front of us. Soon, a sled appeared, and Joseph Shubert was at the end of it.

"Joseph!" Alex exclaimed in surprise.

"Alex, Andrei!" Joseph called out. A wonderful smile lit up his face. I had never seen him so happy before in his life. Of course, I had never been so glad to see Joseph Shubert before either.

"Joe, are you all right?" Alex asked.

"Yes, exhausted and worried, but I am all right." Joseph halted his sled next to us.

"Where have you been? Is there no one with you?" Alex asked.

"No," Joe answered. His smile faded. "As to where I've been; when the snow began, I turned back towards the woods. I was hoping to find someone. Instead, I found the woods and was able to make some shelter from the fallen branches." Joe stopped to take a breath. "I have been traveling for days trying to find Richard and Ellen's cabin and in hopes of finding someone. It's pure luck that I ran into you. I heard your rifle, and I decided to come in this direction."

"Andrei, Sima, and I have been staying at Richard and Ellen's cabin. I found it the morning after the storm. We kept hoping that other men would show up. I am happy we decided to go hunting." Alex smiled at Joseph.

Joseph could hardly return the smile. "I am certainly happy that Sima is also alive, and I will be happy to spend a night with other men. Fear has been my traveling companion for the past two days. I thought that I would be found frozen in twenty years." Joseph then frowned. "My father is nowhere to be seen. I have been searching for him in vain." My heart went out to him; Joseph must have been worried sick. He appeared drained of emotion.

"Joe, I keep hoping that other men will show up, and they might. It took us several days to find you, and the cabin is not easy to find. Let's not worry too much just yet." Even if Alex sounded convincing, I could tell from his expression that he was not sure of his words.

Joe glanced downwards. "Alex, you don't need to play games with me. You know as well as I do that we survived by a true miracle."

Alex put his hand on Joe's shoulder to comfort him. "I agree, but if we survived by a miracle, there is no way that we can say that others did not survive by the same miracle."

"Joe, how about we go? Andrei and I just got some meat; we'll be able to eat some good food tonight. At least for tonight, we're safe." Alex turned back to where we left the deer. I helped him carry it back to the cabin. I realized that again I had to pretend I was Andrei. For the first time since the trip started, I realized how much I disliked my disguise.

*****

Sima was thrilled to see Joe, but I could tell that he was disappointed that we only brought Joseph Shubert with us. Joe Shubert's face had paled and remained pale when we told him about Joseph Smith and Matthew Davis. The tension hung like a heavy storm cloud in the air. Joe's anxiety was more apparent. He was concerned about his father.

Alex and I skinned the deer in the barn and prepared the meat. Both of us were mute as we worked. Finding Joe seemed to bring distress to the forefront of our minds. My thoughts continued to swirl. What would we do if no one else came? I had a feeling that Alex would want to carry on with our journey. I knew that I also wanted to keep going. I was not so sure about Joe Shubert or even about Sima. Sima's home was in Alaska too.

That evening we sat in the main room of the cabin eating fresh venison. I had helped Alex cook it, and we enjoyed the fresh meat in complete silence.

Joseph interrupted the silence in a dull, low voice. "I wonder where Ellen and Richard could be. I hope they also did not get lost in the storm."

"Let's hope not. I think we should wait a few more days; maybe they will show up," Alex said.

"And then do what?" Joe asked, suspicion mounting in his voice. I saw Sima throw Alex a glance that I could not read.

Alex continued to speak. "I am planning to continue to Alaska. There is not much we can do."

"Do you think that's wise?" Joe asked.

"Well, our home is there," Alex answered him.

"How about Andrei?" Joe asked.

"I'm going wherever they go. My home is there as well," I answered.

Alex's gaze met mine at that second. While I had the strongest urge to return to Maine, I did not want to leave Alex or Sima. Also, how would I ever find my parents if I returned to where I had started?

Joe regarded us steadily. "You mean you would continue even without my father? The three of you? On your own? That's brainless."

Sima, for the first time in his life, looked grave. "Perhaps, but we've come so far, all three of us survived the blizzard. What are you planning to do, Joe?"

"I'd like to wait for Ellen and Richard. Then I'll continue to stay here. I can't believe that the rest of the men did not survive." Joe stood up and went over to the fireplace and filled his pipe. He smoked with no presence of mind.

"Look, Joe, we'll wait too, but if no one shows up, it would be better for you to continue with us," Alex stated with a specific gravity in his voice.

Joe's look was thunderous. "To tell you the truth, I don't want to continue. My father bullied me into coming on this trip. I'd rather wait here till spring and return to Maine rather than continue to Alaska. I can't stand dogs, sleds, or snow." All of us were left silent by this speech. I felt that Joe was disrespectful to his father.

Finally, Alex stood up. "It's your decision, Joe. Whatever you choose will be fine with me. Andrei, let's go feed the dogs." Alex strolled towards the door and grabbed his coat. I practically ran after him.

While we fed the dogs, Alex said to me, "That's Joe for you. Even when there are so many difficulties around him, he continues to be selfish."

"I feel sad for him. I wish that this had never happened. I can't imagine how he feels right now." I shrugged.

Alex was standing by me. He placed his hand on my shoulder. "Everything will be fine. Don't give up hope and keep praying, all right?" I turned my head towards Alex. There was a soft look in his eyes. The moment lasted for less than two seconds. Soon Alex was back to feeding the dogs.

"How long do you think we should wait for more men to show up?" I asked.

"Not more than a week, long enough for Sima to heal completely. Not too long, though, or we could remain here forever. If Joe does stay behind, he could send men to continue, and perhaps they would catch up to us. I am sure that they would find our trail. Also, I hope that if we go on, some men might have traveled further, and we might meet up with them on the trail."

"I agree with you. Well, I'm finished. I'll go back to the cabin now."

"Anna," Alex said my name. I turned to look at him.

"Try to keep as far away as possible from Joe. He's not friendly. I also don't want him to know you're a girl."

"I will try, Alex, thank you." I walked out. Although my thoughts bore down on me, my heart was light at that second. Alex cared about me. It meant a lot, especially after losing Matthew.

Night settled on the cabin. Joe had established himself in the big room with Sima. We had found some more blankets for him. Wrapped up in my world of blankets and nightmares, I slept. The day had been long. I awoke with a start because of an unexpected sound in the dark. I heard loud voices in the other room. Frightened, I huddled in the corner of my bed. A knock sounded on the door.

"Who's there?" I asked.

Alex opened the door. "It's me." He looked as if he had woken from a long sleep.

"What is it?" I asked. I tried not to sound alarmed.

"Do not worry. I wanted to let you know that Ellen and Richard arrived. Everything is under control. They were a bit surprised when they found our dogs in the barn and Sima and Joe sleeping in the main room."

"Yes, I suppose we did intrude a bit." I gave Alex a small smile. Part of me was genuinely relieved. However, I was sorry that none of the men had shown up instead.

"Go back to sleep. I apologize if I woke you." Alex closed the door without a smile. I shrugged to myself. I wasn't sure if I should go back to sleep or rise and meet the elusive Richard and Ellen. Since Alex said to go to sleep, I decided to follow his direction and fell back in my pillows.

The following day, I dressed carefully. Two people who should never know that I was a girl were Richard and Ellen. Not only did I not want anyone to have this knowledge besides Alex, but I could also not imagine what they would think of me. They would disapprove of a young girl traveling with so many men. With determination, I walked to the main room. When I entered the room, I saw a thin woman of medium height standing at the stove. She turned to me. I guessed that her age was somewhere around forty years old.

She smiled kindly. "You're Andrei, am I correct?"

"Yes."

"Here you go." She handed me a plate full of food. "You boys must have had such a hard time going through that blizzard. We had heard of the storm and decided not to come here until it was over. As you know, we usually live in Ontario."

I sat and ate my breakfast. The food was fresh and warm. At that moment, Sima and Alex walked into the cabin.

"You sleep too much, Andrei," Sima said with a smile; his kind expression locked on my eyes.

"Sima, you're up and about?" I asked in surprise.

"Yes, I am feeling much better. If you hadn't been sleeping all morning, you would have known that. Of course, you could sleep a bit because we don't need you to cook anymore. We have Ellen here now." Sima put his arm around Ellen.

Alex rolled his eyes. "Ellen, you better be careful. Sima likes to sweep any woman off her feet." While Alex said this to Ellen, I felt as if he was directing the comment at me.

"Alex doesn't know what he's talking about," Sima said and sat across from me. I exchanged a glance with Sima and then looked down at my plate.

I turned to look at Alex, who was speaking to Ellen. "If you do not mind us intruding on your company for a few more days, we will stay. We are hoping to gather some items from your home. Unfortunately, our provisions got ruined during the storm."

"We'll give you what we can, and we'll gladly look after Joe and make sure he returns to Maine. His father is a good friend of ours. I am sorry that this happened to all of you. I pray that they will all show up here, just like you did."

Even if Ellen's hope was the same as my own, no men showed up for the rest of the week. Joe and Richard would go out during the day to look for a trace of the men. Joe continued to look pale and thin. He skipped meals at times due to his agitation. As the days continued to drag by, I realized that we could not put off our departure much longer. Although I did not want to leave the cabin's safety, I knew that we could not stay there forever.

On a cold Monday morning, as Alex and I were feeding the dogs, Alex suddenly said, "I told Sima last night that I think we should leave this afternoon."

I was a little surprised by his sudden announcement. "Oh, I had anticipated that you would let me know at least one day ahead."

"I apologize, but I think we have to get moving. We can't wait here forever."

"That's true. I guess we can't go on living on false hope eternally."

"No, although your hopes may not be false." Alex shrugged. "I think we're all living with the same wish, especially Joe. Even though I never liked him, I can't help but feel sorry for him. His father was a good man. The truth is that I can't bring myself to believe that all of those men aren't alive anymore. Andrew Redlock, Red Fern, Joe Smith..." Alex stopped in the middle of the phrase and turned his face away from me and looked at the dogs. "Let's go inside. We still have to tell Richard and Ellen we are leaving." I wanted to comfort Alex somehow. I could see the lines of trouble had deepened further on his attractive face.

Even if Alex was restless, Richard and Ellen talked us into staying one more night. I did not mind so much. One more night remained for rest in a comfortable bed in a warm cabin.

The following morning we woke at the crack of dawn. Ellen and Richard were kind enough to give us a stash of food, including dried meat, hard biscuits, and some of Ellen's recently baked cake. They were sympathetic and concerned for our safety. Joe, who seemed to be a transparent shadow by now, did not seem to mind our leaving as much. He was too wrapped in his grief to pay any attention to us. For some reason, no matter how much evidence existed that Jason Shubert was not alive anymore, I could not quite believe that the mammoth of a man had not survived the storm while I had.

As our sleds and dogs stood outside of the cabin, ready for departure, Ellen and Richard told us to be careful and wished us luck in our journey.

Joe awoke from his silent sorrow and shook all of our hands. "Who knows when we will see each other again?"

Sima shook his head. "I don't know, perhaps never, but when we reach Alaska, we will try to send a letter by post to let you know if and when we arrive." As Sima said this, a strange expression came to his face.

"When I receive that letter, I will write to let you know how I am faring." Joseph stepped away from our sleds. "God be with you."

"We'll be praying for you and your father," Alex told him.

There was a momentary lapse in conversation. All of us seemed to be rooted to the ground. Leaving this harbor of safety and moving into the desolate Canadian wilderness appeared harder than we expected.

"Let's go!" Alex suddenly called to his dogs. Sima went after him, and I followed.

When we reached the clearing edge, I turned to see Joe standing on the snow-covered ground with his arm raised in a silent goodbye. That was how I would remember him, a lonely shadow of a man standing next to the cabin in the cold, desolate hours of the morning.

PART II
THE JOURNEY

Chapter 9   December 10, 1887

The first day of our travels passed without incident. We unpacked and set up camp. It felt strange to do so without the rest of the men. Sima now occupied Matthew's place in the tent. I did not know how long it would take me to make peace with the fact that Matthew no longer existed.

As we sat eating venison stew, Alex cleared his throat. Sima and I both turned our heads to look at him. Alex cleared his throat again. "I think that since we are all now continuing on this journey together, we should have complete honesty at all times."

Sima's face conveyed confusion. "Alex, what are you talking about?"

I tried to give Alex a look of warning, but that did not work. Alex placed his bowl of stew on the snowy ground. "I think Andrei here should share with you some information."

Sima looked from me to Alex. "What information?"

I sat dumb. Where was I to start? It was hard enough to explain when someone figured out the truth, but Sima appeared to know nothing. My throat felt dry, and my hands turned clammy. I began to worry about how he would react to such news. I let out a heavy breath. Alex cleared his throat again. My mouth could not formulate the words.

Sima interrupted the silence. "Alex, you can stop clearing your throat. I know the truth."

"What truth?" Alex sounded astonished.

"That Andrei is a girl."

The bowl almost fell out of my hands. "When did you find out?"

Sima drank the rest of his stew in one gulp. "I figured it out in Montreal. I suspected something when we crossed the border in Canada. I then began watching you closely. By the time we left Montreal, I did not doubt in my mind that my suspicions were correct."

I stared at Sima. "You knew but said nothing?"

Sima stretched out on his blankets. "What did you want me to say? I figured it would only make matters worse if I said something, and I knew if Alex found out, he would probably tell Mr. Shubert."

"You said you didn't think there was anything wrong." Alex's tone was accusing.

Sima sat up again and faced Alex. "I did not want to deepen your doubts. Since our friend here said nothing, I decided it would be best not to betray her secret. It would be strange if I did not recognize a girl when I saw one. I thought it strange you did not figure it out earlier."

Alex threw Sima a funny look. "It's not my fault that you courted every woman in Boston."

"Not *every* woman." Sima then turned to me. "What is your real name, by the way?"

"Anna," I responded.

Sima laughed a bit. "Anna, Andrei, I see the connection. You know, you're not very original." He then lay down again and pulled out his pocket knife and another ridiculous piece of wood.

I regarded Sima for a few seconds. He often seemed to have no idea what was happening around him. Nevertheless, he had figured out my secret before anyone else and had the sense not to betray me. He had been my ally without my knowing.

Our conversation seemed to have lightened the mood, and we all wished each other a good night. However, the night was not my

friend. I lay listening to the howling wind. I wanted to shut my ears
to it, to shut out the fear that threatened to boil over inside me. I drew
the blankets tighter around me and began to pray. I prayed for the
men who were lost and for their families. As I whispered the prayers
into the inky night, my heart calmed, and I fell asleep.

As I awakened the following day, I heard voices outside. Sima and
Alex were not in the tent. I crawled over to the entrance and listened
to their conversation. It took me a few moments, but I realized that
they were talking about me.

"Alex, we have to do something. She's a girl. We can't just let her
sleep with us in a tent; it just is not decent. She needs privacy." I was
surprised to hear Sima speaking in my defense.

"What do you want me to do? I have no other tent. There is no
other space for her to sleep unless you want her to sleep outside."

"Alex, it is just not done."

"I would think that you of all people would care the least about
this."

I peeked out of the tent. Sima was leaning with one arm against
his sled. Alex stood with his arms crossed in a severe manner, looking
down at the snow with a scowl.

"Alex, you know that I understand decency and respect. The
women I have courted are also not Anna. She is young, innocent. She
lived alone for years and knows little of this world. There is no reason
not to come up with an alternative sleeping arrangement."

I was a bit offended at Sima's words. Only because I had lived
alone did not make me a naïve country bumpkin.

Alex kicked at the snow with his foot and looked up at him.
"I agree with you. I just don't know what is best."

Sima stood straight and crossed his arms as well. "What if we
make a wall of blankets for her? Could we string them up in the tent?
It might be a pain to put up, but I think it is worth it. She might like
us more if we do something for her."

"Do you think she doesn't like us?" Alex asked, his voice sounding curious.

Sima dropped his arms and gave an exaggerated shrug. "Who knows what is running through that one's brain? She thought she could convince a crew of men that she was a boy." Again his words struck a chord of hurt in my chest. I realized he was right, though. What kind of girl would do such a thing? *A crazy one*, I answered myself.

"I suppose time will tell." Alex turned then to the tent, and I retreated to my blankets before he saw me.

That evening, Alex and Sima proposed their plan to me, and I agreed. I tried to sound as kind as possible. I hoped that I could make them believe that I liked them and wanted to be their friend. My only friends had been Mary-Louise and then Matthew.

*****

The sky was a bright blue the next morning when I awoke and peeked out of the tent. Alex was already up, loading our supplies onto the sleds. I rolled out of my blankets, folded them up, and came outside.

"Let me help you," I said as I came up to him.

"It's quite all right." He knotted one of the ropes holding down the supplies on his sled. "Sima awake?"

"Not yet. I'll go wake him." I climbed back into the tent and shook Sima by the shoulder.

He rolled over and rubbed his eyes. "Well, what have you been up to?"

"Nothing, I just spoke to Alex. We're going to start soon."

"Is this something unusual?" Sima asked with a bit of sarcasm.

"No, I guess not." I sat down across from him and started to pack our mugs into my bag.

"Listen, I haven't had my tea yet." Sima stopped my hand with his. His hand shook when he held it out, and he hastily lowered it.

"You can have tea later," I told him. "We're not going to go far, and I'm sure we'll stop for a break."

"Give me a biscuit or something."

I handed him a piece of bread. "Here."

"You know I need something to hold me up. I'm not some type of hero." He finished the stale bread and started to prepare for the day.

I climbed out of the tent again with my pack and walked back over to Alex. "Listen, Alex, are you sure that Sima will be all right?"

"Anna, I hope you are joking. We discussed this already. We waited a sufficient amount of time before leaving."

"Perhaps, but Alex, I just worry that he could become over-exhausted."

Alex gave me a look that I imagined he would give his future children if he were upset with them. "You have as much chance as Sima to become over-exhausted. Also, Anna, if anything is wrong, I think we can come to a compromise and rest some more if we need to." He moved a step closer to me. I looked up into his face. He towered at least five inches above me, and I almost reached six feet in height.

"Listen, we have to get to Alaska, and it is my job to make sure we get there."

"Why is this only your job?" I asked. Without much discussion, Alex had inadvertently become the leader of our three-person troupe.

"It's not, I suppose, but do you think we'd get far if it were up to you and Sima? You would be negotiating with everyone, and Sima would not wake up until noon." He could not imagine that anyone could lead this expedition but him.

I turned from him. "Well, I suppose then it's your responsibility to get us to Alaska. That's at least a weight off my shoulders."

"I'm glad that that is the way you feel about it," Alex said and came up to the tent. "Come on, Sima, we have to leave someday. We still have to take the tent down."

Sima emerged from our sleeping quarters. "What makes you think that I would want to stay here for another day?" I could not tell if he was being cynical. "Now, if you two would be so kind as to help me take the tent down, I would be content." Sima began to take the pegs out of the ground.

"First time in your life that you help take down the tent."

Sima turned to Alex and gave him a strange look. "Why are you talking so much? I thought you said we have to leave someday."

Eventually, the tent was down and placed in Alex's sled. We said a prayer before leaving and then touched off. Our sleds ran smoothly through the snow. The trees' peaks to our right seemed to soar in the sky as we passed by them. I was thankful that Sima and Alex were with me. They had done so much for me already. I realized that even if it seemed that Alex was edgy, he was not obligated to take me along with him and Sima.

I stared at Alex's back as I drove behind him. I wondered what would have happened to me if I had not found him during the blizzard. I would not have known what to do. By now, I might have even not been alive. A shudder ran down my spine, and I shook myself mentally to get rid of that horrendous thought.

"Anna, are you asleep?" Sima asked from behind. I noticed that since I had been deep in thought, my pace had slackened.

"No," I called back to him.

Alex stopped and turned towards Sima and me. "Can we last five more miles?"

"I think so," I responded.

"Sima, can you?"

Sima had pulled to a stop. "Sure, Alex, but let's stop to catch our breath for a bit."

"Let's travel towards the edge of the woods, and then we can take a break," Alex suggested. I was relieved that the tension from the morning had seemed to cease.

"All right," Sima answered, and we continued to travel through the snow. Sima and I traveled at the same speed, while Alex stayed a good ten meters ahead of us. Alex would run and then stand strong and tall on his runners. For some reason, I felt proud of Alex. I could not understand why. I was embarrassed for having such thoughts and came back to earth as I realized that Sima was pulling ahead of me and that I again was falling behind.

We were pulling towards the edge of the woods when Alex stopped. I was not sure why. I yelled to my dogs to catch up to him. "Alex, what's wrong?"

He put his hand up. "Quiet, I'm not sure. My dogs just halted. Something is amiss."

"Hey Alex, what's the matter?" Sima drove up to where he stood.

"I don't know." We all stood without speaking. The dark and mysterious forest seemed to close in on us.

"Let's get out of here. This place gives me the shivers," I said and gave the command to my dogs to move forward.

"Wait." Alex put his hand on my arm. "I think we should find out what is wrong. Maybe some of our men are here. You know, we have not traveled that far from the cabin. I think the dogs recognize a scent."

"Do you think so?" Sima asked.

"Yes," Alex answered as he pulled his rifle out of his sled. "I want us to split up. We won't go far. We can leave our dogs here. Anna, you go to the left, I'll go forward, and Sima, you go to the right. Let out a shout if you see or hear anything. Don't go too far. Come back in fifteen minutes."

Sima pulled out his rifle. "Sounds reasonable."

We split up, and I walked cautiously towards the left side of the woods. While I did not want to admit it, I was terrified. The branches hung low as I snuck forward. I had not gone more than thirty feet when I heard a low growl. Fear of coming face to face with a pack of wolves haunted me. The urge to turn around was strong; still, I advanced.

After a few more steps, I noticed several broken branches in the path. Suddenly, I heard an even louder growl followed by several more. I forgot to be cautious and ran forward. I was confident that I would find some of the men.

After a few more steps, I regretted that I had been so eager to discover the hidden men. I came across an area where no trees grew, and a pack of wolves surrounded some shelter built out of branches. Three dogs lay dead near the shelter. A few others crouched behind the shelter, ears back, teeth bared. The wolves looked ready to rip apart any dog that came near them. Fear as to who I would find in the shelter gripped my heart. I wondered what I could do to dispense the wolves that surrounded the shelter.

Quietly, I reached for my rifle. There were five wolves. They were gradually advancing towards the shelter. I picked out the leader and decided to take a chance. I aimed at the leader and shot. A surprised yelp came from the wolves as their leader fell to the ground. All the mean eyes of the wolves turned to the bushes where I sat hidden. I reloaded and shot again. The wolves did not wait this time and ran in the opposite direction. A breath of relief escaped my lips. Soon I heard more crashing through the woods. In fear, I whirled around to face the coming sound. This time there was nothing to dread Alex and Sima were running towards me. They had heard the shots.

"Anna, what is it?" Sima called. He was a few steps ahead of Alex. Shock and panic were reacting on me and I, unable to speak, pointed to the clearing where two wolves and three dogs lay dead. The remaining four dogs stood behind the shelter, whimpering. Sima stood in silence, and Alex also gravely sized up the situation. A look of fear crossed Sima's face.

"These are Fur Hunter's dogs," Sima stated.

Alex silently looked at the shelter. "I wonder." He bravely stepped forward.

No sound came from the branches, and I feared the worse. My fears came to fruition as Alex lifted the branches of the makeshift tent. Fur Hunter was lying face down on the cold snow. Alex slowly stretched out his hand and touched the immobile shoulder.

He pulled his hand back almost as soon as his fingers had touched the body. "He's dead, frozen." Alex took a few steps back as if those steps would somehow bring Fur Hunter back to life.

"How is that possible?" Sima asked. His voice shook a bit. I could not bring myself to believe what Alex had just said. A ring of ice gathered around my heart.

"Are you sure?" Sima asked.

Alex kept staring at the body on the ground. "Yes." He hung his head.

"What should we do?" I asked. "Should we bury him?"

"The ground is frozen here. There is no way that we could bury him." Alex turned to look at us. All of us were speechless. My body was numb with disbelief. Somehow before this horrendous event had occurred, hope had still lived on in my heart that some of the men were still alive and well, but Fur Hunter should have known better than anyone else how to survive.

"Let's try to cover him up with branches and stones if we can find any. I want to make sure his body is protected." Alex was speaking to us. The look on Sima's face was terrible.

"What about the dogs?" Sima asked.

"Look at them; they are a mess," Alex said and shook his head. "They are trapped tied to that sled." As Alex said this, I realized that the four dogs behind the shelter were still tied to the sled. That was why they had been unable to move when the wolves had come at them.

"Somehow, the other three dogs broke free. These dogs are starving. Fur Hunter has probably been lying here for over a week." As Alex spoke these words, a chill ran down from my neck to my toes.

"Alex, what are we going to do with these dogs?"

"I am going to have to shoot them."

"Alex…" I started but stopped. The look on Alex's face was dreadful. There was no use in trying to drag around injured half-starved dogs. They would be of no use to us.

"Come on, let's cover up Fur Hunter. After that, Sima, you get Anna out of here. I would like you to travel five miles west of here, and I will follow. I will see what supplies we can try to keep."

We worked in silence. My body felt numb. I did not look at Sima and Alex because I thought I would lose any sense of composure if I did. When we finished, we all stood quietly around Fur Hunter's grave. I said a silent prayer for him.

After about ten minutes of standing next to the grave, we seemed to realize that there was nothing more that we could do. Sima and I went to our sleds and started moving west. Neither Sima nor I spoke. I could only guess that Sima's thoughts were the same as mine. After we traveled for five minutes, I heard four shots in the distance, a shot for every dog. Sima and I exchanged a glance, but he said nothing. Tears were threatening to spill over on my cheeks, but I felt that I needed to be brave.

Only later, after Sima and I had set up camp, and I was lying alone in the tent, did I give in to my tears. After at least an hour of crying, exhaustion and sadness had come over me, and I gave in to the comfort of sleep.

I was awakened by someone's hand, shaking me by the shoulder. It took me a moment to comprehend where I was. I turned over on my side and came face to face with Alex.

"I am sorry to have wakened you, but I brought a surprise for you."

"A surprise? What sort of a surprise?" I asked, completely bewildered.

"Come with me, outside."

I stood up and followed him out of the tent. To my great amazement, when I stepped outside, I realized it was early evening. I had not even slept the night. "Did you just get back?" I asked.

"I got back half an hour ago."

"Well, what is the surprise?"

"Here." Alex brought me to his sled. On the sled sat Fur Hunter's dog. He had been his lead dog.

I turned to Alex. "I thought you had shot all of them."

"I could not bring myself to kill this one. I fired and missed on purpose. He was healthier than the rest, and it seemed a shame to destroy such a fine animal. I realized that you were against me shooting the dogs, so I decided that perhaps you would be able to take care of him." Alex looked at me as if waiting for an answer.

"I will take care of him. He can ride in my sled until he is healthier. Thank you, Alex."

Alex smiled at me and said, "I will feed the dogs if you can prepare something for us to eat."

"Yes," I stopped and asked, "where is Sima?"

"He told me he wanted to be alone for a while. He said he would not go far."

"I understand."

Sima did return for supper. Supper was a silent meal. Finally, Alex broke the silence. "It seems strange to me that Fur Hunter was alone and that he would have gotten lost in the blizzard. He was an Indian and one of the best trackers that I knew. That was part of the reason that Jason Shubert had asked him to come on this expedition."

I took a stick and pushed the flames of our small fire with it. "Too bad he didn't have the foresight to know that it would be best not to agree to come on this journey."

"I know it always seems like that when tragedy strikes." Alex's eyes locked on mine, and he continued to speak. "The truth is he was probably hurt. Otherwise, he would have survived. I guess it does not matter that much now."

"No, no, it doesn't." I looked down at the flames. I felt as if I had to turn away from the fiery intensity of Alex's eyes. There were footsteps outside, but Sima did not enter the tent.

Alex looked down at his empty tin plate. "Anna, would you mind going to see if Sima is all right and if he wants anything? I felt as if he did not want to talk to me when I arrived at the camp this afternoon."

"Grief reacts differently on people. I will go to him." I stood up to leave. As I moved past Alex, he suddenly took my hand and gripped it with his. There was strength in his touch, and as I looked down at him, something passed between us. The burning intensity was still in his eyes.

"Alex." His name caught in my throat. He smiled at me in that second and let me go. I quickly stepped out of the tent.

The cold air froze my lungs as I gathered a deep breath of fresh air. My nerves were tight, and I found it difficult to breathe. Then I noticed Sima standing silently next to the tent. His face looked like stone.

"Sima, are you all right? Do you need anything?"

He shook his head. He did not even glance in my direction. Sima's mood unnerved me. He was usually so cheerful. There was not much I could do, so I turned and went back into the tent. Alex was already lying down on his blankets when I returned.

"Sima?" he asked in one word.

"He's all right," I said as I got behind my draped blankets and pulled them around me. My thoughts whirled like a windstorm in my mind, and I could not fall asleep. After lying sleeplessly for about twenty-five minutes, my eyes closed.

In the night, I awoke from a strange sound outside of the tent. I drew back my curtains and looked around the dark tent. Alex slept, but Sima's blankets lay empty. Taking my rifle from my bag, I crept out of my blankets and stepped into the frigid air. Like a glittering chandelier in the night, the fire threw moving patterns of all different shapes and sizes on the pale snow. Sima, who sat on his sled, looked as stiff as the wood he loved to carve. His posture suggested all loss of hope and feeling. A cascade of fear ran through me. How could I comfort him? My emotions reflected a river of breaking the ice. If we were to continue on this journey, I had to find a way to keep the ice from melting. I needed a miracle. With a prayer, I stepped forward.

"Sima," I whispered. He reached out and took my hand with his firm grip. He moved over on the sled, and I sat next to him.

I put my hand around his shoulders. "Sima, you can't do this to yourself."

"I know, but I cannot believe that Fur Hunter is gone. Not only Fur Hunter, but somehow seeing him frozen." He took a deep breath. "This made me think of Joe Smith and Matthew Davis. I can't even imagine Joe Smith lying on the ground lifeless." His body shook with another uncontrollable sob. I held him, afraid to let go. Sima buried his face in my shoulder.

"Sima, there is always some hope. We survived, which is truly incredible, considering what happened to Joseph, Matthew, and Fur Hunter."

Sima nodded. His sobs had calmed a bit. "We better go to sleep. Doubtless, Alex will want to get an early start in the morning." He smiled a bit. A sense of relief came over me. At least he had kept a sense of humor. Sima stood up. "I am afraid that you will think of me as weak. I had not wanted anyone to see my tears."

I stood up as well. "Sima, I will not think any less of you because you were crying."

"Alex has always been stronger than me. I have never seen him break down, not once."

We had been slowly walking towards the tent and now stood at the entrance. Sima put his hand on my shoulder. "Thank you, Anna, for comforting me. I don't know if anyone has ever told you this, but you are a wonderful person."

I squeezed his hand and then dropped it. "Sima, you are too kind. Good night."

The next morning as I was loading my sled, I felt a light touch on my elbow. I turned to find Sima standing next to me. Alex was still inside.

Sima handed me his flask of whiskey. "Anna, I need you to watch this for me. I know that I can trust you not to give it to me. I have never been obsessed with drinking. However, over the past few days, I feel as if I have not been able to stop. I cannot handle my emotions right now. I do not want Alex to know."

I looked down at the flask and put out my hand. Sima handed over the whiskey, and then without a word he went to work on packing his sled. I turned and shoved the flask deep into the canvas folds of my sled.

"It is so cold," Sima said, walking into the tent and pushing his hands toward the fire. Two weeks had passed since we had discovered Fur Hunter, and we kept traveling. We had traveled a fair distance and now were still on our way to Alaska. Not a single person had crossed our paths in the last two weeks. At times, as we traveled through the wilderness, it seemed that we were the only people alive in the world. Also, for the past two weeks, the temperatures had been dropping at a rapid pace. At the end of each day, we would sit huddled for warmth in our tent.

"Yes, I agree," Alex answered Sima. "I thought it would have been warmer by now."

"Really, why?" Sima asked.

"Well, I would think that spring is coming on."

Sima gave Alex a funny look. "Alex, if you have not noticed, there is a lot of snow outside, and nothing is melting."

"Just a thought." Alex shrugged. "I lost count of the days."

Sima laughed. "Unbelievable."

"I know what day it is, or at least I am pretty sure that I have kept count correctly," I put in.

Sima smirked. "Leave it to Anna to keep track of such petty details."

"These are not petty details, Sima. It is December twenty-sixth."

"How is she so amazing, Alex?" Sima asked with sarcasm.

166

Alex gave Sima a guarded look. "You tell me."

"Jason Shubert kept up the calendar pretty well, and then I just kept count from there. It has been about a month since…" I stopped my thoughts.

"It's all right, Anna," Alex said as he put a comforting hand on my shoulder. "You never know where they could be. Some of them could have banded together like us. Just think of it as being split up. When we traveled together, we were split up most of the time anyway. We trailed behind everyone a good mile or so."

I smiled a bit. In the past two weeks, we had grown closer. Still, Sima and Alex liked to tease me about being a girl. "One time when Jason Shubert was yelling at me for falling behind, he too told me to act more like a man and that I was acting like a silly-headed woman."

"You'd be surprised how close he was to the truth." Alex laughed and lay down on his blankets.

"Not silly-headed, surely," I said.

Alex leaned on one elbow, looked at me, and shook his head. "No."

"Maybe stupid," Sima added.

"Sima, enough," I told him and threw a bit of snow at him.

"Stop that," Alex said. "You'll put the fire out."

Sima winked at me. "Alex, the fire is not going to go out because of a little bit of snow."

"It's as if both of you were five years old."

Sima grinned. "Alex, if you stop pretending you are forty, maybe you would realize that we have fun."

"Sima, I do not pretend I am forty. Anyway, this is a ridiculous conversation." Alex turned on his side to look at the tent wall.

"Since you are in no mood to talk, Anna and I can go talk outside," Sima said as he started to stand up. Alex turned back to us and sat up. "Sima, there is no need to go outside in the cold. You can talk to her right here if you need to."

"Cannot stand to have her out of your sight, can you?" Sima asked with a mischievous light in his eyes.

"I suppose I can't," Alex replied. While he meant this as a joke, the look in his eyes made my insides turn within me.

"You see Anna, the danger of you being with us, Alex will fall in love with you." Sima laughed. I could feel my face turn red with embarrassment.

"Sima, please stop. I am not in love with Anna. You are embarrassing her."

"See, the young man cares about you, Anna." Sima laughed again.

"Sima, I think I will soon have a headache," I told him.

"I am only stating plain facts. They are inevitable."

"You wait till we get to Alaska and go our separate ways," Alex said.

"Perhaps that's what you say now, but you just wait until we reach Alaska," Sima said as he smiled. "You might say I predicted the future."

"Sima, how about I make you a proposition?" Alex asked.

"What kind of a proposition?" Sima asked innocently.

"That you keep your mouth shut for the next four weeks."

"I could try that. Good night." Sima lay back on his blankets without a sound.

Alex looked at me and shrugged. "If I knew it was that easy, I would have said that earlier."

"Alex, you know that that is impossible, don't you?" Sima asked with his eyes shut.

"I guess it was too much to hope for," Alex said. "Good night, maybe if I fall asleep, the talking will stop."

"I will be in your dreams, Alex." Sima started to laugh uncontrollably, and I began to wonder to what extent the cold and his emotions had affected him.

When I lay down, I began to think about Sima's motive. He joked a lot, and he never again had mentioned Fur Hunter. When we spoke of the men, he usually would change the subject rather quickly to something light. In a way, it was not surprising that he and Alex were friends. Alex hid his emotions behind strictness and serious nature. Sima seemed to hide his feelings behind a light attitude.

The next few days continued to be cold. Traveling was becoming even more challenging every day. The weather made it hard to breathe sometimes, and we would have to stop every half hour. The cold hurt my throat. Ice would cover the scarf that I wrapped around my face. At times, our dogs were covered with ice; there would be ice all around their mouths, and we would have to chip off the ice with our hands.

One particular day, the weather had dropped to such a frigid chill that Alex had been unsure if we should travel that day. However, we gathered our meager belongings, and we touched off. Almost as soon as we started, I knew that this was a bad idea. My legs kept numbing out as soon as I had moved my feet. My entire body ached from the cold. I wondered how Alex and Sima could even move. They seemed to be traveling along without a problem. They rode a bit ahead of me and talked easily about the next few days and hunting. While they spoke, I lagged and drove on my runners. My brain became numb, and I looked at the snowy ground and felt that I would be all right if I just lay down for five minutes. Darkness crept into my eyes, and the light of day disappeared as I looked at the grey sky.

I awoke to a bright fire shining on me, and I realized I was covered from head to toe in blankets. Even though I felt warm, my body started to shake, and my teeth shattered. I could not figure out where I was or who was the person who sat next to me. I wondered if I was dreaming. Suddenly, the person turned around, and I realized it was Alex. His comforting hand found mine, and he smoothed back my hair with one hand.

"Anna, how are you feeling?" he asked.

"Warm, but I can't stop shaking," I told him.

"Here, Sima made some tea. Drink it." He helped me sit up, and he propped several blankets up behind me to support me. I took the tea that he held out to me and wrapped my fingers around the mug.

"What happened to me?" I asked.

"I am not sure, but Sima had turned around to ask you a question, and you were about twenty feet behind us sleeping on the ground."

"I don't remember falling asleep."

"I hope not," Alex said as he smiled. "From now on, you will be driving in front of us in case you fall off again."

The shaking in my body started to calm as I drank the hot tea. "This is good tea."

"Yes, one good thing that Sima can make."

"I think you give him far too little credit." My eyes locked on Alex's. I could not seem to take them away from his ever-changing blue eyes.

My heart almost melted as Alex grinned at me and said, "Yes, I suppose I am hard on him, but I have known him for a long time."

"I know, here, take this," I said as I handed Alex my empty mug.

"Now you lay down again, or you will get sick."

"The strength in my body is returning."

"Please rest some more. I need you to be well so we can continue to travel." Alex rearranged the blankets behind me and helped me to lie down.

"Rest now." He held my hand in his for a quick second. "I need to go get some supplies now, so please try to sleep. Tomorrow I think we will not go anywhere."

"All right, Alex." I smiled at him and closed my eyes. I could hear him walk out of the tent. When he left, I opened my eyes again and focused my vision on a small hole in the sloping tent ceiling. Thoughts began to swirl through my mind.

Furthermore, after seeing Alex, my nerves were tight and raw. I could hardly breathe. I knew that maybe this line of thought was dangerous and not practical, but I knew that I liked Alex a lot. There was no way that I could help my feelings. These emotions had been coming on gradually ever since and maybe before we had left Ellen and Richard's cabin. I knew I was young, though, only coming upon my eighteenth birthday, while Alex was twenty-two. Still, my heart could not rest when he looked at me and smiled.

For now, I decided to try not to engage these thoughts. While it did not seem that Alex minded my company, I was somewhat unsure whether he liked me. Therefore, I decided to try my best to hide my true feelings until I was sure of his. After taking a few deep breaths to calm myself, I closed my eyes and tried to sleep. I never fell asleep. Sima and Alex returned to the tent.

"Are you asleep, Anna?" Sima asked as soon as he walked in.

"No," I answered and moved my blanket curtain aside.

"You gave us a fright," he told me.

Alex reached out his hand to me. "Here, Anna, have some crackers. They are from Richard and Ellen's cabin."

"Do I want them?" I asked Alex as I regarded the dry crackers with distaste.

Sima gave Alex an exasperated look. "I thought you said Anna was weak… one of those crackers will make you sick for about another ten days, here, Anna." He pulled out some dried meat from his bag, unwrapped it, and handed it to me.

I took it gratefully. "Thank you, Sima."

"Sima, make some more tea," Alex commanded. He seemed annoyed and sullen.

"Can't you?" Sima asked.

"No," Alex answered and sat down. "It does not seem that anyone appreciates anything that I do or offer."

Sima rolled his eyes. "All right, nobody appreciates you at all. Nobody cares about you. You never do anything." Sima was frighteningly sarcastic. I had no idea how to stop this verbal battering.

"Yes, and you do so much." Alex was equally sarcastic.

I found my voice. "Both of you, stop it!" I guessed I sounded rather commanding because both Alex and Sima halted and looked at me.

Sima just laughed. "It's all right, Anna, just friendly argument."

"Well, I would rather that you not argue," I told him.

"Yes, we better stop. We shouldn't upset Anna for now." Alex got up and walked out of the tent.

Sima shrugged. "He gets like that sometimes."

"Yes, I noticed," I answered. I finished the food that I held in my hand and lay down again.

"Sima, please smooth things over with Alex. We do not need extra arguments on this trip, or we will never get anywhere."

"Yes, that's true. I'll talk to him. I know how to cheer him up."

"Please." I closed my eyes as I heard Sima walk out of the tent. I tried to understand Alex's mood. The only conclusion that I could come to was that Alex and Sima were getting sick of each other. Traveling in such close quarters would cause anyone to lose his or her mind. I fell asleep, hoping that the next day our spirits would be higher.

We experienced no such luck, though. The next day proved to be colder than the day before. Alex kept the fire going at full blast the whole day. He and Sima would take turns running out of the tent to get firewood; this did little to brighten our spirits. Even if there was a hole in the top to let the smoke out, the tent was smoky. Alex seemed gloomy, and the few jokes that Sima tried to make were not funny. There was hardly anything we could do but sit in the tent with smoke billowing around us. By night time, we all sat in sullen silence and did not say a word.

Then Alex spoke, "I think we might have to bring the dogs in for tonight."

"Bring them in here?" I asked.

"No, leave them outside; what do you think to bring them in means?" Alex asked.

"I am sorry. I just thought we would not have enough space in here," I answered him.

"She does have a point, Alex," Sima thankfully backed my argument.

"Well, it will be warmer, and they may die in the cold weather outside, and then we would have to walk across Canada, which does not sound intriguing at all. Inside we will be warmer, and they will keep us warm as well."

"All right," Sima agreed.

"Come on then," Alex said to Sima. They both walked outside. One by one, they started to fill the tent with dogs. The smell inside the tent got worse and worse as the dogs piled in and infiltrated the tent. Soon there was only room for us to lie down on the blankets.

"We'll have to stay up tonight to watch the fire," Alex said.

"Do we even need the fire?" Sima asked. "I think the dogs will keep us warm enough anyway. I do not even know if there is room to make a fire."

"Yes, there is, and the dogs will not go near the fire." Alex started to move the dogs out of the way. When I sat down, I could not see Sima, who sat opposite of me.

"I guess we'll just have to yell over the dogs," I said with a chuckle.

"I think we might have to explore other options," Sima added. I agreed with Sima. Caesar was standing with one paw on my knee, and Bobick licked my face.

"I'll try to think of a different plan tomorrow," Alex told us.

"Who says we'll get any sleep tonight? Might as well think of a plan tonight," Sima commented.

"Sima, please, I am trying to light the fire. Hold Star, get her out of my way." Alex tried to push the brown dog out of the way of the fire.

"Alex, this is not working," Sima told him unnecessarily.

"Thank you, Sima, but I think that hardly helps at the moment."

"Honestly, Alex, I think you can leave the dogs outside. Wolves survive all winter up here." I thought this was ridiculous.

Alex finally managed to start a flame. "Yes, well, they have caves where they stay at times, you know."

The dogs had now sort of settled all over the tent. In a way, the tent was much warmer this way, but there was hardly any place to move. I lay down in between four dogs.

"I'll take the first watch," Alex said. "I'll wake Sima, and he can wake you when it is your turn to watch the fire, all right?"

Sima nodded. "That sounds fine. I do not know if I will even fall asleep with Caesar breathing on my face."

"Sima, stop complaining and go to sleep." Alex was cross again. I could understand his mood, any crack in the tent let in a gush of cold air, and there were twenty-two dogs in our tent.

"We should write a book after this trip is over," Sima said over the panting of the dogs.

"What would you call it?" I asked.

"*Three Men and Twenty-Two Dogs*," Sima answered.

"You seem to forget that I am a woman," I told him.

"It does not sound as good if you were to write; *Two Men, a Woman, and Twenty Two Dogs*." Sima laughed.

"Yes, I agree, but there must be another alternative."

Sima started to laugh again. "Fine, *Alex in the Lead, and Sima and Anna Follow*."

"How about, *Lost in the Wilderness?*" I suggested.

"But we're not lost," Sima countered.

"True, but we were lost for a bit."

"How about, *In Search of Alaska?*" Sima snorted, laughing irrepressibly.

I was about to answer, but Alex put a stop to our nonsense. "Would both of you please be quiet?" he asked in utter exasperation.

"See, Alex, you never have fun. That is why you are so angry all the time," Sima told him.

"Yes, well, I cannot take it anymore. One more title for a book, Sima, and I will hit you."

"Very adult behavior," Sima observed. I thought they were both going to lose their sanity. I had a good title for a book, *A Normal Girl and Two Rather Insane Men*.

"Please, let's just go to sleep. Wake me up when I need to watch the fire." I turned on my side and tried to sleep. I had difficulty getting used to Eagle's panting. Eventually, I fell into an uncomfortable sleep.

When Sima awakened me, I could barely keep my eyes open. Still, I sat up and watched the flames. My bones felt heavy, and even if dogs filled the tent, I felt the cold creep into my stiff body frame. Even if I had not done much the day before, I was exhausted. My eyelids began to close, and I tried hard to keep them from closing. I decided just to close my eyes for a second.

The next thing I knew, my shoulder was shaking. "Anna, what are you doing?" It was Alex. I realized that I had fallen asleep, fallen over, and had hit Alex's leg and that his foot was underneath my head.

I jumped up quickly. "I am sorry." I looked at him in embarrassment.

He just shook his head. "Weren't you supposed to watch the fire?"

"I fell asleep," I told him.

"Wonderful, do you know how dangerous those flames are? We could have gotten burnt to a crisp."

I tried to avoid looking at him. "There is no harm done."

"Can't trust you with much, can I?" Alex asked.

I glared at Alex for the first time in the last month; I was furious with him. I felt my frustration rise to my lips. "What is that supposed to mean?" I asked. He did not answer. "Alex, I am sick of you. All you do is get angry. All right, I fell asleep. I made a mistake. You are far from perfect." I could not believe that I sounded so irritated.

Alex just looked at me in surprise. Tears were stealing into my eyes. I did not want him to see me cry, so I stood up and walked out of the tent. Once outside, I sat down on my sled. In frustration, I put my head in my hands and started to cry. The cold outside made my tears sting, so I hurriedly wiped my eyes. Unfortunately, I turned, and there stood Alex. I closed my eyes.

"Anna, look, I am sorry, I spoke out from anger. I did not mean what I said. Stop crying."

I stood up and looked at him. He looked so guilty at the moment that I forgot my fury. "Alex, I am sorry too. I lost my temper. I think this cold is playing games with my brain."

"We have been together, all three of us, for over three months. I can understand why we are losing our minds." Alex gave a genuine laugh.

I looked at him with astonishment. "We better figure out how to avoid problems, or all of us will eat each other alive, not literally, but you understand."

Alex came up to me and put his arms around me in a hug. "Look, Anna, I promise you that I will do everything that I possibly can to not get angry at you again, all right?"

I nodded. "What about Sima?"

"Him too, if he does not drive me too crazy."

I looked up at Alex and smiled. "I can live with that, and please let's figure out what to do about our dogs and how to keep them sufficiently warm at night."

"Let's get back in the tent. I do not want us to freeze out here." Alex released me from his arms. We crawled into the tent. The smell of the dogs hit me as soon as I got in.

"Alex, this is revolting."

"Yes, should I kick Sima to wake him up, or do you think you can wake him up in a civilized manner?"

"I will. You cannot risk the chance of his strange jokes again." I leaned over to awaken Sima.

*****

The next day proved to be brighter, and Alex's mood improved. I felt as if a new bond had formed between Alex, Sima, and I and that we grew closer every day. We traveled few miles that day. Even if the sun was shining brightly, the air was icy, and we were afraid of freezing to our sleds. We stopped after traveling five miles and decided to take a rest. This time Alex and I devised a plan to put our dogs in a warm place outside the tent.

We set our sleds close together and then laid down extra blankets between the sleds. We then placed blankets and stretched them over the sleds' tops. With the blankets drawn over the sleds, it looked as if they formed a small cave.

"I don't know if this will be any help," Alex said. "Let's hope they will be a bit warmer together."

"Yes, but then tomorrow we'll have to take down our tent and all our blankets off the sleds," Sima chimed in.

"Sima, no one ever said that this trip would be easy." Alex turned to look at him.

"No, of course not. When Jason Shubert spoke of this trip, it sounded like we would have to find ten checkpoints and then somehow miraculously reach Alaska and Fort Yukon. This would all be a bit easier with Jason Shubert." A sad look came into Sima's eyes for a second. He then seemed to shake himself mentally. "How about we get a good rest today? We hardly got any sleep last night."

"That's true. We should keep the fire going hard tonight. We can take shifts to watch it again," Alex suggested.

"Yes, I think that we can manage," I told him.

He smiled a bit. "Just make sure not to fall asleep again this time."

I laughed in response. "I'll do my best not to."

"Maybe we are going too hard for you," Sima stated. "You keep falling asleep everywhere."

"No, I will be all right," I reassured him. Even though I assured Sima that I was fine, I felt that perhaps he was right. Every day I began to feel weaker than the day before. I did not want to admit this to Sima and Alex, though. I felt as if I had to keep up with them because I had gotten myself into this mess after all. A fear that we would never reach Alaska sometimes came upon me at night. There would be no one to rescue us if we fell into some kind of danger. Nobody would know, and we would end up like Fur Hunter. When these thoughts came to mind, I tried to think of other things or to distract myself by talking to Sima and Alex, but I spent several sleepless nights imagining the nightmare that lay before us. I tried to shake off these thoughts, but they seemed to persist. I was more than glad to turn in early that evening, and I wrapped myself in several blankets and, to my relief, slept soundly.

We continued to travel the following day. After a good sleep, I felt much renewed. Still, by the end of the day, my energy sagged. For a week, we traveled northwest, continuing to reach our goal of Alaska. That Friday evening, I sat in the tent all alone while Sima and Alex were outside. My body felt broken. Alex had said that it would be better if we rested for the next two days, and I agreed with him. Alex and Sima said they would go hunting. We were running short on food, and Alex thought we needed considerable amounts of food to keep us going. I wanted to tell Alex how sick I was of the food that we ate. We hardly had any regular food besides meat. Many times after dinner, I would feel sick to the stomach. I dared not complain. There was no reason to worry Sima and Alex. When I picked up my bag, my hands shook.

Even after traveling a week, it did not seem as if we had made considerable progress. Perhaps, I thought, it was because everything looked the same. All the trees were bare, and no leaves appeared on them. At times, there would be vast plains of white snow. I never wanted to see snow again. It was cold, white, and ugly. I thought of how I used to love the snow and run out into it, but now everything was the same monotonous white color. All three of us would travel through the wet, freezing snow for the entire day and then fall exhausted onto our blankets at night. Nothing changed, and I felt as if we were traveling to an unattainable goal.

I lay down to sleep, and my back hurt as I turned over. Alaska seemed to be so elusive. For some reason, when I had left, I had been naïve enough to think that there would be an adventure and that I would find my family and my parents without a problem. I tried to keep in mind why I came on this journey in the first place. Now that I was so far into this expedition, I was beginning to doubt the fact that I would ever find my parents. There was almost no point. They were strangers to me. It seemed that Alex and Sima had become more of a family to me. The sound of their voices outside provided comfort. I began to realize that I cared about them more than anyone I had ever known before.

Chapter **11** January 10, 1888

When I awoke the next day, I found Alex sitting on his blankets and looking at me.

"Is everything all right?" I asked.

"Yes, I just wanted to let you know that Sima and I are going hunting again. I did not want to leave you here alone without knowing where we have gone."

"Would you like me to go with you?" I asked as I sat up.

"No, you can stay here and mind the camp if you want. We might be back late, though, so do not worry if we are not back in time for lunch." Alex began to load his rifle. "You seemed a little bit pale last night. Are you all right?"

"Yes, I am quite all right. I have just been thinking, Alex, would it not be wonderful if we had fresh hot bread and some fresh food and not all this salted meat?"

He stood up to go. "Of course, but there is not much we can do about that, is there?"

"No, of course not. Do you know what the other checkpoints on Jason Shubert's maps were? Perhaps we may be able to find a town or something nearby."

"I do not think that there is anything nearby, not for another hundred miles. Most of Jason's checkpoints are landmarks or something of that sort."

"What's the nearest town?" I asked.

"I am not sure. I will have to look at the map again," Alex said. "Anyway, I already fed the dogs with Sima. You can rest a bit more if you like." Alex smiled at me. "Also, if you want to keep busy, you could patch some of the blankets and also Sima's extra coat."

"I will do my best to help out. It is a bit boring to sit here without much to do."

"All right, we will see you later." Alex walked out of the tent, and the flap closed behind him. I lay back on my blankets and closed my eyes.

I do not know how long I slept, but I knew that I had slept a while longer than I had expected. I stood up and stretched. Sleep had revived me and calmed my nerves. The blankets that I needed to sew were on my sled, and I proceeded to retrieve them. I busied myself with the repairs that took me about an hour. I could not find Sima's extra jacket, though. Afterward, I made some hot tea. I sat sipping the warm liquid and observing the dancing flames. Time crawled. I was sorry that I had not had the foresight when I was back in Maine to bring a book with me to read. I guessed I would have probably finished it by this time anyway.

I did not start to worry until the hours began to pass by one by one. I made myself some lunch and fed the dogs. Still, Alex and Sima did not come. I went outside and walked a bit out of the camp to see if I could spot their tracks. Alex, of course, had said that they would be late, but I did not think that they would be gone for more than four hours. I began to worry incessantly about their return. At first, I thought I should look for them, but then another hour passed, and darkness began to settle. I became frightened at the thought of setting out to search for them.

The gray shadows in the forest began to dance about in the setting sun. A frightening thought came to me. What if Alex and Sima had decided that they did not want me to go with them? What if they had decided to leave me? They had their sleds, rifles, and supplies.

They could easily leave me and continue the journey on their own. They knew that I was weakening. Panic filled me as two more hours passed. Fear exploded like a volcano within me. I knew my only chance would be to catch up with them. I decided that if they did not return in two more hours, I would pack up camp and go in search of them. I would find their trail and continue behind them. They could not leave me in the wilderness; I would not give them a choice. I would not let them out of my sight for one second.

In a dreaded silence, I waited for the most prolonged two hours of my life. Sima and Alex did not return. All hope that I clung to in desperation disappeared in those two hours. With tears in my eyes, I began to get the dogs ready for the journey. The tent came down, and I rolled the poles and the canvas into my sled. I was about to yell to my dogs to move out when I heard barking in the distance. My spirit lifted at the familiar sound. Soon Alex and Sima arrived at the campsite. They had two large bucks lying on their sleds. They stopped short when they saw me.

"Anna, what is happening?" Alex asked. "Why did you take the tent down?"

I looked at both of them, guilty. Now that they had arrived back at camp, I realized that my worries had been unfounded and that Alex and Sima would never abandon me. Why the thought had come to my mind in the first place did not make sense. I gulped. How would I explain to them what I had been thinking?

"Well," I started, "I thought maybe we could move to another location. I don't like it here?"

"You just decided that at this moment?" Alex asked. "You know you would have had all day to do this."

"I was waiting for you to return." I tried to pretend to explain to them.

"Good lie," Sima said sarcastically. "How about you tell us the truth?" Sima and Alex got off their sleds and began to let the dogs out of their harnesses.

I gulped. "I thought that you had left me and that you weren't coming back. I decided to go follow you." I shrugged my shoulders. There was not much else that I could tell them. It appeared that I had to tell the truth.

"What?" Alex came over to where I stood by my sled. He seemed more distraught than angry by what I said. "How could you even think that?"

"You were gone for so long," I explained unconvincingly.

"As I recall, this morning I told you that we would be gone for a long time."

I looked down at the snow. "I didn't expect it to be this long."

"Unpack the tent," Alex ordered. "We have to skin the deer and pack the meat. We'll talk more of this later." My heart felt heavy. Both Alex and Sima seemed to be hurt by what I had said. How could I have thought they would leave me?

With cold hands and a heavy heart, I unpacked the tent and began to set it up. Alex and Sima started to unload the deer. They laid them out. After I had set the tent up, I went over to help Sima and Alex. No one spoke. I was afraid of looking at Alex.

Alex decided to create a smokehouse for part of the meat and smoke it for two nights. The other meat we saved and packed in boxes that we placed on the snow outside. Frigid temperatures meant the meat would stay fresh. Sima also took some of the meat and began to cook the stew over a fire that he lit. Throughout this whole time, nobody said a word. It was rather dark and late by the time we finished. We sat down to eat supper. We sat outside the tent because we had a large fire burning. I was hoping that no one would mention my stupid conduct, but I had no such luck.

After I had finished my first bowl of stew, Alex brought up the subject. "Anna, what made you think we would leave you?"

"I don't know." I shrugged. Actually, I had no idea what came over me earlier. "Alex, please forgive me. I made a mistake. Fear made my reasoning irrational. "

Alex regarded me with a severe look on his face. "I just want you to know that you can trust us. I hope you can believe that."

"All right, Alex, I do believe you. I just panicked."

"I suppose this trip can have strange effects on people." Alex shrugged and then reached for another serving of stew.

I looked at Sima, who had been oddly quiet throughout our conversation. I felt timid as I glanced at Sima. "Sima, will you forgive me?"

Sima looked up at me from his stew. "Of course, we all know you're a bit strange." His face lit up with a smile. "I just cannot believe that you would think that I would leave behind the only woman between here and Alaska."

"Oh, stop it." I looked over at Alex almost instinctively. He was laughing at Sima. I had never felt so relieved to be forgiven.

Fortunately, my impractical behavior did not seem to have any adverse effects on our relationship. The following two days passed without an event. We packed the meat and got ready for the rest of our journey. The snow was still white, and the temperature was still well below freezing.

We left mid-morning. I felt much rested. However, I still did not feel fully recuperated. I did not think that I would ever again feel healthy. We pressed on. I did not have any idea of when we would reach Alaska. Alex said that it might take another three months or even longer. My head spun when I thought of another three months on the trail. We had already been traveling for three months. What else could happen? Sima and Alex drove on at a steady pace. I wondered if they felt as drained as I did. Sima never seemed to tire, even though he had sustained the most injury out of all of us.

While I worried endlessly about what would happen, the next few days were peaceful, and we traveled at a steady pace. Alex and Sima never brought up the fact that I thought that they had left me. Our constant movement made all of us weary. Even Sima joked a bit less.

Silence surrounded us that evening as we sat in our tent. For some reason, no one spoke. It seemed as if we had run out of things to say to one another. We all went to sleep relatively early. I fell asleep without a problem, but in the night, I awoke. I could hear the dogs growling. I tried to ignore the sound and go back to sleep, but I could not. I was not sure of what to do. I decided to awaken Alex. The growling sounded dangerous. I climbed out from behind my blankets and shook Alex by the shoulder.

Alex turned over on his side. "Anna, you better be awakening me for a good reason."

"Alex, there is something wrong with the dogs; I did not look yet," I whispered with urgency.

"You could have checked before wakening me. I'll go look." Alex took his rifle and coat and looked out from the tent. As soon as he lifted the tent canvas, he bolted outside. He started to yell like a man gone mad. I at first thought that he had lost his mind, but when I peeked out, I realized the need for urgency. A whole pack of wolves had surrounded our dogs. Alex's lead dog was growling, and a nasty-looking wolf was clenching its throat. Star, one of my dogs, was lying on the ground in a pool of blood. I grabbed my rifle and loaded it in haste. Sima still slept. Alex's actions appeared irrational. He ran towards the wolves and started to throw rocks at them.

"Get out of here!" he yelled.

"Alex, get away from them!" I called to him in a panic.

I aimed at the wolves and shot one of them. It was not the leader, and the wolves seemed to have not even noticed that I had been shooting. I quickly reloaded the rifle and fired at a wolf closer to the rest of the pack. The wolf fell to the ground with a yelp. As Alex also aimed his rifle at the wolves, they turned their fury on him. I noticed that Alex's lead dog lay on the ground. For some reason, Alex did not shoot, and as I reloaded my rifle, a wolf jumped at Alex with a low growl. I screamed.

Alex fell to the ground from the force of the wolf's attack. He was able to hit the wolf in the jaw and jump up again. The wolf, however, clenched Alex's arm between his strong teeth. The other wolves were closing in. I, afraid that Alex would soon be the wolves' dinner, aimed my rifle at the wolf that was now holding Alex's arm in his mouth. I could not imagine the pain that Alex experienced as he tried to struggle with the wolf. Fear of shooting Alex by accident made me hesitate. Still, a moment more, and Alex might not be alive at all. I shot. The wolf flew off to the side. Alex grabbed his rifle, his right arm now torn apart, but he shot another wolf in one rapid movement. Another shot came from behind me. I turned around. Sima now stood near me. Now that four dead wolves lay on the ground, the other four wolves scattered.

Time seemed to stand still. Alex turned to look at us. There was a massive scratch on Alex's cheek, and his coat and his arm were torn up. I thought I would be sick to my stomach. Sima and I looked at each other.

"What do we do now?" I asked.

"Well, we must do something quickly, or he will bleed to death," Sima answered me. "Get some bandages and start boiling some water." He sounded frightened to death, but his tone invited no argument. I ran off to follow his instruction.

Sima helped Alex inside and lay him down on the blankets. I was boiling water and had already laid out the bandages. Sima took the water from the fire to clean Alex's wound. I closed my eyes to avoid looking at the open gash and the skin that was torn open.

Alex looked at me. "Are you all right, Anna?"

"Yes, Alex, I am more worried about you at the moment."

His face looked pained, but he did not complain. "I'll survive."

"You better survive, Alex," Sima said. "May I ask what you were trying to accomplish by charging a pack of hungry wolves?"

"You know, Sima, I was not thinking."

"I could tell. I awoke, and I thought the whole world had gone crazy. You were yelling. Rifles were firing off in every direction." Sima pressed down on Alex's arm with a bandage.

"Here, Anna, make yourself useful. Hold this," Sima directed. I gingerly held down the bandage and watched in disgust as Alex's blood seeped through it.

"You need to press down hard to make the blood stop, Anna," Sima commanded. Although I was utterly sick by now, I held down the bandage as hard as I could.

"Alex, I am going to try to clean the wound with hot water, and then I'll try to sew it shut." Alex nodded at Sima.

"Sima, what do you mean sew it shut?" I asked, terrified.

"I have a needle, and I have thread unless we want Alex to have half his skin hanging off from his arm for the rest of his life." I closed my eyes after Sima said those words and tried to get rid of the image that had just formed in my mind.

"Thank you for that image Sima," Alex said cynically.

I grabbed another bandage because the other had seeped through with blood. "Alex, are you all right?" I asked.

"I am fine, a little dizzy."

"I am hoping that this blood will stop soon," Sima said as he dipped a bandage in water and began to clean Alex's arm.

"That stings," Alex stated.

"It is not my fault you decided to try to be an irrational hero," Sima replied casually.

"You should be pleased that this is not you in this situation. Anna might have woken you up first."

Sima laughed a bit. "Well, I am happy then that Anna thinks more of you than she does of me."

"Yes, that is my good luck." Alex chuckled a bit and then grimaced as Sima cleaned his wound.

"I had to act quickly. I did not know what could be happening outside." I defended myself to both Alex and Sima.

"Do not worry, Anna. We are only joking," Sima told me, but he frowned as he looked at Alex's arm.

"Alex, I will do my best to sew this up, but I am not sure how it will turn out."

I began to feel sick to my stomach again. "Do you mind if I leave?" I asked Sima.

"Yes, I will mind. You need to help me."

"That's what I was afraid of; what do you want me to do?" I asked.

"Get out my needle and thread from my bag. I brought it along to sew the tent up in case there were any rips in the tent. I hope it works on Alex."

"You know, Sima, I have a feeling that you are not sure of what you're doing," Alex told him.

"Alex, I will do my best. After all, I did attend two years of medical school before I quit."

"That's true, but that still does not mean that you know what you are doing." Alex closed his eyes for a moment. "I am ready when you are."

I swallowed hard. "I'll help."

Finally, we had Alex all sewed up and bandaged. We felt drained after the experience. Alex had not complained or even made a single sound the whole time, although his face looked terrible.

Alex regarded both of us. "Thank you," he said. "Now, I will try to sleep."

"Yes, that would be good. I'll wash and tend to the dogs. I'll try to get everything cleaned so the blood will not attract more wolves."

"Sima, if the dogs are hurt, just shoot them. We really cannot afford to lose dogs, but we cannot carry around extra baggage, and there is no point in making them suffer any longer." Alex sounded distressed. His lead dog was probably lying dead already.

"All right, Alex." Sima walked out of the tent with the dirty bandages and the water. He picked up a rifle on the way out. I sat next to Alex in uncomfortable silence.

I cleared my throat. "I think I will go help Sima." I started to stand.

Suddenly Alex took my hand in his. "Anna," he said my name quietly.

"We can talk later, Alex. You need your rest now." I reached my hand down and moved some hair that had fallen into his face.

"We'll talk." Alex squeezed my hand and then let me go. My heart beat as if it would leap out of my chest as I walked out of the tent to assist Sima. When I saw the mess that the dogs were in, my spirits fell. I came over to Sima as he stood looking at the ground. Star lay whimpering. She had a huge gash in her stomach.

"What do we do now?" Sima asked.

"Do what Alex told us to do," I said. My throat felt tight. I knew there was no reason for us to keep Star alive.

"It's all right, girl," I said, kneeling next to the dog and patting her head.

"Could we not sew her up?" I asked.

"We could," Sima said. "However, I do not think that would be doing the dog any justice. Anyway, let's get all the other dogs out of here." We did so. A horrible feeling of dread washed over me. Alex had shot some of Fur Hunter's dogs, but thankfully I had been able to stay away. Once we moved the other dogs out, I sat next to Star and pet her as Sima loaded his rifle. He closed his eyes, and I did the same. I held Star tightly. The shot reverberated through the air. Two hot tears rolled down my cheeks. I did not think that I could deal with any more death, human or animal. I opened my eyes and looked up at Sima, who stood quiet regarding the now-deceased dog.

"I hate this," he said. "Come on." He held his hand out to me and helped me stand up. Both of us carried the dogs far into the woods and buried them under branches and rocks. Then we leaned upon each other as we walked without a word out of the woods towards our tent.

*****

We stayed in place for the next few days. Alex did not feel well and needed his rest. Despite the adverse circumstances, I was relieved to have another break. The days seemed to drag by for us. Alex appeared to be in no hurry to leave. I feared that his arm would become infected. However, after a few days, it seemed to begin healing.

Alex was sleeping one afternoon when Sima came into the tent. Two days had passed since the attack. Sima looked worried.

"What's the problem?" I asked.

"When do you think Alex is going to get better?" Sima asked, looking to where Alex lay.

"I don't know."

"Look, I have a feeling we are not going to get to Alaska."

"What?" I asked, surprised. Although, what Sima said only reflected my thoughts.

"Think about this," Sima stopped his words for a second and then continued, "we have food for now, but what if there is another cold spell? Animals hide during the cold too. It took us so long to find meat that last time."

"Sima, believe me, I have thought about all this already. There is nothing we can do but travel on."

"Well, I think we should try to follow Jason's map and find a few of those checkpoints that were not landmarks. There were a few forts on there."

"We have been following the map Sima," I replied.

"Yes, of course, but we are mostly heading in that general direction."

I looked at him, confused. "Yes, of course."

"What I am saying is that Alex has not considered even stopping at any certain checkpoint along the way."

"Would we find them?" I asked. "I truly think that only Jason knew where those checkpoints were found."

"Yes, some of those checkpoints were landmarks, but some of them are towns or forts. We should try to locate them."

"We can always try. Where do you think would be the closest checkpoint?" I asked.

"Do I know?" Sima asked with a smirk. "We should ask Alex. He is the one with the neatly folded map."

I laughed and then became serious. "How will we talk Alex into this idea? It might be better just to follow his lead."

"Look, Anna, Alex may not want to go on some hair-brained scheme of mine, and he may not want to deviate from our trail. He knows as well as we do that we need to stop and get new supplies. We also need to get a few new dogs." Sima picked up a mug and gulped down the remaining liquid. I just wanted to get to Alaska, no matter how much we needed supplies. I did not want to continue delaying our journey.

When Alex awoke, we proposed the plan to him. He took out his map, and we all sat studying it. "I truly do not know where we might be exactly. I can only guess that the nearest checkpoint from here would be Churchill."

"If we find the bay, then we should be able to travel along the bay and find the Prince of Wales Fort. That is one of our checkpoints," Sima suggested as he pointed to the map.

"Yes, but we truly do not know exactly where we are," Alex said with a note of doubt in his voice. He looked at both of us. "Of course, I agree with you about the need to stop somewhere and get new supplies."

"Will there be anyone at the fort in the middle of a winter?" I asked.

"Yes, well, that is part of the Hudson Bay Trading Company; trappers' trade furs there," Alex told me.

"How do you know this?" Sima asked Alex skeptically.

"If you had paid attention when we worked for Jason Shubert, you would have realized that a lot of the people that came to his store to trade were men from the Hudson Bay Trading Company. Jason traveled with them a lot during the winters."

"Only because I am not tiresome enough to pay attention to minute details does not make me stupid." Sima grinned at me. "I had much greater interests at the time."

"Yes, girls and drinking," Alex interjected.

"Not that you never drank. You took out that Harris girl out often enough too," Sima kidded.

"What Harris girl?" I asked suspiciously. A surge of jealousy that I had never experienced came over me. I shrugged off that feeling. After all, Alex was in no way tied to me.

I noticed Alex throw Sima an irritated glance. "No one worth mentioning. She did not mean much to me. We just went out together with a few friends at times." While Alex did try to sound nonchalant about it, I noticed that he appeared flustered.

Sima just snickered and shook his head. "That's what he says now. A few years back, Alex assured me he would marry her if he had a chance."

"Sima, enough!" Alex's voice was a bit more commanding now. "How about we figure out how to get to Churchill before you tell Anna about everything stupid that I once did in my life?"

"Suit yourself. Anna will find out someday anyway. One day you or I will tell her everything."

"We'll see," Alex cut Sima off and turned to the map. Alex's curt answers to Sima's comments made me hope that he perhaps was beginning to care for me as much as I cared for him. No matter how much I tried to put the thoughts that I truly was beginning to like

Alex more and more every day in the back of my head, I could not keep them at bay. The reasons why I liked Alex did not matter to me anymore. The mere fact that I just liked him almost bothered me. I had no fundamental understanding of love or how I was supposed to act. I could not be sure of Alex's feelings, and I did not think that the middle of the Canadian wilderness was the place to tell him about them. I still had to travel with him for at least two more months, telling him how I felt could result in a rather uncomfortable situation if he did not reciprocate my feelings.

"Anna, are you listening?" Alex's question pierced my daydreams.

I jolted back from my thoughts. I looked at Alex with embarrassment. "I am sorry, I am not listening. What were you saying?"

"I was just wondering if you think we should go to Churchill."

"While I do not want to stop over somewhere for too long, I see the need to regroup. We are taking a risk if we do try to find this fort and deviate from our trail."

"Since we are not following any real specific trail, we might as well give this a try. I think we would need to head north about fifty miles." Alex looked at us for approval.

"Yes, I think we should go then," Sima agreed. "Anyway, if we get lost, we will just have to head northwest, and we should reach Alaska."

"That's true," Alex said. "At the moment, I have to admit we are a bit lost. I mean unless heading in a general direction means that we know what we are doing."

"Are you trying to tell us that even if we reach Alaska, it might take us a while to find your home because we won't know exactly where we are?" I studied Alex skeptically.

"Look. Hopefully, we will reach the trading town right on the border of Alaska and Canada. From there, there is a trail that leads to Fort Yukon. I remember where my home is in relation to Fort Yukon. I have been to Fort Yukon even though it was twelve years ago."

"That is if we find the trading post," I told Alex.

Sima looked at me. His eyes were troubled. "That is another reason to reach Churchill. We can then hopefully follow the trapper trail to Yellowknife, the next checkpoint on our map. We can then head to the trading post from there."

"That is if we find all of these checkpoints," I told him. Then I turned to Alex. "Alex, why did you not mention that we were lost before?"

"Because we are not lost," Alex retorted. "If we follow our trail, at the moment, we would still reach Alaska. I see the need to re-supply and the benefit of following an actual trail, so that is why I agreed to go to Churchill." Alex looked tired, and I knew that I should not press him about our position on the map.

"So when should we head to Churchill?" Sima asked.

"How about tomorrow?" Alex asked.

"Tomorrow?" I questioned. "Are you well enough to travel so soon?"

"Yes, tomorrow," Alex answered. "You know, Anna, I can never understand why you always question why I do something. After all, I never questioned more than once why you came on this journey, even if you are a girl."

"Alex," Sima interrupted, "why are you bringing up this subject? There is no reason for this."

Alex's words startled me. I looked at him, hurt and embarrassed. "I thought you said that it did not bother you that I had come. I hoped that you had enough sense not to mention the subject." I stood up. "I think I should go tend to the dogs and begin to get our supplies ready if we are to leave tomorrow. Also, Alex, you have questioned my coming on this journey more than once." I glared at him and walked out.

As I left the tent, I heard Sima say to Alex in an angry tone, "Well done." I did not wait for Alex to answer.

While I was throwing supplies on the sled and tying them down with rope, I heard footsteps behind me. I turned in hopes it was Alex ready to apologize, but it was only Sima. Sima looked at me for a second and did not say anything. He just leaned over and began to help me.

"What?" I asked.

"Alex had told me that he agreed with you not to argue."

I threw another box of bandages on the sled. "That is easier said than done."

"Yes, with Alex, that is most difficult." Sima straightened out and looked at me. "Listen, all of us have gone through a lot on this journey, but I do not suppose that always questioning Alex's actions is a good idea."

I stared at Sima in surprise. I had expected sympathy from him, not a lecture. "Do you mean to tell me that I was wrong? I was just concerned for Alex's health."

Sima smiled at me. "For now, pretend you were in the wrong." He grinned and tied some of the leftover boxes to the sled.

"You mean that I should tell Alex that I was wrong?"

"You could let your pride go once in a while, could you not?" Sima gave me a questioning glance.

I smiled in response. "Yes, I suppose I could."

"Why don't you go talk to him? You know Alex, he does not stay angry for a long time."

"Yes, I have gotten to know Alex well enough by now."

"Probably more than you ever wanted to know."

I shrugged at his comment. "I do not mind so much, you know."

Sima nodded. "Yes, I thought so." Then he just smiled. "Why don't you go talk to Alex right now?"

"All right, I guess I can let my pride slip once or twice and tell him that I was in the wrong." I turned towards the tent.

"Only once or twice?" Sima asked.

"Yes," I answered.

Sima shook his head. "Good luck." He put his hand on my shoulder and then let go. I grinned back at him and walked towards the tent. When I climbed in, I found Alex was sitting staring at the fire and smoking his pipe. He had a serious look in his eyes. He looked at me for a moment when I entered and then looked back towards the flames.

"Alex," I started and then swallowed.

"Yes?" he asked.

"I apologize. I did not mean to sound the way I did."

"It's all right, and I am partly to blame." I wanted to tell him that he was to blame in full, but I did not want to start another argument.

I sat down not far from him. "I thought we said we would not argue."

"Yes, we did say something like that, did we not?" Alex grinned. "I suppose I just have a flaring temper, which is not good, of course."

"No, I suppose I get annoyed rather quickly too." I hugged my knees to my chest. We both then sat in peace.

Alex let out a loud sigh. "You know, I understand that you were just trying to be nice by asking if I was well enough to travel."

"Yes, well, if you were not so stubborn."

He looked at me and smiled a bit. "You are rather stubborn, too, you know."

"I am. I do not deny it." I laughed a bit. "But will your arm be all right, Alex? I am sure that you are in a lot of pain."

"Even if I am, it does not mean that my arm will not be well. But I do have a favor to ask of you." His voice softened at the moment.

"Yes?" I asked; my heart started to beat harder in my chest.

"I do not mean to put more work on you, but could you sew up my jacket?"

My heartbeat slowed down. "Oh, is that all?" I asked with a note of disappointment in my voice. I do not know what I had expected him to say. I had rather hoped he would say something more romantic.

"Did you expect me to say something else?" he asked.

I shook my head. "No, I suppose not."

"Here is my jacket anyway." Alex handed it to me. "You see, I would rather trust it to you than to Sima. I saw what a good job he did with sewing up my arm."

"Do you think your arm will ever be normal again?" I asked as I took the jacket that he handed to me.

"I think if it heals, there should just be a scar. I fear that it might get infected."

"Perhaps if we get to Churchill, there will be more supplies."

"I am not sure that there will be supplies or that we will even get there."

"We can hope that we make it."

"Yes, I certainly hope that we will. If not, we will just have to travel on and hope to reach Alaska sometime soon."

"That seems like such a remote possibility at this time. I do not believe that that will ever happen." I reached for my bag and started to pull out thread and needle.

Alex placed his hand over mine. "Do not even think such things. For some reason, we have made it this far."

I pulled the needle through the coarse jacket material. "I try not to lose hope, Alex. I just do not want to go on forever. All my energy feels as if it has drained from me."

"I can understand your feeling." He packed more tobacco into his pipe. Then silence fell on the tent.

Then I said, "You know if your arm does become infected, we could always ask Sima to amputate it." While I said this as a joke, the thought of Alex losing his arm made shivers run down my spine.

"Do not even say such things. The horror of losing an arm is bad enough. To have Sima cut it off is terrifying."

"That is certain." I laughed. "I hope that we do not have to ever consider that option."

"Listen, Anna, please do not mention to Sima that I am afraid of infection. He never appears to worry much, but I know him well enough to know that he does worry more than he lets on."

"He is lucky to have you as a friend, Alex." I gently touched Alex's hand. Alex looked at my hand on his with a cool glance.

I took my hand away. "I am sorry."

"Nothing to be sorry about," he said in a severe tone of voice. Then he stood up and said, "I guess I will call Sima back in, now that you have finished apologizing." Alex laughed.

"Did you hear Sima tell me to apologize?" I asked him.

"No, I just know Sima well enough to know exactly what he told you to say. You both think you are so sly."

"Yes, both of us are probably terribly predictable too."

"Sometimes." He smiled down at me and walked out of the tent.

Chapter 12   January 12, 1888

The next morning we touched off. Alex managed to harness his dogs even if he could hardly move his arm from pain. We traveled with little progress. Even after a few days of respite, my legs still felt heavy. The weather was warmer compared to what it had been. The comparable warmth did not in any way make traveling for long periods any simpler. After about five miles, we stopped for a rest.

"How many miles would you like to travel today, Alex?" Sima asked as he sat down on his sled.

"At least twelve," Alex answered.

"Yes, let's hope we can pick up some trail towards the fort."

"I doubt that would be possible. The ground is covered in snow," Alex told him.

Sima rolled his eyes. "I can see that."

"What I meant to say is that there might not be anybody traveling through this area right now and that finding a trail might be difficult."

"I understand," Sima said, laughing. "If we find the bay, we could travel along the shore and from there find Churchill."

"I certainly hope so," Alex answered.

Sima started to laugh again. "See, I am smarter than you thought. The ground is covered in snow."

Alex got up. "Oh, let it go." My eyes followed his movements. I noticed that at that moment Sima's eyes were upon me. I looked at him, and he just smiled at me. I shrugged my shoulders. He grinned.

It was disconcerting that Sima knew my feelings for Alex and understood them better than I did. I shook my head at him.

"We better get started again," Alex said. He had not observed our silent conversation.

"Yes, let's go." Sima and I got up and gathered our belongings.

We did not travel fast for the rest of the day. The sun peeked through high clouds, and the white ground reflected a bright light into my eyes. There were no trees in sight, and the white plane seemed to stretch for miles at a time. We all drove in a long line. Alex in front, I was in the middle, and Sima traveled in the back. Our dogs seemed to feel no urgency in reaching our destination. I almost felt as if I was enjoying driving and that I could go on like this forever.

That evening we sat resting around a fire outside of our tent, drinking hot tea. I leaned against my sled, letting the warmth of the hot tea run through my veins. We had picked up firewood along the way. The fire grew.

"How many more days do you think it will take before we reach Churchill?" I asked Alex.

"Probably three more days, if we even reach it," Alex answered.

"We can only pray and hope that we will," I said and pushed a stick towards the fire.

"Yes, I can't wait to get to Alaska," Sima said as he leaned back against his sled.

"Do you miss your parents?" I asked him. For some reason, until that moment, I had not thought much of Sima's parents or Alex's parents, for that matter. They had mentioned them before, but not enough times for me to even contemplate them.

"You know, I don't know." Sima gave a sort of half-shrug. "I mean, I have not seen them for almost over twelve years. What I remember of them is not even that pleasant."

I looked at Sima in shock. I had not expected such a strange answer from him. I was about to ask him something else when I caught Alex's eye, and he shook his head at me.

I decided to switch the subject over to Alex. "What about you, Alex?"

"You know, I suppose I do not remember them much, but I did have a wonderful childhood. I have tried to correspond with my parents as well as I possibly could, although my mother never learned how to write in English. You might remember that I mentioned that Sima and I lived near each other as young children. We had a wonderful time playing tricks on the girl my parents had taken in. I must have mentioned her before, Katya is her name."

"Yes, I remember, you did mention her." I wondered what Sima and Alex had looked like as children. I was jealous of both of them. They both knew their parents, and they both could remember them. I was even more jealous of Katya for having Alex as a friend.

"I wonder what Katya is like now," Sima spoke.

Alex looked over at where Sima was sitting. "She probably is beautiful. She was a pretty girl, you know."

"Yes, probably; I was too busy playing tricks on her even to remember. Of course, you spent more time with her. I do not think that she liked me much."

"Remember the time when we tied knots in her hair during the night?" Alex asked.

"Oh yes." Sima started to laugh. "I could hear her crying in her room from my cabin. I got into so much trouble that day. I spent the whole day without meals and the entire week doing chores in the barn. I must say it was worth it. Honestly, I do not think that Katya will be happy to see me if we do ever get home."

"She always asked about you in her letters to me," Alex told him. I felt resentful towards Katya.

Sima shook his head and smothered another laugh. "Yes, doubtless she asked about me just to know if I am healthy. She probably wants me to be healthy so that if I ever come back, she can pay me back for all the awful things I did to her as a little boy."

Alex reached over for the tea kettle and refilled his mug with hot water. "Katya sounds as if she has grown into a kind young woman. I doubt she has anything like that on her mind."

My jealousy towards Katya seemed to increase with every second. "I hope that your family will not mind me coming to stay with you," I told Alex.

"Of course, they won't mind. I will explain to my parents that you are staying there temporarily until you find your family." Alex regarded me over the flames of our fire. I felt a dull ache in my stomach. I had rather hoped he would say something different, but now I knew what he expected.

"Yes, of course." I regarded Alex with what I was sure was disappointment in my eyes.

Sima placed down his empty bowl. "They will not care. Alex's parents are very kind and generous. When my parents moved to Juneau, they let me stay with them and then helped me get to school with Alex. I will be staying with them for as long as I wish, and I am sure that they would not mind such a beautiful girl as you." Sima smiled at me. I gave him an appreciative smile in return. Sima always made me feel better about myself.

Of course, I knew that if we ever were to reach Alaska and find Alex's home, I would feel guilty about having to impose on Alex's family. I also did not know what they would think of me when they would find out that I had dressed up in boy's clothing to come on this ridiculous journey. At that moment, I realized that we had all gotten quiet. I glanced up at Alex, who I noticed was looking at me. His eyes met mine. I felt my insides light up. I felt as if he could see right through me. Sometimes I wished that Sima would go hunting on his own so I could just sit and talk to Alex. I wondered if I could somehow approach Sima with this subject. I knew that he suspected that I had feelings for Alex, but I was unsure if I could open my heart to him. He was still Alex's best friend, and I did not know if he would tell him anything if I spoke to him about how I felt.

"We should retire for the night," Alex stated. "We still must concentrate on getting to Churchill."

"Yes," I said and started to roll out my blankets as well.

That night I could not sleep. Thoughts of my parents kept creeping up on me. I was beginning to realize that I had decided to go on a wild goose chase. It seemed as if there had been no real reason for me to come on this trip.

The next morning, we traveled at a faster pace at Alex's suggestion. I could tell that his arm was still in pain, but he did not admit to it. As we traveled, trees began to appear in more significant quantities. The bare branches stretched out covered in a layer of light ice—the branches glittered like crystals in the cold sun that lit the way. The further north we traveled, the rockier the terrain got. We traveled by large boulders spread apart by lines of wild bushes.

Alex, who was traveling in front, turned back to us and yelled, "I think I can see the bay from here!" Excitement leaped into my heart. If we had found the bay, perhaps we would discover Churchill.

"Hurry up," Alex called again. Sima and I sped ahead. The weariness seemed to melt from my limbs. Alex's train of dogs had now pushed through several tall bushes, and then he came to a stop. "Come look at this!"

I had never heard such awe in his voice. Sima and I pushed through the bramble with our dogs.

"This better be worth all our troubles, Alex," Sima remarked. Then he stopped in his tracks with me at his side. The sight that I beheld I will never forget. The gigantic frosty waves of the bay broke against the tall rocky walls that we now stood on. Frosted snow covered the rocky structures below our feet. We seemed to have stepped into a scene from a storybook. The muddy sand below was covered in patches of cobwebbed frost. I let out a breath.

"Well, we at least found something worthwhile to look at," Sima observed. Alex and I both stared at him as soon as he broke the silence.

"I apologize," Sima said dryly. "I did not mean to ruin the moment."

"You did ruin it," Alex said, but then he laughed. "We might as well keep traveling west against the shoreline. We are bound to find Churchill from here."

Sima pulled up the brake from his sled off the frozen ground. "We at least found the bay. Let's give ourselves some credit."

Soon the light of day began to fade, and bright pink and violet colors stretched across the evening sky. The cold nipped the tips of our noses, and I was sure that mine was invariably bright red. The cold began to sting my cheeks, and I pulled my dark brown scarf higher up on my face. The silence around us seemed to be deafening, and the soft patter of the dogs' paws was the only sound upon the soft icy snow.

As we were about ready to start to slow our pace and search for a place to spend the night, Alex's dogs, who were in the lead, stopped dead in their tracks. My dogs came to a halt as well.

"Bobick, what's wrong?" Bobick looked back at me. Then he turned and cautiously sniffed the air. Another one of Sima's dogs began to whine. Sima, Alex, and I exchanged glances.

"Is it wolves?" Sima asked in a whisper. Alex shook his head and motioned for Sima to be silent. A minute later, as our dogs remained paralyzed, we learned why the dogs refused to move. Some fifty meters ahead of us, the brush moved, and a large white bear crossed our path. I felt void of air. I was relieved that Alex was in front of me. Alex slowly reached for his rifle. The polar bear was giant. It thudded across the snow with its gigantic paws. The mouth of the bear hung open, and we could hear him breathing from where we stood. We stood rooted to the ground like the ice sculptures back in Montreal. The bear seemed to take no notice of us and kept walking.

Finally, when the bear was a good five hundred meters to our right, Alex whispered, "Let's get moving." We pulled ahead with caution. My legs trembled. We urged our dogs on quietly. The dogs moved reluctantly. Gripping the handle of my sled was difficult. My arms felt like oatmeal.

When we had traveled a good three miles from the spot where we had seen the bear, we stopped. The cold frozen water seemed to whisper from the bay, and the icy wind whipped our faces.

Sima spoke, "I am happy we did not end up being dinner for that bear. It seemed not even to notice us."

"We are so far from any kind of civilization that that bear may have never seen humans before," Alex told him.

"It is also possible that there could be more of them out here and that they don't care if we are humans or not," Sima responded.

Alex got off his sled and started to unpack. "We should take up shelter in a safe place then and keep watch tonight."

"That will help," Sima answered sarcastically. "What do you propose we do if all of a sudden this bear decides to charge whoever is keeping watch?"

"We should build a big fire. The bears should not come near the fire."

"Judging by the size of that thing we just saw, it could snuff out any fire that we build in a second," I piped in.

Alex gave me an exasperated look. "Thank you, but do you have any better ideas?"

Sima and I exchanged glances. "No." Sima laughed. "It's just fun to annoy you."

"Aren't I lucky?" Alex shook his head and motioned for us to keep moving.

Of course, that evening, I was the unfortunate one to keep watch first. For some reason, it made sense to Sima and Alex to put me out into the face of danger first. I sat next to our massive fire with the rifle clutched in my hands. I stared out across the frozen bay. Millions of stars dotted the night sky. The sky seemed to go on for miles. The night felt cold, but the welcome heat of the fire kept me warm. I leaned back against the sled. Bobick whimpered next to me. I patted his head and rubbed behind his ear.

I sighed. "Bobick, since I am out here alone, you might as well protect me."

"What? Are you talking to your dogs again?" a voice asked from the tent. I almost jumped out of my skin. It was then that I realized how taught my nerves were. I turned around.

"Alex, is it necessary to creep up on me this way?" I asked.

Alex chuckled. "I thought you might want to feel safer out here. Of course, I did not know that you were already occupied talking to your dog."

A slight warmth crept into my cheeks. "Yes, well, there was no one else to talk to."

Alex stood and looked across the bay. "Can you imagine the beauty that is here on this earth?"

"I don't have to imagine. It is right here in front of our eyes. It seems like we are the only people in the world tonight."

"Except for Sima, who is snoring in the tent," Alex said as he looked down at me. "Do you mind if I sit down?"

I felt a sudden shyness creep over me. I moved over to give Alex space to sit on the blanket. We sat close enough to touch.

"Are you cold?" he asked.

"No, the fire keeps me warm," I answered.

"I doubt that." Alex put his arm around my shoulders. "Now, you should feel warmer." I gazed up at him and smiled. His eyes were twinkling down at me. I was afraid he would feel my heart beating against him. He looked up again at the sky, his arm still around me. I dared to lean against his shoulder. He did not move away.

"Do you ever feel that there are moments that you want to keep alive forever?" Alex asked.

"I have not had much of those moments until I met you and Sima."

"Really?" Alex asked in surprise.

"Yes, you are the only friends that I have ever known. You are the only people who I can trust not to leave me."

"I have never felt the need for companionship." Alex looked up at the sky. "But I guess I have never been without friends or people that cared about me."

I felt comforted by his deep voice and his strong arm that held me. "Alex, I want you to know that even if we never get to Alaska, it was a pleasure to meet you."

"Do not talk that way." Alex's arm tightened around my shoulder. "I am convinced that we will reach Alaska."

"Truly?" I asked.

"Maybe I have my doubts, but I might as well be positive."

"You are not always very positive, you know. In fact, Sima seems to be more positive than you." I regretted the words as soon as they left my mouth. I feared Alex would get upset and leave, but he did not move.

"That is perhaps because Sima and I have a different temperament. I have to work on being carefree. I envy Sima. I always have. He always seemed to be able to get away with so much."

"Alex, there is no need for you to envy Sima. You are just as good as he is. No one thinks any less of you."

"No," Alex said and continued, "but then when I mention the fact that I try to be positive, you decide to tell me that Sima is more positive than I am." Alex looked down into my eyes. The blue in his eyes seemed more profound because of the light coming from the dancing flames.

"I am sorry, Alex." My heart filled with guilt. It was good to know, though, how he felt.

"That's all right." Alex leaned down and kissed my cheek. "I'll go wake Sima. He has the second watch. You go inside and rest." He pressed me against him for a second and then stood up. I wanted to tell him not to go, to stay there with me, but I could not muster the courage to say any more words to him.

I fell asleep with my head floating in a cloud of doubt and happiness. There were no words to express the feelings that I held for Alex. Even though I had never been in love, I was sure that I was on my way to falling in love with Alex.

In the morning, the sun's rays spread across the icy bay. Apart from my romantic interlude with Alex, nothing happened that night, and no polar bears had decided to visit our camp. Sima admitted to me that he had been frightened to sit out in the dark in front of the fire. I also let him know that I had been half scared to death. Something stopped me from telling Sima about my conversation with Alex. In truth, there was nothing to say to him. Still, I decided to keep quiet. If Alex wanted Sima to know, he would tell him. I had a feeling that if I spoke, the wonderful feeling that I had in my heart would disappear.

Traveling that day was simpler. We traveled along the shoreline. Of course, there were areas of large rocks and boulders that we had to avoid. Alex said there were probably about two days left until we reached the fort. I hoped that we would reach it soon.

Later that afternoon, as we traveled along an icy pass, Alex paused. "Look," he said as he pointed to something that looked like a trail about twenty feet ahead of us.

"What do you think it could be, Alex?" Sima asked.

"It looks like it is some kind of trail," Alex answered. "Perhaps it is a fur trapper's trail."

"Be careful," Sima piped in. "It could also be some kind of path made by bears."

Alex looked at him and then back at the trail. "I suppose you could be right."

"You only suppose?" Sima asked mockingly. "Ah well, I guess if we get eaten by bears, that is better than freezing to death."

"If it comes in between choosing those two, I am not sure what would be better." Alex grimaced.

My insides shuddered at the thought. "Let's get off this morbid subject," I told them. "We might as well take a chance and follow the trail."

Sima drove forward a bit. "Listen to Anna, Alex. You know she is smarter than both of us together."

"We can be sure she is brighter than you," Alex commented. "All right, let's go then." Alex moved forward. He pulled his rifle out of his sled and slung it over his shoulder. We traveled ahead with caution. As we continued to travel along, it was a relief to see that the trail seemed to be human-made.

"You know we might be closer to the fort than we thought," Alex called back to us.

"That could be the case," Sima answered him. "But as you see, there is nothing close to being civilized around here unless you count yourself as civilized."

"If I remember correctly, Jason Shubert mentioned that this fort is quite isolated."

Sima looked over at me with a grin. "I don't think Jason would be the first one to make that observation."

Alex turned to look at Sima. "Sima, while we realize that you are hilarious, your comments hardly help."

"Yes, well, it helps to be funny sometimes. Honestly, Alex, you should try it."

"As you see, Sima, Anna is smart enough to keep silent."

"Yes, that makes her brilliant, Alex, doesn't it?" Sima retorted.

"I think you should stop calling back and forth to each other, or you will yell yourselves hoarse," I told both of them.

"You see Alex, but when she talks, she always says something smart, unlike you," Sima called to Alex. Alex, who traveled just a few steps ahead of my dogs, shook his head. For a while, we traveled in silence. Then it seemed to me that I heard voices.

I hesitated for a moment. "Listen," I whispered to Sima. He was closer to me than Alex.

"Yes, what is it?" Sima asked.

"Shhh!"

Sima was silent. The voices seemed to get louder as we traveled further.

"Are those human voices?" Sima asked me.

"No, Sima, it's two bears talking to each other," I answered him with sarcasm.

"Yes, I thought as much. You never know; we are so far from civilization that perhaps these bears do know how to talk." Sima raised his eyebrows in mock surprise. "It's a wonder that brilliant Alex hasn't heard anything."

Alex turned his head towards us. "I heard that, Sima."

"Don't you hear voices?" I asked Alex.

"Apart from the ones in your head?" Alex turned his head to the side for a moment and then gave a shake of his head. "No." Then he grinned. "Yes, I did hear them. Let's go. Anna, be careful. We might have to call you Andrei."

"Just as I was getting used to calling her Anna," Sima remarked with disappointment in his voice.

"Sima, please." Alex smiled a bit. "Let's travel quietly now."

My hopes lifted. Perhaps the people ahead of us were part of our original group, although I could not be sure. The voices got louder as we traveled on. Alex motioned to us that we move with attention. Snow crunched under us. The voices that we heard were not recognizable, and my heart sank as we drove up to a small encampment nestled between the rocks and scraggly snow-covered bushes. Two unknown men sat around a small fire. They had a makeshift shelter of branches set up not five feet from them. Both of them looked up almost automatically as we drove up.

"Hello," Alex greeted them. I heard the smallest amount of hesitation in his voice that I had never heard before. The surprise on both men's faces was apparent. I did not blame them. They may have thought we were some kind of apparitions.

"Hello, who are you?" one of the men asked. He had a dark, disheveled beard. He looked to be at least ten years older than his counterpart.

"We are traveling to the Prince of Wales Fort," Alex answered. I understood why he decided to dispense with the details.

"Ah, we are just on our way there. We came out here to hunt and collect some furs. Why do you not join us? We are only about ten miles from the fort. We decided it might be too late to travel further today."

"Yes, we have been trying to reach the fort for a few days now. We were not sure if we were on the right track," Sima told them as he pulled his sled up to Alex.

"My name is Stefan," the older man said to us. "This is my friend Robert." Robert gave us a shy smile. He seemed young. However, there appeared to be a certain resilience to his features that was difficult to explain.

"My name is Alex. These are my friends Sima and Andrei." Alex gave me a look as he said that name. I nodded to him in understanding.

Stefan motioned for us to move closer. "Come join us by the fire. You all look worn out."

Sima, Alex, and I exchanged glances. Then Alex stepped forward. "Since you are heading towards the fort, we might as well join you."

An awkward silence settled upon us. It did not seem as if any of us knew what to say. Alex, Sima, and I kept throwing each other wary glances. Finally, after we set up camp, we decided to sit down with the other two men. We settled down around the campfire that they had made.

"Whereabouts are you from?" asked the older man.

Alex and I looked at each other. Sima cleared his throat. "We are from Maine," Alex answered as diplomatically as he could.

Stefan looked at us as if we had said we had come from the sun. "Maine?"

"Yes," Sima answered a bit testily. "You have heard of it before?"

"Of course, but what are you doing here?" Stefan asked.

"We are on route to Alaska," Alex answered.

"I have a feeling you are lying," Stefan told us.

"We aren't," Sima answered defensively.

"Truly you have come from Maine?" Robert questioned.

"Yes," I answered, losing my patience. I noticed the two men exchange glances as if we genuinely had lost our minds.

"At the moment, you are heading towards the Prince of Wales Fort, correct?" Stefan asked.

"Sir, we are not lying. We have lost the rest of the men that were with us. You may have heard of one of the men, Jason Shubert." Alex looked at me, and I gave him a shrug. While our trip seemed to be preposterous, I had not thought it entirely insane until I saw the look on those men's faces.

Robert suddenly perked up. "I have heard that name before."

His tone of voice lifted some hope in me, but Stefan only smashed that hope. "Of course you have. That man is a legend. He has made the trip to Alaska from Maine at least twice before."

Sima gave them an admonishing look. "You see, we are not as crazy as you think we are."

"Yes, but all of you look as if you would be the first ones to get lost," Stefan stated. Alex looked somewhat offended at the moment, and I did not blame him.

"It would do you well to stay at the fort until spring and then travel by horse to Alaska," Robert suggested.

"Perhaps, but we would love to reach Alaska sooner rather than later."

"Do you realize how far you still have to go?" Stefan asked.

"No, we did not look at any maps," Sima answered him in a somewhat cynical tone.

"Did not mean to offend you." Stefan laughed a bit. Suddenly, I had a great dislike toward the man.

"Well, you did," I stated. Alex turned his head quickly toward me in a warning.

"We did not mean to," Robert said, sounding apologetic.

Alex stood up. "Yes, well, I think we better turn in. We are rather tired."

"You have some nice dogs there," Stefan observed.

"Yes, they must be strong to have gotten us here from Maine," Sima said in a mocking tone. He then turned to me and rolled his eyes. I had to hide a giggle.

Once we were in our tent and heard the other men turn in, Alex said to us, "You two could have been a bit kinder."

"I do not trust that man," I told him.

"There would be no reason not to trust him. After all, we are in the middle of the Canadian wilderness, and he is heading towards the same place we are."

Sima began to spread out his supplies. "You do have a point there."

"I just want them to show us where to find the fort. We have to depend on them. So in the morning, please be nicer." Alex turned over on his side and faced the tent wall. "Let's go to sleep now. I am a bit tired."

I closed my eyes. "As Stefan said, we all look as if we will soon fall over, so I suppose sleeping would be the best solution."

Chapter **13**   January 15, 1888

The following day, I awoke with a lazy yawn. As I stretched my arms out, an uneasy feeling came over me. The camp seemed to be too quiet. I turned over on my stomach and opened the flap from our tent. Shock came over me. The two men and their sleds were gone. I sat up as quickly as I could. I turned to Alex and frantically shook him by the shoulder. He reluctantly opened his eyes, and his eyes seemed to take a few moments to adjust and focus on my face.

"Anna, this better not be about any wolves."

"Alex, those men are gone."

"What?" Alex sat up swiftly and pushed his blankets aside. He jumped up and looked out of the tent. He turned to me, his face crestfallen. "Did you hear them go?" he asked.

"No, I just awoke and noticed they were gone."

Alex swiftly turned and shook Sima by the shoulder. "Wake up."

As soon as Sima had awakened, we all ventured out. We noticed straight away that something was wrong. The men seemed to have left in a hurry, and our sleds were a mess. It was only when I came closer to the sleds that I noticed that Bobick was gone. I began to panic. My heart started to beat hard, and my hands began to shake.

"Where could he be?" I asked aloud.

"Who?" Sima asked.

I pointed to the empty harness. "Bobick, he's gone."

"One of my dogs is gone too," Sima said in a deflated voice. He walked up to the empty harness that was lying next to his sled.

"Those men, they stole our dogs?" I could not believe that for a moment. Why would they want to steal our dogs?

"That is rather stupid of them," Alex said. "If they are heading towards the fort, they cannot be naïve enough to believe we would not find them."

Sima turned to us. "They did not seem to be too bright. I would not put it past them. We better locate them."

"Do you think we would be able to catch up to them?" I asked.

"Since none of us have any idea of when they left, we cannot be too sure. We can still follow their trail. Hopefully, their trail will lead us towards the fort."

Sima turned back to the tent. "Let's pack up and get moving then."

We tore down the camp in haste. It took us a while to pack up our supplies since they were strewn all over the place. We discovered that several other items were missing. Some medical supplies had disappeared as well as some of our meat.

"When we find those men, they will be sorry they ever meddled with us," Sima said in a threatening tone.

"There can't be that many places that they could hide in the fort," I observed.

Alex rolled up some blankets. "Yes, if they are at the fort. They could have just gone to the town of Churchill, and then who knows."

"I will find them. They have no right taking my dog." I was surprised at the forcefulness in my voice.

Sima laughed a bit. "We better keep Anna at a distance, or she might get violent."

"Sima, this is nothing to joke about." Alex was serious.

"I know, this situation really is ridiculous," Sima said. He tried to sound lighthearted, but I could see he was worried too. There was something genuinely upsetting about the fact that those men had taken our things and snuck off.

"Come on, let's start moving. If we want our dogs back, we better catch up to those men." Alex commanded. All of us climbed on our sleds and touched off. Parts of the trail seemed to be visible while other areas were covered with snow. The air seemed to be getting colder as we moved on. We were afraid that we would need to stop before nighttime. Still, we plodded on through the snow, aware of the fact that if we did not reach the fort soon, we would never find our dogs. We just hoped that the men had gone to the fort as we predicted. We moved at lightning speed, although it was difficult to maneuver without a lead dog.

The break that we took at midday was relatively short, and then we pressed on. We drove on and on, and finally, we saw a break in the trail and the shoreline seemed to widen. The bleakness of our surroundings for the past hour diminished, and we came to a coastline with ice-covered rocks sticking out over the edge of the shore. I narrowed my eyes. In the distance, there appeared to be a rather large and broad structure. The structure seemed close to the bay. The rugged beauty of the place took my breath away. I stared at the bay and let out an icy breath. All of us had stopped at the same time.

Alex reached to touch my shoulder. "We better move forward." Unfortunately, the tracks we had been following stopped abruptly a few hundred feet before. We continued to travel ahead with the hope that we would find something at the fort. I had a somewhat nervous fluttering feeling in my heart since I had woken that morning. I was frightened that Bobick would not be at the fort, and I feared that I would lose my faithful dog. Although on this trip, I realized that dogs were more expendable than I had imagined.

Standing near the fort were many makeshift shelters and tents. I wondered if we would ever have any luck finding out who Stefan and Robert were and where they had gone. We all stood rooted to the ground.

"Where should we go now?" I asked.

Alex shrugged his shoulders. "I am not sure. There must be someone who is in charge of all the activity that goes on around here."

"We won't find out, standing here all day," Sima said as he let his dogs know that we should start moving. We followed him. It was the first time that I had seen Sima take charge. "You know what bothers me the most is that these men lied to us. They might as well have said we can't trust them," Sima said as he traveled forward.

"There is not much they could have done if they had told us the truth." Alex pointed out to him.

Sima threw off that thought with another shrug of the shoulders. "Yes, well, I suppose you are right, Alex."

I did not say anything at the moment. I remembered I had lied for a long time to both Sima and Alex, although the fact that I had lied to come on this journey hardly seemed to matter anymore.

Alex moved ahead, and we followed. "Let's see who we can find inside that could perhaps help us."

I was becoming apprehensive about the whole situation. As we neared the entrance to the fort, I noticed many men who were peering out of their tents looking at us in curiosity. I doubted that we would be able to find anyone here. People milled around like ants. Makeshift shelters with large towers of wooden logs to block out the cold Canadian wind stood everywhere.

"Perhaps there is a place to stay inside the fort," Sima wondered aloud.

"I certainly hope there is," Alex answered him. "I do not trust the looks of the men out here."

We traveled towards the entrance. An armed guard stood there with a rifle. "What do you want?"

"We are looking for our stolen animals," Alex told him. "We have reason to believe that the men who stole them are at this fort."

"We cannot let just anybody enter this fort. Who are you anyway, and where did you come from?" The man's tone of voice was threatening, and I wished we had not come.

Sima came up from behind Alex. "We were traveling with Jason Shubert. We are on route to Alaska."

"Jason Shubert?" the man asked. "I have heard something of him. I will let you speak to the general who is in charge of this fort. Move along quickly." The man moved aside. Sima, Alex, and I went through the high doors.

Sima looked at us with triumph. "All you need to do is to use your head."

Alex turned to him. "It is surprising that you used it just this once. Now we should find the general."

It took us at least an hour to locate the general, but we did reach him. In the center of the fort's location, there was a large pole with a flag. On each side of the flagpole, there were long walls that resembled corridors. We were told the general was located in the halls to the right. We were asked to wait in a cold brick-laid room. Alex, Sima, and I stood waiting. We had tied our sleds and remaining dogs outside in the courtyard.

"Listen, Anna, for your safety; we better pretend that you are a boy. There is no reason for you to let anybody know the truth at the moment. Anyway, if they find out that we were with Jason Shubert, they could suspect you of fraud." Alex looked anxious, which was surprising to me.

"Poor Anna, we can't seem to make up our minds about who she is," Sima said with a chuckle.

"It was Anna's choice to come, Sima."

"I am not sorry that she came at all," Sima said as he winked at me.

Alex gave Sima a shuttered look. "Neither am I."

Sima just looked at me and said, "Don't worry, nothing will happen to you. Even if you do wind up in jail, we would be happy to spring you from there."

Alex opened his mouth to say something, but the door opened. A young soldier who I thought could be no more than eighteen looked at us from the entrance. "General Wilkin said he will see you now." The three of us followed him into the next room. Several soldiers were standing in the room. All of them seemed too young.

"What are the three of you doing here?" General Wilkin asked in a gruff voice.

"Sir, our first intention of coming here was to find some shelter," Alex answered. His voice was clear. He seemed to show no signs of wavering, although the man behind the desk frightened me. He was not a broad-shouldered man, but he sat erect, and his gray eyes seemed to pierce through us from behind the desk.

"You seek shelter? There is no reason that any one of you should be traveling in the middle of Canada in the winter. You three must be daft."

"Sir, we were traveling with Jason Shubert and with many other men. Unfortunately, all of the men became separated. We think that we are the only three, except his son, who chose to stay behind, that are still living."

General Wilkin looked at us. "Jason Shubert, you say?"

All three of us nodded in unison.

"You may be glad to hear this news."

I looked at the man in anticipation.

"What news?" Sima asked with a note of distrust in his voice.

"Jason Shubert was alive one month ago. He was here, devastated because he thought he had lost all hope of ever finding the rest of his men. Two men were with him, Steven Lake and an Indian. I cannot remember his name."

Sima, Alex, and I looked at each other in awe. "Did they say if they were going to continue to Alaska?" Alex asked with a certain lightness in his voice. Other men had survived!

"No, I told them they were out of their minds. Jason Shubert is a legend, of course, but this has been a hard winter. There was no reason for them to continue, and there is no reason for you to go on either."

"Sir, we fully intend to proceed with our journey," Alex said in a firm voice.

"Is Jason Shubert still here then?" Sima asked, his voice full of anticipation.

"No," the man answered. "They intended to travel to Winnipeg and then to return to America after the winter. The supplies they were carrying will be sent to Fort Yukon in the summer months. Should you wish to continue, your supplies could be left here, and we would see that they arrive safely at Fort Yukon. That way, you would not be loaded down with them when you travel."

"That is kind of you, sir, although we do not have many supplies left. Two men stole many items from us, including two dogs, while we were on route to this fort. They went by the names of Robert and Stefan." While Alex was speaking, I studied the soldiers around the room and wondered why they would ever come to such a desolate place.

My thoughts were interrupted by the general. "Young man, we cannot inspect every man who comes here. You should have watched those men more carefully. You should know that men cannot be trusted." Sima and I exchanged glances. This inquiry was not getting us anywhere.

Alex could not hide his annoyance. "Well then, do you know if we could buy other dogs?"

"There are some natives just outside the fort that perhaps could get you some other dogs. You will need to barter, but seeing that you are at least part native and your friend is a native, you could perhaps talk them into giving you a lower price. Otherwise, I cannot help you much. Perhaps we can find a place for you to stay. Although, you cannot stay longer than three nights. Re-supply and get out of here. Natives, even ones that know Jason Shubert, are not of much interest to me." Something in my throat began to hurt. Alex's eyes flashed, but I knew that it was better not to argue and to take any offer we can get.

"Where could we stay, sir?" Sima asked.

"Across the way." He then pointed to the young man who had shown us in. "William here will show you."

"Thank you," Alex said, and we all walked out and followed the soldier to another cold hallway about fifty steps away from the general's quarters. William opened the door to a rather large comfortable room with a fireplace. The room had four cots and a small table. When the door closed, we all looked at each other.

"Jason Shubert has been alive all of this time?" Alex asked. "Strange that he did not come to Richard and Ellen's cabin."

I sat down on one of the cots. "That is strange. He should have known the checkpoints better than we did."

Sima nodded. "I do not understand."

"Could that man be lying?" I asked.

Alex looked at me with a puzzled expression. "Why would he lie about that?"

"I do not know. Of course, he did give Steven Lake's name, and the Indian that was with him must have been Red Fern."

"It must be true," Sima said. "But I have a feeling that Jason Shubert perhaps had plans that did not include the rest of us."

"What are you talking about?" Alex asked. He sounded angry.

Sima's eyes had turned hard. "Why did Mr. Shubert lead us into that storm? Then he never showed up at Richard and Ellen's cabin. That was the established checkpoint. Even his dimwit of a son found it. Then he comes here, leaves all of his supplies, and continues on

to Winnipeg. There is no guarantee that they will reach the fort,
you know."

"You imagine things, Sima. I have never thought that Jason
Shubert was conniving, and what good would this do him? At the
expense of so many men's lives, even his son's?"

"Look, I am not saying that he wanted us all dead, but I do not
think he ever intended for us to reach Alaska."

Alex gave Sima a cold stare. "Why would he lie about this? It just
doesn't make sense. Now stop this nonsense, Sima."

"I apologize; I should not speculate so." Sima turned towards the
door. "I will go tend to the dogs and get the supplies that we need for
the next three days."

When he walked out, Alex and I regarded each other.

"I do not think he is right either," I told him. "All of this just does
not add up, you know."

"Yes, I think the strain has been too much for Sima. I doubt,
though, that we will get our dogs back, especially without any help."

"Yes, why help natives?" I asked with frustration as I took off one
of my boots. I just wanted to lie down. "I do hope we will be able to
get more dogs, though. We can hardly reach Alaska with a limited
amount of dogs. Also, we have so far to go still, and look how many
we have lost already."

"All right, I will go help Sima. You stay here and rest."

I stood. "I can help too, you know."

"Yes, I know, but it is nice to have a break once in a while, isn't it?"

"Yes, it is nice to rest once in a while." I smiled at him as he walked
out.

When I was left alone, I looked at the small room. A small fire
burned in the fireplace. I sighed, took off my other boot and coat,
and then lay down on the cot. It was not soft, but it felt a lot more
comfortable than the blankets we had been sleeping on. I do not
remember falling asleep, but I opened my eyes to find the room

darkened. I surveyed the room; Sima sat by the fireplace, and Alex was nowhere in sight.

"Where is Alex?" I asked.

"He went to look for some dogs for us to buy."

"On his own?"

"Well, is that not what Alex likes to do, be on his own?" Sima asked.

I looked at him to see if he was joking or kidding around. He did not seem to be joking. His voice sounded serious. He sat there on the floor with a sullen look on his face.

"Sima, what is the problem?"

Sima turned his face to me. His eyes appeared darkened by worry. "I'll tell you, Anna." The coldness in his voice frightened me. "Why do we have to keep going? You heard what General Wilkin said; it is sheer madness to continue. Why does Alex get to make all of the decisions? We won't reach Alaska before springtime anyway. We could stay here and wait for the spring."

"But you heard General Wilkin; he said we could not stay for longer than three days."

"We could camp outside the fort."

"That's monotonous; we would just be sitting here." I could not understand why I was arguing the point when I secretly agreed with Sima.

Sima stood up. "Why do you always defend him?" His anger made me uncomfortable.

I sat up on the cot. "I just think that perhaps we should move on. There is not much point to staying here."

"No, you agree with me. I know you do, but you defend Alex because you have feelings for him. He sometimes can be foolish."

"Sima, he's your friend." I began to wonder if Sima could be jealous. "Why do you think I have feelings for him?" I asked with caution.

Sima snorted. "Anna, it is written all over your face. When he walks by, you stare at him as if you have never seen him before."

"Sima, I don't understand why you are so angry about this. What's the matter?"

"Nothing, perhaps you and Alex are from the same thoughtless pool of people. Why listen to me at all? I cannot even have an opinion. If I say anything, you laugh at me."

I had never seen his side of Sima before. "Sima, you joke all the time. That is why we laugh."

Sima came towards me. "Yes, well, maybe you should learn to listen a little better."

I moved away from my cot. "Sima, we should talk about this later; you are upset now."

"Yes, we should. You never talk much anyway. We would not get anywhere if we talked now, would we?"

"Sima, you are not making any sense. I hope you know that."

"Oh, I don't make sense to you either now? First Alex, then you, I am sick of listening to you and Alex. Look, if you want to go, fine. I am staying right here. Why risk our necks for something we can't achieve?"

"Sima, we still have to make this trip. Don't you want to get home to your family?"

Sima stopped and looked at me. "My family cares almost nothing about me. There is nothing for me in Alaska."

"Sima, you don't know that. I am sure that's not true."

"Yes, well, they dumped me with Alex's family. I lived with his family before coming to study in America. They wrote to me twice while I lived there, once when I started school and six months before I left to go on this ridiculous journey."

"Sima, I am sure they wanted what's best for you. You should go back to Alaska and try to mend things with them." I was at a loss of what to say to Sima. He seemed so hurt at that moment. I had never wanted to upset him.

Sima crossed his arms across his chest. "And you know so much about family, now, don't you?" Sima's eyes were bright with frustration.

"Sima, I care a lot about you, and I would not want to leave you here." At that moment, I thought I had heard a noise, but I did not look to the side because I was staring at Sima.

"Yes, you and Alex would leave, wouldn't you? You have feelings for him so you would go with him. Even though I am your friend, you wouldn't stay."

"Sima, we have to stay together. You can't just stay here. Alex, you and I are kind of like our own family. We care about each other and look out for each other. I won't let you stay here. Anyway, I don't even know why you keep talking about Alex as if I were getting married to him. He hasn't said anything to me, and perhaps I do care about him a lot, but that doesn't mean I don't care about you."

"Yes, but you can't marry two people now, can you?"

At this point, I realized that both of us were speaking quite loudly, almost yelling. I was about ready to launch into a new argument when I caught a glimpse of someone in the room. I turned my head. Alex stood at the entrance. Sima had followed my gaze, and he now turned to face Alex as well. My face burned when I realized he must have been standing there for quite some time.

"What is happening?" Alex asked with confusion in his voice. "You were yelling so loudly I could hear your voices from two hundred feet away. Sima, I am not sure what your problem is at all, but I wish you would stop with this ridiculousness. All three of us are going to Alaska, and that is not a debatable question."

"Yes, that's what I thought," Sima spat out the words and stalked out of the room. I stood facing Alex. I was sure my cheeks looked like a bright red sunset.

"I think that Sima just needs to have some time to himself. There has been too much pressure lately. Now that we found out that Jason Shubert is alive, it is quite too much of a shock."

I was afraid to look into his eyes. "Yes, I know."

"Listen, I think you should talk to him. Calmly you know, it does not help to yell back."

"His anger threw me off, and I was not sure how to react."

"Yes, Sima usually is never this angry. He said things he didn't mean."

"That's true. I overreacted too. Anyway, where were you?" I wanted to change the subject. I wondered how much he had heard, and I did not want to discuss the argument I had with Sima.

"I did buy two new dogs, and I got you something as a surprise."

"A surprise for me?" I now looked into his eyes, and I only saw kindness there. He didn't seem to be at all worried about the fact that I perhaps cared about him. "I want to look at the dogs that you got and this surprise."

Alex smiled a bit. "All right, come on."

I followed Alex out into the yard. There, next to our sleds, stood two beautiful dogs. One was large and black with short fur. The other had long silver fur.

"You can choose first since Sima has disappeared."

"Do you blame him for disappearing?"

"No, I suppose that was rather uncomfortable."

"Yes, I think I will take the black one. He will never replace Bobick, but he looks friendly enough." I knelt and put my hand on the dog's head.

"He looks strong too. What will you name him?"

"I don't know yet."

"Please don't name him Bobick number two."

I smiled at him. "Where's the surprise?"

Alex took a blanket out of the sled. "Here." In the blanket lay a tiny puppy. He was brown with white markings.

"The man who was selling the dogs did not want him. I decided that it was better to take him with us than to leave him."

"I promise I will take good care of him." I took the puppy from Alex. "He can travel in my sled. Fur Hunter's dog has healed and can help pull now. Perhaps we could leave most of the supplies going to

Fort Yukon here. It would be easier for us. Although, I know Sima feels there is something wrong about the whole situation."

"Yes, well, even if the supplies did just stay here, it might be better. We have already used up half of the supplies meant to go to the fort. Right now, I just want to get home."

I put my hand on his arm. "Me too. Thank you, Alex."

He put his hand over mine. "You're welcome."

"I think I will go talk to Sima now. Can I take my puppy with me?"

"Of course, don't scare Sima with it."

"I won't." I patted the puppy's soft fur and went to find Sima.

*****

Sima sat behind the building leaning his head against the brick wall. He was smoking his pipe and whittling away at a piece of wood. He did not look at me as I approached.

"Hello," I said as I walked over to him.

He looked up at me and stood up. "Hello." He was now looking down at me.

"I came to show you the surprise Alex gave me." I opened up the blanket with the tiny puppy in it.

Sima laughed. "Quite the surprise." His gaze then shifted down to the ground. "Anna, I want to apologize. I should not have done that. I was upset, and I shouldn't have taken out everything on you."

"No, you shouldn't have," I joked.

Sima smiled. "I have been so worried lately, and the news of Jason Shubert is quite distressing."

"Yes, I am worried about continuing on in this winter weather, but I think I would rather reach Alaska sooner rather than later. It might be more difficult in the spring."

Sima kicked at the snow. "That is true. We would not be able to take the dogs and may have to pay money which we are sadly lacking."

"I think we should continue on. I have my doubts, but I do not see a lot of reasons for staying here either. Anyway, living outside of the fort in a tent would probably be the same as traveling."

Sima leaned against the stone wall. "Just safer and closer to civilization."

"This is not a very civilized place. Why there is a fort here in the first place is beyond me."

"You know, I have actually wondered about that."

We both stopped speaking, and I cleared my throat. "Sima, please let's not have this argument come between us."

Sima grinned. "It won't. I apologize if Alex heard anything that he should not have heard."

"It's all right. He probably doesn't care. I do not think that he cares about me in that way."

"I think he might. I am his best friend, you know."

"We'll wait and see, right?"

Sima laughed. "With Alex, that is all you can do." He then hugged me. "Don't ever think that Alex or I would leave you. Also, I would never let you leave without me. But please, if you disagree with Alex, tell me the truth."

I tilted my head to look back at him. "All right, Sima."

*****

That night I fell asleep with a calm feeling in my heart. I realized how close I was becoming to both Alex and Sima, and the comfort of knowing that someone cared about me reassured me. I was wrapped up in thoughts of Alaska. Sima had assured me that he and Alex would never leave me, but what would happen when I reached Alaska? I was not sure what would transpire. I did not ever want to be separated from them. I fell asleep with worries still tumbling about in my brain.

The next day I awoke late. Sima and Alex were not in the room. I wondered where they could have gone. After preparing for the day, I walked out into the courtyard of the fort. My stomach rumbled. I wanted to eat something warm and fresh for a change. I was tired of salted meat and the stale crackers that we always ate on the trail. I looked for Alex and Sima but could not locate them. I went over to my dogs and was about to settle for some stale bread and crackers again when I caught the fresh scent of bread. I saw smoke coming from one of the outer buildings towards the edge of the fort. I decided to head in that direction.

After walking about fifty steps towards the building, I noticed the backside of a large oven. I peered inside the building. What I observed made my mouth water. On the windowsill, there were huge loaves of light brown fresh bread. A woman of large sizes was taking several more loaves and pies out of the oven. I stared through the glass. I decided to walk in and ask if I could buy one.

The door hardly made a sound as I entered. "Excuse me, ma'am. Can I buy a piece of bread?" I asked timidly. I did not have much money, but I would barter if needed.

The woman turned towards me. "You can have some for free. I have scraps anyway. The rest has to go to the army and the men they keep cooped up in that jail of theirs."

"Oh, thank you," I said as I took the bread. "There are men in jail here?" I could not imagine why they would want to put anyone in jail here. There was nowhere to go.

"Yes, they do. Two men got jailed this morning."

I stared at her. I hoped that it was not Sima or Alex. However, I had a sinking feeling that it was them.

"Well, here is the bread," she said as she handed me a bag with several fresh pieces of bread in it. The smell was heavenly.

"Thank you very much." I took the bag and walked out the door. I jogged back to our room in a panic. The room remained empty. I ran outside again. I noticed William, the young soldier, walking across the yard.

"Can you be so kind as to tell me where they keep prisoners around here?" I called as I ran to catch up to him.

"You must be looking for your friends. Come with me."

My heart sank. William led me towards the back of the fort. He showed me to a door in the wall and entered. The area was gloomy. I followed him down a dark corridor, and then I saw a lone light and the beginning of small jail cells carved into the walls. Several men were sitting in those cells. I did not notice Alex or Sima. There were soldiers standing inside the long corridor. I continued to follow William. Finally, at the end of the passage, I spotted Alex and Sima. As I neared, I noticed they both had expressions of guilt on their faces. I stared at them.

Sima gave me a sheepish smile. "Hello."

"Sima, this is not funny," I said unnecessarily.

"Come on, An..." Alex stopped mid-sentence when he noticed William was standing there. "Andrei, this is not our fault."

I came up to the bars. "Then why are you here?"

"We found Stefan and our dogs," Sima told me.

"Did you get them back?" I asked with anticipation.

"Obviously not," Alex answered with a smirk.

"Why is this funny?" I asked.

Sima laughed. "You just look so furious." Alex tried to hide the fact that he was laughing behind his hand.

"Well, what are we going to do?" I asked, looking back at the soldiers.

"We have to appear before the general this afternoon, and then he decides what will happen to us."

"Will they let you out?"

"We don't know."

"That doesn't help us if we are trying to reach Alaska."

"We can see that." Alex looked at me with a mocking expression.

"What did you do to Stefan that made you end up here?" I asked.

"He called the guards on us. Unfortunately, the general saw what happened. We tried to explain that it was our dogs that got stolen. All we did was try to convince Stefan to give them back."

"Why is Stefan also not here then?" I asked.

"They let him go." Alex's eyes narrowed. "Look, everything will be fine. We will explain the whole situation again to the general. He has to let us go. We can promise to leave right away."

"I will come to see what happens. Is the hearing supposed to happen in his office?" I asked.

Alex nodded.

"Here." I took some bread out of the bag. "I was given some fresh bread this morning. I thought you might want some."

"Yes, they did say they were supposed to feed us some time, but they didn't."

I handed the bread to them through the bars. Alex squeezed my hand. "Thank you." He smiled at me.

I quickly smiled back and then turned to William. "Please take me out of here." He obliged, and I followed him out.

When we were outside, William turned to me. "I think you may have realized that the general is not very fair. He is rather cruel, actually. I did not want to say anything in the presence of the other soldiers. You would probably be better off if you got them out of there and all of you left."

"How am I supposed to do that?" I asked. "The prison is guarded."

William's expression turned serious. "I like you and your friends. All three of you are different from the usual men that pass through these parts. I want to help you. I will let you know if they put me to guard the jailhouse tonight. I will help you get them out if that is the case."

I gave him a grateful smiled. "Thank you," I said and walked away with some relief.

*****

That afternoon I went to the general's office. There were a handful of soldiers in the room. Sima and Alex got escorted inside. Their hands were tied, which I thought was ridiculous. I saw William on the other side of the room. I then looked at Alex. I could tell he hated standing there in shame with his hands tied. His eyes shifted and met mine, and then he hurriedly turned his eyes to General Wilkin. Sima looked as if he had been in this kind of situation before and that it could not bother him any less that he was standing there.

"I knew you two would cause trouble around here," General Wilkin began.

"Sir, all we were trying to do was to get our dogs back. I think it is ridiculous that we are not being helped," Sima spoke out. Alex attempted to motion for Sima to stop talking, but Sima did not appear to notice.

General Wilkin stood and came up to them. "You are the ones who started to hit this man and yell at him."

"It was because he was a scoundrel," Sima again spoke out of turn. Alex just rolled his eyes at Sima.

"Sir, if you let us go, we will leave your fort and never come back," Alex said.

"You will leave this fort, but not right away. Two more days in a jail cell and thirty lashes each will teach you a lesson." Sima's expression turned hard as stone after hearing these words.

Alex just looked as astounded as I was. "We did not do anything so terrible," Alex argued.

"You have to learn that fighting is not allowed in this fort."

"Sir, if we never come back, what difference does it make?" Sima asked in an impudent tone.

Suddenly, General Wilkin hit Sima across the face. Sima's eyes were blazing now. His usually warm features had gone cold. General Wilkin glowered at Sima. "The difference is that I run this fort and that you are no one to me."

I was ready to start yelling at him but held my tongue and tried to hide as far back in the room as possible. I feared I would also end up in a jail cell with Alex and Sima.

"This punishment is ridiculous," Alex said calmly.

"Not to me. Sleep well tonight, because tomorrow night you will not sleep because of your whipping. Now get them out of here." General Wilkin turned around.

My heartbeat sped up. What was I to do? I had to get Sima and Alex out of the fort that night. I saw Sima and Alex exchange glances. Sima shrugged his shoulders. I noticed Alex look again towards me. I tried to give him a reassuring smile, but I think I failed to be encouraging.

*****

I went back to our quarters which seemed hollow. About twenty minutes later, there was a knock on the door. I opened it to find William standing there. He nervously looked over his shoulder. I motioned for him to come into the room and closed the door behind him as he entered.

He whispered as he spoke, "We are in luck. I am on duty at the jailhouse tonight. Many soldiers in this fort do not like General Wilkin. The men at the gate will make sure to let you out. I have already spoken to them."

"What about you, though?" I asked. "Won't you get in trouble?"

"Perhaps," William said as he lifted his shoulders. "But I think you will have bigger problems than I will. Anyway, I can make it seem like an accident, or I will pretend that I was knocked out. Meet me at the entrance to the jailhouse at around midnight, and I will help you."

"I am not sure why you are helping us," I said to him. "I have no other choice right now but to trust you, thank you."

"Do not worry. Make sure that their dogs are ready too. You will have to make a quick escape."

"Here." I handed him a bit of money that I had.

"I don't want this money."

"Keep it. I don't know that I will ever use it," I replied.

*****

That night I sat anxiously awaiting the stroke of midnight. I had silently packed our sleds in darkness and harnessed the dogs. The dogs were mercifully quiet. They, too, seemed to sense the urgency in the air. I quietly ran to the jailhouse just a few minutes before the strike of twelve. A soldier I did not recognize stood at the door. The minutes seemed to drag by. I began to wonder if William would show up. Then I saw William approaching. He said something to the guard, and then the other soldier walked away. I crept over to where William stood.

He noticed me and gave me a little wave. "I have the watch tonight. We should be quite safe, but you have to move fast. You have about five minutes. It might be difficult to get out without being noticed by someone. The gates are unlocked tonight. Come on." He gestured in the direction of the jailhouse.

A bell rang on the clock tower that stood in the middle of the fort. Five minutes. The time would run out before I knew it. I crept down the dim, narrow aisle. The cell compartments seemed to be even closer to each other in the dark. All of the prisoners appeared to be sleeping. At the end of the hall, a lone bare lantern signaled the place where Sima and Alex sat prisoner.

I crawled to the door of their cell. The cold from the ground penetrated my trousers.

Three minutes now. I looked in. Alex lay on the ground snoring. Sima sat leaning against the wall whittling away at another confounded piece of wood. I wondered where he had found it.

I leaned my head against the heavy metal bars. "Sima." My whisper seemed to reverberate through the hall.

He raised his eyes, rested his head back against the wall, and grinned. "I knew you'd come."

"We don't have much time," I said as I fumbled with the keys. "The guard is about to come." The key slid into the keyhole, and the door opened.

Sima crept over to the door and squeezed my hand. "Good girl." He then turned towards Alex and shook his shoulder.

Alex sat up with a puzzled look on his face. "What's wrong?"

"Anna's getting us out. We have to go."

Alex pulled himself up without hesitation and followed Sima and I down the narrow hall. Half a minute, that was all we had. The three of us stole out the door and stepped into the fresh air of the courtyard.

We were halfway across the yard when we heard a voice behind us, "Halt! Where are you going?"

I dropped the keys on the ground, and the three of us tore across the rest of the distance to our sleds. I could hear a rising commotion behind us. Fear threatened to take over me. If we got caught, I did not know what would happen.

We jumped on our sleds in record time. Our dogs seemed to sense our determination to leave and took off towards the gates. The gates still stood open. William had pulled through for us. As we passed through the large gate, I heard a shot ring out behind us. Loud shots echoed through the night as we charged out of the fort. The dogs flew like eagles across the snow.

We did not stop until we were well outside the boundaries of the fort. The shots from the fort had died down, and the soldiers did not seem to think we were worth the effort of a chase. It appeared that we had traveled ten miles within an hour.

After pulling our dogs to a stop, we all took a deep breath. I felt my heartbeat calm. Alex pulled out the brake on his sled and, without a word, came over to me and drew me into a big hug.

Sima also ran up to us and threw his arms around the both of us. "Anna, you have saved the day. What would we do without you?" He then kissed the top of my head.

We stood there celebrating like little children. The tension of the past hours dissipated, and relief flooded through me. Not only the three of us were safe, but I finally felt as if I belonged and had a purpose. I was not only a welcome guest but a close friend.

*****

Several days later, we were well away from the fort. We had broken camp. The past few days had been filled with travel. Fear that some of the soldiers may decide to follow us had forced us to push on without much rest. At last, we had felt that the situation was not as dire as we had thought and decided to take a more extended break.

After supper, I stepped outside of the tent. I picked up the new puppy that I had nestled inside of my sled. I sat down on top of my sled and held the puppy tightly in my arms. A deep sigh escaped my lips. I missed Bobick. I felt responsible for the fact that he was stolen. I did not know if the men that had taken him would treat him well or if he even understood why I was not there anymore. Nothing could replace Bobick. A tear ran down my face. I tried to wipe it away, but another tear followed.

"What's the matter, Anna?" I felt a hand on my shoulder. I turned. Sima stood there with a look of concern on his face.

I shook my head. "Nothing, I am being silly."

Sima sat down next to me. "You would not be crying if it was nothing. Come on, out with it. You said you would be truthful." He then put his arm around my shoulders.

A few moments passed before I could speak. "I miss Bobick. It seems silly after all the horrors we have been through to cry about a dog. However, he has been my companion for several years now."

Sima took his arm off my shoulders and pulled his legs onto the sled. "It's not silly. Dogs become part of our family. I have not for one second rejoiced in the fact that our dogs have been stolen or injured beyond repair." Sima stopped and took a deep breath. "Bobick was, of course, important to you. You talked to him more than you talk to us." Sima smiled a bit. "Don't ever feel that crying about him is wrong, all right?"

"Thank you, Sima." I wiped away another tear. I was thankful Alex had not found me in such a state.

Sima turned to scratch the puppy behind his ear. "What will you name this one?"

"I'm not sure. I was thinking of naming him Snow Spots because his spots look like snow."

Sima looked at me and studied my face for a bit. "You are not original. I think that is a good name, though."

I looked down at the puppy that had now settled into my lap. "I like the name. This puppy I will guard, and no one will take him from me."

Sima scratched the puppy's ear one more time and then stood up from the sled and stretched. "You have to realize, Anna, that you cannot stop bad things from happening."

"I know, but sometimes I feel like the whole world has fallen into shambles and if I don't hold on to everything, I will become lost."

Sima turned towards the tent. "That's why we pray. Good night."

I watched Sima as he climbed into our tent. For some reason, it had never occurred to me before that night that Sima was a good person.

Chapter 14   February 5, 1888

Weeks had passed. We had been able to get away safely from the fort without anyone catching our trail. We plodded on step by step, mile by mile. I felt as if we were no closer to our goal than we had been three weeks back. Sima, Alex, and I felt spent. There seemed to be no end to our road. At night we would sit and speak of Alaska and our homes in Maine. The weather by now seemed milder, and the air did not even seem frigid. We broke for an early dinner. We had been pushing hard and decided to take an early break. All of us sat quietly in our tent.

"Seems like it will never end," Alex said in a dull voice.

"If you weren't such a sourpuss, perhaps it would seem like the time would go by faster," Sima replied.

"I was just saying it seems like we go on for miles day after day, and nothing happens."

"You are right. It does seem that way." Sima bit into some stale bread we had kept from the fort.

"I would rather nothing else happen and that we get safely to Alaska." I looked at both of them. "Too much has happened."

"That is true." Alex looked at me for a second before turning to Sima. "So what are we planning to do tonight besides sit by the fire?"

"Sleep," Sima answered quite determinedly.

Alex laughed a bit. "Yes, we could do that."

Sima pulled off his blankets and stood up. "I am turning in then."

"Already?" I asked.

Sima gave me a knowing look. "Anna, I don't know about you, but this trip is making me extremely worn out." He had a smile on his face, but I could tell that he was telling the truth. It seemed impossible, but Sima had started to look thinner lately. Sima's narrow shoulders did not seem to be able to hold the strain. Alex, on the other hand, still appeared as robust as ever.

"I see what you are saying, but I would rather sit and talk to Alex for a while."

"I understand." Sima smirked and turned away from us. "Well, have a nice chat. I need sleep." Sima was soon snoring away. I marveled at his ability to fall asleep within seconds of bidding us good night.

I sat with Alex by the fire. My heartbeat quickened as I regarded his handsome face.

Alex cleared his throat. "So, how are you feeling?" It seemed like an irrelevant question since we were just talking and saw each other all the time.

"How are we all feeling, Alex?"

"True, I suppose it was a pointless question." I smiled and leaned back on my elbows.

"There is no one else here besides me to hear what you are saying."

"You know Anna. I think that even if you Sima and I lived out here for the rest of our lives, we could be rather happy."

"Do you really think so?" I asked.

"Yes, well, both of you are my closest friends now, and I cannot say I have known anyone better than you or Sima."

"Me too. I never had anyone really except Mary-Louise. I am out here chasing a dream of some sort."

"Every dream is worth chasing, don't you think?" Alex regarded me with his clear blue eyes.

I swallowed hard. For some reason, I was starting to feel somewhat embarrassed. "You are turning into quite the philosopher, aren't you?"

"Nothing else to do around here except travel forward and think," Alex said as he moved over and sat next to me.

"True, I like traveling on dogsleds, though. It can be rather exciting at times."

"That is true. It can be exciting but rather dull after several months. When I reach Alaska, I intend to sleep for ages."

"You could catch up on some sleep now as Sima is doing." I was trying hard not to focus on Alex, and I put all my energy into focusing on some point beyond the fire.

Alex gave me a sidelong glance. "Are you all right?"

"I'm fine," I answered the question. I tried to sound nonchalant.

"If you say so, but you know, you shouldn't try to hide anything from me, Anna."

I turned to look at him. What was he trying to say? "I am not hiding anything. Well, I think I will go to sleep now."

"Already?"

"Yes, as Sima said, we are all tired."

"I am not sure that he said that."

"I am paraphrasing, I suppose." I pulled my blankets around me.

"Go ahead and rest then," Alex said. He did not seem to mind too much that I had decided to retire for the night.

I shrugged to myself. Whenever I thought that perhaps Alex would say something or something good would happen between us, nothing occurred. Alex seemed to be content only to be my friend. I wrapped myself in my blankets in my curtained corner of the tent. I closed my heavy eyelids. I wondered if I would ever stop feeling fatigued.

The next day, I still was weary when I awoke. Exhaustion seemed to hit me full force. My feet dragged. I got ready for the day and hauled myself out of the tent. I gathered a bucket of food that Alex had probably prepared when Sima and I were asleep. There were things that I really liked about Alex. One of them was that he was always so responsible and ready to do the right thing. No matter what happened, Alex would be as steady as a rock. Anyone could always depend on him.

I bent down to feed the dogs. I pet the new dog that Alex had gotten for me. I still dearly missed Bobick. I hoped he would bite his new owners often. I hugged the new dog to me.

"I wish I could call you Bobick number two," I said to the dog. "However, I think that Sima and Alex would not stand for it." It was while I was talking to the new dog that I heard a noise in the woods. I stood up and grabbed the rifle that was leaning against the dogsleds. I stepped forward with caution. I crept into the brush. Whatever was in the woods appeared to be enormous. Perhaps it was a deer or something that we could eat for lunch. As I came closer, my foot hit a branch, and it made a loud crack. Suddenly, out of nowhere, a gigantic moose reared its huge antlers in my direction. I yelled out in fright. For whatever reason, the moose decided that I was his mortal enemy. I felt paralyzed with fear.

The moose snorted loudly. I just gaped at it, my feet frozen to the ground. The moose bent its head low. My only instinct was to run. I forgot all about the rifle that I carried in my hand. I ran for my life and did not look back. I could hear a thud of hooves behind me. The only thing I could think of at that moment was that there was no possible way that I could outrun a moose. There was a loud shot. In distress, I did not stop to think as to who could be shooting. I, for some reason, thought that someone was shooting at me.

As I ran, I heard a loud shout from Alex, "Anna, climb a tree!"

I think I flew up a tree. Just as I grabbed onto the tree branches, I felt a stabbing pain in my back and leg. The moose then withdrew its antlers, and there was another loud shot. There was a thud behind me. I turned my head around with caution. The moose lay unmoving on the ground. Pain shot through me, and I could feel blood running down my leg.

"Don't move, Anna!" Alex shouted to me. I held on to the tree for dear life. I was afraid there could be another moose.

The snow crunched as Alex ran up to me. "Why didn't you shoot at it?"

"I didn't have time to think," I answered. "Can you please help me down?"

"Yes, here, let go slowly." I released the branch and fell back into his arms. He held me tightly and made it quickly out of the forest into the clearing.

Sima ran up to us. "Anna, what were you doing? You could have been killed!"

"Thank you, Sima, for stating the obvious." I turned my head towards Alex's chest. My head was throbbing.

"You're hurt," Alex said, stating a fact that was quite apparent.

"Yes, I think the moose got me with part of his antlers."

"I think he more than got you," Sima said with panic rising in his voice. "Alex, she's dripping blood all over you and the snow. Come on, get her into the tent."

Alex wasted no time and carried me to the tent. He placed me down in the corner on top of all of my blankets.

I looked at Alex's stained clothes. "I am sorry, Alex, I didn't mean to cause such a mess."

"Do not worry about it. This is not your fault."

"Don't fall asleep, Anna. What are we going to do?" Sima's voice had more than a note of fear in it.

"Take care of the wounds," Alex said in a serious voice.

"Why did you go into the woods by yourself?" Sima raised his voice.

"Sima, this is not going to help right now," Alex cut him off sharply.

"All right, Anna, I'll turn you over so I can see what happened." Alex gently lifted me and turned me on my stomach. I felt so much pain at that moment that I almost cried out. I took a deep breath.

"It's all right, Anna." Sima put his hand on my head and stroked my hair.

"Here." Alex took off my jacket and gave it to Sima. He looked at the wounds. "Sima, run and get some hot water and some bandages, quickly." Sima left.

Alex took my hand. "Are you all right?"

I gave him a weak smile. "Of course, I am not all right."

He smiled just a bit in response.

Sima sprinted back in. "Here are the bandages, and the water is boiling."

"Start wiping away all the blood," Alex said to Sima. Since I was lying on my stomach, I was glad not to see the wounds.

"I am happy I shot that moose," Sima said. "He deserved it. Why would he chase Anna anyway?"

"I have no idea," Alex answered.

"Anna, listen, the wound on your back is not very deep, which is good, but the wound on the lower part of your leg is quite deep. I am afraid I will have to sew it up. Can you stand the pain?"

"Alex, I am in so much pain at the moment that I do not think that I would notice."

"Sima, can you please get the boiling water?"

The ordeal of being sewn up was horrible and more painful than I had imagined. I just stuffed a blanket into my mouth so as not to scream out. Tears flowed freely from my eyes. Sima held my hand and tried to comfort me. Finally, Alex finished. My leg felt as if I would never move it again. Alex told me to try to sleep. I did not think I could sleep, but I did not think I could stand the pain any longer. I closed my eyes and was enveloped into the deep comforting darkness of sleep.

I opened my eyes to find Alex sitting next to me and looking at me with a concerned expression. "How are you feeling?" he asked.

"How do you think I'm feeling?"

Alex grimaced. "Probably as good as I felt after having my arm sewn up."

"We are like sewn-up twins," I said, trying to joke. Unfortunately, my joke turned unsuccessful, and I berated myself for making such a stupid comment. I was almost happy that Alex did not answer that remark.

Instead, he changed the subject. "I made some hot tea for you," Alex said. "Here, let me help you sit up." He handed me the hot tea.

"Thank you." I took the cup. My fingertips brushed his, and I wondered if he had let my fingers touch his on purpose. I highly doubted that, especially after my silly comment.

"Now I have a question for you, Anna."

"Yes, what is it?" I asked.

"I want you to get well, but I am unsure of how you feel. Do you think you will be well enough to travel, or would you like to stay here for a few more days and rest?"

I looked straight into his blue eyes. "I want just to travel forward, even if it is just a few miles per day. Anything is better than sitting in one spot knowing that Alaska is so far away."

Alex smiled at me. "I am happy that you said that because then I do not have to convince you to move forward even if you are hurt."

"Alex, I knew that you would want to keep traveling. Thank you for asking, though."

"If you start to feel weak, we will stop right away and rest."

"I will do my best to tell you if I feel weak or hurt."

Alex regarded me for a second and said, "All right then. I will let Sima know that we are going. Although I think he will have a fit."

I laughed. "He never wants to go anywhere anyway."

"That's very true, but he is always very concerned for you. You are seriously the only person that he connects with besides me. "

"I am happy that I have you and Sima here to help me. It's strange, though. Sima seems to be so full of life all the time and so friendly. I would never imagine that he has a difficult time connecting to others."

"Yes, well, he is friendly; he has more in his head than it appears at times."

I gave Alex a mischievous smile. "I certainly hope so." He grinned at me and then left.

I looked at the sloped tent ceiling and wondered if I would ever actually look at the roof of a house again. I felt as if nothing would ever change. My leg hurt, and truthfully I did not think it would be a good idea for me to continue on this trip for a few days. I could understand Alex's determination. Who would not want this monotony to come to an end?

In a few minutes, Sima came storming into the tent. "I can't believe Alex. I think he wants us all to depart from this life. Does he have no consideration for you at all?" Sima sat down next to me.

"What do you mean?"

"I mean, why does he think that he can just keep dragging you on when you have been through such an ordeal?"

"I told Alex that it is all right if we keep going."

"You told him that because you want him to like you. Come on, Anna, you and I both know that you would do anything for him."

"Sima, that might be partly true, but I do want to reach Alaska. I know the difference would only be a few days, but we just cannot stop too many times, or all of the snow will melt, and we will be dragging our sleds to Alaska."

"I have a feeling that the snow will never melt up here. It's cold all the time."

"Yes, but we have to keep going."

"All right, I realize there is no arguing with you and Alex. Both of you are made for each other. If he does not marry you when we get to Alaska, I will be upset with him."

"We have to get to Alaska first. Let's not jump ahead that far."

"You just wait and see." Sima gave me a mischievous smile.

"I'll keep hoping, and you keep planning." I lay back on my blankets. "I am tired now. I need some rest."

"Sleep well." Sima got up and walked out.

I sighed and lay back down. I now regretted that I had not told Alex something different. I wanted to tell him that I would not be able to continue. I just wanted to stay in one spot forever and never travel again. I fell into a deep sleep.

When I awoke on the following day, Sima and Alex were not in the tent. I could not understand what time it was. I sat up and moved gingerly over to the tent opening. I lifted it and looked outside. Sima and Alex were working at the sleds. They appeared to be tying the sleds together and attaching the dogs to pull two sleds at the same time.

"What are you doing?" I called out to them.

"Look, Anna, this way, you do not have to stand or run at all," Alex told me.

"We are rather ingenious if you ask me." Sima grinned in my direction. "Although Alex thought of this, of course."

"Yes, well, I believe you. You would not have thought of it."

Sima smiled. "You have to give me some credit, Anna."

"Anna, get ready. We will help you get situated." Alex waved at me to get back in the tent. Seeing Alex and Sima working so hard to make me comfortable renewed some of my energy.

Alex and Sima helped me get settled into a sled. The way they had tied the sleds together was a good idea, but our progress proved to be slow. It was pretty cumbersome for the dogs to pull two sleds at one time, even though there were two teams of dogs.

"Alex, I am not sure that the dogs are going to hold up much longer," I told him when we stopped for a quick lunch.

"I would rather have the dogs be tired than you not able to move at all. We would never reach Alaska then. Sit tight for a few days, and then we will let you move again." Alex looked so stern when he said those words. I hoped that the fact that he was stern was because he was actually worried about me.

"Alex, you sound as if you are putting a jail sentence on the poor girl," Sima teased him. He sat down next to me on the old log that I was sitting on.

Alex looked a bit flustered. "I just want Anna to be all right, Sima."

"I knew I'd get it out of him," Sima whispered to me and winked. I looked into Sima's kind brown eyes and winked back.

"Sima, what are you whispering about?" Alex asked.

"If it concerned you, we would not be whispering." Sima then laughed and fell back into the snow from the log.

Chapter 15   February 28, 1888

It took three weeks for me to feel as if I could regain normal function. My leg had healed well, and the pain had ceased. Both Sima and Alex had been attentive to me. They took great pains to make me comfortable, and I could not be more grateful to them. Sima kept making jokes to make me feel better, and Alex brought hot tea and made hot stew for us to eat. At night we would sit around a fire and talk. Somehow the incident with the moose had united us even more. We now never seemed to run out of things to say about our travels. Sima and Alex never seemed to lack a sense of humor. They told me a lot about Alaska and their school days.

On a night such as this, I lay on my sled covered in blankets watching Sima and Alex. At this time, they were the dearest people to me on earth. There had never been anyone who cared as much about me as they did.

"We should probably start thinking of what we will do when we reach Alaska," Sima said.

"Don't you think we have plenty of time to think about that later?" I asked.

Sima leaned his head back against his sled. "We keep coming closer and closer to our goal. Before you know it, we will reach our destination."

"Let's hope so," Alex replied.

"First, we have to locate your home, don't we?" I asked. "There's no use reaching Alaska and then not having a place to stay."

"I think I remember how to get home, actually," Alex said. "If we follow our map, we can reach an Indian settlement right on the border of Canada and Alaska. From there, I remember the road. My father and I went there to trade furs."

"Weren't you very young?" I asked.

"Yes, but that has remained in my memory."

"Alex has the memory of a turtle," Sima remarked.

I laughed. "Sima, I don't think that turtles have good memories."

Sima chuckled. "I just thought it might be a funny thing to say."

"Sima, sometimes you are just not that funny," Alex told him.

"The most important thing, Alex, is that I try to be funny. See, you don't even try to be funny."

"Sima, Alex, and I don't have to try to be funny. We just are hilarious by ourselves."

"Why are we talking about this?" Alex asked.

"I don't know. Why do we talk about anything?" Sima asked.

"I think we ought to turn in," I said. "This conversation is getting a bit strange, and we still did not decide what will happen when we get to Alaska."

"I guess it doesn't matter." Sima sent me another wink. "We'll decide that when we get there."

Alex stood up and stretched. "I think I will go to sleep now. Good night."

"Good night, Alex." I watched him walk into the tent.

"Anna, you really like Alex, don't you?" Sima asked when Alex was out of earshot.

"Is it that apparent?"

"Yes, but I think Alex is not aware of your feelings."

"Has he ever said anything about me to you?" I asked.

Sima sat up a bit straighter. "I don't have to tell you that."

"I know, but please, Sima, I would feel better if I knew something."

"Anna, he has never said anything about you that I would consider romantic. I am telling you this as a friend. I am not sure that he likes you in the way you want him to like you."

"He sometimes acts as if he is interested, though," I argued. I so much wanted Alex to like me.

"Let me tell you something, you are the only female he has seen in the past two months, and you are darn attractive, especially now that your hair is growing out. Alex has always thought you were pretty. True feelings take time to build. He has had a lot more experience with women than you have ever had with men. Follow my advice and be friendly for now. I hopefully can help nudge him in the right direction as well. You would have to wait to Alaska to get married anyway."

"Now I feel as if I am silly. You are right, Sima." I was surprised at how perceptive Sima seemed at times.

"It's not silly to fall in love, Anna." Sima's brown eyes clouded for a second. "Anyway, if Alex doesn't marry you, I will."

I laughed at him and climbed out of my sled. "I hope you won't have to make that kind of sacrifice. I better go to bed. Thank you, Sima." He stood up as well.

I hugged him. "Can you truly nudge him in the right direction?" I asked.

"Anna, believe me, I am capable of anything." He wrapped his arm around me. "Good night, and don't you worry about a thing."

The next morning I awoke early and walked outside. I started to feed the dogs and get them ready for the day. As I was about to feed the last of Sima's dogs, I began to feel a bit dizzy. I leaned down to pick up some more food, and I felt myself fall forward, and everything went black. I opened my eyes to find Alex looking down at me.

"Are you all right?" he asked.

I looked back at him. "I do not think so."

"Here, let me help you sit up." He pulled me into a sitting position.

At that moment, Sima came out of the tent with a cup of hot tea. "Drink this. You may feel better." Sima handed me the teacup.

Alex gave me a critical stare. "You know, you should have never been out here feeding the dogs on your own. You are not strong enough yet."

"I know, Alex. I wanted to be of some help, and I felt just fine this morning."

"It's not her fault, Alex," Sima cut in. "All of us are weak. We do not have enough food to eat, and we are wasting a lot of energy traveling so hard every day."

I gave Sima a grateful smile. "I suppose all of us must be extra careful. Anna could have frozen out here. I think we should not go anywhere on our own, even outside of our tent."

There was truth to what Alex said, and after that episode, I decided to listen to his instructions. The memory of Fur Hunter lying frozen in the snow came back to me. The fear of the same thing happening to me, Sima, or Alex paralyzed me.

How many more weeks could I stand of this endless dreary travel? No matter how much I liked Sima and Alex, I was not sure I would be able to endure. Also, for some reason, my feet had begun to hurt more. We had more important matters to think of at that time, so I decided to ignore all of my aches for the moment and push on. Sima and Alex's presence comforted me, but I knew that if anything happened to either of them, I would not be able to keep going.

As the long weeks continued, we did not meet with any bad weather, and the temperatures seemed almost warm, we traveled for many hours a day, and our spirits lifted considerably. My feet, however, continued to hurt. It began to get painful to even step on the sole of my foot. I knew that this problem had to be fixed. However, I was afraid to remove my boots. I realized that I had not taken my shoes off or changed my socks in a very long time. None of us had. It was too cold, and we usually slept in our boots. There were no extra wool socks to wear either.

I took my chance when Sima and Alex went hunting. I felt embarrassed to show Alex and Sima my feet. I also hoped that I could take care of the problem on my own. When I settled myself into the tent and took my boots off, I was horrified to see that there were about four large holes in each sock. I also noticed that in every place there was a hole, a big blister had formed. When I removed my socks completely, I saw that other blisters had formed in some other areas of my feet and that some of them were oozing blood.

I could hardly look at my feet. I understood how stupid I had been, not even to check and see the problem when my feet began to hurt. I did not know what to do. I just sat there staring at my feet in disbelief. I was about to put my socks back on when Sima burst into the tent.

He stopped as soon as he walked in. "Anna, what have you done to yourself now?"

I looked up at him like a guilty child. "I don't know how this happened, but my feet began to hurt, and I decided to see what the problem was."

"You mean you haven't checked this whole time?" Sima asked in surprise.

"Well, if you haven't noticed, it has been a little bit cold lately," I told him. I was irritated.

"Hey, Sima, what's the hold-up? Did you tell her that we got a deer?" Alex came into the tent and stood behind Sima.

"I did not get a chance to tell her that, no," Sima told Alex.

Alex now also stared at me. "What happened?"

"She has nasty blisters, Alex," Sima said as if he had not been staring at me for exactly three minutes now.

"The only thing we can do for now is bandage your feet. Why didn't you do that before?" Alex asked.

"I didn't think of it before," I told him.

"I do that every other day." Alex kneeled on the ground and started to pull bandages from his bag.

"Why didn't you tell me?" I asked. I had never seen him or Sima changing bandages. They must have done so when I was not around because they also may have been embarrassed.

"I thought you would have thought of that yourself."

Sima gave Alex an exasperated look. "Listen, genius, we are not all as smart as you. There is no need to insult Anna."

"I was not trying to insult her," Alex said defensively. "Anyway, Sima, get some more bandages from my sled and get some snow that we can boil." He then turned to me and said, "We'll wash your feet before bandaging them."

"No, I thought we would leave them the way they are," I snapped at him. I could not help being a little sarcastic.

"Sorry." Alex looked at me for a second and then left me alone again in the tent.

I felt like I would cry at any moment. I worked hard to keep my composure because I did not want Alex and Sima to think of me as a little girl who needed to be comforted and constantly cared for. I already had a feeling that they believed that. I did feel silly for not having thought of taking care of my feet on my own. I was beginning to realize that I struggled with a lack of judgment.

Alex came back in, and Sima did as well. Together they helped me clean and bandage my feet. Alex had a look of disgust on his face, although I saw that he was trying to hide it. I had to admit that I was a bit hurt by how he acted; he was not my father.

After my feet had been bandaged, he turned to me. "It's not your fault. This weather and your boots definitely do not do anything in your favor."

"Unfortunately, I do not have other boots to wear."

Alex sat down across from me as Sima started to pour hot tea. "Yes, it was quite ridiculous for all of us to believe Jason Shubert when he said we would make it so far. He did not prepare us at all for this trip."

Sima handed me a cup of tea. "I have no idea why I am even going to Alaska," Sima said and then started to swallow his hot tea as if it were the coldest drink in the world.

Alex studied him for a second. "Come on, Sima, you know that your family is there, and you would be left alone in Maine if you stayed behind."

"I know." Sima held his empty teacup and stared into it. "It is just that I do not think my parents even want me. Also, look at us; every one of us is beaten up. Poor Anna is hardly going to be able to move after this trip is over."

I took another sip of tea. "Well, there is nothing we can do but to go further."

"Yes, just keep on going." I studied Sima for a second. He sounded very cynical at the moment.

Alex gave Sima a stern look. "You know you will have to face your parents at some point in your life, Sima."

"Yes, well, I think that when we reach Alaska, I'll be so happy that we finally got there that I will not mind talking to my parents."

"Sima, you can always forgive your parents. Tell them that you want to be closer to them and that you felt that they abandoned you," I exclaimed this and was not sure what made those words leave my mouth.

Sima studied me for a second. "I haven't talked to my parents in about ten years. We hardly ever wrote to each other when I was in Maine. Alex's family is more of a family than my parents. They left me with Alex's family and moved to southern Alaska. They felt that going to New England would be a good opportunity."

"They probably wanted what was best for you."

"Yes, but everything worked the wrong way. I would rather have stayed with them all those years than having wasted my time studying and then gone on this ridiculous journey."

"Everything has a purpose Sima," I said gently.

"Anna's right; there is a reason for everything."

"A reason that almost all of our friends died?" Sima spat out.

"Even that." Alex put a hand on Sima's shoulder. Sima turned to look at Alex and gave him a wry smile.

I decided to interject. "This conversation is getting a bit too sad. We won't get anywhere if we sit around moping. At least we are alive, and there is a reason for that too."

Sima then smiled at me. "Thank you for trying to make me feel better. You are the one who should be sad. You have got the most wounded feet of anyone I have ever seen."

"I'll make it to Alaska, Sima." I smiled back at him.

Sima stood up. "Now there is a girl with spirit, Alex. She will probably make it to Alaska before we do. Anyway, there is a reason we got a deer today; we do not want to starve tonight. Anna, get that pot boiling since I hope you can stand now, and we will have some venison stew tonight."

That evening, our sad mood of the morning had dissipated. We ate and watched the puppy that Alex got for me play in the snow. We had decided to keep the name Snow Spots. He was still so small. We threw him bits of venison, and he chased them around and ate them up. We laughed as he chased them and then ran to us and wagged his tail as if begging for more. I loved my little puppy and was ever grateful to Alex for buying him for me.

Sima and Alex also sang a few songs. I loved the melodies, but I did not know them. They were old Russian songs that they had learned from their fathers when they were younger. I ended up humming along to them. Finally, we all turned in, and I again felt as if this was the life I was meant to live. However, I was not sure that I wanted to remain in the middle of the wilderness for the rest of my life. I still hummed one of the melodies in my head as I drifted off to sleep behind the cover of many blankets.

The next day, we traveled further. We hoped that we would find Fort McMurray. According to Jason Shubert's map, it seemed that we could not be more than three weeks of travel from the fort. Still, I felt that it was impossible to find a relatively small trading post in the middle of the wilderness. However, Alex believed that he knew everything and was unwavering in his confidence that we would find the fort.

That evening, when Alex and Sima were outside feeding the dogs, I came into the tent. I did not complain to Sima and Alex, but the pain in my feet was horrible. I took some bandages from my sled and boiled some water. I peeled off my boots. I was horrified to see that blood had seeped through the dressing. I unwrapped the bandage and sat washing off my foot. I was so disgusted and tired that I had trouble fighting off tears.

Suddenly Sima walked in and stopped to look at me. "Do you need any help with that?"

"No." I tried to avoid his eyes.

"Anna, what's the matter?" Sima asked and sat down across from me.

"Nothing," I blurted out as an unexpected loud sob escaped my throat.

"You wouldn't be crying if nothing was wrong."

"Just look at this mess," I said as I pointed to the pile of bloody bandages that I had pulled off my foot. Then I put my head on my knees, and the tears spilled out of my eyes. I was indeed in a lot of pain, and I finally let out all of it.

"Now, Anna, pull yourself together. I'll help you." Sima picked up a bandage and took my foot, and started to wrap it. "You see, if you ask others to help you, the task is so much simpler."

I gave Sima a watery smile. "Thank you, Sima."

Sima took my other foot then and began to wrap it. He did so in an expert fashion. "Look, Anna, I do apologize, but honestly, this is one of the worst cases of blisters I have ever seen." He said this with a smile, but I noticed he had no trace of disgust on his face. I was grateful to him, and I felt ten times better because of the kindness that he showed me.

"Thank you."

"Here, you stay sitting. It won't do you any good hobbling around. I'll go get rid of this mess." He patted my foot and stood up, and gathered all of the bandages. I wondered what he was planning to do with them, but I guessed it did not matter.

"Well, my dear, I am also going to get you some food to eat," Sima said as he got ready to exit the tent. "You stay here."

"Sima, do you think that we will get to Fort McMurray?"

Sima looked down at me and shook his head. "I don't think so, but so far, we have gotten everywhere Alex wanted us to go."

I gave Sima a mischievous smile. "Perhaps we should listen to him and put more trust in him then."

Sima laughed. "There's no reason to do so. Anyway, it's much too fun to poke fun at him. He's too serious all the time." Then Sima stopped and gave me an apologetic look. "I am sorry, I forgot you like him."

"It's all right, Sima. I like poking fun at him too."

He raised his eyebrows. "I wonder why."

"Oh, stop it." I laughed.

"I have to go, or you'll be hungry. I'll be back." Sima walked out. I felt much better after talking to him. I lay down on my blankets; however, my feet remained in pain. Sima had done an excellent job, and I tried not to think of my feet too much.

Soon Sima and Alex entered again. Sima handed me a cup of venison stew. I held the warm mug in my hands, treasuring the warmth as it seeped through me. The waft of scent that I got from the stew did even more to lift my spirits.

"How are you feeling?" Alex asked as he sat down.

"Better," I answered him. "Sima helped me bandage my feet, and I feel so much better."

"Sima seems to be turning into quite a doctor," Alex observed.

"I know, sewing people up and bandaging feet. I'll be able to be a doctor at Fort Yukon too by the time we get there if we keep up at this rate."

"Everyone at Fort Yukon will be cured of every single disease they had by the time we get there," Alex replied.

"Not one of us has escaped a close brush with death," I put in.

"Let's just hope that's the end of it," Alex stated.

"Definitely," Sima said. "I didn't enjoy smashing my head up."

"We can't afford for you to hit your head too much," Alex said. "You're strange enough as it is."

"Ha, speak for yourself."

"You know what they say; it takes one fool to recognize another," Alex said.

Sima lay back on his pillow. "Who says that?"

Alex chuckled and lay down too. "I heard it somewhere."

"I wish that we were already in Alaska," I commented.

"Why is that?" Sima asked.

"Because then I would not have to worry about losing either of you."

Sima turned on his side to look at me. "That's sweet, Anna."

"Don't worry about losing us," Alex said. "I think I would be more worried about losing you."

Sima gave me a meaningful look, while Alex was not paying attention. I just shook my head at him. I could not explain, though, how elated I felt when Alex spoke like that. I hoped that Alex would grow to love me just as much as I loved him. Even the slightest look could send my heart into a beating fit. I hoped Sima was right, that he could point his friend in the right direction. I snuggled deep into my blankets, and after a short prayer for safety, I fell asleep.

Chapter **16**   March 25, 1888

A few days later, as we traveled on, I noticed a strange shape covered with snow. "Alex, look." I pulled at his sleeve. "What do you suppose this is?"

Alex called for his dogs to halt. "Don't know."

"What is it?" Sima asked as he pulled up from behind.

"We are not sure." Alex grabbed his rifle. He came up to the mound he kicked it with his boot. There was a loud clunk, and the snow fell from a large rusty metal trap. Sima and I exchanged glances.

"What could that be doing here?" Sima asked.

"It seems old," I observed.

"We could be somewhere near the fort," Alex said.

"Alex, this is one trap in the middle of nowhere."

"Yes, that might be true, but let's turn and head this way. If we don't see anything else, we will turn around and follow our original route.

"Another one of Alex's brilliant plans," Sima whispered to me. I smiled at him.

Alex turned his head towards us. "What's that, Sima?"

"Oh nothing, Alex, I think it's a good idea."

We made a decision, and we followed Alex as he led the way. Much to Sima's chagrin, Alex's instinct was correct. Soon there was a trail of half-hidden traps. Some of them looked old, but then some new ones began to appear as well.

"Whoever set up these traps can't be too brilliant," Sima observed. "There are no animals in these traps, and they are all ridiculously close together."

"Perhaps, it is more than one trapper."

"We could be nearing Fort McMurray," Alex said, his voice was hopeful.

I shrugged my shoulders. "Maybe."

We decided to push on through the day. We traveled a few miles further and found no more traps. This began to worry us, and we were afraid that we had turned off course for absolutely no reason other than for some inconsequential traps. Alex urged us to try to go on one more mile, and then if our search proved fruitless, we decided to return to our original trail. With wary hearts, we plodded on through the heavy snow. After traveling about three-quarters of a mile, we heard voices to our right.

"Listen," Sima said as he put a hand on my shoulder.

"I hear it."

"Careful now," Alex warned. The memory of our last meeting with trappers still lay fresh in our minds, and we certainly could not afford to lose supplies or dogs this time. We slowly traveled towards the sound of conversation and soon came upon a frozen river. Not far from the bank sat four rather ragged-looking men. I realized, however, that we probably looked worse than they did. One of the men who seemed to be in his late thirties turned in our direction and appeared rather startled at the sight of us.

"Who are you?" he asked suddenly as he motioned to his companions to look towards us.

"We are looking for Fort McMurray," Alex answered them.

The man stood up and came towards us. "You's didn't answer my question."

"We do not need to answer it," Sima told him.

"You're a great help," I whispered to Sima.

"I'm Matthew Roberts." The man told us when he was standing about two feet from us.

"Hello, Matthew," Alex said and gave him a short nod. "Now, I am not sure why it would make any difference to you who we are. All we want to find out is where the fort is; if there is a fort near here."

"Well, whoever you are, we was just trying to be friendly." The man then turned to his companions. "These boys is looking for the fort."

One of his companions snorted. "If you call those run-down shacks down the river a fort, then it is about a mile away if you follow this river."

Alex nodded. "Thank you, sir." He turned back to us. "Let's go."

We were about to pull away when one of the men called out to us. "You boys sure are not friendly."

"We just really require supplies and rest."

We were about to move forward again when one of the men called to us. "Come on back, we won't hurt you, and we do have some fresh-baked bread from the fort and some fish stew. The stew's fresh."

Alex, Sima, and I stopped in our tracks. "That does sound appetizing," I told Alex.

Alex nodded. "All right, let's turn around." We came back to the men and joined them for a meal.

"Keep your head down," Sima whispered to me. "We can't have them know that you're a woman."

I nodded in agreement and sat silently throughout the meal. I felt as if I was eating the most scrumptious meal of my life. I allowed the warmth of the stew to seep through my body slowly. The men told us that they had been staying at the fort trapping since October. They told us that in about another week, they would be heading east with their furs.

"I's tired of sitting around here cooped up like a bird in a cage," Matthew Roberts told us.

I thought at the moment that I would not mind sitting like that for the rest of my life. There was certain predictability in a situation like that. All I wanted was to feel as if I knew what the next day would bring.

"So, where are you boys headin'?"

"Alaska, Fort Yukon," Sima responded quickly.

One of the men studied us quizzically. "Where's you comin' from?"

I saw the look of hesitation on Alex's and Sima's faces. I knew that we probably sounded plumb crazy to everyone. I knew Alex did not want to impart too much information to these men. "Prince of Wales Fort," Alex told them firmly. "Thank you for the soup; we really must get going." He then stood up and nodded to us. Sima and I stood as if Alex had trained us to do so. I understood that he did not want history to repeat itself, and the less time we spent with people we did not know, the better. We moved to our sleds and started getting our dogs ready to leave.

"You boys better remember to be a bit friendlier. Men around here don't like unfriendly folk."

Sima and I exchanged glances. We knew what happened when someone became too friendly.

Sima gave them a smile that looked more like a frown. "Thank you for letting us know."

We then pulled away as quickly as possible. When we were out of hearing range, Alex said to us, "I am not sure whether I am just nervous from the last time that we met men on the trail or not, but I did not trust those men."

Sima laughed. "Of course, they is just friendly folk."

Alex's serious expression softened a bit as he smiled. "All right, perhaps we should follow their advice. I do not know that we have a better option."

I laughed at Sima's accent. "I just hope that there are no men like that up at the fort."

Sima winked at me. "I agree with you, uncultured, I would say."

"We certainly won't find much culture up here in the middle of nowhere," Alex told us. I mentally agreed with him. Although I did not think Alex, Sima, or I were the best judges of culture.

Soon the fort came into view, and those men were undoubtedly correct. This place was not much of a fortress, but a cluster of wooden buildings sat at the river's edge. Some of them were not much bigger than my cabin in Maine. My heart sank. We were supposed to get some rest here. I hoped to sleep in a warm cabin for at least two nights. It did not seem as if we would have a room, let alone a cabin.

"We had better find the commanding general," Sima said as we got closer.

"If there even is a commanding general," I countered. As it appeared, there was one. A man came out on the front step of the first cabin that we saw. He seemed to be too friendly.

"Hello there! Captain James Francis here!" he called out and waved his arms wildly in the air as if he was waving to a lost ship.

"Perhaps we should turn back," Sima whispered to me under his breath.

"They aren't only friendly but half crazy," Alex added quietly.

"Stop before he hears you," I added.

We cautiously pulled up to Captain James Francis. He jumped from the step of the cabin and sprinted over to us.

"You boys out trapping?" he asked with an enormous amount of energy.

"No, sir, we are just stopping by on our way to Fort Yukon."

"Fort Yukon?" The man's eyes almost fell out of his head because he opened them so wide. "You've got quite to go from here."

"Yes, we have come a long way too," Sima told him. "We are from Maine."

"Maine? The United States?"

"No, outer states," Sima answered with just the right measure of seriousness.

"Sima," Alex hissed a warning under his breath.

"Don't know where those are, that's for sure. I think you boys are just pulling my leg." Then Captain James Francis proceeded to laugh so loudly I thought I would go deaf. Sima, Alex, and I just exchanged awkward glances.

"Guests such as you should have a place to stay, that's for sure! I'll call someone to take care of your dogs. You boys come in and have some hot tea and cake."

We were bustled into the captain's cabin, and before we knew it, we had cups of hot tea in our hands and large pieces of cake. We had not even had time to take our coats off, and the blazing fire that came from the fireplace built of rock seemed a bit too warm to me, although it was quite a relief after the cold of the outside. While I traveled, I thought that I would forget what it was like to be warm. The tea also seemed a bit too warm, and the cake felt dry. I could not even figure out what the flavor of the cake was supposed to be.

"So, what is there that we can do for you boys?" asked Captain Francis.

"If it's not too much trouble, we would like a place to stay for two nights," Alex said.

"Not too much trouble!" Captain Francis exclaimed with too much enthusiasm. I wondered if he ever spoke calmly. "There is a place where all of you can stay, about a half-mile from these buildings. There are a few cabins. One of them is empty. It is not very large, but you could fit the three of you comfortably in two rooms and also have some space for your dogs."

"All right, that is all we could ask for." Alex nodded at the two of us as Sima, and I mutely nodded back. I felt a bit overwhelmed by the captain's enthusiasm.

"Also, would you happen to have a medic here?" Sima asked suddenly, as if a thought had shaken him out of his mute state.

"Yes! My wife is the medic here!" The poor woman, I thought. I wondered if her head ever hurt as horribly as mine hurt at the moment.

"You have a wife?" Sima sounded as surprised as I felt. I saw Alex nudge Sima.

"Yes, quite a beautiful woman, ELSIE!!!" The windows shook as he called for her. I almost fell out of my chair. Out of a side door, a young woman of about twenty-five appeared. She looked too young and too beautiful to be the wife of such an energetic captain.

"Yes?"

"One of these boys needs a medic, I assume," he told her and then turned back to us. "Which one of you is it?" I sat as still as stone. I was not sure why Sima had asked about a medic.

"It's Andrei, his feet are hurt, and he needs serious care," Sima told him.

"Well, then follow me." She motioned to me to follow her. I stood up timidly, set down my teacup and cake on the table, and followed her to the next room. The room she led me to was clean and bright. I had never been in a doctor's office, but I imagined that a doctor's operating room might look like this.

"I studied to become a nurse in the East before marrying James," she told me. "I was the only one who knew anything about medicine out here, and trapping is a hard job. I learned as I went along. After living in this place for three years, I have learned quite a lot. I could be a doctor, but I doubt that anyone would allow a woman doctor into a hospital." I nodded, silently agreeing with her.

She pointed to the table. "Here, sit."

I sat on the table and realized that I was still wearing my coat. "Do you mind if I take my coat off?"

"Of course not."

I slowly removed my coat and tossed it on a nearby chair.

"It's your feet?" she asked.

"Yes, bad blisters." I tried to answer as quietly as I could. I did not want anyone to realize that I was not a boy. I raised my feet on the table, and she removed my boots and looked at the bandages.

"These bandages are done well," she said to me.

"One of my friends," I answered quickly.

She started to remove the bandages, and I saw the look of horror that she tried to hide. "This is not good. Not only are the blisters terrible, but there is also an infection. I'll wash your feet first. This situation happens if you travel far and have not given your feet the proper time to heal. I have a salve against infections that I will give for you to use." She started to wash my feet with warm water.

As she washed them, she kept looking at me curiously, and then she finally looked straight into my eyes and asked, "Why are you lying? You are a girl, aren't you?"

I looked miserably at my hands and nodded.

"What are you doing in this place?" she asked with a horrified expression.

"Please do not tell anyone. I am traveling to Alaska with these boys because I had nothing left back in Maine. They know the truth about me, but no one else discovered the truth, and we have done our best to keep it a secret."

"Are you going to marry one of them?"

"I hope I will. He does not know how I feel."

She shook her head and smiled. "I hope he will marry you. I can't believe how brave you are."

"What about you? You came all this way and have lived here for three years."

She took out a towel and dipped it into a liquid that stung when it touched my foot. "I knew what lay ahead of me, and I had a man who loved me. I knew he would take care of me." I could not imagine wanting to be with the captain, and I hoped I could keep a straight face.

She took the salve from the shelf and started to put it on my feet. "Yes, he is older than me by fifteen years, and he is not what anyone would expect as a romantic suitor. Nevertheless, he has always been kind to me and has loved me more than I could ever imagine. My dear, make sure that the man loves you before you give your whole heart to him."

I started to feel miserable. I knew that my heart would just tear apart if Alex did not respond to my feelings. I did not know if I was being wise. I said no more on the subject.

"I will give this to you to put on your feet every day. I hope you will be able to heal even with traveling. I will also give you a whole year's worth of bandages, supposing that you can fit them somewhere on your sleds." She smiled then. "It is nice to have another girl to speak with. There are very few women, only male trappers."

"It is nice to see a woman too, after being surrounded by men so long," I told her and finally dared to smile back.

"Do not worry," she said as she finished bandaging my feet. "Your secret is safe with me. I do not usually keep secrets from James, but I will tell him after you leave. He tends to spread news without even meaning to do so." The way she smiled when she spoke about him was so pleasant. There was no sense of worry in her voice, and she seemed to be so much in love with this loud, enthusiastic man. Love was a strange phenomenon.

I put my coat and cap back on as we walked out of the room. As we entered, Sima and Alex were getting ready to follow the captain to our home for the next few days.

The cabin that the captain brought us to was bigger than our tent, and Alex and Sima insisted that I take a room to myself and said that they would bunk with the dogs. It was rather pleasant to have more privacy than a simple blanket as a wall in front of my bedspread. Although the mattress was rather hard, it was much softer than blankets on the ground. I plopped myself down on it and fell asleep without planning to do so.

I was awakened by Alex shaking my shoulder lightly. "Do you want something to eat?"

"Already?"

"Yes, you've been sleeping for four hours."

I sat up quickly. "I am sorry, Alex. I did not mean to fall asleep. I did not even help with the dogs."

Alex smiled and shrugged his shoulders. "It does not matter. Sima and I took care of everything. Sima and I will be waiting for you. Mrs. Captain Francis brought some food for us. Our supper is in our room."

"She is a nice lady," I told him.

"Yes, I agree. Captain Francis is a lucky man, albeit a little odd."

"You know yourself that living out here in the wilderness will do strange things to anyone."

"Ha, you must be right. Although I am sure of one thing, it certainly makes you hungry, so don't be too long getting ready for supper." He exited the room.

I smiled and hummed to myself as I brushed through my hair with my fingers. I was happy that there was no mirror in the room. I was afraid to look at myself. I could feel that my cheeks were sunken and that my arms were thinner than I ever remembered them. Still, I could not help feeling lighthearted at the prospect of staying in a place with a mattress for two nights.

When I walked into the room, Sima and Alex were already sitting at the table. The small table was laid out with a platter of fish in sauce and fresh rolls of bread. The smell of the food was tantalizing. I had to do everything in my power not to run to the table and start stuffing food into my mouth.

"That man is lucky. Every man needs a woman who can cook," Alex said to Sima.

"How about we stop talking and eat? That food looks too good to sit there for too long," I said to both of them. They both nodded their heads in agreement.

We all stood and said a prayer. Then we sat down to the most delicious supper of my entire life. The fish seemed to melt in my mouth, and the bread was soft and warm. There was complete silence for at least fifteen minutes as we enjoyed the feast.

After the break of silence, Sima stood up. "I think I have to get some food to the dogs."

"Why don't you eat some more?" I asked him.

"No, I am full. This food is very filling." He stood up and took his coat and then turned to look at me and gave me a meaningful look so Alex would not notice. I smiled back up at him. I adored Sima for trying so hard to make things work between Alex and me.

As Sima walked out, I turned to Alex. "So, how long are you planning to stay here?"

"Don't you think that is up to all of us?"

"No, not necessarily, you have made that decision on your own before."

"Well, I think that we are all essential, don't you? Anyway, let us wait a few more days, perhaps than originally planned, so your feet heal a bit more. I do want you to be able to walk when we reach Alaska."

His smile melted my heart. I was flattered, and a bit surprised that he was becoming so much more considerate. Perhaps he had become more aware of the fact that this trip was never-ending. At that moment, Sima returned, and he gave me a questioning look as he entered. I just shook my head quickly at him, so Alex would not notice. He came over and sat down at the foot of his bed.

"That must be record timing for you to feed the dogs," Alex observed. I hoped I heard a bit of disappointment in his voice at the fact that Sima had returned so quickly.

Sima shrugged. "I have had a lot of practice. Anyway, I wanted to get back in time to show Anna the surprise that Mrs. Captain Francis baked up for us." He then reached under the bed and pulled out a plate covered with a towel.

He nodded his head in my direction. "Pull the towel off."

I did so, and underneath the towel, I discovered a cake iced with white topping. "Quite the culinary wonderworker."

Sima laughed. "Yes, in this hole in the ground."

"It's a fort, my friends, a fort," Alex added. We then proceeded to laugh hysterically. For some unknown reason, everything seemed much funnier than it was. I believed at times that we had already all lost our minds and did not realize it. Perhaps we were even crazier than Captain James Francis.

Chapter **17**   March 29, 1888

After some discussion, we decided to stay at Fort McMurray for four nights and then continue. It was a nice uneventful break during our trek, and I felt less emaciated due to Mrs. Captain Francis. Her cooking held us through the few days. I was in awe of her kindness. She would trek a half-mile through the snow to bring us meals, and I felt that what she provided to us was the best that they had. Also, sometimes Mrs. Captain Francis would stay after she brought us our food, and she and I would chat. I relished having female company. However, I had never had any company really before I had come on this journey.

Still, it was so pleasant to talk to her, and I hoped with all my heart that there would be other girls that I could talk to when I reached Alaska. Alex had spoken of his adopted sister, Katya, in Alaska several times, and I wondered if she would be as lovely as the captain's wife.

The evening before we left, Alex, Sima, and I sat together in our cabin enjoying the last pieces of yet another wonderful cake baked by Elsie. I relished the savory taste of each morsel in my mouth. With my eyes closed, I felt the taste of butter from the cake fill my mouth. Sima's laugh interrupted my enjoyment. I opened my eyes and found Alex and Sima both staring at me.

"What are you doing?" Sima asked with a smirk.

"Just enjoying the cake. I am sorry, I did not realize I had an audience."

"Yes, well, Elsie promised to make us some more for the road."

"It won't be fresh, and I have become so tired of dry food."

Alex raised his mug of hot tea. "I agree to that."

"Anyway, Anna," Sima started, "Alex and I are relieved that you have had a chance to rest during these last few days. Now you won't drag us down for the rest of the trip."

I looked up at him, surprised that he would say something so inconsiderate. When our eyes met, I realized that he was teasing. "Well, you two have truly been so helpful. I know I have given you a lot to put up with."

"Don't worry about it," Alex said. "Sima and I have a bit of a surprise for you to keep your spirits up during the last leg of our long journey."

"A surprise for me?"

"Yes, we do like you, Anna. We are happy that we have a beautiful girl with us all the time."

"I am not sure that I am so beautiful, especially after so many days of travel."

Alex waved his hand in dismissal at my statement. "After you get to Alaska and put on a few pounds, you will be fine."

"Anyway, this is from me," Sima said as he pulled a little pouch out of his pocket and handed it to me. I looked at it. The stitches were obviously hand sewn, but I could see that he had made an effort to make it look nice.

"Look inside, why don't you?"

I peeked inside and found a beautiful carved wooden heart that was about an inch in height and an inch across. My name was carved into the heart.

"This is beautiful." I let out a breath as I held the heart in my hand. I was in awe of the intricate detailing.

Sima cleared his throat. "Here is a string to put through the knob on the top." He pulled out a string from his pocket. "I just wanted to give you something nice to wear all the time. You might feel more like a girl with some kind of jewelry."

"It's lovely, Sima." I put the string through the loop and then asked him to tie it around my neck.

Sima looked over at Alex. "Now it's his turn."

I could tell that they were both not comfortable with presenting me with gifts. Alex pulled out something wrapped in paper and handed it to me. It was a soft package. I opened it and found two pairs of colorfully knitted pink and blue socks.

"I apologize about the color," he said self-consciously, shrugging his shoulders. "Those are the only colors that Elsie said she had."

"He knit them himself," Sima said with a laugh.

"Mrs. Captain Francis did have to help me with most of it."

"It is the best present I have ever received." My heart burst with happiness at the thought that Alex had spent time knitting socks just for me. "Thank you, Alex." I suddenly forgot myself and hugged Alex with all my might. I was surprised that he hugged me back.

Sima cleared his throat and stated, "I'll go make sure the dogs are comfortable."

I pulled back from Alex with a sudden pang of guilt. I had not even thanked Sima. "Wait." I put my hand on Sima's shoulder.

He turned to me and grinned. "I think that you were just too overwhelmed with the beauty of my gift to thank me." While Sima was smiling, I was not sure if I could detect just a hint of dejection in his voice.

"I am sorry, Sima." I touched the heart that now hung around my neck. "It is stunning."

"I knew you'd like it." Sima smiled again and walked out of the small house.

*****

Upon Sima's return, I turned to both him and Alex. "Before we leave, I have to write a letter."

Sima looked up from the piece of wood he had just begun to chisel. "Whom are you writing a letter to?"

"To Matthew's wife. He asked me to do so a few days before the blizzard."

Alex tilted his head at a curious angle. "Why?"

"Matthew told me that he felt something could go wrong."

Sima placed his knife on the small table that stood next to the entrance to the cabin. "What are you thinking of writing?"

I sat down. "I have no idea. He gave me a letter to enclose in mine. I have no clue how long it will take a letter to reach Maine from this desolate place. However, I just thought that I should still send it while I have a chance." I fingered the letter from Matthew that lay in my shirt pocket.

Sima looked at the ground with a sad expression on his face. "His poor wife."

Alex stood. "I wish this had not happened. We can look back and think of every option, but the truth remains, that we have to let Matthew go."

"Unfortunately, it's a depressing truth."

I looked towards Sima. "I feel like I want to hang on to this letter. I feel as if this letter has kept Matthew alive for me. Somehow writing down these words and mailing his letter only makes everything more definite."

Alex walked towards the door. "It might help to put some closure on the situation. I have to get our dogs ready for tomorrow. Let me know if you need help."

I stared after Alex as he shut the door. "Somehow, that did not help me feel better."

Sima walked over to me and touched my elbow. "Listen, you knew Matthew the best of all of us. You know he was a good man who stood up for you when you needed him the most. You can't do anything else but write from the heart. You've got one of the best hearts of anyone I know."

I sent Sima a fleeting smile. "I doubt that. I'll try to write from the heart."

That night in my room, I agonized over every word before putting pen to paper. My letter was finally finished when the clock on the wall had chimed one in the morning. I sealed Matthew's letter in mine. The action felt so final and horrid.

"I've done what you wanted, Matthew," I whispered into the night. I hoped that wherever he was, he heard me.

✶✶✶✶

Early the following day, I walked to the cabin where Elsie had told me that they collected the post. A post cart would travel through every few months. I decided it would be best that Matthew's wife receive the letter no matter how long it would take to reach her. I had no idea if I would have a chance to mail the letter ever again. After taking a few measured steps across the open field, I heard someone walking behind me. It was Alex.

"Where are you headed off to?" I asked as he came up to me.

"I decided to send a letter to Joseph Shubert. I wanted to let him know that we had heard the news of his father. Also, I am forwarding him our address in Alaska. Hopefully, he will write to us if he has any news."

I clenched the letter to Matthew's wife in my hands. "I hope that he will write to us that the news is good. I have had enough of bad news lately. Does the post travel from your home?"

"Not really. We would usually have to take our letters to Fort Yukon and then travel to the fort every so often. Usually, if one person from our neck of the woods would travel to the fort, they would collect all the letters from their neighbors and then send them out all at once."

"I can't wait to see your home."

"I'm looking forward to it as well." Alex reached over and opened the door to the cabin that contained the mailroom.

I turned to glance back across the field before entering. I noticed that Sima stood outside our lodgings. He was leaning against the wall smoking a pipe. I felt a bit disconcerted since his eyes appeared glued to us. I gave him a little wave, and he responded with a short wave of his hand. Afterward, he put out his pipe in his mouth and re-entered the cabin. A wave of guilt washed over me. I could not understand why. Perhaps I needed to ask Sima if something was bothering him.

After leaving the letter on the mail cabin's table with a note and an address, I felt a sense of relief. I had completed the task that Matthew had set out for me. I headed back to our cabin to finish packing. Alex walked towards the sleds to ready them for our journey.

Sima was tying up his supplies into a bag as I entered. He glanced up as I walked in. "Good morning."

"Good morning. Is everything all right?" I was careful to keep suspicion from my voice.

Sima looked back at his bag and seemed to pretend to be busy with the string. "What do you mean?"

"It's just that when you were outside before, you seemed to be preoccupied with your thoughts."

Sima gave me a fleeting smile. "You seem more observant than usual this morning. My thoughts must have just trailed off. I had just stepped out for a quick smoke."

I reached for the bag that stood next to his. "What were you thinking about?"

Sima pulled a final knot onto his bag. "That is none of your concern." He grinned and then walked out of the cabin with his brown cloth bag. I looked after Sima, thoroughly confused. It was unusual for him to keep secrets or to seem to act mysteriously. Of course, Sima always loved to joke around, and perhaps he was just being silly.

I stood next to Elsie as we prepared to leave. She made sure that I had packed the salve for my feet and carefully instructed me to put it on my feet every day. She also gave us what seemed like endless amounts of food to keep us going. After I placed the food into my bag, I turned around and hugged her.

She returned my embrace. "You are so brave to be going out into this crazy wilderness."

"No, you are the brave ones. I do not know how you have survived here for so long."

"I will miss you. If I am ever in Fort Yukon, I will look for you."

I smiled and felt a stab of sadness in my heart. I knew that the chances of me seeing her again were minimal. They did not even exist. How many friends had I made and lost in just a matter of months? The numbers were astounding, yet for some reason, I lived and continued on. I turned to go.

Unexpectedly, Elsie placed a hand on my shoulder. "I forgot. I wanted to give you a book to read."

"Oh, that would be wonderful! I have not read a book in months."

She turned on her heel. "I will be right back!" She then ran into the house.

Sima came up behind me. "What is she running away from?"

"She's not running away. She said she wants to give me a book to read."

Sima leaned over and pet one of his dogs. "Hopefully, it is something good. We can take turns reading it out loud to each other."

"I agree. That could be fun." I smiled at Sima. I just hoped the book would be on a subject that would interest all of us.

Elsie came back and handed me the book. "I found this quite riveting. It was new on the market last year, and one of the trappers always brings new loads of books." I looked at the cover, and Sima looked over my shoulder to read the title. I almost laughed out loud. The cover read, *Phosphorescent Light and its Origins.*

I swallowed hard. "I am sure this will be quite stimulating." It was a nice gesture. I could not envision how this book could be exciting.

Sima coughed. "Alex will certainly enjoy this."

I could hear the humor in his voice. I looked over at Elsie, and she did not appear to notice that we were both trying hard to contain ourselves. She now had tears in her eyes. I came over to her, and I hugged her one last time.

Captain James Francis and his wife stood waving at us as we pulled away from the fort. At first, I smiled at the fact that the Captain was waving as wildly as when we had arrived, but then I thought of Joseph Shubert standing at Richard and Ellen's cabin, a lonely figure in the wilderness, and a chill ran down my spine. A thought occurred to me then that had never arisen before, why did people go through all of these problematic trials when it was so much easier to just stay in a safe place? I did not know the answer to that. I could not at that moment understand why I drove on with these two men who had become the closest people to me in the world. Why could we just not stay?

The day dragged on as we pulled on through the miles, I felt like we were going nowhere, although I did feel much less tired, and the pain in my feet had diminished. I had put the socks that Alex made for me on my feet, and just the thought of them made my feet feel like they could fly. I was worried that the sores on my feet would get worse again.

All of us seemed to be preoccupied with our thoughts, and we barely spoke, calling out commands only to our dogs. My parting with Elsie had made me think of all of the friends I had lost. I especially, for some reason, kept thinking of the last conversation I had had with Matthew. I began to think of Joseph Shubert and what he was doing at this moment. Was he still at Richard and Ellen's cabin in Canada?

"Anna!" I heard Sima call. I looked up and noticed that I had fallen behind Alex and Sima.

"Hike!" I yelled to my dogs, and they sped up.

"I am sorry."

"We can't wait for you all day, you know."

"I said I was sorry." I was surprised at how annoyed I sounded.

"I was joking," Sima stated. He then raised an eyebrow. I just shook my head in response, and we traveled on in silence.

That evening as we set up camp Sima and Alex joked between each other, but I could not find the energy to joke and remained silent.

"Are your feet holding out?" Alex asked.

"I already told both of you that I am fine." I looked away and silently stroked my lead dog's back.

"All right, if you want to be left alone, we don't have to talk." Alex turned and headed towards Sima. "Finish with the tent. I'll get dinner started. She's just in a bad mood."

His words hurt me. I knew that I was not usually so quiet, and perhaps it had thrown him off, but he had to understand that I had feelings and emotions and that it was not so easy to brush them off. I began to miss the comradeship I had felt with Elsie, and while I cared about Sima and Alex deeply, I realized that not having another woman around was quite tricky. The evening continued quietly, and we did not have much conversation. Alex and Sima both told me that they wanted to turn in early, and I sat alone in the quiet of the night with my thoughts. As I lay on my back, I realized that it was not as cold as it had been even two weeks earlier. I decided to clear my thoughts and go outside.

I crawled out of the tent with a blanket. I laid the blanket out on the snow and sat on top of it, and stared at the sky. The stars were bright as diamonds. I thought I could get lost in their brilliant fire. I began to wonder if Fur Hunter was up in heaven looking down on us. I hoped he was. I could imagine that his stern expression was now a smile. As my thoughts began to dwell again on the people we had lost, I felt tears rolling down my face. I buried my face in my hands and cried. After a while, I felt a movement next to me.

"Mind if I join you?" I looked up. It was Sima. He towered above me as I sat on the ground. I quickly brushed the tears off my face and hoped that he did not see them. I moved over, and Sima lowered his lanky figure onto the blanket.

He sat quietly next to me and looked up at the sky. "Look at those stars, beautiful."

"Yes, they are. I was admiring them myself."

"How could you be admiring them? Your head was buried in your hands."

"Well, before that." I started to pick at the blanket. I did not necessarily want to explain myself to Sima. I had a feeling, though, that he would not leave before I gave him an explanation.

Sima suddenly put his hand on top of mine. "Would you stop picking at the blanket? You're making me nervous."

I looked up at him. I realized that I was indeed ripping the blanket to shreds. I gave him a sheepish smile. "Sorry."

Sima cleared his throat. "Now, Anna," he said, sounding like someone's father before giving them a long lecture. "I am not trying to take Alex's side, but you have to try to put your bad moods behind you. If we are to survive for the rest of this journey, we cannot just cry in the night for two hours. I know that this is difficult, but we cannot pity ourselves so much. We are alive."

"I am trying, Sima. I am not so upset most of the time, but I feel that when I get close to someone, they are taken away from me. Anyway, you have been upset before." I felt a tear roll down my cheek.

"Oh no, and now you are crying again." Sima put his arm around me and pulled me closer to him. He held me tight as tears again started to pour uncontrollably out of my eyes.

"Alex and I hoped that our presents would make you happier, that it would be easier for you if you saw how much we care. Alex snapped today. I think because he thought you were angry at him for some reason."

I smiled at that thought. "Oh, Sima," I laughed a bit now. "The reason I liked Fort McMurray so much was that there was a female I could talk to. Sometimes girls just cannot speak to men about the same topics. I was just sad to lose that friendship so quickly. I highly doubt that I will ever see Elsie again."

Sima nodded in understanding. "I guess you also realized that you did not have any real women in your life. You have missed a lot." He took a deep breath and exhaled slowly. "Unfortunately, Alex and I cannot help you in that department, although it would be nice if you just told us right away what is bothering you. We are just concerned for you because I, I mean we…" Sima suddenly broke off his sentence and looked again at the sky. "It is getting late, and if we are both exhausted tomorrow, Alex will throw a fit. Please just remember what I said. I know we are male, but you do have to cooperate here."

I smiled at him again. "Sima, I promise you that I will try to be more pleasant."

"That would be nice. Also, remember, if you do need a shoulder to cry on, I am always here. Although I think I may just make matters worse at times."

I squeezed his hand and gave him a quick hug. "Sima, you are a true friend."

"Yes, I am. Now, let's do something to drive Alex crazy tomorrow." Sima offered me his hand and helped me to stand up. I thanked him as I got to my feet and then gathered up my blanket. I smiled and felt almost lighthearted. I thought about what Sima said as I snuggled into my blankets. It was not good to just keep my troubled thoughts inside and not let them out. It did not help to keep them bottled up and take it out on Sima and Alex. They were both kind people. They wanted what was best for me.

Chapter 18   April 5, 1888

"Do you realize that it is now April?" Sima asked me as he drove up from behind me the next day. I looked over at him and chuckled at the question. It seemed strange to me that it was April. In Maine, the snow would have started melting by now, and the green blades of grass would begin to peer out from patches of melted ice. The thought of it made me homesick for my Maine cabin. The idea that I missed Maine astounded me. There were days where all I longed for was to wake up in my Maine cabin or go and take long walks to town and never think twice about going anywhere. I thought back to my brave decision to go to Alaska. While part of me felt foolish, another part of me realized that I had no future in Maine. Also, I could not imagine my life now without Alex and Sima. I did not know how I had lived before without them.

"I did ask you a question, Anna," Sima's voice broke through my thoughts.

I shook my head. "Sorry, Sima, I just lost my focus. Your question made me think back to what I missed most about Maine."

"What do you miss the most?" Sima asked curiously.

"Spring and the soft grass popping up through the ground when all of the snow had melted," I answered him.

"You know that is what I miss most too. There is grass in Alaska, although the summer months are shorter than in Maine. Also, it can be quite a bit cooler, even in the summer."

"Yes? Well, I look forward to a time when we can rest and not ever think of trying to get to Alaska again."

"To be in Alaska forever," Sima stated and shook his head.

"Perhaps not forever, forever sounds so definite."

Sima chuckled. "Please do not tell me that you are planning to go back to Maine. I would not recommend it."

I looked at him and laughed. "You know that is not what I meant."

"Of course not," Sima said and grinned at me. "Anyway, I have an idea of how to make Alex crazy out of his head."

"Sima, I am always afraid of what you may suggest next."

"I think that you should pull forward on your sled and then halt. I will then pull ahead and halt, and then you will pull in front again."

"Why are we doing this? Please remind me."

"For the sake of sanity, there is not much else for us to do around here."

"I guess I agree. Alex is going to be angrier than a wet rooster."

"Oh well, I like to rile him up from time to time." Sima flashed a smile in my direction and pulled ahead of me. I looked back at Alex, who at that moment seemed to be just enjoying the scenery as he drove several meters behind us.

When I turned forward, I saw Sima halt suddenly, and I yelled to my dogs to speed up. My dogs sprinted, enjoying the speed. I was almost afraid that they were going too fast and that I would lose control of the sled. I yelled for them to halt. The dogs slowed and stopped. Then Sima yelled again to his dogs, and I saw them dashing forward. He also slowed and stopped after about two hundred meters. It was at that moment that I could hear Alex yelling at us from behind. I decided to tease him a bit more and gave my dogs the signal to go. Again the sled flew at an incredible speed. I felt exhilarated by the wind blowing in my face. I felt free.

When I gave my dogs the order to halt, I turned around to see Sima. Alex, who had caught up to him, was now coming towards me.

The look on Alex's face told me not to attempt to speed up again. I felt the urge to feel the strength of the wind on my face. Even so, I stood rooted to the ground.

When they drove up to me, Sima said, "I told you he would not be happy with us."

"Anna, what made you think of this idea?" Alex asked me.

My eyes met Sima's, and he gave me a mischievous smile. I glared at him. "This was not my idea Alex. Why do you not ask Sima to tell you what he decided to do?"

"Well, you were the one who kept going. You could have gotten hurt." Alex's blue eyes flashed as he spoke.

"Yes, but I did not get hurt, Alex. We were just having a bit of fun at your expense, you know." I then saw Alex's face light up with a smile. That momentary smile made me wish that he would smile more often.

"I guess you are right, Anna. I just wish you would not always decide to tease me about things."

"You are just an easy target, Alex, that's all." Sima laughed. "Why do you not join in?"

Alex seemed to hesitate for a second and then grinned. "Why not?"

All of us then yelled together, and our dogs flew forward, and then we took turns halting and moving forward. After a while, we had to slow down. We were breathless from laughing, and we wanted to give our dogs a break.

After our run, the dogs happily rolled in the snow. They must have enjoyed the speed after plodding along with us endless hours and days. Their trust in us was unfailing. I regarded their play with a smile on my face. The little puppy that we had gotten back in Churchill played as well. Although we had not yet started to train him to run with the team, he was getting bigger. Alex had suggested that we wait until we reach Alaska to teach him. I shrugged off the thought that we perhaps would never have the opportunity to train him.

After we caught our breath, we continued slowly through the snow, cutting a path. The rest of the day proved to be reasonably calm. The four days of rest had given us the energy to travel forward. I wondered how soon we would reach Alaska. I knew that the snow here would not melt too soon. However, already there seemed to be less white, and the fact that it was April worried me. I wondered if Jason Shubert had any idea of what he was doing before he set out.

I brought the question up as we sat around our supper; some bread that we brought from Fort McMurray.

"You know, hopefully, the snow will only really melt in May," Alex said.

"May?" I asked. "Then what do you suggest we do?"

"I have thought about that, and I am not sure."

Sima gave Alex a meaningful look. "I hope we don't have to wait until next winter to finish our journey."

"Don't be ridiculous. I think we should just push harder and not take too much time to rest at Fort Nelson; that is if the two of you agree."

"We still have to cross the mountain range," Sima added.

"According to Jason's map, there is an area of the mountain range that is less steep and easier to travel through."

Sima leaned back against his sled. "Considering that we are the only three men still traveling and Jason Shubert organized this expedition, I am not sure that I trust his map."

Alex stood up from the ground and brushed some snow off his pants. "To be fair, we have found all of the checkpoints so far."

"Yes, and we almost got shot at Prince of Wales Fort."

"That was not Jason Shubert's fault," I said pointedly. "Anyway, what is this mountain range? I, unfortunately, am not familiar with the geography of Canada."

"Is anyone familiar with it?" Sima asked sarcastically.

"Montaignes de Roches," Alex answered.

I just stared at him. "Pardon me?"

Sima rolled his eyes. "Alex, please do not speak French."

"I apologize. I just misunderstood," I said this in order to defend Alex.

"It's all right. Alex hasn't understood either. He just likes to pretend he knows more than he does. In our terms, it means mountains of rock."

"That sounds dangerous." At that moment, fear and pressure were building inside of me. I was afraid that one more obstacle would just send me over a cliff in my mind.

"You have a look of pain upon your face," Sima said and laughed.

I shook my head. "It's nothing. I just had a wave of panic hit me when I thought about going over a mountain range."

Sima grinned and stood up. "Do not worry about anything. We are right near you. We won't leave you behind on a cold lonely mountain."

"The one good thing is that the snow does not melt so rapidly in the mountains, and we will reach them near the time when snow will be melting everywhere else."

"And when we get off the mountain?" I asked.

Sima crossed his arms in an official manner. "We might as well get a move on, as Alex suggested. I do not want to end up dragging our dogs and sleds through the grass of the Canadian wilderness."

"Yes, let's go." Alex turned to leave.

Sima reached down to help me stand up. "We are forgetting our beautiful lady on the ground here."

He gave me a dashing grin. "My Lady."

"And you didn't want me to speak French?" Alex asked. "You are ten times worse. You definitely would never pass for a medieval knight."

"I am just courteous." Sima winked at me as he said this. I gave him my hand and stood up.

"Why did you speak French?" I asked Alex.

"Because the first man to come up with the name for the Rocky Mountains was French." Alex paused and gave us an all-knowing look.

"Trust Alex to know such a strange fact," Sima said, and then he sighed as he leaned down to harness his dogs to the sled.

From that moment on, we pushed hard. However, as we had known, pushing hard was not going to be an easy task. Despite using Elsie's medicine daily, my feet still hurt. Some of the sores remained, and I had a feeling that those sores would remain indefinitely. Alex's socks provided a nice cushion for my feet, and they were warm. Although I changed the bandages every night, I realized that my socks would not last long. After two weeks, they began to look threadbare and somewhat dirty. Devastated, I showed them to Sima while Alex was out hunting.

"Why don't you wash them?" he asked. "I can help you melt some snow. I can even assist you in washing them."

"Too bad we do not have a scrubbing board," I observed as I followed Sima outside.

Sima turned to me with a questioning look. "A scrubbing board?"

"To wash clothing," I told him. "You mean you don't know what that is?"

"Anna, I am a man. I have never washed clothing with a scrubbing board. At school, it was always collected, and after that, I always paid to have it cleaned. Sometimes Alex washed it for me. I only started to wash clothing after coming on this trip."

I shook my head. "Then how do you suppose that you could help me? Why did Alex wash clothing for you? He is a man too."

"Let's just say that up until I came on this trip, I was a lazy cad. I think that it is about time I learned to complete simple chores. It can't be that hard."

"It's not. Do we have any soap?"

"We have some shaving soap left."

I shrugged good-naturedly. "I guess that will have to do."

"My mother would probably be horrified at this conversation. Do you know how long it has been since all three of us have had a proper bath?"

"You mean washing with old washcloths in front of a fire from a bucket of melted snow is not a proper bath?" I asked as I grinned at Sima.

I was horrified at the thought. I also wondered what I would say to my daughter if she had not appropriately bathed in several months and traveled through the Canadian wilderness with a pair of rather strange men. I knew the answer, and I knew that what I would say to her would not be pleasant. I unexpectedly thought back to the beautiful women at the hotel where we had resided in Montreal. I knew that they would never consider my behavior proper. How I wished I could have their magnificent dresses, their shining hair, and glistening jewelry. I remembered the way Sima had tried to flirt with those girls. I wondered if I would ever be able to look like them. How would Alex react to me if I looked like that? I instinctively reached to touch my short locks. They had gotten about three inches longer. Still, I missed the dark slick beauty of my long hair.

"Hey, daydreamer," Sima's words interrupted my thoughts. "I found the extra shaving soap." He was leaning over the sled and rummaging through the contents.

"Will Alex be upset?" I asked.

"Who cares? He can be upset all he wants. This is about a woman's dignity and keeping her socks clean. He gave them to you. He would want you to keep them clean."

"True." I lit a small fire and began to melt a large bucket of snow over it. I looked at Sima, who had gotten a blanket for us to kneel on as we washed. He did not seem to think me to be strange in any way, and he was so open to me and to everything I needed. I sometimes wondered what he honestly thought of me.

"Sima, do you remember those beautiful girls in Montreal?"

"What girls in Montreal? Do you remember something that I do not?"

"No, those girls that you said were pretty, at the hotel."

He leaned over and worked the shaving soap into a rich lather. "Oh, those girls, I almost forgot."

"Do you think that I could ever be as pretty as they were?"

Sima gave me a surprised look. "Anna, Alex himself said you were beautiful, and you are. It is not always what you wear that makes you beautiful." Now it was my turn to be surprised. I had not expected such a profound observation from a man who hardly ever washed his clothing.

"Don't act so surprised, Anna. I may have been a good-for-nothing scoundrel for a good part of my life, but I have learned a few things about women. Those girls are a dime a dozen. Not one of them would enjoy a good adventure through Canada's untamed wilderness."

"I would not call you a scoundrel, Sima. In fact, I think you are the nicest person I have ever met. I'm also not sure that I am enjoying this adventure."

Sima just smirked. "Alex, now that is an upstanding young man. Me, well, I just lounge around and do my best to keep out of trouble. Here, give me the sock."

I handed him one of my dirty socks. I noticed with disgust that blood had broken through some bandages and left some stains on the sock. Sima happily scrubbed away with the shaving soap.

"For someone who has never washed clothes before, you are not so bad at it."

He looked up and smiled at me. "This is just a sock, you know."

"I apologize that it is so dirty."

"There is nothing we can do about it, Anna. We just have to make the most of what is at this moment."

"True, I just can't seem to shake off this feeling of grief that lingers about."

"Really?" Sima asked with a hint of mischief in his eyes.

"What?" I questioned suspiciously.

"Will this make you happier?" Sima took a handful of shaving soap and threw it at my face. It hit my jacket instead as I bounded to the side.

"Ha!" I laughed. I took some of the soap and threw it back, and it landed in his hair.

"Now you're in for it?" Sima laughed and lathered up some more soap and threw it in my hair. I took two handfuls and smeared his face with the shaving cream. We were both laughing hysterically, and of course, at that exact moment, Alex decided to return to camp. He brought his dogs to a halt right near us and just stared. We were both covered in shaving soap and could hardly stand from laughing so hard.

"What are you doing?" Alex asked.

"Washing socks," Sima told him.

"What is all that white stuff?"

"Shaving soap, we had no more regular soap," I explained.

"Well, you probably used up the last of the shaving soap." Alex sounded as exasperated as he looked.

Sima let out another laugh. "It is not so bad. We may have to look a bit scruffier, Alex, but only Anna is here to notice, and I do not think she minds."

"All right, you suit yourself. You two seem to have a knack for coming up with ridiculous ideas. I am not going to join you in this shaving soap throwing party or whatever you call it."

"You don't have to join us," I told him haughtily. "We are having fun without you."

"I can see that." Alex shook his head. "You are also wasting all of the shaving soap."

"At least we're clean now." Sima laughed and wiped the soap from his face with his sleeve.

"I was able to hunt out a few rabbits for us." Alex changed the subject abruptly. I saw two snow-colored rabbits on his sled.

"Thank you, Alex. I will help you skin them and prepare them for supper." I looked over at Sima, and he nodded at me.

"I'd appreciate that," Alex said to me and turned to his sled.

"He's such a turnip," Sima whispered to me.

"A turnip?" I asked in a hushed tone with a giggle.

"Not always friendly."

"I did not realize that turnips are unfriendly. You know, he's a good person, Sima. In his defense, he was out hunting while we were fooling around."

"I know. Anyway, if you are determined to help Alex, how about you wipe that shaving soap out of your hair? That's not the most attractive look on you. I never forget where your interests lie."

"Shhh," I shushed him and looked over to where Alex was standing. He did not seem to be interested in our conversation and was preoccupied with preparing the rabbits. I swiftly wiped the soap out of my hair and looked at Sima for approval.

His eyes twinkled. "You always look good. You go, and I'll finish with the laundry here." I smiled at him in appreciation and walked over to Alex.

That evening we ate a delicious meal of rabbit stew in comfortable silence. There was not much to discuss at the moment. There was no recent news, and it seemed that we still were quite far from Fort Nelson. Even if there was a comfort to the evening, there was always the overarching sense of worry that we would not reach Fort Nelson. I wondered if I would ever in my life feel a sense of true calm and if ever again, I would feel with certainty that I would survive the next day.

Chapter **19**   April 30, 1888

S everal weeks passed as we continued to travel towards Fort Nelson. Nevertheless, to our great chagrin, we did not seem to see any signs of the fort or a trail. Instead, we reached a densely wooded area. There also seemed to be less snow, and we traveled slowly through the forest. We worked hard to avoid the branches that threatened to hit us in the face. Several days were spent just breaking through the dense foliage. We spent many days in focused silence, and then we would just collapse and sleep when we had reached our destination for the day. After traveling in such a manner for four days straight, we came to the sad conclusion that we probably could not reach Fort Nelson. It was the first checkpoint that we missed. After much discussion, we decided to continue to Alaska without searching further for Fort Nelson. I still hoped that by some minor miracle, we would be able to find it.

After a few more days of travel, we were sure that we would not reach Fort Nelson at all. We spotted mountain ranges in the distance. As we neared the gigantic peaks, the fear seemed to tighten around my heart. Despite my worries, the sun reflected magnificently against the cliffs. It was truly awe-inspiring to travel with such a sight in view. The mountains were a refreshing sight compared to the flat tundra and deeply wooded birch wood forests in which we had spent most of our days of travel. The thought of crossing over the mountain range caused my head to spin.

In the evening, we sat in the shadow of the mountains. I had taken out Elsie's book and had begun to read it to myself. Phosphorescent light did not interest me in the slightest. However, I felt as if the pages of that book kept my fears at bay. I could focus on another topic and forget that I now lived in the wilderness, that I had no home, and that I doubted that I would survive much longer.

"Hey!" Sima's voice interrupted my thoughts.

I placed the book in my lap and looked up. "What?"

"Would you mind reading out loud? It feels as if we are just sitting staring at you while you read in silence."

I shrugged. "I'm sorry, I did not mean to ignore you. I just thought I could read, and you would talk amongst yourselves."

Sima laughed and glanced at Alex. He then pulled out a piece of wood and a knife and continued carving. "Alex and I have been talking to each other for the last fifteen years at least. Now, read out loud."

"All right, I don't think it is just that interesting."

Alex chuckled. "It sure is probably a lot more fun than anything else around here."

"Sure." I began to read.

After about a chapter, Sima interrupted me, "Are the northern lights a source of phosphorescent light?"

We all sat in silence. I had not given much thought to the northern lights. I just marveled at their beauty whenever they appeared.

Alex tossed a stick at the fire. "Who knows? I just know that they are beautiful. I think that they are a reminder to us that beauty still exists on earth."

Sima stood then and put the stick he had been whittling into his pocket. He held out his arms. "I think everything around us is a reminder that beauty still exists on this earth. Even if we lose our lives on this adventure, we can't say it has not been well worth the scenery."

I stood as well. "Perhaps that book will answer our questions about the northern lights and about other dull topics we never wanted to study in the first place."

Alex stood then and put his arms around the both of us. "I think the real beauty is the three of us. We have survived and remained friends, and that love cannot be replaced."

We all stood and embraced each other. My heart filled with delight. I could not remember a time when I felt more love in my life. I wanted to stand like that forever. I knew this night would not be one that I would soon forget.

*****

The cold weather began to break as we neared the shining peaks of the mountains. We found a river that was flowing from the mountain, the banks of ice were breaking, and pieces of ice that looked like giant shards of glass moved at a remarkable speed as the unrelenting current of water pushed them.

"We need to get over those mountains as quickly as possible," Alex stated as he stared at the gigantic slopes.

"That's almost the same as saying that we should get wings and fly," I remarked sarcastically. Sima gave me a sidelong glance as I spoke.

Alex turned to me. "Feel free to stay here then."

I turned my eyes to the ground. I felt like a child in grade school. I knew that Alex was only echoing the concern that we all had. What would we do if the snow melted before we reached Alaska?

Alex glared at me. "Let's go."

We pulled ahead, staying as far away from the riverbank as possible.

"Don't say a thing like that again. Alex has a lot to worry about," Sima whispered to me.

I felt my cheeks get hot. "And I don't?" I asked this in an angry whisper and then clamped my mouth shut. Angry emotions tumbled inside of me like rocks during an earthquake. Sima just gave me an annoyed glance. I yelled to my dogs and pulled ahead of both Sima and Alex. My anger blinded me, and I felt ablaze with uncontrollable emotion. I felt some relief from the speed at which the dogs carried me.

Unexpectedly, I felt my sled stop. I flew against the handle of my sled and fell to the ground. I tried to gather my footing while I landed. However, the river bed was icy, and I slipped towards the river. A streak of fear shot through me. I frantically grabbed at the ground, trying to hold on. I saw the river coming up, and I prepared myself for the worst. Unpredictably, the ice suddenly broke near the river bank, and before I knew it, I landed in a slippery muddy puddle that slightly sloped down from the river. I felt as if I was about to get sucked into the mud hole. It was then that I heard a voice coming from above me.

I looked up to see Sima leaning over the ice ledge that had formed when the ice broke below me.

"Anna, can you give me your hand?" I struggled to pull my hand out of the mud. A chill began to form at the base of my spine. I had a horrible vision of myself sliding down the dark muddy bank into the deep river. I wondered how there could be so much mud below a ledge of ice.

"Alex, hold on to my legs!" Sima called to Alex, who it seemed was behind him. I saw Alex grab Sima, and Sima leaned over the bank and grabbed onto my shoulders with both of his hands. He was now covered with mud from his hands to his elbows. He gripped my shoulders tightly and then yelled, "Alex, pull us out!"

Alex pulled with all his might, and I began to feel the mud let go of its slimy grip on me. Finally, both Sima and I got to safety. All of us sat on the ground, breathing hard. I was afraid to look at Sima and Alex. I blamed myself for the entire situation.

"What a mess," Alex commented as he looked at my dogs and then at me.

"Thank you for stating the obvious," Sima said as he rolled his eyes. "Here, Alex, you go on and start setting up camp," Sima said, with unusual command. "I will help Anna clean the dogs and the sled."

"Why do we constantly get into a mess because of her?" Alex asked as he gave me an angry glance and stalked off towards his sled. I looked after him. Tears welled up inside my throat. I blinked furiously so Sima would not notice.

However, nothing ever seemed to escape Sima's notice. He looked over at me as soon as Alex was gone. "Look, you know Alex is a big windbag. There is no reason to get upset. It wasn't your fault, by the way."

"I know he doesn't mean it. Nonetheless, it does hurt when he makes comments like that."

Sima came up to me and put his arm around my shoulder. "You know you aren't always a piece of cake either."

I smiled at him, but I felt a tear travel down my cheek and over my lips. I furiously wiped my tears with my hand.

Sima took off a blue wool glove and brushed the tear off my cheek. "Your face is covered in mud," he said with a grin. "You should see yourself."

I sniffled. "Wonderful, a muddy crying pig."

"Oh, stop that. You look pretty, even when you have had such an unfortunate mishap."

"Thank you. You are a good friend." I put my arms around him in a hug.

He hugged me quickly and then let go. "I'll soon be covered in mud too from head to toe if I do not stop hugging you. Then we'll both get an earful from Alex."

"That's true. Alex will be happy to know that he was right about the fact that we should have saved the shaving soap." I wiped my face with the back of my glove.

Sima headed over to his sled. "I'll wash your clothes while you wash. I'm getting better at washing every day. Let's get back to the camp before it gets too dark."

"Yes, we should get started on these dogs and the sled. I think most of the supplies on those sleds are ruined."

"We'll salvage as much as possible. Anyway, if any of these provisions reach Fort Yukon, I would be shocked."

"Sima, do you really think that we may never reach Fort Yukon?"

"No, I think we will reach it. The supplies, well, I think it would be embarrassing to bring them to help people, don't you agree?"

Chapter 20

It took hours to wash and clean off the clothes. Alex had actually boiled some water for me by the time Sima and I returned to the camp. The mud seemed to be everywhere. It was caked in my hair, under my fingernails, and between my toes. I sighed as I scrubbed with one of the cloth bandages found in the sled and had decided to use it as a towel. Alex had not said anything to me since I got back to the camp. I had not been able to muster the courage to say anything to him.

I finally finished my haphazard bath. I dressed in the extra clothes that I had in my bag. I looked at them in disgust as I realized that I had been wearing the same basic clothes for months now. I focused on the task at hand and gathered all of the bandages now covered in mud. I knew there was no sense in washing them. I decided that I would dig a hole and bury them somewhere. What use was it to keep them? I walked out of the tent and saw Sima and Alex drying out my other clothes near the fire. There was also a pot of stew standing on the log next to them.

Alex looked up at me. "I was able to catch the rabbits while you were still out with the dogs."

I hesitated before opening my mouth. I cleared my throat. Sima, who was kneeling next to the fire, looked up at me.

"I wanted to apologize to both of you." I stopped then. I had no idea what to say further. It seemed to me that I had run out of excuses

299

as to why I was angry. I had lived on my own for so long that I felt that I was just learning how to talk to people.

Alex, who was sitting on the log next to the fire, stood up and smiled. "Forgiven and forgotten, hopefully, the next time you get irritated, you will not decide to drive right next to the river bank." He smiled a bit as he said this. "My true worry is that the snow will soon be gone. The snow luckily is not melting yet on the mountain slopes."

"I agree that we have to hurry, or we will have to drive our sleds through the mud."

"That would be quite an adventure. I think Anna especially would enjoy it." Sima then let out a loud burst of laughter, and we all lost control of our composure.

*****

It took us about three days to reach the top mountain peak. We set up camp at the top. Looking down at the valley was exhilarating. Vast open spaces interspersed with dark forests created a magnificent picture. I had a hard time believing that we had covered so much land in our travels. All three of us sat marveling at the sight that lay below us. The afternoon sun created a mosaic of color as it sent its brilliant rays across the earth. I tried to take a deep breath. However, breathing seemed quite tricky. "I wish we could see your home from here, Alex."

"We'll see it soon enough. I predict it's not much more than three weeks travel from here."

Sima stood up and stretched his arms above his head. "I almost can't believe that we will reach your home."

"Let's not speak too soon," I stated. "The path down the mountain looks treacherous."

Sima gave a wave of his hand. "As long as we're careful, we should be able to navigate down the mountain quite easily." Despite his reassurance, worries about our downhill journey still plagued me. The thought that so much could go wrong concerned me.

After breakfast the following day, we sat and took in the mountain view one last time. Alex asked me to read a bit from our book before we started. I felt a strange tug at my heart as I was reading. What would happen after we got to Alaska? We had all grown close, and now we sat on the precipice of a new life—a life that seemed as uncertain to me as the life I had had in Maine.

After reading about a chapter, we finished packing our sleds and stood in a position to head down the mountain's icy slopes. Alex said he would go first. Sima and I both watched as he made slow but steady progress down the hill. He broke an excellent path for us with his sled. I breathed a little easier. It seemed as if the ride down would be effortless. I looked at Sima, who now was preparing his dogs for the ride down. Sima looked over his shoulder at Alex, who now kept moving towards the clearing at the bottom of the mountain.

Sima looked back up at me. "I'll wait for you. I can catch you if you fall."

I laughed. "I hope that will not be necessary."

Sima jumped on the back of his sled and whistled to his dogs. I watched as he moved down the slope. His progress down the hill was faster than Alex's. Alex had done an excellent job of breaking the path. Suddenly, Sima's sled seemed to slide to the left. I watched as the dogs jumped to the right to counteract the pull of the sled. However, their efforts were not successful. The entire sled flew to the left, and Sima catapulted off the sled. I watched in horror as his helpless body flew against two large gray boulders, and he fell in a heap on the pale snow. The sled and the dogs now slid towards Sima. The mad scrambling of the dogs did not seem to be enough to stop gravity. The sled flew into Sima with a thud and then broke to pieces as it hit the jagged rocks. The dogs now yelped in fear as they panicked and got tangled in the gangline.

Time seemed to be frozen. The world around me flipped over. After about five whole seconds, a surge of adrenaline hit me. I jumped on my sled and, with extreme caution, guided my dogs down to where Sima lay. I jumped off the sled and tore over to Sima.

Sima's head was turned to the side. The gash on his forehead was oozing blood. The amount of blood seemed to be never-ending. Sima's hip was also exposed, blood was intertwined with the tattered bits of clothing. I removed my jacket in haste and tried to tie it around Sima's waist to make the bleeding stop. Whether or not he was alive, I knew not.

"Alex!" I screamed. I desperately hoped that he would hear my cries.

"Please don't die, please don't die," I repeated frantically as I tore off my scarf and wrapped it around Sima's head.

"Alex, hurry!" I let out such a wild screech that I was surprised at its force.

Finally, I finished with my makeshift bandages. It was hard to tell if I had tied them with enough pressure to stop the bleeding. The biggest fear would be internal bleeding, if it even mattered. Fearing a loss of control, I did not scream again. I put a final tie on the scarf that was now covering Sima's forehead. I pulled off my gloves that were soaked red. I grabbed Sima's wrist. His pulse still beat; however, it seemed unsteady and fainting.

I put another tie on the scarf that was now covering Sima's forehead. I looked towards my sled and my dogs. Would I be strong enough to carry Sima to the sled on my own? Would moving him cause any damage? There seemed to be no reason to move him now. I would never forgive myself if I caused him more damage by trying to transport him on my own. It would be better for me to head a bit down the slippery slope and try to call Alex again. I realized that he would begin to wonder why we had not arrived yet.

"Alex!" I screamed all over again.

"What?" It was Alex. He had left his dogs behind and now ran up the hill on his own. When he turned the corner, he stood motionless.

"Sima fell." I looked up at Alex helplessly. Alex was a doctor. I only hoped he had what it took to save Sima.

Alex moved over to Sima with great speed and felt his pulse. "We have to get him off this mountain. Get a blanket from your sled. We will put him on it as carefully as possible and pull him down on it."

"Won't that hurt him more?" I asked as I stood to follow his direction.

Alex looked exasperated. "Do you have any better ideas, or do you propose we leave him to die on this mountain? I have no time to argue, Anna, follow my direction."

I nodded and ran off to the sled.

After what seemed like hours later, we finally reached the base of the mountain. Alex had already begun to set up camp while Sima and I had been traveling. With caution, we placed Sima in the tent. After we had laid Sima flat on the ground, Alex left the tent.

Alex returned with his doctor's bag. "Anna, listen carefully. I need you to boil some water and start to clean his wounds. We will need to try to sew up his head and his hip as fast as possible to stop the bleeding. I may need to cut him open if his hip bone is, in fact, broken and jutting into another organ. This procedure may not help."

I nodded without a word. I pretended to be brave, but the thought of cutting Sima open in the middle of the wilderness terrified me to the core. What if Sima passed away while we operated? I got everything ready and began to clean his wounds with shaking fingers.

Two hours later, I sat outside the tent on my sled with a feeling of numbness spreading throughout my body. We had cleaned Sima's wounds, and then Alex had cut open his hip. I could not get the feeling of disgust out of my body as I thought of the fact that I had held parts of Sima's hip together as Alex cleaned the wound and then sewed him up. As these thoughts raced through my mind, I lost my stomach's entire contents on the white snow. I stared without feeling at the food I had just lost and then stood and buried it under the snow. Alex remained in the tent, and I did not want him to be a witness to my miserable existence. I curled up in a ball on my sled and closed my eyes. Exhaustion took over me, and I fell asleep.

I awoke to Alex shaking my shoulder. I sat up and noticed that he had taken our tent down and had transported Sima to his sled. "Anna, I think I know where we are. There should be a trading post about two days ride from here. We need to get Sima to a more stable environment. I think we can get there faster if we travel at a reckless speed without stopping."

My body seemed to be void of emotion. I thought that I would rather just die than continue. I looked over at Alex with a total blank in my soul. "I suppose we should go. What does it matter?" I then prepared my dogs and followed Alex.

Describing the next excruciating twenty-four hours would be almost impossible. We ran for hours on end. We stopped only long enough to feed our dogs and throw cold snow on our faces to stay awake. We traveled through the night and then into the day. My legs had lost all feeling as the next day began to come to an end.

"Are you sure you know where this place is?" I asked Alex.

"Yes, look." Alex stopped his sled and pointed to the fresh footsteps in the snow in front of us.

"It's human," I told him.

Alex laughed for the first time in hours. "Yes, most certainly human. Let's go."

In an hour, the trail of footprints increased, and a mile later, a cluster of buildings and trading stalls appeared in front of us. Alex and I both sped ahead to the most prominent building on site.

After parking the sleds, Alex hopped off. "You stay here. I'll see what I can find out." Alex ran off inside the building. I marveled at the fact that he had even remembered how to find this remote trading post.

A wave of relief hit me. At least we had found the place. I looked down at Sima. He still breathed, but I could not tell if he would live much longer. His breathing seemed shallow, and his lips looked blue. I pulled out some more blankets from my sled and covered him. I then took his hands and rubbed them in mine. His hands seemed too cold. Several men walked by and gave us curious glances, but no one stopped to help though. A sense of loneliness came over me. I put my head on Sima's chest, his heart still beat. I sat there for what seemed like hours and rubbed his hands while praying the whole time.

"Anna," I heard Alex's voice behind me. A man walked with Alex. "I found a doctor. As luck would have it, he only arrived a week ago. He is more experienced than I am, and he said he would be happy to take a look at Sima."

I looked over at the doctor. "At this point, we need a miracle."

The doctor, who seemed to be in his late thirties, gave me a perplexed look. "Both of you look like death itself. I will take care of your friend. There is a boarding house down the street. You go there. I will come to find you when I have more to tell you."

I held tight to Sima's hand. "I cannot leave him. He's going to die."

Alex came over to me and gently took my hands off Sima. "Anna, he is in good hands now. We have done everything we can. Come on, let's go rest." He then unhitched our dogs, and we walked towards the boarding house.

Fortunately, two beds were available. Regrettably, they were located on opposite sides of the room. After paying the woman in the front room, I fell on the bed in an exhausted heap and slept as I had never slept before.

Chapter 21   May 8, 1888

I awoke hours later. I looked to see if Alex was on his bunk. I did not notice him. Several other men lay snoring on the bunks around me. I stood and stretched. I stepped outside of the boarding house. I had no idea which building contained Sima. I hoped he was still alive. Without hope, I sat on a log in an alley outside the buildings. A dark feeling of dread weighed on my shoulders. I felt too numb to cry, too scared to show emotion. I just stared at the white ground. At that moment, I thought that I just hated everything. I hated the snow, the dogs, and I hated Sima most of all for falling. I could not bring myself to fathom what my life would be without him. I could not imagine how I ever lived without him before. Snow crunched near me, and I looked up to see what made the sound.

It was Alex. "I was looking for you." At that moment, a strange thought hit me. I had not thought to seek him out. I stood up and brushed snow from my pants.

"The doctor says he sees no change. He was not sure if there is internal bleeding in his head. If there is, he's done for." Alex leaned one arm against the building as if in support. He breathed heavily.

I came closer to him. "Alex, don't lose faith."

"It's just like Sima to keep getting into accidents," Alex said in an exasperated tone. "Why must he keep hitting his head?" Genuine concern burdened his every word. I had a feeling that the real Alex, the one that cared more than he ever dared to show, lived somewhere deep inside, too deep for me to reach.

I put my arm around his waist. "Alex, don't do this to yourself. Whatever happened is all for the best. You have to believe that miracles happen. We did not come all this way and remain alive for no reason."

"That's just it. I can't believe that we came all this way only to have Sima die now."

"Well, he's not dead yet," I said coldly.

My voice seemed to snap Alex out of his depressed state. "Anna," he whispered. "You have always been so comforting. You are a source of inspiration to me. This journey is hard enough for a man, but for a woman? I still think you are the bravest girl I know." He put his arm around my waist and drew me closer to him.

I was suddenly overcome by emotion and held Alex tightly. I reached up and touched his face, and the next thing that I knew was Alex's lips came down hard on mine, and he was kissing me with what seemed like all the strength he could muster. At that moment, I felt that I had lost my mind and returned his kiss with little control.

We were interrupted by a voice coming from around the building. "Alexander!"

Alex let go of me so quickly that I almost fell to the ground. I hastily ducked behind a barrel that was standing near the door.

"Yes?" I heard Alex turn.

"Come with me quickly," the other doctor spoke.

"Is everything all right?" Alex asked shakily.

"You better come with me."

"Yes, let's go."

I heard their footsteps retreating quickly through the snow. I stood up and watched their shadowy forms walking toward the building where Sima lay. My heart beat hard in my chest. What if Sima had passed away? I looked again at Alex's form, now entering the building. I knew that we had only kissed because we had both lost our sanity somewhere along the way to Alaska.

*****

The next day, I sat by Sima's bedside and held his hand. He was not dead, and the doctor had called Alex away so suddenly the day before because Sima's temperature had risen significantly. However, during the night, his fever seemed to have broken. Alex told me that if his temperature did not rise again, he might yet have a chance. Alex had spent the night by Sima's side and now had gone to rest. I was glad to be away from Alex's company because I was thoroughly bewildered after yesterday's kiss. Also, I was delighted to be alone with Sima. I wanted to be with him in case he woke. He slept peacefully now. I stared at his pale face as if my gaze would somehow wake him from his deep slumber. He barely moved as he slept. I kept my ears strained for the faint sound of his breath.

"Sima, please wake up. Please, please, just don't go away. I do not think that I could imagine life without you. You have been such a good friend. I could not imagine anyone better than you." I pressed his cold hand against my cheek, and I began to pray. I prayed that he would live. I knew that my life without him would be bleak and dismal. Also, I needed him to be there for me for the rest of the journey. He made traveling so much more enjoyable. I felt that all of my efforts to rouse him seemed to be useless.

Finally, I just put my head down on the table next to the bed and started to cry. My mind kept repeating the same prayer; Sima could not die. The hours of traveling and the sleepless nights of the past several days reacted on me, and I fell asleep.

I awoke in what seemed hours later. My body felt stiff, and the room was freezing. I sat up, stretched, and rubbed the back of my neck. My immediate instinct was to look over at Sima. He was still asleep. I swiftly rushed to the corner of the room and got another blanket for him. I also put more logs on the now diminishing fire glowing in the hearth. I came over to Sima and poked his shoulder.

"Come on, Sima," I let out a vehement whisper. I shook his shoulder with caution in order not to hurt him further. Sima, however, seemed to be determined to sleep as long as he needed. I wondered where Alex and the other doctor were. The fact that no one seemed to have any idea how long it would take Sima to recuperate bothered me. Thoroughly discouraged by my efforts to awaken him, I again sat by his side and buried my head in my hands. Suddenly I felt someone's hand rest on the top of my head. I lifted my head and met Sima's perplexed gaze.

"Sima!"

"Where are we?" Sima asked, thoroughly confused. His eyes darted about the room as if trying to find an object that he recognized.

"Sima, you've had an accident," I said as I took his hand.

Sima touched his head with his free hand. He winced as he felt the sutures that were on the top of his head. "What sort of accident? I can't seem to remember what happened."

"You fell on the mountain and hurt your head. Your hip is also severely damaged." I did not tell him that the doctor feared he might never walk again.

"Where's Alex?" he asked suddenly. His eyes were beginning to focus, and he seemed calmer now and more aware of his surroundings.

"He's resting."

"You're here, though."

"Yes, I'm here, and I am not going anywhere."

Sima sighed heavily and closed his eyes. "I must have hit my head something awful." He closed his eyes. "My head hurts as if ten bricks smashed against it."

"It might as well have been ten bricks," I told him. "You hit your head on an extremely sharp rock.

"I really must stop hitting my head. I do not think it will make me any brighter."

I smiled with relief at the fact that he had not lost his sense of humor.

He opened his eyes again and looked at me seriously. "How long have I been unconscious?"

"About five days. Alex and I have been running hard day and night to get you here. Luckily we found a place to stay."

"Where is here?"

"A small trading post on the Alaskan border. It was our last checkpoint," I answered. "Listen, Sima. It may be a good idea for me to get Alex and tell him that you awoke. He has been so worried about you."

Sima looked at me and nodded. The enormous dark circles that had formed under his eyes terrified me. I did not want to leave him from the fear that he had just awakened momentarily and that he would leave this world while I was away.

I almost flew into Alex as he was walking into the building. "Alex, Sima just awoke!" I exclaimed excitedly.

He grabbed me by my arm. "What? How long ago?"

"Not more than five minutes."

"Let me go see him." He brushed past me. I hurried after him.

Sima was still awake and gave Alex a weak wave. "I apologize for causing such a mess."

"No, Sima, this is not your fault." Alex sat down next to him in the chair that I had sat in before. "We are just both relieved that you are alive."

I came up behind Alex, and we both regarded Sima with great love, and a wave of relief swept through me. I was not sure where we would go from here. I had never felt such an urgent need to reach Alaska and the Milichkovs' home.

"I can't move my legs," Sima exclaimed suddenly. His voice had a note of panic in it.

"No, Sima, one of your legs is broken, and also your hip has been smashed," Alex told him.

"So what are you trying to tell me?" Sima looked at Alex seriously as he tilted his head back against the pillow.

"Sima, we do not know when you will heal or if you will be able to walk again," I said to him.

Sima's eyes seemed almost lifeless. "I certainly have a fine talent for making a situation a hundred times worse than it already is."

Alex put his hand on Sima's shoulder. "All we need right now, Sima, is for you to get better. I will go find the other doctor." Alex then walked out.

I looked at Alex for a second as he walked out, and then I turned my gaze back to Sima. His face appeared to be a light shade of green. He held out his hand to me, and I took it. He squeezed it lightly and closed his eyes. I held his hand in hopes that my strength would somehow flow into him.

He then opened his eyes, and for a second and his gaze focused on my face. "Anna, even if I die, I am so relieved that I was able to see you one more time." He then closed his eyes again, and he fell asleep. It was then that I realized that I was clenching his hand tightly in mine.

Within the next few days, Sima started to improve. It was easy to tell, though, that he was going to have a long recovery. The other doctor said that we would have to wait at least two weeks before moving him anywhere. I knew that the snow would not wait for us. The days were starting to get longer, and the sun was in the sky for a long time. I felt that if we got to Alex's home, we could all get complete rest and not just sit around and wait for the unknown. I thought it would be better to stay one week instead of two. I knew I needed to speak to Alex. However, since we had kissed, I had hardly had a chance to talk to him. We had also barely had an opportunity to speak to each other. We both took turns watching Sima. Both of us were beaten, and the strain of the past weeks was beginning to take its toll.

I decided to speak with Alex the next chance I had. I awoke early the next day and went to the building where Sima lay. Alex had said that he would stay the night with Sima, and I had slept at the boarding house. I got up from my bunk, went outside, and checked on our dogs. I let them lick my face, and I hugged each one tightly. My muscles were sore, and every time I moved, my bones ached. I stood on my knees and let my bones sink into the dogs' soft fur. I then stood up and, with a prayer, went over to the building where Sima lay.

As I walked in, I saw Alex sitting next to Sima's bed. His head was in his hands, and as I walked over to him, I saw that he slept. Sima dozed as well. I could see the slow rise and fall of his chest. I breathed a sigh of relief. The fear that Sima might die at any second still haunted me. My gaze shifted back to Alex. I gently touched his shoulder. He did not awaken. I shook his shoulder. "Alex," I whispered. His head jolted up, and his shoulders straightened out. He looked over at me with embarrassment on his face.

"I'm sorry if I frightened you."

"No, it's all right. I did not even notice that I had fallen asleep." Alex stood up quickly and started to walk towards the door without another word.

"Alex, I need to speak with you," I said as I followed him outside.

He turned and gave me a wary look. "About what?"

"We need to decide what we need to do next. What else did you think I wanted to talk about?" I phrased the question carefully. I felt that I needed to leave the door open for further discussion if he wanted to discuss our kiss. A certain feeling of boldness came over me.

Alex had a concerned look on his face. I could tell that the kiss that we had shared was the furthest thing from his mind. "Yes, I agree we have to decide what to do next. I am worried that if we stay here much longer, we will never get home. I am afraid all of the snow will melt." I crossed my arms across my chest and leaned back against the building.

Alex did the same and looked at the snow. "I think if we secure Sima in one of our sleds, we can make sure that he does not get hurt."

Alex kicked at some snow on the ground with his boot. "Yes, however, I think we should leave Sima's sled behind and take out all of the supplies that we do not need." His gaze did not focus on me.

"We will not have any supplies left at all to take to Fort Yukon," I said hesitantly.

Alex looked at me, and his eyes flashed with annoyance. "Listen, we cannot worry about that right now. We need to get Sima and ourselves to safety before we all die from exhaustion and concern."

I nodded my head in agreement. "We should probably not wait much longer than three more days. How long do you think it will take us to get to your home?"

"Do you think you can rest enough in the next three days to be able to push for five days without much sleep?" Alex's gaze was serious. I gulped. I had not anticipated the fact that he would want to push so hard. Something about his whole demeanor at the moment made me feel as if I should not say no.

"Are you sure we can reach your home that quickly?"

"Although I was young at the time, my father and I used to make the trip in about eight days. I think I remember the trail well enough. At least I hope I do."

"As Sima would say, you have the memory of a turtle." I laughed a bit as I remembered the phrase that Sima had used before.

The expression on Alex's face lightened a bit, and he gave me a tight smile. "I think in Sima's mind that means that I have a good memory."

"Yes, something like that," I said with a laugh.

Alex just shook his head. "All right, I think we agree. However, I think you should be the one to tell Sima about our plan. I think he may be more partial to it if you tell him."

"Why would he be more partial if I tell him?" I asked.

"Because I always tell him what to do, and you're the one who suggested this whole plan," Alex said with a smirk and then walked away, leaving me alone by the building. I had nothing else to do but to step in and tell Sima our idea.

Later, when Sima awoke, I relayed our plans to him. He regarded me with a severe look in his eyes that I had not seen before. The scrutiny in his eyes made me squirm in the chair that I occupied.

"What's the matter?" I asked.

"Anna, have you taken a good look at yourself lately?" he asked slowly.

My head filled with confusion. "What do you mean?"

"I just have a feeling that you will kill yourself trying to save me."

"Why?" I stared at him. When he should have been most concerned about himself, all he seemed to have was a worry for me.

"Because you look like you could use several weeks of sleep and that you should probably eat several large elks before going anywhere. You have no fat left on your bones. Alex's parents will not even realize that you are there if we ever get to his home. You will just be a shadow of a person. Alex has not traveled this road in at least ten years."

"Unfortunately, Sima, we cannot take a chance on waiting, and we have to trust Alex."

"Oh, I trust Alex, just not his memory." Sima sighed and regarded me through half-closed eyes.

"Sima, we have to take a chance. Don't you want to feel secure? We've come so far together."

"I would feel better if I knew you were safe." He then closed his eyes as if he was tired of talking to me.

"Why are you so concerned for me all of a sudden?" I asked while studying his tired face.

Sima opened his eyes and looked straight at me. Something in his gaze started to make me feel uncomfortable. "Because I would rather be the one who's hurt. I would have a hard time seeing you in the position that I am in now. Alex doesn't understand. He doesn't feel as I do. He never thinks with his heart. Oh yes, he's got a lot of logic up there in his head."

I looked into Sima's brown eyes, and I began to feel immeasurable guilt for having kissed Alex. I could not understand why. "Regardless of what you say, Sima, we are leaving in three days. Unfortunately, you do not have much choice in the matter."

Sima's eyes narrowed. "You both are stubborn fools. You have to promise me one thing; that nothing bad will happen to you."

I smiled at him. "I am more worried about you at the moment."

"No matter how sweet your smile is, Anna, I still think you should think about your actions a little more before you jump in and do something foolish."

I stared at him. I wondered why I felt that he was talking about my feelings for Alex rather than our plans for our future journey. "I'm not foolish," I muttered.

"You can stop staring at me. You know what I am talking about." Sima did not seem to be in a jovial mood. I wondered if he had somehow figured out what had transpired between Alex and I. Sima did not say anything else, though, and I did not press him any further. He had closed his eyes again, and he did not seem to be in the mood for more conversation. Perhaps his accident was affecting him more than I thought.

The sleds were packed and ready to go. Sima's voice haunted me. Every time I took a step, my legs quivered. I was not sure if it was from nerves or exhaustion. There was nothing more that I wanted than to get to Alex's home. According to him, we could reach it within the week. We unpacked even more supplies to make travel lighter. Also, we cleared Alex's sled completely and padded it with blankets so Sima would not get jostled around as we drove.

The doctor came to help us carry Sima out and place him on the sled. "Make sure he moves as little as possible, or you will cause more damage."

"How will we move him to the sled?" I asked, concerned. As much as I thought it would be best for all of us to be settled at Alex's home, I did not want to do anything that would compromise Sima's health even further. When we had awoken Sima that morning, he had looked positively green, and his usually sandy blonde hair had looked gray. The dark shadows under his eyes also revealed a fear that he did not usually show. As we entered his room, he gave us a weak smile. I could tell that he did not want to leave. Alex had convinced me that it was for the best. Still, looking at Sima made me wonder if siding with Alex had been the best idea. I felt, though, that I had to trust him. After all, he had gotten us this far.

Alex and the doctor slid a board under Sima as I stood to the side, silently watching the process. Sima grimaced as they lifted him off the bed and carried him to the sled with unhurried steps. I ran ahead and finished harnessing the dogs to the sleds. We also harnessed the dogs that were still functional from Sima's sled to our sleds. The doctor said he would take two of the ones we had saved but were too injured to continue. As soon as Sima was settled and secure, I ran over and hugged the doctor.

"You do not know how thankful I am for you!" I exclaimed and ran back to my sled.

Alex looked over at me. "Are you ready?" I could not read his expression. I nodded at Alex. He nodded back and then yelled to the dogs to move. We touched off.

The following two days were excruciating. We only stopped every five hours to rest for an hour and then move on. The weather, though, held in our favor. I was happy that the temperature had risen, although I could see patches of grass starting to come through in places. I hoped we would not have to cross any water. I knew that we would have to go around any lakes or streams if that were the case. Sima slept most of the time.

After two days of hard travel, I lost track of the miles we had trekked. Alex and I sat resting against his sled and sharing a piece of bread. It had been good that we had stopped at the trading post. We had been able to pick up fresh food that we did not need to catch. We could hardly talk from exhaustion, and we just passed the bread silently to each other and nibbled on small bites. I felt my eyes closing, and I felt my head nodding off.

"Alex, let me sleep for a bit." I turned my head and put it on his shoulder.

"Sure." He stood up slowly and propped me up against the sled. He got some extra blankets and tucked them around me. "I'll tend to the dogs."

He walked away as I closed my eyes. It, however, did not elude me that he had avoided contact with me quite gracefully. I was too tired to be hurt. I marveled at Alex's stamina. I was not sure that I had even slept for the past forty-eight hours. I slipped into a delicious sleep.

Too soon, Alex did wake me from my slumber. I opened my eyes and shook my head, and hid my head under the blanket. "I can't; I just can't."

"Anna, come on, I let you sleep for four hours. We need to keep going. We're going to be home soon."

"Alex, let her sleep," I heard Sima say from the sled.

"No!" Alex almost yelled.

I jumped up from my sleepy state. "Alex, what's wrong?" I asked.

"We have to go, or Sima will die. I am responsible for all of us here."

I watched Alex with caution as I stood up and brushed myself off. The look on his face was not one of fear but of guilt. I walked over to the side of the sled so that I could see Sima.

"Alex, it's not your fault that I fell," Sima stated weakly. "Anyway, if we keep traveling at this rate, maybe I will not die, but Anna just might. You may be responsible for me, but I can take care of myself. You are tired too. Both of you get some sleep. I'll hold the gun and keep watch for a little."

"What if you miss?" I asked.

"Then all of us will get eaten." Sima smiled a bit. "Now, no more arguing, or I'll shoot both of you."

Alex looked at both of us and shrugged. "I guess there is no arguing. Anna, you sleep on your sled. I'll put some blankets out on the ground."

I went over to my sled and was about to get in it when Sima said to me, "You better take the food out, or you'll squish it."

"It would still taste better than anything we have eaten so far on this journey. However, I have to agree that it would be best to take it out." I snuggled into the sleigh after removing the food and looked over at Sima in the attached sled. I could hear Alex already starting to snore.

"Sima." I cautiously touched his hand.

"Yes?" He looked over at me. His face looked almost transparent.

"I'm happy you have survived so far. Please keep living for me," I said quietly as I closed my eyes.

I felt Sima take my hand. I was not sure what he said as I started to tumble into sleep, yet it sounded as if he had said, "You are worth living for."

Chapter 23   May 22, 1888

I woke to find the sun hanging high in the sky. I rubbed my eyes and looked over to where Sima lay. He looked so peaceful. The rifle still lay over his chest. Sima was asleep, and Alex snored away. I could not believe that he even slept. I clambered out of the sled and stood up and stretched. After taking a deep breath and yawning, I walked over to Alex and shook him by the shoulder. Alex woke slowly and gave me a confused look as he came out of his stupor.

"What's going on?" he asked. "Is it wolves or dog thieves again?"

I smiled and shook my head. "No, it's midday. Don't you think we should get going?"

Alex sat up quickly and looked at the sun. "Yes, why did you not wake me earlier?"

"I just awoke myself."

Alex quickly strode over to his sled and took out some bread, and handed it to me. Then he noticed Sima sleeping in the sled. "A fine protector he is." Alex grinned as he said this. "Let's go." He climbed on the back of his sled, whistled to the dogs, and touched off. I followed.

*****

Our campfire burned low that evening. Alex and I sat huddled near Sima's sled. Sima had his eyes closed in a deep sleep. Alex handed me the last piece of stale bread.

320

I handed it back to him. "Alex, I can't have it."

He shook his head and turned his head to look over to where Sima lay. "We should be in Alaska by now."

Those words should have made me jump for joy. However, for some reason, a slow ache started to build in my stomach. I looked over at the low flatlands, the half-frozen river, and the melting snow and sighed. "How soon do you think we will reach your home?"

"Probably no more than a day's worth of travel if you think we can sprint, I would feel better if Sima was in a more stable environment."

I gave a little laugh. "I think all of us would feel better if we were all in a more stable area."

Alex stood. "You rest. I will put the tent together." I nodded at Alex.

I did not remember getting into the tent or falling asleep. Exhaustion got the better of me. I awoke the next day to find Alex already packing the sled. I stumbled over to him.

He looked up at me as I approached. "I am happy to see that you are awake. It saves me the trouble of waking you."

A stab of pain shot through my heart. "It really can't be that much trouble to wake me."

"Here," Alex said as he handed me a piece of crusty bread. "Do you think you can keep going?"

I bit into the bread. I could feel the dry pieces travel down to my empty stomach. "Give me some tea, and then I'll be ready."

Alex handed me the mug that he had been drinking from. I finished off the tea in an instant. "Thank you."

He held out his hand to me and helped me get onto the sled. Before, I thought this to be a romantic gesture, but now I found it necessary. My legs were weak, and I felt my strength leaving my body with every waking minute.

Alex pet his dogs before jumping onto his sled. "Just one good run left, boys."

I hardly noticed the scenery as we took off. I held onto my sled. The road to Alex's home curved and moved. I had run on empty, and with my remaining strength, I held onto the sled as if it was only wagon wheel left to safety.

That afternoon as we reached another bend in the never-ending river, Alex paused. "I'm not sure that we are headed in the right direction."

I felt my heart drop. My legs screeched in pain, and my body felt as if I went any further I would collapse and never get up. I glanced at Sima, who had fallen asleep again. "Listen, Alex, I need to rest, and I don't know if it is a good idea to keep going with Sima in this state."

Alex appeared to be deep in thought. "I do not want to stop, but I think it might be a good idea for you to stay with Sima here, and I will try to find the trail."

"Will you be all right?"

Alex gave me a wry smile. "I'll be fine. I don't plan on being gone for more than an hour. You set up the tent and get Sima settled. I'll be back soon." He then called to his dogs and drove off before I had the chance to say anything.

I looked back at the small clearing behind me. I felt alone and decided to awaken Sima even if he needed rest. I needed him at that moment. "Sima." I shook his shoulder. "Sima."

"What?" He turned to me. "Where is Alex?"

I kneeled next to him. "Alex lost the trail, and he said he would go look for it. He said for us to set up camp here and wait for him."

Sima shook his head. "We should stick together. Alex thinks he's invincible."

I felt my insides breaking up. I just wanted to lie down. The thought of setting up the tent made me want to lose the stale bread that I had eaten for breakfast. However, the image of sitting out in the cold wind propelled me forward. "Sima, let me help you out of the sled."

Sima took my hand. "You get the tent up first and then help me. I'm fine here."

"All right."

After what seemed like an hour, but in reality, it was twenty minutes; everything was ready. I then helped Sima lie down in the tent on the blankets. I propped his head up as best I could.

He smiled at me. "I am sorry for making you work so hard for me."

I returned his smile. "Please, this is in no way your fault."

Sima raised both his eyebrows. "Somehow, everyone else managed to get down the mountain without flying down headfirst."

I moved some hair out of his face. "You did your best, the same as all of us."

Sima turned his face from me and looked dejectedly to the side. "Apparently, my best is no good."

I laughed and shook my head. "You're too hard on yourself."

Sima touched my cheek with his finger. "You need to lie down, sleep a while. I've slept enough."

I nodded. "Thank you." I crawled over to my blankets. "Wake me if Alex returns or if you need any help."

"Don't worry. I will."

I closed my eyes and fell asleep in an instant.

*****

When I awoke, I found Sima looking into space. I turned over on my side. "Hello."

Sima looked over at me. "You slept for a while, and Alex is not back yet." Concern passed over his tired face.

I propped myself up on my elbows. "Do you know how many minutes it has been?"

Sima gave me a wry smile. "It has been hours."

I bolted up. "Hours? I need to go look for him."

Sima shook his head. "Listen, I don't want to lose you too. I am sure Alex will return, but you, I am not sure. You do not look well enough to go look for anyone."

"All right." I stood and straightened out. "I need to at least check the perimeter."

Sima gave me a half-smile. "You check the perimeter, soldier."

I picked up my rifle. "I'll be right back."

Sima reached out his hand. "Do you mind handing me the other rifle?"

I handed him the other rifle, and he began to load it as I stepped out of the tent. I surveyed the area, and I felt a shiver run down my spine. The dogs huddled together by the sleds, and Star growled as I approached. I shrugged and then moved toward the trailhead. A loud crackle in the woods behind me made me jump. I turned towards the noise, and my heart stopped. An outline of a large animal lumbering through the woods made me tear towards the tent.

"What's the matter?" Sima asked as I flew into the tent.

I took a deep breath. "I think there is a bear out in the woods."

Sima grabbed the rifle that lay next to him. "Anna, run out and let the dogs free of their harnesses and then grab the extra rifles."

I hesitated. "Let the dogs go?"

"Anna, just do it. We have no time for debate and discussion," Sima snapped.

I nodded, taken aback by Sima's tone. I charged out of the tent and released the dogs from their harnesses with shaking fingers. The sound of the crashing branches seemed to be getting closer. "Hurry, get out of here," I yelled and pushed the dogs away from the sled. I then hurried back to the tent.

I handed the extra rifle to Sima and then huddled next to him. "It's coming closer."

Sima put his arm around me. "I apologize for snapping at you before. Now listen, if the bear comes into this tent, you shoot, and then I'll shoot again. We have to shoot to kill, or he will become injured and just destroy us."

I tightened my finger on the trigger of the rifle. I could hear the crashing continue and then stop for a moment. "It's all right, Sima, I understand." The crashing got louder, and then the sound of tearing ripped through the air.

I looked over at Sima. Sima sat propped up with his rifle at the ready. "I think the bear found our sled."

I crawled over to the tent entrance and watched in horror as an enormous bear ripped through the belongings on the sled.

I turned back to Sima. "Well, I suppose our sled will not be of much use to us anymore."

Sima narrowed his eyes a bit. "Get over here, or you won't be much use anymore either."

I clambered back over to where Sima was sitting. Sima took one of my hands in his. My arm was shaking. "Sima, what if we die?"

Sima planted a kiss on my forehead. "If we die, then there is no one I would rather be with than you."

I gave Sima a grateful glance. "Do you really mean that?"

Sima grinned in reply. "Of course." He then moved the rifle over. "Now, do you want to try to shoot the bear now or only if he comes near the tent?"

"Let's just wait it out." I shrugged. "He must be hungry after hibernating. Could we fire and try to scare him off?"

Sima lifted his shoulders slightly. "I don't know if that would work. Check what he's doing now."

I crawled back over to the entrance and lifted the tent flap ever so slightly. The bear had finished destroying our sled, and now he sniffed the premises.

Please let him leave, I prayed in silence. The bear continued to lumber around our camp. He sniffed the prints left in the snow by the dogs. The dogs had all disappeared. The bear then stopped and fixed his gaze on our tent. My heart ripped and pounded inside my chest. Without a sound, the bear appeared to change his mind and then turned back to the forest. He walked away from the camp into the dense growth.

"He left," I said in an excited whisper.

Sima placed his rifle on the ground. "I am sure that Alex will be excited to know that the entire sled is now destroyed."

"Should I go and get the dogs?" I asked.

"No, let's wait a while to be sure that the bear left for good."

I returned to where Sima sat and huddled on my knees next to him. "Not time for us to die just yet."

Sima shook his head. "For some reason, we keep living. I have no idea as to why."

I took his hand in mine. "We should give a prayer of thanks that we are still alive."

"You're right Anna, I've been upset about my injuries. I did not think much about how lucky I am. Poor Joseph Smith, Matthew, and Fur Hunter, they never had a chance."

A shudder ran down my spine. "At least I like to think that they are in heaven, watching us travel."

Sima smiled. "Perhaps they have better things to do than watch us travel."

I laughed a bit. "Perhaps."

Sima tried to prop himself up on his elbows. "Let's say a prayer of thanks."

We both bowed our heads and prayed. Never had I thought that this is where my journey would lead me, kneeling on the cold snow in a cold tent, giving thanks for the mere fact that I still breathed.

Sima and I had both dozed off afterward. We awakened to loud barking outside our tent. I grabbed my rifle. "I hope it's not the bear again."

Sima put a hand out to steady me. "Hold your horses, Anna. It might be Alex. Let's not shoot him while we are at it." I paused with the rifle still in hand.

"Anna? Sima?" Alex's terrified voice rang through the camp.

I jumped out of the tent and tore over to Alex at a breakneck speed. "We're here. We're alive!"

Alex embraced me. "What happened with the sled?"

"A huge bear destroyed it. Sima and I are unharmed. The dogs are in hiding. Where were you all this time?"

Alex turned back to the edge of the clearing. I only then noticed a tall man standing there. Behind him stood a colossal sleigh tied to two horses. "I found my home and asked my father to come to help me get you back to our cabin safely."

An inexplicable feeling of joy overcame me, and I jumped into Alex's arms and wrapped myself around him. "You found them? You found safety?" I kissed his forehead in ecstasy. Alex unwrapped me from his arms and placed me on the ground in silence. I stepped back, embarrassed by my unchecked display of emotion. I then noticed Alex's father now walking towards us.

Alex cleared his throat and then turned to him. "Father, this is Anna."

"Anna?" Alex's father's voice told me everything. Alex had not yet disclosed the fact that he had been traveling with a girl.

"You had said your friends were here. You never told me that you had a girl with you. Are you married to her?" Mr. Milichkov sounded confused.

Alex shook his head. "Oh no, she's not with me. We did not even know each other before this journey had started."

Alex's father looked from me to Alex. "I see."

"Honestly, father, there is nothing between us," Alex assured him. My heart began to hurt. The way I had just thrown myself at Alex probably made Mr. Milichkov have some serious doubts about me.

In confusion and pain, I turned back to the tent. "Sima is in the tent."

Mr. Milichkov followed me. "How is he doing?"

I did not answer his question and pulled back the tent flap. My cheeks burned in humiliation. "Sima, they are here."

Sima looked up at us as we entered. "Yes, I could tell from your screams."

I took my arms and wrapped them around his. "Alex's father is here with a huge sleigh. Sima, we made it. We made it!"

Sima grinned. "That is a good thing. I have no idea how we would have continued to travel on just one sled."

Mr. Milichkov stood behind us in silence and then got down on his knees next to Sima. "How are you, Sima? You have changed so much."

Sima gave him a weak smile. "I am sure that the multiple hits to the head have not helped. You don't know how relieved I am to see you, sir." The vulnerable expression on Sima's face made something deep inside of me break. I did not understand the feeling. I felt as if I needed to step out of the tent.

Mr. Milichkov put his hand on Sima's shoulder. "We're taking you home."

"Thank you." Sima then looked at me. "You can start looking for the dogs if you want."

I stood, but Mr. Milichkov put out a hand to stop me. "You go lie down in the sleigh. You both look as pale as winter snow. I'll take care of the dogs."

Sima and I were both safely in the wagon in no time. I lay down and closed my eyes. Mr. Milichkov had brought several blankets, and I made a burrow deep inside them. In the last few months, I had never felt so comfortable. Sima lay a few feet from me. Alex had gone to gather the dogs.

Sima put his hand out to me, and I took it. "We made it, Anna."

"We did." Tears started to run down my cheeks.

"Shhh." Sima rubbed my hand with his finger. "It's all right now. It's all right."

The pain and fear of the last few weeks overwhelmed me. My tears did not cease until we reached Alex's cabin.

When the sleigh came to a halt, I sat up to look over the edge of the sleigh. Lights coming from the large cabin spilled out over onto the snow. The warmth of the chimney seemed to reach the barn. I wiped my tears away with the back of my hand. I looked back at Sima. He seemed to have dozed off again.

I regarded the cabin's gigantic proportions. I could not remember when a sight such as this had been more welcoming. Alex had driven up behind us on his sled, with all of our lost dogs following behind him. Alex came over to me and helped me to climb out. Sima looked over at us as Alex helped me to stand.

Once I stood safely on the ground, Alex turned to Sima. "I'll help you in just a few minutes."

I opened my mouth to thank Alex for helping me when the cabin's doors flew open, and a woman, who I assumed was Alex's mother, ran over to us and hugged us all. It was then that I noticed a young woman following behind her. My best guess was that this could only be Katya, the young woman that Alex had told me lived with his parents since she was a young girl.

She ran over to Alex now and threw her arms around him. "I'm so relieved you have returned."

Alex returned her hug and held her for a while longer. A surge of jealousy tore through me. She's like his sister, I assured myself. As Katya stepped back from Alex, I noticed the expression in her eyes and wondered if something else did exist between them. I recalled that Alex had said that he had written to her for years. I shook my head.

Mr. Milichkov helped me into the house. As I entered, Mrs. Milichkova handed me some hot tea. Waves of exhaustion swept through me. The teacup in my hands began to shake. Holding the teacup became impossible.

Mrs. Milichkova came up to me and steadied my hand. "Are you all right, dear?" She, unlike Mr. Milichkov, did not seem at all perturbed by the fact that I was a girl. I looked around in a daze. The room seemed to fill with fog. Sima now lay on the couch. I tried to keep my focus on him, but the whole room began to spin. I put my hand on my head and closed my eyes.

Alex put a hand on my elbow. "Anna, I think you need to go to bed."

I nodded at him. "Yes, yes, I agree."

"I'll help her." Mrs. Milichkova took my arm and then led me down the hall to an empty room. She put me into bed and covered me with several blankets. The whole room continued to spin, and I could barely utter the words, "Thank you."

"Sleep now, my dear," Mrs. Milichkova said as she smoothed back my hair. I was relieved to be in a safe place. I fell into a deep slumber.

PART III

ALASKA

Chapter 24   May 30, 1888

The morning after we arrived, I slept like a rock. I could not remember a time that I slept so peacefully. I awoke only to find the sun streaming through the windows. I blinked several times to orient myself. I had not had much chance to look around the room. Also, I was wearing a beautiful nightgown. Something that I felt I had not worn in years. The carved wooden door was closed, and the room was sparsely furnished. However, the room felt cozy. I had a brightly colored red and blue quilt on my bed, and to my right, I found a washstand with a mirror standing on it. A small wooden table stood next to my bed, and a braided rug lay on the floor. As I regarded the room, I sat up with a start. Where were Sima and Alex? Also, I did not see any of my clothes. I vaguely remembered being helped into the room by Alex's mother. I was unsure of what to do, and I did not want to venture out into the cabin's main room in my nightgown.

I decided to get up from my bed and open the door and call out to someone. I swung my legs over the side of my bed, and my feet touched the floor. As soon as I put pressure on my feet, I yelled out in pain. I looked down to see that the bandages were gone. I was disgusted by what I saw. Since we had traveled so hard for the last few days, I had not thought of putting salve on my feet. Bloody blisters covered the top and the bottom of my feet. Some looked as if they had burst. As I regarded my feet in disgust, someone knocked on the door.

"Who is it?" I called.

"It's Mrs. Milichkova, my dear."

"You may come in," I said and quickly tucked my feet under my quilt and covered myself with a blanket. The door opened and in walked Mrs. Milichkova, a small beautiful woman with dark black hair. She had the kindest smile. I could not imagine how such a small woman could have a son as tall as Alex. Her hair was tied in a bun at the back of her head, and she had loose strands that surrounded her face. She was dressed in a plain dark blue dress. The dress's simplicity did not distract from this woman's beauty.

She smiled at me and held out her hand. "We were not properly introduced last night. Welcome to our home."

I accepted her hand. "I do apologize if I am a nuisance. I know that you probably were not expecting me."

"We were not expecting anybody last night at all. We thought that we might never see Alex again. We knew he was supposed to come back, but we thought he might decide to stay in the states." The woman smiled at me. Her voice was so soft and kind, and she did not look like she ever worried.

"Alex would not let us stop," I told her. "His main goal was to get back to you."

"That is wonderful to know." She then smoothed some hair back from my face.

"And you, my darling, why did you come?"

"My parents, I think they may be somewhere in Alaska. Although at this point, I am not sure that I will find them." I knew even then that my reason did not sound like it had any foundation behind it.

"Right now, you need to rest. Afterward, we can think about your parents. I will talk to my husband. Alex told me a little bit about you. We can ask around in the neighboring areas about you and if anyone knows anything of your family. However, I do not want you to worry about it right now." She smiled gently and then said, "I took off your bandages last night. You were already asleep. I think your feet may need to breathe to allow them to heal properly. I wanted to come and wash them off for you. I have a basin of water just outside the door."

"You do not have to," I responded, thoroughly embarrassed.

"Also, my husband will bring in the large tub in here so you can wash appropriately. I was quite horrified when my son told me this morning that neither one of you has had a bath in about seven months." I looked down at my hands, and my face burned. I had no idea what kind of impression this woman had of me.

"I did not expect everything to turn into such a mess. I had not thought anything through when I started on this journey," I whispered.

"Young people usually never think anything through. That is why being young is so wonderful. You get to have a lot more adventures that way." I looked at this woman and smiled. She made me feel much more at ease.

"Do not worry, Anna. I do not think that you have done anything wrong. I am happy that you are here. Katya has not been able to have a true friend her age. There are few women around here."

"Is Sima all right?" I asked.

"Yes, he slept just as long as you did. Katya is making breakfast for you both. However, I would recommend that both of you stay in bed for a while. I do not want you to try to walk around. You seem very weak. The three of you seemed to have pushed yourselves to the limit."

"We needed to get here."

"I understand."

It was at that moment that Mr. Milichkov peeked into the room. "How is she this morning?" His deep voice rumbled through the room.

"All right, come in and bring in the tub," Mrs. Milichkova told him. Mr. Milichkov walked in carrying a large tub filled with water. He was a man of gigantic proportions.

"What a fine mess you landed yourself in," Mr. Milichkov said to me in a stern tone as he put the tub on the floor. I felt myself shrinking under his hard gaze. His wife seemed a lot happier with the fact that I was there than he was.

"I have instructed Anna to stay in bed until she regains strength," Alex's mother told him.

"I feel that that is for the best," he said and then turned to go. He then unexpectedly stopped, kissed his wife on the cheek, then walked out and closed the door. Mrs. Milichkova turned back to me and then smiled. She must not have realized before that I was now terrified of her husband.

"Do not worry about him," she said. "He is happy that you are all here. He is just worried about all of you. It is a lot for him to take in right now. It is overwhelming to see your son after so long." Yes, with a couple of unexpected visitors, I thought to myself. I also began to wonder what Mr. Milichkov looked like when he was angry.

Mrs. Milichkova then helped me to get out of bed. She left while I washed. She said she would get me a lovely dress to wear. I got into the warm water and felt so relieved. Every aching muscle in my body seemed to relax. I leaned my head back against the metal tub. I took the soap that Mrs. Milichkova had given me and rubbed it into my skin. I felt like I could scrub forever. The layers of dirt on my skin seemed to be endless. I was again thoroughly disgusted with myself. Finally, when I was clean, Mrs. Milichkova returned with a dress. She helped me put it on and helped me to dry and brush out my hair. The dress was Mrs. Milichkova's, so it was a little bit short. However, all of the material sagged. It was too big on me. I studied Mrs. Milichkova and could not believe that I was thinner than her.

I looked into the mirror and stared. My cheeks were sunken, and my wrists seemed awfully small. I did not know how I had not noticed that I was so thin. However, I loved the plain green dress's soft material, and I did like how it accented my eyes.

"You look beautiful," Mrs. Milichkova said.

I turned around and hugged her. "You are too kind."

"Now lie down, and I will see what I can do about your feet," she said to me.

"Mrs. Milichkova, I know you want me to get better, but I really need to talk to Alex and Sima or at least see them. I promise I will listen after that."

"That is fair enough," she said. "Here, you can wear my slippers."

I walked gingerly out of the room and turned to my left down the hall to the main room. I leaned against the wall for support. I came to the next room and saw a door leading to a bedroom. It was Sima's room. When I saw him, my heart began to beat wildly in my chest. I panicked and was afraid that I was going to faint. I leaned against the doorway.

"Anna, are you all right?" I looked up and saw Sima grinning at me from where he sat on the bed. I felt silly suddenly and righted myself. The faint feeling passed.

"Yes." I slowly came towards him. "You?"

"As well as I could be, I am thankful to be alive. I am not sure when I will be well enough to walk, though."

"I think it may take a while," I told him truthfully.

"I agree with you," Sima said, sounding disheartened. He then took my hand. "You need to gain some strength too, you know, you look like a pile of chicken bones. Katya and Mrs. Milichkova cook well. Believe me; I just had breakfast."

I smiled at him. I was beginning to see the old Sima coming back. "I believe you," I told him.

"Anna, what are you doing in here?" a deep voice behind me asked. I turned to see Mr. Milichkov standing behind me. "I thought my wife said you should stay in bed. Sima needs rest too."

"Mr. Milichkov, she just wanted to say good morning. I promise you that afterward, she will go right back to bed. We haven't been apart for seven months. It's kind of hard to be separated, you know,"

Sima said with his usual boldness. I always wondered how he was so brave. He did not seem to be scared of anyone.

"Well, in that case, I'll let you speak for a while longer if you want," Mr. Milichkov said this, grinned, and walked out. It was nice to see that he may have a sense of humor.

"He is so intimidating," I said to Sima once Mr. Milichkov had left.

"Why?" Sima asked. "He's just a big man with a loud voice." He then looked at me and smiled. "You look wonderful in that dress, by the way."

I was surprised at this comment. "Thank you. I would twirl around in it for you. However, my feet hurt too much right now for any type of physical activity."

"It's a little bit short on you." Sima grinned at me and leaned back against his pillow.

"This is the best Mrs. Milichkova could do. It's not my fault that I am so much taller than her."

"It's great to see you in a dress. You look very clean too."

"So do you," I said. I had just noticed that Sima had shaved and washed his hair.

"Yes, well, the fact that we have not washed properly in seven months should probably remain a secret."

"Unfortunately, Alex told his mother this."

"How could he betray us?" Sima chuckled and then closed his eyes. "I am sorry, Anna, I feel like an elephant ran me over."

"I think all of the tension from our journey has now hit me full force since we have a chance to rest. I am not sure I feel much better than you do," I told him.

"We probably should get some rest, as Alex's father instructed. Of course, if you want to stay, please do."

"No, I agree with you. Anyway, I am scared of disobeying Mr. Milichkov."

Sima opened his eyes and shook his head. "All right, go ahead. Promise me that you will come in at least once a day. At least you can walk."

"I promise." With this said, I squeezed Sima's hand and walked out of the room. I wondered where Alex was. It seemed strange to me that he had not come to see me at all. I walked warily towards the main room. I heard two voices speaking. One of them was Alex's, and the other voice I recognized was Katya's. I felt that it would be rude to interrupt the conversation, so I walked back to my room. I guessed that Alex and Katya had a lot of catching up to do.

In my room, I found a tray of food on the table next to my bed. There were fried eggs and waffles and a large piece of venison. I sat down on my bed. However, my head buzzed like a swarm of bees. If Sima had felt that an elephant had run over him, I felt like I had been treed by a moose all over again. My stomach made loud growling noises. I realized I had not eaten much since the morning before. I had been so exhausted upon arriving that I had hardly been able to touch the food Mrs. Milichkova had served. I devoured the food that someone left for me in less than five minutes. I could not remember the last time I had eaten so well.

After polishing off what felt like the most delicious meal I had ever eaten, I lay back onto my pillows and closed my eyes. Suddenly a wave of nausea hit me, and I sat up quickly. Then I felt all the food that I had just eaten come up, and before I knew it, my breakfast was all over the floor. I feebly looked at my overturned breakfast and started to cry. I was too embarrassed to call for help. I just sat on my bed and sobbed.

Suddenly I heard a voice at the door, "Anna, lie down." I looked up and saw Mr. Milichkov standing there.

At that moment, I wished myself back to the Canadian tundra. "Mr. Milichkov, I am so sorry. I will clean this up," I told him tearfully.

Mr. Milichkov then did something unexpected. He came over to me, gently moved me back onto the bed, and covered me with the quilt. He then took the wash towel that hung on the dresser in my room and wiped off my face. "There is a reason why I told you not to walk around too much. You should not have eaten so much food. Katya should have known better than to give you so much to eat."

"I am so sorry," I kept repeating.

"Look, there is nothing to apologize for. You are sick and exhausted. You will regain your strength, but it will take time."

"This mess, though," I said feebly, looking at the floor.

"I have to clean out stalls every day," Mr. Milichkov said with a laugh. "This is nothing." I wondered if he purposely had just compared me to a horse.

"You relax and close your eyes. I will have this cleaned up in a minute." I lay back. There was nothing I could do. It was useless to argue.

"Katya!" I heard him yell out.

"Yes?" I opened my eyes to see Katya standing at the door with wide eyes.

"Please get me some warm water and some more towels." She quickly turned and left the room. She was back within a matter of minutes with the items that he requested.

"I am sorry," she said to Mr. Milichkov. "I did not realize Anna would get so sick." Her voice sounded full of remorse.

"It's all right," Mr. Milichkov answered. His voice had a considerably softer tone to it now. I was surprised that he did not call her out and tell her that she should have known better. How different he was from Jason Shubert. I closed my eyes again.

"Katya, how is Anna?" I heard another voice at the door, and my eyes flew open. Unfortunately, Alex was standing at the door. He also now stared at the floor. I just closed my eyes and pretended that I was in Maine.

"The both of you can stop gaping like fish and help me clean this up," Mr. Milichkov said quickly.

"Yes, we can," Alex answered. I was surprised at the cheerful tone in his voice.

I opened my eyes and looked over at him. "I apologize, Alex. I would help if I could."

"Do not worry, Anna. You know we have been through worse." He said nothing more and helped his father and Katya clean the floor. Alex and Katya then carried the towels out of the room, and Mr. Milichkov stood up and looked at me. A tear ran down my cheek. I felt humiliated, and I was thoroughly disgusted with myself. I did not understand why I felt so weak and sick now. Mr. Milichov's gigantic figure loomed over me. A bear, I thought. He looks like a bear.

"Anna, from now on, you are not to get up without my permission. You need to get better, understood?"

"Yes, sir," I whispered.

"Stop crying," he said and wiped the tear from my face. "You gave too much of yourself on this journey, and now you are paying for it dearly. That is not your fault. Now you rest, and I will go call my wife."

"All right," I said and wiped the tears from my face. Mr. Milichkov walked toward the door. I then remembered my promise to Sima.

"Sir?"

"Yes?" Mr. Milichkov turned around and looked at me.

"I promised Sima I would go see him every day at least once a day. I can't see him if I can't get up. Could you tell him, please?"

Mr. Milichkov grinned and said, "Of course I will tell him. I think he will understand." He then walked out.

It took over a week for me to be able to stand up again. I still, however, did not feel strong at all. During that week, an intense fever took over me. It seemed that everything around me was in a deep gray mist. Sometimes, I would see Mrs. Milichkova sitting next to me in that mist. Sometimes it was Alex, at times it was Katya, and other times it was Alex and Katya. I felt like I had cotton in my mouth and had great difficulty speaking. It was good to have Alex next to me. Although in my feverish state, I could not say anything to him. He would put a cold cloth on my forehead, and I could see the concern in his face.

It was the following Tuesday morning on which I woke up and felt a renewed strength. It was at that moment that Katya came in. I looked at her. I marveled at how beautiful and poised she was. I felt pretty inadequate around her. I had not really spoken to her since I met her. I was not sure that I could be friends with her. She seemed to be so quiet and calm. I, on the other hand, felt as if I created a mess everywhere I went.

"Good morning," she said, smiling. "How are you feeling today?"

"Much better," I told her. I tried to prop myself up but found it challenging to sit up. She came up to me and propped the pillows up behind me. She then supported my back as I sat.

I smiled at her. "Thank you."

"Alex's mother and father have been so worried about you. They have hardly slept."

"I do feel like I am causing a lot of turmoil. I feel like I should not even be here."

Katya looked at me with her large blue eyes. She seemed to be calculating what to say next. She looked as if she agreed with the statement I had just made. "Well, I have never heard of a young lady journey across all of Canada to reach Alaska. You were very brave to do so. It was quite a bold move on your part." Her voice was soft, and I wondered if she ever spoke any louder. She always seemed to talk in a quiet, calm voice. At that moment, it was grating on my nerves. I tried to calm myself inwardly.

"Thank you for asking about me, Katya. However, I need to dress right now, and I was hoping to walk out to the kitchen and get a bite to eat. I am very tired of being cooped up in this bedroom. Can you come back in five minutes to help me walk to the main room?"

"Yes, however, I will ask my father, I mean Mr. Milichkov, if it is all right for you to get up. He gave me strict instructions not to let you get up without his permission."

I sighed. "All right, I guess since I am enjoying your family's hospitality, I should listen to directions."

Katya smiled and said, "I guess you should." Then she walked out. I did not understand her. She seemed to be an excellent person. However, everything she said appeared to be calculated and pointed. I also had a sneaking suspicion that my dislike towards her was because she seemed to spend a lot of time in Alex's company. I told myself that she was almost like his sister. Nevertheless, in reality, she was not his sister.

After she left, I got dressed slowly. Then, as I sat down on my bed, I heard a knock on my door. "Yes?"

"Anna, may I come in?" It was Alex.

"Come in."

Alex opened the door. He was so tall. After meeting Mr. Milichkov, I understood why Alex was so gigantic. He also looked particularly handsome that morning. My heartbeat quickened.

"It is good to see you are looking alive this morning," he said as he walked over to where I was sitting and leaned over and kissed me on the cheek. I was taken aback. My eyes met his for a brief second, but I could not read anything in his eyes though.

"It is good to be alive," I told him with forced cheerfulness.

"Sima's been asking about you every day," he said. He pulled up a chair and sat down while looking at me. "Katya said that you wanted to get up out of bed this morning, and she went to ask my father if it is all right."

"I do want to get up. I feel cooped up in here. I do not want to disrespect your father, though. He has already put up with a lot because of me."

"My family loves having you and Sima here. They seldom get visitors. They told me that you both could stay for as long as you both need to stay."

"That may be a while," I told him as I picked at the quilt on my bed. "I do not imagine that my parents are even within one hundred miles of this cabin. When I started on this journey, I did not think that Canada and Alaska covered so much space. I was rather inexperienced. I thought it would be easier to find my parents."

"I think that all three of us were rather naïve when we started this journey. Do not worry. My father is an influential man in these parts. He is going to do everything he can to help you. He has already started to write letters and has sent men to the fort to find out if anyone has a missing daughter."

"That is very kind of him. I do not know how I will ever repay your family."

"There is no need to repay them." He then paused and looked as if he wanted to say something else. We were interrupted by Katya, and she came up to where Alex and I sat and stood close to Alex.

"My father said that if you would like to get up, it is fine, as long as you do not stay out of bed for longer than an hour."

"I have to see Sima. He will be worried about me."

"Let's have you eat breakfast first," Alex said. He then slightly touched Katya's arm. "How about Katya, you support Anna from the left side, and I will stand on the right? We can walk you to the kitchen." He took charge like he always did. They helped me stand and led me to the main room of the cabin. I peeked into Sima's room as we passed and saw that he was dozing. When I was safely seated on the bench in the main room, I felt much relieved. The room seemed so large compared to my small bedroom. Alex sat on a chair, and Katya began to busy herself by the large stove.

"How is Sima?" I asked, concerned. I saw a look of understanding pass between Alex and Katya. I thought that I had never read Alex's thoughts as Katya seemed to be doing now.

"He seems to be gaining health back by the day. He doesn't look as green anymore. However, my father is not sure that he will ever walk again. Also, Sima seems to be almost depressed lately. He is not his usual self."

"I hope I can cheer him up and make him feel better about himself."

"We've tried, although you seem to be able to make him laugh better than the rest of us."

"I have not noticed that I have some special touch." I looked at Alex. I wanted Katya to leave. At the moment, I just wanted to talk to Alex, to ask him about Sima, and to come up with a plan of what we should do next. The camaraderie and the strength we had seemed to share the last few days of our journey seemed to be gone.

Katya turned from the stove and came over to me. "Anna, here is a plate for you. I only toasted some bread with butter. Please let me know if you need anything else. I thought that I should not give you anything too heavy to start with." I hoped that she would not even mention that whole embarrassing episode again. I looked at my plate with hot cheeks. All I could mumble was a thank you. I ate my toast slowly. Katya then started to walk over to the water pump with a pot from the stove. As she walked by Alex, I saw him ever so slightly touch her skirt. I was pretty sure that I had not imagined that he had done so on purpose. I did not think it was meant as a brotherly gesture either. My heart sank in my chest. I probably felt as depressed as Sima did. I suddenly felt a desperate need to talk to Sima. I just wanted to get out of that room. I ate half the toast and then asked Katya and Alex to escort me to Sima's room.

Sima was awake when they helped me in, and Alex brought a soft chair for me to sit on. I sat on it. Alex walked out then, and Katya followed right on his heels. Sima had sat in silence until they left. He then gave me a mischievous grin.

"So, I hear you have been creating a mess next door."

"Oh no!" I exclaimed, and my hands flew to my cheeks. "Who told you?"

"No one told me. I am next door, remember? I heard you lose your lunch. When Mr. Milichkov passed my room, I called to him and told him that I thought that it would be a good idea to check up on you."

"This whole time, I have been so humiliated about the whole situation. Alex saw it too."

"There is no need to feel that way. It is natural. At least you did not lose your breakfast because you had one too many drinks." He then winked at me. I was not at all shocked by his speech. Sima was Sima, and I knew that he could not be a better friend even if he sometimes made strange comments.

"So, how have you been spending your time?" I asked.

"Reading and talking to Alex and Katya, I actually think I have done more reading here than in the whole time that I spent at the university. However, I did quite a few other things at the university that I would never do here or ever again.

"That is all past now. Although Alex said, you were feeling depressed."

"It's because I could not see you," Sima said. I looked straight into his eyes. I could not tell if he was serious. He just smirked. "Well, it's been rough. Still, I am determined to walk again. I know that it was a horrible injury. I think, though, if my head got better, that my hip will heal as well."

"I will pray for it every day," I told him.

"I would appreciate that. I need all the prayers I can get."

*****

The next few weeks continued quietly. I slowly continued to regain strength. I was not sure if I would ever feel completely healthy. I would wake up in the morning and, at times, look in the mirror. I remembered how I used to look before I came on this journey. The girl who looked back at me from the mirror was not who I once was. The healthy glow in my cheeks and the beautiful black hair was gone. Instead, I saw what Sima had called "a ghost of a girl." There was no color in my cheeks, and instead, my face looked dull and pasty. My hair had turned into a mop of black that hung just past my cheeks. I was lucky it had grown some, but all of the edges looked dull and frayed.

Furthermore, my bones stuck out all over the place. My cheekbones looked higher than before. I guessed that I had lost at least 30 pounds, and I had not been that large before. After a few days of studying myself, I decided to give up on mirrors and just do the best with what I had.

The bright point of my days was Sima. I would walk by his room, usually to find him napping. When I saw him awake, I would go to him, and we would talk. He never seemed to run out of funny stories or exciting thoughts that he had. I yearned more than anything to speak with Alex, though. Whenever I saw him, my heart beat wildly in my chest. I could not seem to forget the kiss that we had shared. He would sometimes walk by me and smile, and I would smile back nervously. Still, I hardly had any conversation with him. He seemed occupied in the barn. It would not have bothered me so much if Katya also did not seem to have an increased amount of chores in the barn.

Katya's perfection bothered me. She was the most beautiful person I had ever seen. She never raised her voice. She was always respectful towards Alex's parents. Whenever I compared myself to her, I found I could not rival her. No wonder Alex seemed to prefer Katya to me. I once even prepared water and biscuits to take to Mr. Milichkov and Alex while they worked and found that Katya had beat me to it. While Alex stood there speaking with Katya in low tones, Mr. Milichkov, who seemed to sense my disappointment, took the biscuits from me and grinned his thanks. I shrugged and walked away.

Evenings at the Milichkov home were terrific. Mrs. Milichkova, who never seemed to stop baking and seemed to eternally stand at the stove, would make a gigantic meal, and the entire family would gather for supper. Sima was still not strong enough to join the family for supper, but it always felt so good to be part of a family. I could remember nothing of my family or ever being as close to someone as the Milichkovs were to each other. Even if Alex had been absent so many years, he seemed to fit right back into the family life. I, at first, felt like an outsider looking in. Eventually, I began to feel comfortable and as if this were my home. I still felt guilty about imposing. I said so to Mrs. Milichkova one evening after the rest of the family had retired to their rooms.

She put a hand on my back. "You are not imposing."

"You have done so much for me," I told her. I could not tell how much longer I would need to stay. As of yet, Mr. Milichkov had not heard anything about my family from any of his contacts. For some strange reason, I did not seem to mind. I was not even sure if they would want to take me back. Now that I had arrived in Alaska, the anticipation of meeting my family decreased. Sima and Alex felt more like my family. The Milichkovs began to feel like my family. Something about them made me think I was part of a more extraordinary loving family and that I belonged.

"And where would you go, might I ask?" Mrs. Milichkova asked, drawing my thoughts back to the conversation.

"I have nowhere to go right now," I told her.

"You are welcome to stay here as long as you need. I have always wanted a second daughter. I would not mind if you stayed forever. You are a good person. Alex has told me how much you risked for Sima and him." My spirits lifted at her words. At least Alex seemed to remember who I was. I then leaned over and hugged her. This woman was such an inspiration. She had such a kind, calm and loving way about her. She indeed did not seem to have a mean bone in her body. There also appeared to be some sort of strength in her. I had seen the same strength in Captain James Francis's wife.

*****

The next day I was determined to at least try to speak with Alex. I just wanted to talk to him. I felt that if I could only speak to him, the connection we had between us would somehow ignite a spark. I had a strange nagging feeling that I was losing that spark. I felt that I had to grab at any chance possible to keep it alive. I casually asked Mrs. Milichkova where I could find Alex. She told me that he was out in the clearing in the back of the cabin helping his father set up a fence. I walked around the end of the cabin. When I reached the clearing, I stopped. Alex was casually leaning on one of the posts and looking up at Katya, who stood on the newly built fence. She was laughing. I turned back to the cabin with my head down. I wondered how any work ever got done with Alex so occupied. It also baffled me how Katya seemed to move so swiftly.

Chapter 26
June 15, 1888

A week later, after supper, Mr. Milichkov approached me. "Anna, may I please speak with you?" I looked over at him cautiously. He always made me feel as if I had committed some heinous crime.

"Yes?" I asked warily. I felt as if I was being called to task by Mr. Shubert.

Mr. Milichkov smirked a bit as though he could see my discomfort. "How about we sit down?" He sat on the sofa, and I sat down on the armchair across from him.

"What's the trouble, sir? Have I done something wrong?" I could not think of anything I had done.

"No, of course not," he said with a smile, and I felt my shoulders relax. "Still, I think we should talk seriously about this business of your parents." I sat up expectantly and listened to him speak.

"Alex has helped me pen several letters to my contacts in Fort Yukon and several towns south of here. Since we do not have a direction, I feel as if we are looking for a needle in a haystack. So far, my search efforts have yielded nothing. No one in the radius of two hundred miles seems to have heard of a Mark and Lubov'. No one even seems to know of anyone who may be missing a daughter. That is not to say that they could not be somewhere else."

I regarded him carefully. The whole reason I had set out to Alaska initially had been to find my parents. I had set out in search of a family, to find a place where I belonged. Life in Maine had been mundane and complex for me. I had come to Alaska and had gotten more than I had bargained for. Mr. Milichkov looked at me as if he expected an answer. I swallowed. I had no answer for him, and I was not sure how to respond. The hope of finding my family had been what had driven me the first few months of our journey, somehow, though, during the trip, my focus had shifted. Still, I felt it was vital for me to locate the people to whom I belonged.

"Are you even sure your parents are in Alaska?" Mr. Milichkov asked. I shook my head. He must think me ridiculous, I thought. I knew that when I had left Maine, I had gone in search of family. *Maybe you have already found your family*; the thought caught me off guard.

I glanced at Mr. Milichkov, who looked as if he still expected an answer. "I don't know what to say to you right now, Mr. Milichkov," I told him truthfully. "Please let me think about what you said." I stood up swiftly and walked to my room. While he had been very kind the whole time, I did not know how to tell him my thoughts. I believed he was a very knowledgeable man and could help if I needed it. Still, I was not entirely sure of how to approach him. I needed someone else to talk to.

After gathering my thoughts in the quiet of my room, I walked over to Sima's room and knocked on the door.

"Come in," I heard his reply from the other side.

I slowly opened the door. He was sitting up in bed. An empty supper tray lay on the table next to him. Sima grinned as I walked in.

"Sima, I need to speak with you."

"I'm always ready to talk with you, Anna." Sima motioned to the chair, and I sat in it.

"I am not sure how to start." I looked at my hands. How could I tell Sima that I did not feel that I needed to keep looking for my parents? He would think I was crazy. How would I explain to him that I thought that I had found a place where I belonged?

"Try starting with the truth," Sima said quietly. I raised my face to look at him and our eyes locked. For a second, I thought that he looked nervous. I could not figure out why.

"Sima, I wanted to speak to you about the search for my parents." My words came out slowly. A look of disappointment flitted across Sima's face, but then he seemed to give himself a mental shake, and he nodded.

"What about them? Have you heard any news?"

"No, I haven't. The truth is Mr. Milichkov said that he has not found even a trace of them and that it is like looking for a needle in a haystack."

"That's not very comforting, is it?" Sima questioned.

"No, not really, but you see, the problem is that I don't seem to mind so much."

"What do you mean?" Sima looked at me curiously.

I took a deep breath and tried to form my thoughts into words. "When I joined Mr. Shubert's group, I went in search of my family. I feel as if I found the place where I belong. Somehow in the middle of Canada, I stopped focusing on people who I do not know and started to focus on those who were right there with me all the time."

Sima looked at me carefully and then brushed his hair away from his face with his fingers. "So you want to tell Mr. Milichkov to call off the search?"

"Yes, of course, I would love to meet the people who brought me into this world. However, I have so little to go on, and I sense that I would not connect with them. Mr. Milichkov has also already done so much for me. If I decide to keep looking, it will have to be on my own."

"Perhaps one day you'll locate them. I think they would be happy to see that their daughter has turned into such a beautiful woman."

"I wish that I could just even have the smallest memory to go on. Still, it is so strange; it is as if I am some sort of lonely person who just happened to land in Maine."

Sima gave me a wry smile. "Just remember, you will always have friends now, no matter where you go. I will never forget you."

"Thank you, Sima, for letting me speak to you." I stood to leave.

"When has speaking to me ever been a problem?" Sima asked. His tone seemed changed, more serious.

I smiled at him. "You are the person with whom I feel the most comfortable. You are my true friend." I walked to the door. I felt Sima's eyes still on the back of my head. I turned and found that I was right. Sima was sitting up, and his eyes still gazed at me. A strange feeling crept up on me as I stood there watching him.

"You can speak with me whenever you want." He grinned. "Even if you have to wake me up in the middle of the night." Emotions that were not new to me started to flutter around my heart. I quickly shook them off. I was sure that I was silly. That night, though, I lay deep into the hours of darkness, unable to fall asleep.

The next day I happened to walk into Alex by accident. I was just headed out the door into the vegetable garden when I flew into him. He seemed to be hurrying into the cabin.

He stopped and said, "What's the rush?"

"Oh nothing, your mother just asked me to get some cabbages from the garden."

To my great surprise, Alex said, "How about I help you?"

"Sure," I answered and walked out the door. Alex followed me. Mrs. Milichkova had a large vegetable garden. Second to cooking, she seemed to spend the most time in her garden. I glanced over at Alex, who stood by me next to the neat rows of vegetables.

"How many cabbages did my mother want?" he asked.

I set the basket that I had carried outside on the ground next to me. "She said three." I leaned over and started to gather the cabbage.

Alex knelt as well and pulled at one of the vegetables. We worked silently for several seconds, and I relished the fact that I was alone with him. The camaraderie between us had not seemed to have died.

The friendship between us seemed to remain the same as it was; a friendship and nothing more.

"How are you feeling lately?" Alex asked, breaking the silence.

"I've been well. There are days when I still feel weak, but in general, I feel much stronger than I did."

"You look a lot better too," Alex said.

I was astonished that he had even noticed my appearance. I peeked over at him. I wanted to say more. I hoped that he would say something further to me. He had never mentioned the kiss that we had shared. I wondered if he even remembered that he had kissed me. The thought that this behavior was rude crossed my mind. I did not understand him. He had to have some feeling for me. I handed him the cabbage that I had just picked, and he placed it in the basket.

"How have you been?" I asked in return. My voice sounded hoarse.

Alex shrugged. "As well as can be expected, I also have some bad days. I am sorry that you and Sima seem to be struggling so much more than I am. I am glad to see that you are back on your feet."

"You were stronger, to begin with," I said quietly. I regarded him from the corner of my eye. I realized that he was wearing short sleeves and that I had not ever seen him without heavy clothing. His arms were strong, and his muscles visible. They also seemed to be enhanced by his olive-colored skin. No wonder Katya was attracted to him. Still, I felt that I had the advantage. I had spent the last nine months with him.

"Unfortunately, I could not share some of my strength with you," Alex said and straightened out his back. We had enough cabbages in the basket, and he now held it in his arms. My eyes met his icy blue gaze. I felt that if I was ever going to say anything, it had to be now. He stood there as if he was expecting me to do so. I was about to open my mouth to speak when I heard someone calling Alex's name. It was Katya. I listened to her voice coming from the direction of the barn.

Alex looked over his shoulder and then back at me. "I'm sorry, I have to go."

He handed the basket over to me and then turned on his heel and strode towards the barn. I wanted to call him back, to tell him that I needed to be with him. I could not let go of the feelings that I had when he was around me. My mouth remained shut, however, as I stared after him. With tears in my eyes, I walked towards the cabin.

Mrs. Milichkova waited inside for me, and I quietly handed her the basket of cabbages that I had just picked with Alex. I tried to keep my face away from her so she would not see the fact that tears were threatening to fall down my cheeks. Mrs. Milichkova started preparing dinner, and I began to set the plates on the large wooden table. Life seemed to be so unfair at the moment. A tear rolled down one of my cheeks. I quickly brushed it away. A touch on my shoulder made me turn around.

Mrs. Milichkova was looking at me with concern in her eyes. "What's the matter, my dear?" she asked.

I just shook my head, and the tears continued to fall from my eyes. She then took me into her arms and held me. The comfort of her arms made me wish that I knew where my mother was. She did not speak and just patted my back. It seemed as if she understood that was what I needed at that moment.

"The strain of this journey has been too much for you," she said finally. I regarded her quietly; if it were only the strain of the journey.

"Also, my husband said that this morning you had told him not to continue to search for your parents. I understand that you have had much to think about lately."

I just nodded silently. She was so kind and understanding. I was not sure, though, that I could explain to her the whole depth of my feelings. She loved Alex and Katya more than she did me. She also probably hoped that they would be together.

"How about you go and lie down in your room until supper time? My husband will come to get you." I smiled at her and then went to my room.

By the time Mr. Milichkov knocked on my door, I felt much better and had a chance to take a few deep breaths and calm myself. I opened the door and walked to the main room for supper. Mrs. Milichkova gave me a reassuring smile as I entered. I returned her smile. Alex and Katya came into the room, and we all stood for prayer. After praying before the meal, we sat down. Mrs. Milichkova and Katya filled our plates with meat stuffed into cabbage leaves. While I was struggling emotionally, I realized that I did have to be thankful for what I did have. I thought back to the men who had lost their lives during our journey, and suddenly the feelings I had for Alex did not seem so important. I at least had a place to stay and people who cared about what happened to me.

After supper, Alex turned to Katya and me. "Let's take Sima's supper to him all together. I think it would be good for us to cheer him up a bit. He seems to be lonely in his room."

The ungrateful thought that Alex could talk to Sima more often came into my head. I had noticed a long time ago that Sima was lonely and probably more emotionally drained than I was.

When we walked into Sima's room, he was sitting up in bed reading a book. He looked up at us and smiled. The green tone of his skin had greatly diminished in the past few days, and his smile lit his whole face. He glanced over at me and gave me a discreet wink. I quickly winked back at him.

"We brought you supper," Alex told him triumphantly. He sounded as though he were some sort of hero.

Sima took the supper tray from Alex's hands and placed it across his lap. "It is wonderful to see all of you. Unfortunately, I do not have enough space for everyone to sit."

"That's all right," Alex said. "Katya can sit on this chair here." He pulled the chair out for Katya. I remained standing and looked around awkwardly after Katya sat down.

Sima gave Alex a scathing look. "Anna, how about you sit on the end of my bed?" I sat down on the edge of the bed. Alex remained standing. He did not seem to notice Sima's angry stare.

After I sat down, Sima looked down at his food and said, "This looks delicious."

"Of course, it is delicious," Alex said. "My mother made it. Everything she makes is tasty."

"Maybe it's just better than anything we had on the trail," Sima said as he bit into a piece of his food.

"Perhaps it just proves that we are not good cooks," I said with a snicker.

"It's not as if we had much to cook with," Alex answered me.

Sima, Alex, and I laughed. I looked over at Katya. She sat silently and did not join in. I was glad that she was not able to contribute to the conversation. I felt guilty for thinking so. She indeed had not done anything to hurt me on purpose.

"Thank you for all coming in to cheer me up. I have gotten a bit lonely here. Although, Anna has kept me company for many days now." I gave Sima a grateful look. He always had a kind word for me. Sima raised both eyebrows at me, and his eyes twinkled.

"I apologize that I have not been able to visit with you more often, Sima. Father has kept me busy working in the barn," Alex said.

Sima nodded his understanding. Nevertheless, I wondered if I imagined a flicker of hurt in Sima's eyes. He noticed me observing him, and he shrugged slightly. We spent about another half an hour in lighthearted conversation. Katya did not add much to our discussion, but she laughed whenever Alex said anything.

When Sima finished his food, Alex took his tray and said, "I'll take this to mother."

"I'll go with you," Katya said and stood up. Sima handed Alex the tray with his plate. Alex headed out the door, and Katya followed him.

"Alex and Katya seem to be spending a whole lot of time together lately," I said after the two of them had left the room.

"Yes, they have," Sima agreed and gave me a pointed look. I knew what it meant. My hopes of ever being with Alex were slowly wilting.

"You, Sima, are the only one who knows how I feel."

"Did you talk to Alex?" he asked even though he already knew the answer.

I shook my head in reply.

"I think you should tell him. At least that way, if he has any romantic feelings for you, he will know how you feel. He may not even realize that you are interested. Katya may just seem more attracted than you are." I looked at Sima gratefully. My spirit lifted a bit. Although I felt that Alex already knew what his choice would be.

"I think I may be too late," I said sadly, as I looked at Sima.

"Anna, why don't you marry me?" Sima asked suddenly. "I told you I would marry you if Alex didn't."

"I remember, but are you sincere?" I asked, utterly stunned by his proposal.

Sima studied me carefully and said, "Anna, for the longest time, I have thought that you were one of the most beautiful women I have ever met, and I do not just think so because I have not seen many women in a while."

I stared at him for a second. I felt tears stinging my eyes. I had wanted to hear those words from someone for such a long time, but unfortunately not from Sima.

I cleared my throat. "Sima, do you love me, though?"

"Anna, what is love but caring about someone so deeply that you could not bear the thought of not being with that person? I am not sure when it happened exactly, but I am very much in love with you."

"Sima, do you really feel that way?" I was so astonished that those were the only words I could utter.

Sima, for the first time since I had met him, suddenly looked bashful. He gave me a sort of shy half-grin. "Would I say it if I didn't mean it?"

"I don't know what to say. Why didn't you say anything earlier?"

"I don't think I have to explain that one," Sima said, looking straight at me. I knew the answer. My love obsession with Alex had stood in the way.

"Now that you think that Alex will not marry me, you have decided to tell me this?"

Sima took my hand. "Yes."

"So you want me to marry you?" I just stared at him. His brown eyes met mine, and I had to use every ounce of my strength not to look down. There was something in his eyes that told me that he was completely honest about his feelings.

I looked straight back at him. "Sima, I care so much for you, but I do not know if I love you. I don't know if I can think of you that way. Please give me some time to think about it."

Sima's hand tightened on mine. "Anna, no matter what you decide, remember that I will always respect and love you. I think you should talk to Alex anyway. Tell him about your feelings and see what he says."

"I will, Sima. I'll go now." I leaned over and kissed him on the cheek.

He touched my shoulder. "Hopefully, I'll see you later."

I gave him a small smile as I walked toward the door and laughed a bit nervously. "In such a small house, it seems unavoidable."

I walked out of his room, feeling more confused than I had ever been in my entire life. I started to feel faint. I needed some fresh air. I escaped out onto the porch and sat on the wooden bench next to the door. I leaned my head back against the wall of the cabin and took a few deep breaths. I closed my eyes and tried to clear my head. I opened my eyes a few minutes later as I heard footsteps walking up the porch steps. It was Alex.

"Hello Anna," he said as he walked over to me.

"Hello," I answered, swallowing a large lump in my throat. My heart began to beat faster, as it was accustomed to doing while he was around.

"May I join you?" he asked.

"Of course." I moved over on the bench allowing him to sit next to me.

He sat down. I moved away carefully so as not to allow myself to touch his arm.

"Anything wrong?" he asked.

"No, I was just thinking," I answered.

"Hmm, anything interesting?"

"Yes, actually about you." I had to be honest. That was what Sima had urged me to do.

Alex looked at me in surprise. "Really? What were you thinking about me?"

"Just about everything we have been through and how close we've grown."

Alex took a deep breath. "Yes, there is that. We have grown close. Anna, what if I brought someone else into our friendship? You know it seems like you, Sima, and I are sort of bound together, but eventually, we have to move on." I, unfortunately, understood precisely what he was trying to say, and my heart began to sink deeper and deeper into my stomach.

"Are you talking about Katya?" I asked. "Are you in love with her?"

"Yes, I am, Anna. How did you know that?"

"Alex, I have eyes in my head, you know."

He laughed a bit. "Has it been that obvious?"

"Well, it was evident to me," I answered him.

"Really?" Alex had a suspicious note to his voice. I kept my eyes down and studied my worn-out hands.

"Alex," my voice came out in a squeak. I cleared my throat, embarrassed. "Alex, have you ever loved me?"

"Loved you?" Alex almost sounded shocked. I was a bit injured at how he made it sound ludicrous.

"Yes, because I love you." I could feel my cheeks flaming. I could sense Alex's eyes on me, but I could not look up.

"Anna, I never loved you like that. I care about you a lot, but I do not love you in that way. I'm not even sure that you love me. I think you think you love me, but I am the first man you met. I am not sure you realize the difference between love and infatuation." I could feel my heart in my stomach, and tears were starting to pour down my cheeks.

He suddenly took me by the chin and turned my face towards him. "Look, Anna, I know that this is hard for you, and while I am not much older than you, I do have some more experience. I was afraid of something like this, but I know I could not be with you for the rest of my life. We are different people, and quite simply, I love Katya, and she does love me."

I forced myself to look at him and said, "Alex, I am sorry, and I apologize for embarrassing you."

"You have not embarrassed me, Anna, and I wish you all the happiness in the world. I will always look after you as a friend, and if you ever need any help with anything, let me know."

I gave him a watery smile. "Alex, thank you."

He hugged me tightly then and kissed my cheek. "Good luck." He then stood up and walked into the cabin.

After he walked away, I felt a physical break in my heart. Tears started to course down my cheeks. I sobbed in silence until I could not sob anymore. I had to forget about him, but I could not just use Sima as my escape. I needed time to pray and to think. I did not want to marry someone that I did not love. After a few more hours of loneliness, I walked inside and fell into bed. I kept praying for clarity until I fell asleep.

*****

The following day, when I awoke, I could hardly open my eyes. My whole body felt emotionally and physically exhausted. After morning prayers and breakfast, I came back to my room, sat down at the small table next to my bed, and took out some ink and a piece of paper. I started to fill my pen and make a list of things that I liked about Sima and then a list of things I liked about Alex. As I wrote, I noticed that the lists were almost the same length. On Alex's list, I wrote; *sometimes funny, responsible, caring, and kind.*

On Sima's list, I wrote; *always makes me laugh, caring, sometimes responsible, and always tries to make everyone feel better.* As I looked at Alex's list, the word, *boring,* crossed my mind, and I realized how many times I had squashed it and had tried so many times not to let that thought cross my mind because my feelings had been so strong. I thought of all the times that Sima and I had laughed at Alex's perfection and at the fact that Alex was ready to do the right thing all the time. By this time, I had mulled over the conversation that I had had with Alex last night about a thousand times. The more I thought about it, the less I liked him. It was the first time I had opened up so emotionally to him, and he had acted as if he had had nothing to do with it. He also had said that he had a lot more life experience. I did not believe that. I had to live on my own for years and had traveled through all of Canada with him. Still, my feelings could not leave so quickly, and I could not stop my heart from beating when I heard his voice in the hall. I put my head on the table and began to cry.

*****

After a few days of emotional breakdowns and dodging both Alex and Sima, I decided to clear my head and get away from the cabin as far as possible. I took Snow Spots with me if, as Mr. Milichkov had said, there could be bears around. My dog walked calmly next to me as tears kept dripping down my cheeks. No matter how hard I tried, I could not stop the tears from falling down my face. My dreams of Alex could not just dissipate. Also, the thought of Sima being in love with me was too overwhelming at the moment. I had lived in a bad dream for the past two days.

I walked about two miles from the house when I saw a small waterfall formed between the rocks on the river. I sat in a patch of wildflowers and tried to drink in the clean air that smelled of wood and flowers. It was then that I heard voices that seemed to be behind the rocks that were to my right. I climbed the mossy rock and looked down to see who it was. I had not thought twice, and I did not think anything about the fact that the conversation had just stopped.

As I looked down, I regretted ever climbing that rock. Alex and Katya sat below, kissing passionately. Of course, to my great chagrin, Snow Spots had climbed up beside me and started to bark. Both Alex and Katya looked up before I even thought to move. The color in my cheeks must have been visible three miles away. I slid down the rock quickly and ran as fast as I could all the way home with the dog at my heels. I ran to my room and closed the door. I stared at the table and opened the drawer where I held the lists I made about Alex and Sima. I took Alex's list and tore it up.

What was the point of making a list when he had never been mine to have? I would never be with him now unless I took Katya into the woods and got her lost. I doubted that was a practical idea. I lay in my bed curled into a ball. What would Alex think of me now? He probably suspected that I had followed him there. I stayed in my room until Mrs. Milichkova knocked on my door and told me it was supper time. I trudged into the kitchen with my head down. I tried to look at everyone's shoes and avoid eye contact. I noticed Mr. Milichkov was not present.

He suddenly came in and announced, "Sima feels strong enough to join us for supper." My heart froze. I did not know how I could face Sima today.

"I'll help you carry him, Father," Alex said. My heart thudded against my rib cage as Alex walked by. I could feel his animosity as he passed by me. He must hate me, I thought.

Alex and Mr. Milichkov carried Sima into the room. He was sitting propped up in a chair wrapped up in blankets. My heart went out to him. I was sure he wanted to walk so much. Mr. Milichkov and Alex moved Sima up to the table. We all said a prayer and sat down to eat. I was hardly able to look at the food that Mrs. Milichkova placed in front of me. I pushed it around aimlessly on my plate.

No one else said anything until Mrs. Milichkova, in her infinite kindness, asked, "How was everyone's day today?"

Everyone's eyes remained glued to their plates. "Good."

Mrs. Milichkova appeared not to notice the general discomfort in the room. "Alex and Katya, you went for a walk. How was that?"

I could feel my cheeks burning as Alex answered, "We weren't the only ones who went out for a walk today."

"Was there a ghost?" Sima asked, laughing. I felt a laugh come up in my throat, but I forced myself to keep quiet. I willed myself not to glance in Sima's direction.

"Yes, who else went for a walk?" Mr. Milichkov asked.

"I did, sir," I answered quietly, feeling as if I sat in a courtroom. I forced myself to look up. Alex, who sat across from me, was sending me a look that could have frozen water. Sima shot me a look from the head of the table. I could see him trying not to laugh. I felt as if he probably knew exactly what had transpired. Katya sat in silence. She was perhaps as mortified as I was.

"Did you see each other, or did you all walk together?" Mrs. Milichkova asked innocently.

"No," I answered. "I walked on my own, and I bumped into Alex and Katya."

"That's an understatement," Alex mumbled from across the table.

"What was that, son?" Mrs. Milichkova asked.

"Oh, nothing, it was fine, Mother. Anyway, Father, what are you planning to do with the furs we have collected so far?"

Mr. Milichkov, who did not seem to miss anything, looked relieved to change the subject. Sima sat there with his hand at his mouth. I looked at him, and he rolled his eyes. It took every ounce of strength in my body not to start laughing. I grabbed a mug of hot tea and hid my face in it until I calmed. I knew if I lost my composure, Alex's whole family would think that I was a lunatic.

After a long, drawn-out supper that seemed as if it would never end, we finally were able to leave the table. Alex and Mr. Milichkov helped Sima back to his room and went to feed the animals. I decided to go to my room. I mumbled good night to Katya and Mrs. Milichkova. I could not bring myself to look at Katya. Who knew what Alex had told her about me?

I shut the door and changed for bed. I lay thinking of Sima that night. I had felt connected to him that whole time at the table. I had felt as if he knew everything that I was thinking. He always made me feel better. I thought about how much I wanted to tell him about what had happened with Alex. I wanted to hear his assurance that I was not stupid and that no one thought that way about me. Talking to him had always eased my fears. Also, I began to think about what life would be like if I married him. I could imagine that we would be happy. I knew that we could sit through many suppers and send each other looks and know precisely what the other was thinking. I did not want to stay on my own.

I knew that I could be with Sima and be happy. I could not give myself a reason not to marry him. Alex no longer stood in my way. Also, his anger at me for seeing him and Katya had helped to put a stop to my romantic thoughts. Sima knew more about me than any other person, and I was happy that he did. I thought of his smile and his beautiful brown eyes, and I realized that my heartbeat had increased several times when he had looked at me. I also thought about how I felt when Sima lay on Canada and Alaska's border in a small fur trading town fighting for his life. I had thought then that I would lose my mind if Sima died. He did not die, and he was here. We needed each other. There was no way that we could part and go our separate ways now. Not after everything we had lived through together. I prayed again that I would be sure of my decision.

Chapter 27 June 18, 1888

The following day, I awoke with a desire to talk to Sima more than ever before. I wanted to tell him my decision. I had no idea how to approach his room, and I walked by his open door quickly so as he would not see me. I had to time my entrance. I could not walk in with my fingers shaking.

As I ate pancakes and meat pie for breakfast, Mrs. Milichkova said, "Sima was not feeling too well this morning. He must have become overtired at supper last night. I did not think it was good for him to sit up so long last night. I brought him breakfast this morning. Anna, after you are done eating, could you be a dear and go get his plates from his room?"

I looked at her and wondered if she said it on purpose. She seemed as innocent as a lamb. I did not know if she realized four confused lovesick men and women lived in her house. Then again, she was Alex's mother and probably did not miss a beat. I was also worried about Sima. How long would he be so weak that he would get tired from just sitting up?

I timidly walked toward his room after breakfast. I stood next to his door for a few moments and then peeked in. What I saw surprised me. Sima was leaning heavily against his washstand and trying to stand. I ran to his side and put my arm around his waist.

"Sima, what are you doing?" I asked as I made him sit down in his bed.

Sima sighed. "I was hoping to stand."

"But Sima, your limbs are not healed yet," I told him.

"I just hoped that if I could walk, I would be able to see you," he told me as he moved back and leaned against his pillows.

"Sima, I..." I started, and my voice choked in my throat.

"I thought you said it was hard not to see each other in this house. I thought I had asked you a sort of important question."

I looked at the floor. "Sima, I know. I needed time to think."

"I'm sorry, Anna. Come sit up on the bed. I feel awkward sitting while you are standing."

I sat on the bed, and he held out his hand, and I took it. "Sima, I have been thinking, and I realized that I don't think I love Alex, and I think that I want to marry you."

A slow grin spread across Sima's face. "Anna, I love you," he said, and his grip on my hand tightened.

"Sima, last night I felt so connected to you. It was as if you could read my thoughts, and I thought I could not lose you. You know everything about me. I care for you deeply. I want to be with you."

"I know what you mean," Sima said as he leaned against his pillows. "Anna, while I am ecstatic that you agreed. I want to ask you something. Do you love me?"

"I wish I could say yes. I know that I have a deep affection for you and as I realized, I have a deep connection to you, but my feelings can't just switch over so swiftly."

I could tell that there was a look of disappointment on Sima's face, but then he smiled. "I feel a little bit selfish marrying you just because I love you. I do not want to monopolize your feelings." Sima let my hand go for a second.

"Sima, I think that I am a bit selfish as well. I don't want to hurt you by not loving you, but I also don't want to be left alone. Besides you and Alex, I have no one. You are the person that I feel most comfortable with."

"Suppose when we are married you meet someone else?" Sima studied the quilt on the bed, avoiding my eyes.

I reached out and touched Sima's shoulder. "Sima, I could never hurt you. Quite honestly, there are not that many young men around here."

Sima laughed a bit at my comment. "That is quite true. I can only hope that you will learn to love me like you loved Alex." What he said struck a chord in my heart.

"Sima, I do not know if I ever loved Alex. I was blown away because he was the first man I had ever loved. I was obsessed with the thought that I wanted to be with him, and I never stopped twice to think that I should be with someone else. When I saw him kissing Katya, I started to lose my feelings for him. If I loved him, I wouldn't have lost my feelings for him so quickly."

Sima laughed aloud suddenly. "I thought that is what happened. Alex looked angrier than a wet hen."

I laughed too. It was good to laugh and let the severe tension in the room break into pieces. "Alex probably thinks I followed them there," I told Sima as I wiped away tears of laughter from my eyes.

"Ha! It would serve him right. I can't lie, I think he led you on and just changed his mind when he saw Katya."

"Sima, that is kind of you to stand up for me, but one cannot choose whom to love."

Sima touched my cheek at that moment. "Aren't you making that choice right now?" he asked gently.

I looked straight into his attractive brown eyes. "I suppose I am."

"Look, Anna, I would love to kiss you, but I promise you that I will not kiss you until you ask me to, even if we're married before that."

"All right." I nodded my head slightly. I could slowly feel the heat rising to my cheeks. I wondered what it would be like to kiss Sima.

"Anyway, Alex has nothing on me in that department. You should count your lucky stars that you ended up with me." Sima grinned when I looked at him with raised eyebrows.

"How would you know?"

"Experience," he replied with a chuckle. I was a bit shocked by his statement. I had never thought of how many girls he may have courted before me.

"Sima," I started slowly, "how many girls have you kissed?"

"Um, let me see now, probably five or seven, perhaps it was seven. That's a lot better than Alex's two." At that comment, the heat rushed to my face, and I looked down at the quilt.

I could see a hint of a grin from Sima. He chuckled and crossed his arms. "Should I make it three?"

"It was a mistake," I answered in a barely audible whisper.

"A mistake?" Sima questioned. He laughed good-naturedly. "Anna, as much as I have kissed girls, I can safely tell you that it was never a mistake."

"I mean, we were both overcome with emotion. It was when you were unconscious, and we did not know what would happen to you." My cheeks were burning, and I was quite ashamed to admit the events to Sima.

"Quite a suitable solution to the problem," Sima said dryly.

"That did not sound right, Sima. Please believe me. I really do not think I have any feelings left for Alex."

"Let's hope not." Sima smiled.

"Well, you should not be talking, you and your seven girls you kissed."

Sima shrugged. "I was young and stupid. I can safely tell you I haven't kissed anybody in the last nine months."

"That's a great comfort, Sima, considering Alex and I are practically the only two people you have seen for most of those nine months. I am not sure about all of those girls, you know." I stopped for a moment and then continued, "I am sure you left a lot of them heartbroken. I am not sure how I feel about being the eighth one." I laughed a little, but at the same time, I began to realize that I had wanted to be the first girl that he had loved.

"At least I had no little escapades while you were lying somewhere unconscious." Sima looked at me. I could tell that his eyes were laughing. I blushed and looked down, avoiding his eyes.

"You know it's all right, Anna," Sima said, gently touching my arm with his finger. I still looked down.

"Anna, look at me and listen to what I say." I raised my eyes. The feeling in his eyes made me suddenly feel as if I should look down again.

"All of those girls, I honestly don't remember half their names, but if I kissed you, I would remember." My heart stopped for a second. I felt as if I was becoming drawn more and more to him by the minute. I almost thought that I could kiss him now, but I felt suddenly uncomfortable and cleared my throat.

"Thank you, Sima. I am not sure that I deserve to be loved so much."

Sima suddenly touched my hair and gently pulled me to him. I leaned my head against his chest. His lips kissed my hair. "Anna, you will not regret marrying me. I will do everything to give you all the love you deserve. You deserve to be loved." It was so comforting to lean my head against him. I could feel his heart thudding through his shirt.

I looked up at him. "Thank you." We held on to each other for a few minutes longer, and then I said, "I think that I need to go, or Mrs. Milichkova will begin to wonder what happened to me."

Sima hugged me a bit and then let me go. "Come back after dinner. We can talk some more then."

"All right." I felt shy, and I hastily gathered his plates and walked out of the room.

I thought my cheeks must be the color of the red morning sun. I needed to talk to someone. I had to admit that I was apprehensive in accepting Sima's proposal, but it did make a lot of sense. I had no idea who to talk to, though. Mrs. Milichkova seemed to be too unsuspecting and too kind to delve out the hard truth. Suddenly I thought of Mr. Milichkov; he seemed like a strong man who would not be afraid to tell me the truth.

I walked out of the cabin, and of course, Alex was approaching the house. I wanted to run back inside, but Alex approached me rather calmly. "Good morning."

"Alex, have you seen your father?" I asked in a steady voice.

"Yes, he's in the barn. Everything all right?"

"Oh yes, I just needed to ask him something."

"Good, see you later then." He walked into the house. I shrugged my shoulders. He had acted as if nothing had happened in the last few days. I hoped that he had forgotten my multiple awkward moments and hoped that we could end up just being friends. I knew it would be quite a few weeks before I could feel comfortable around him again. I headed towards the weathered barn doors.

My courage failed me as I got nearer to the barn. I entered. I saw Mr. Milichkov standing in the dark barn. He was in a far stable brushing one of the horses. I approached slowly. Mr. Milichkov did not see me until I was only a few feet away.

He looked up from his chore and smiled. "Hello Anna, have you come to help me?"

"I can help you," I answered. "However, I had a question for you." I stood there awkwardly. I did not know where to start.

"You know what? You do not have to help me." He put his brush down and came over to me. Mr. Milichkov now loomed over me. "What is your question?"

I cleared my throat and focused my gaze on the barn floor. "I am not sure how to start."

"I have a feeling that this has something to do with yesterday's conversation at supper." Mr. Milichkov was an intimidating figure, but as I looked up at his face in the shadows of the barn, his blue eyes radiated kindness.

"Well, yes and no," I told him.

"Then how about we take a walk towards the river? It might help to clear our heads, and it will get me a break from this old barn, just a second." He closed the door to the stable.

He started to walk towards the barn doors, and I followed him. He then strolled towards the cabin and knocked on the door.

Mrs. Milichkova came out onto the porch. "Yes?"

"Anna and I will just take a walk. I wanted to let you know if we are not back early enough, you can start supper without us." A look passed between Mrs. Milichkova and Mr. Milichkov that seemed to be one of mutual understanding. I wondered how much they knew of what had happened. I stood there uncomfortably. Alex's parents were the kindest people that I knew, and I felt like an imposter.

"Don't come back too late. I do not want both of you too hungry, and Anna is probably still a bit weak."

Mr. Milichkov looked at his wife with what I thought was a look of unreserved adoration. "Don't you worry, we won't get hungry, and I will take care of Anna."

I still wondered how I was going to explain everything to him. I felt a lump rising in my throat. Then Mr. Milichkov leaned over and kissed his wife on the forehead. It was so simple, yet it touched my heart. He was such an intimidating, large man, yet he loved his wife so much. Mrs. Milichkova was a lucky woman to have him love her so, *like Sima loves me,* entered my mind. It stood true. I wondered if I should consider myself fortunate.

"You better go ahead then." Mrs. Milichkova smiled and waved to us.

We hiked down the path that led to the river in the woods. When we were far enough from the house, Mr. Milichkov looked down at me. "So, what did you want to ask me?"

"Well, sir, I am a bit confused emotionally." My heart was beating hard. I had never discussed any kind of problems with older people. Quite frankly, I seldom talked to them.

"What is confusing you?" Mr. Milichkov asked. He did not seem to be surprised that I was confused. He probably thought I was the strangest person he had ever met.

"I loved your son," I blurted out. Mr. Milichkov stopped and looked at me from his full height.

"Yes?" he prompted me to continue.

"I don't think I ever truly loved him, but now Sima asked me to marry him, and I agreed." This statement came out in one hurried breath.

Mr. Milichkov looked at me seriously. He probably thought I had taken leave of my senses. "Anna, let's sit down." We sat down on a mossy log. He then looked at me and said, "Marriage is quite a serious decision, but I would say that Sima is quite a good choice. I am not sure that you would get along well with my son, and I have sensed that you and Sima get along quite well."

"So, you do not think that I am ridiculous?" I asked him.

"No, I would say you do not have that many choices for your future, and you need someone that could be with you and someone you can help as well."

I breathed a sigh of relief. I began to realize that I had wanted him to approve of the marriage. The truth was that I wanted to marry Sima.

"Do you love Sima?" Mr. Milichkov asked.

"I don't know," I answered truthfully and then started to pick at some green moss on the log furiously.

"I see." Mr. Milichkov gave me a sidelong look as if he were debating to say something and then said, "You know, I did not really love Alex's mother when I asked her to marry me. I came here on a Russian ship to trade furs. I did not know what to expect. I was lonely after the first year. I knew I needed to stay for another three years, so I decided to get married. I then met a beautiful native girl who was kind and gentle. I asked her to marry, she, of course, as you can tell, said yes."

Mr. Milichkov then gathered a deep breath and went on, "We got married only a year later, and within that year, we talked every day. I would work, she would make me supper, and then we would go to her family's village or to the harbor to eat. We developed a strong friendship that grew into a rather deep love. It was different than I expected, but I cannot imagine loving anyone else more."

I looked up at him, amazed by his story. "Did she love you?" I asked.

"Yes," he answered.

I looked down at my hands. I was flattered that he had shared his story with me. "Mr. Milichkov, thank you for telling me all of this. I feel now that I am not as crazy as I thought I was."

Mr. Milichkov chuckled. "Anna, you are not crazy; you seek adventure, something new. This does not make you crazy."

"Do you think it is all right for me to marry Sima then?" I asked, hoping for his consent.

"Yes, Anna, but I think you need to have time to get to know him. I know you know him very well because you have spent so much time with him, but now you need to get to know him on a more personal level. Learn more about his morals and his moods. Take that time. You will be a lot happier when you are married if you have fewer chances for surprises later."

"Mr. Milichkov, do you think I will fall in love with him?"

"I think that you are already on your way to falling in love with him. You would not have agreed to marry him had you been completely impartial to him. If you do get to know him better and realize that it would not work, then tell him you can't marry him. It would be better for him as well to move on, even if he loves you." Mr. Milichkov stopped and looked at me as if he expected me to say something.

I shrugged my shoulders. "Thank you, Mr. Milichkov, for helping me. I appreciate your advice. I think I will try to spend at least an hour a day talking to him from now on."

"Hopefully, it becomes more than an hour." Mr. Milichkov smiled and then reached over and hugged me. I had never spoken so seriously with someone so much older. I felt as if he had somehow become a father to me now.

"Let's head home," Mr. Milichkov said as he stood up and brushed off the bramble from his pants. I stood up as well, and we turned to the path towards home.

After that day, Sima and I spent every evening together after supper talking and laughing. I began to enjoy talking to him more and more. It was different, as Mr. Milichkov had said. We were getting ready for a life together, not just traveling across the Canadian wilderness. There was so much to discuss. He shared more about his family and his parents. I learned he had only received an occasional letter from them while at school, and then he had not wanted to communicate with them because he had felt they betrayed him and left him. I knew how much I longed to know my parents, and I began to talk him into reestablishing his relationship with them. It took a few days to talk him into writing to them and letting them know he was in Alaska. I realized he was stubborn in some ways, but I did not necessarily see this as a fault.

I shared a lot with Sima about my life, as uneventful as it had been. He seemed to admire me for everything I had done, although

I had not thought it had been so much. It was nice to feel respected, and also, it was wonderful not to have to worry that I would have to face years of loneliness in a cabin somewhere on my own with a dog.

A few weeks later, I was in the barn cleaning out the horses' stalls when I heard footsteps behind me. I turned, and Alex stood there. I was astounded that my heartbeat did not quicken.

"You seem cheerful," he said to me.

"Oh?"

"You were singing just now. I have never heard you singing alone before," Alex told me.

"Well, I am feeling a lot better and healthier." I tried to focus on the task at hand. I still felt awkward around him. It seemed as if I had not talked to him in weeks.

"It wouldn't have anything to do with the fact that you seem to spend almost every single waking moment of the day with Sima?" he asked suspiciously.

I looked up at him. He was still handsome, yet I was not drawn to him. I realized I had never been entirely comfortable around him. I did not think I could have ever discussed with him what I discussed with Sima. Still, he was a good friend, one of the best friends I had ever had. I thought it was time not to keep him in the dark about my betrothal. So far, only Mr. Milichkov knew.

"Well, Alex," I said as I cleared my throat, "Sima and I are engaged."

Alex looked stunned for about five seconds, but then he smiled and said, "I wondered when it would happen. I just did not think it would happen so soon."

"You mean you thought we would get married?" I asked, confused.

"Yes, you two seem to be made for each other. I don't even understand why both of you think some things are funny."

"Did you know Sima loved me?" I asked.

He shook his head. "No, I did not know. He never said a word. Perhaps he did not think he had a chance."

"No, he didn't think he did. I was confused, Alex. I had never spent time in the company of men, and I did not realize the difference between real love and infatuation."

Alex laughed. "I think it takes a lot of time for anyone to figure that out. You are not alone."

I smiled back at him. "You know, Alex, it is good to talk to you again. Please believe me; I did not follow you and Katya to the forest that time."

Alex cleared his throat. "That's all forgotten now. Katya calmed me down and told me that it was unlikely that you would have done that."

"You know, Alex, I hardly know Katya because I would not let myself like her. I felt as if she had taken you from me, but now I feel as if I am missing out on a friendship."

"Well, we are not going anywhere for now." He grinned and then put out his hand. "Let's be friends, as we always were."

I took his hand. "Yes, Alex, I hope that you and Katya will always live close to us as well."

"I hope so. Listen, I'll go congratulate Sima," Alex said, smiling, and walked out of the barn.

As I looked after him, I thought about what I had said to him. I had not realized the difference between real love and infatuation. My feelings were real now. I thought about Sima daily. I wanted to go now and tell him about my conversation with Alex. I loved Sima. My hands shook a little as I put down the pail I had been cleaning. I had, for some reason, not let these feelings come out before. I was afraid of how I felt. This love was a different kind of love. This seemed so natural. I washed my hands and walked out of the barn. I headed towards the cabin. It was quiet when I walked in, and I was glad everyone was outside doing chores.

I came to Sima's room, and I noticed him sitting up in bed reading. I stood at the doorway, afraid to walk in. Sima loved me. There was no reason to feel frightened. Sima looked up at that second and saw me.

"Come in," he said, although he did not smile, and his voice sounded a bit cold.

"Sima, what's wrong?" I asked as I walked towards him.

"Why did you tell Alex?"

I stopped for a second. I did not think that he had wanted to keep the whole thing a secret. "I don't see any real reason to hide the fact that we are engaged," I told him. I was now even more nervous because he seemed upset with me.

His look softened. "It's not that, Anna; I just hoped that we could tell him together. It was something special I wanted to share."

I felt terrible for not thinking of Sima's part in it at that moment, but I knew why I had told Alex. I had wanted Alex to know. It was during those minutes that I realized how much I loved Sima. I swallowed and took a deep breath. "Sima, I did not mean to offend you, and I should have waited to tell him, but I wanted to tell him because I am proud of being engaged to you."

Sima smiled, and the twinkle returned to his eyes. "I am happy to hear that. I wish though that you loved me."

"Sima," I said as I walked closer to him and sat down on his bed so I could be at eye level with him. "I do love you. That's why I wanted Alex to know."

Sima looked at me, his eyes serious. He reached out and touched my hair. "You can't imagine how much I wanted to hear that." His hand rested on my shoulder. "Would you mind if I kissed you?"

I looked at him, and my heart started to beat hard against my chest. "I would like that very much."

"Help me stand up then."

"Is that necessary?" I asked.

"It will just be more romantic," he said smiling. I helped him stand up then. His arm rested on my shoulders, and his other arm came around my waist. He leaned over, and his mouth came down on mine.

My hands came up to his shoulders, and I kissed him back. After a bit, he let me go, and my head rested against his chest.

"That wasn't so bad now, was it?" he asked against my hair.

"No, not at all," I answered quietly.

"Would you like to kiss again?" he asked.

"Yes," I answered and looked up at him. After a few more kisses, Sima sat down again. I sat next to him, and we held hands. We did not talk for a while. I was afraid to ruin the silent happiness that enveloped us.

Chapter 28

As the days continued, Sima started to become stronger. He would often sit in a chair out on the porch. He still looked thin, and I tried to bring him as much food as possible. We would sit out on the porch and talk about our plans for the future. The Milichkovs had a small hunting cabin not far from their home, and we decided to make it our own after we got married. It was on such a day after we finished discussing plans that Sima told me that he wanted to try to walk.

"Sima, has it been long enough for you to heal?" I asked with concern.

Sima looked over at me and said, "I feel like I am only weaker because I am sitting around so much. Also, I do not think that I can sit any longer or I will go crazy."

I smiled at him. "Yes, I know how difficult it is for you to just sit around without creating some kind of chaos."

He grinned. "Listen, I am serious. Please help me walk. I don't care what Mr. Milichkov says. I now understand why Alex is so bossy all the time. I forgot what it was like, being away for twelve years."

I smirked. "It must be genetic. Alex was not around his father enough to pick it up."

"I, however, do not think that I am anything like my parents," Sima said to me as he put his arm around my shoulders.

"I hope they write back to you."

"Me too; I do hope they remember who I am."

"Of course they do." I leaned my head against Sima's shoulder. "If I thought of my parents for so many years without knowing who they were, I am sure your parents have thought of you often."

"You never met my parents." Sima looked out towards the woods. "It's strange how both of us met. In a way, we are truly similar. We both have not had much contact with our parents and have had to fend for ourselves."

I contemplated Sima's statement. It was accurate, and despite my attraction to Alex at first, I had formed a stronger bond with Sima. "That's true, you know. It is odd how life works out. When I started on this journey, I had no thought of romance on my mind."

Sima looked at me with a smirk. "It seems you had it on your mind for the rest of the journey."

"Yes, unfortunately, I think it would have been better if I had not had it on my mind."

Sima laughed a bit. "How could it be avoided? A beautiful girl with such fine handsome men was bound to cause sparks to fly."

"You are ridiculous," I said with a smile and then stood up. "Now, how do you want to handle trying to walk?"

Sima only took a few steps that day. He leaned heavily against me the whole time. With my support, he held on to the railing and walked down the porch steps. After that, he was able to take a few steps across the grass with my support. We had to sit down soon on the grass. He looked at me unhappily as we sat down. I could tell that it bothered him that he was so weak. He never really complained and seemed to take everything in good stride. However, the wistful look in his eyes told me that he wanted to be healthy and mobile. I had always seen Sima as such an energetic person.

As we were sitting on the grass, I saw Mr. Milichkov walking over to us. "What are you doing out here?" he asked. He did not look happy with us.

"I asked Anna to help me walk," Sima told him nonchalantly.

"You know I said not to try walking for another two weeks," Mr. Milichkov said with reproach in his voice.

"I know, sir. However, with all due respect, I do not think that you are the authority on when I should walk. I feel as if I do not walk, I will go crazy. I also think it will be better for me."

Mr. Milichkov looked as surprised as I felt that Sima had spoken to him this way. I wanted to hide my face in my hands. I never understood how Sima had so much confidence.

"Sima, I think that you should know that you are living under my roof, and since I am entrusted with your care, I suggest you listen to me. Nevertheless, you seem to be as stubborn as I am. I will help you walk again. I just do not want Anna to help you by herself since she is not strong either. So tomorrow, if you both meet me out here, I will help both of you." With that, Mr. Milichkov turned and walked away toward the cabin.

I looked after him and then looked back at Sima. "Sima," I started, thinking of how to best tell him that I did not believe that he should speak to Mr. Milichkov in such a manner. I hesitated and then said, "You know, I think you should be more respectful of how you speak to Mr. Milichkov." I could feel my cheeks getting hot.

"Why?" he asked. He looked astonished by my statement. "I got what I wanted, didn't I?"

"Yes, but Mr. Milichkov, he just wants what is best for us." I started to rip at the sharp blades of grass under my hands. I was becoming increasingly uncomfortable under Sima's gaze.

"He's just bossy. Mr. Shubert was scarier."

"Yes, Sima," I said slowly and then continued, "but he's not Mr. Shubert. He would never have led us into a storm and left us to die. I think he loves us."

Sima looked away from me silently and did not answer for a few seconds. I felt like he was going to tell me that he didn't love me anymore. I felt, though, that Sima had to relinquish some of his hard pride. He always fought for everything. I often wondered why.

Sima then looked at me and gave me a small smile, and took my hand in his. "I guess you are right. I do not trust anybody beyond you and Alex. It's hard to admit that sometimes."

I reached up and touched Sima's cheek and looked into his eyes. "This is a new start for both of us." I wondered how much Sima struggled and how much he hid from the world. I remembered the night in Canada when I had found him crying outside of our tent. He had felt abandoned too many times. He had also lost several good friends in the Canadian wilderness.

"Look, Sima, I promise I will never leave your side."

Sima's face broke out into a grin, and he leaned over and gave me a quick kiss on the cheek. "That is exactly why I decided to marry you."

*****

That evening, after washing dishes, I sat with Sima in the main room of the house. We sat quietly holding hands and looking at the fire playing in the hearth. It threw shadows all over the room. Despite the warm summer days, the nights got relatively cool, and I had wrapped a blanket over my legs. Sima had propped his legs up on a chair. Mrs. Milichkova had retired to her bedroom, and Alex and Katya had gone out for a walk. I felt as though we were already married, enjoying a calm evening at home. It was about twenty minutes later that Mr. Milichkov walked into the room. Sima cleared his throat, and his grip tightened on my hand.

"Sir," he said rather quietly. Mr. Milichkov did not seem to hear him and nodded at us and started heading to the kitchen's water pump.

"Mr. Milichkov," Sima said in a clear, loud tone.

"Yes, Sima?" Mr. Milichkov turned and came to sit in the armchair across from us. "What is it?" he sounded almost impatient.

"I don't usually apologize. However, I wanted to apologize to you. I should have never been as rude as I was this afternoon. Anna told me that I should not speak to you that way." I could see Sima's eyes focused on the far wall past Mr. Milichkov's head. He did not, however, lower his eyes.

"I accept your apology. Although I did not feel you were rude. I can understand why you would like to walk. Everything must be difficult for you." Mr. Milichkov leaned back in the armchair. His long legs stretched in front of him.

Sima looked over at me, and he smiled a bit. I covered his hand with mine. I could tell how hard this must be for him. "Anna and I are grateful for everything you have done for us, sir. We could never repay anything."

"Sima, your parents, entrusted me to care for you, and Alex has brought with him two friends. I could never turn you away. I have everything I need to care for you." Mr. Milichkov stood and stretched. "I will leave you two here. Don't kiss too much," he said with a laugh and walked down the hall.

My cheeks burned with embarrassment. I was afraid to look at Sima. I remembered how Mary-Louise had once told me that girls should not kiss before they were married. Yet I had already kissed two men, and I was not married. Mr. Milichkov did not seem to mind. I lifted my eyes to meet Sima's gaze. He had a mischievous look on his face.

"What's the matter?" I asked.

"All the lecturing from you made me so worried, and Mr. Milichkov said he did not even mind."

"Well, you know I am right."

Sima sighed. "Unfortunately, you are right." He then put his arm around my shoulders and kissed my forehead.

*****

In the days that followed, Mr. Milichkov kept to his promise. Every morning he helped Sima outside and helped him walk. I sometimes assisted, and during other times I watched quietly from the window of the cabin. It must be a significant blow to any man's pride, I thought, to have to be helped and taught how to walk. It was on such a morning, as I sat watching Sima take halting steps from Mr. Milichkov to a tree in the yard, that I felt a touch on my shoulder. I was startled by the touch. I then realized Katya stood behind me. I gave her a nervous smile. We had never really spoken to each other without anyone else present, and I could not even start to imagine what she thought of me.

She looked apologetic. "Anna, I am sorry that I frightened you."

The tension in my back eased, and I smiled at her. "It's all right. I just did not see you right away."

She fingered her skirt, and her eyes avoided mine. "I had not wanted to bother you. You looked so peaceful."

"Do not worry. I was just watching Sima. I hope he gets better soon."

"I am truly sorry about everything that happened to all of you. I cannot even begin to envision what you went through."

"I was rather naïve when I started." I looked down at the floor. I thought that Katya must believe that I was rather brash and stupid.

Katya gave me a restrained glance. "I wanted to apologize to you, Anna."

I looked at her in surprise. "For what?" I was taken aback by her words.

Katya did not respond right away. She, however, continued to pull at her gray skirt without speaking. She then cleared her throat and said, "For taking Alex away from you. I noticed when you came that you were interested in him. Still, I continued to pursue his affection."

I was so astounded by what she said that I was not sure that I could respond. I put my hand on her shoulder. "Katya, please do not worry. If Alex had been interested in me, he would not have liked you. Also, I am in love with Sima. I was just too silly to see it at that time. I think

Alex was pre-disposed to like you from the start. He had mentioned on our journey here that he corresponded with you while he lived in Maine."

Katya stopped fingering her skirt, and a slow smile spread across her face. "I am happy, Anna, that you came. I always thought that we could be friends."

"I would love to be friends with you. I met a woman on the way here, and I thought she would be a wonderful friend. I was sad to leave her. Other than that, I have never had a true female friend before. Also, I apologize that I had not reached out to you earlier; I was rather self-obsessed."

"Apology accepted. Anyway, the real reason I wanted to talk to you this morning is that I wanted to see if you wanted to sew our wedding dresses?"

"Wedding dresses?" I raised an eyebrow.

Katya suddenly looked flustered. "I mean your wedding dress." She then stopped and took a deep breath. "I guess I can tell you, Alex and I are getting married too. He and I just wanted to tell everybody tonight at supper, so please do not tell anybody."

I grinned and hugged her. "I would have never guessed that the two of you planned on getting married," I said in a playful tone.

A light shade of pink rose to Katya's cheeks. She was such a beautiful girl. It was no wonder that Alex fell in love with her. She then took my hands and said in an excited whisper, "I'll show you where Mrs. Milichkova keeps the fabric."

*****

For the next several weeks, we sewed every morning. Alex and Mr. Milichkov spent many hours outside in the barn. Sima practiced walking every morning, and he was beginning to get a lot stronger. Mr. Milichkov had fashioned a large wooden staff for him to lean on when he walked. Sima would also help in the barn. He would sit and help saw or build.

Alex and Katya had told everyone of their engagement the night after Katya and I had spoken. I thought that they looked as if they were the perfect couple. Alex never seemed to make any mistakes. Katya also appeared to be ideal. She had not even thought to judge me for my decisions. I had decided that evening to become more like Katya. I had a feeling, though, that I had a long way to go to become like her. We busied ourselves with the sewing of our dresses. Our dresses were not white, however. Mrs. Milichkova told me that we had to make do with the material we had. She said that back in April, when she and Mr. Milichkov had traveled to the fort to trade, she had not expected two weddings. She had just bought bolts of fabric that she could find at the time and some lace. Katya said that she was going to wear Mrs. Milichkova's veil. I had no veil at the moment. I guessed that I would have to sew it myself. Katya was much better with the needle than I. She helped me immensely with my dress. I chose a beautiful blue-colored fabric, and Katya chose dark green.

It was on such a morning that we sat and sewed. We had spent three weeks on the dresses, and the task was close to completion. I was standing in the middle of the room with Katya pinning up the skirt of my dress.

"I just have to hem this skirt and take in some material at the waist," she said through a mouth full of pins. She stood and tightened the material around my waist.

"You are so thin, Anna. You need to eat more."

"Well, if I add more weight, I will not be able to fit into this dress." I laughed. Despite my joke, I still looked down with regret at my tiny waist. Although I had gained some weight, I could still count all of my ribs, and I wished to look like Katya. She had a figure, but she was slender as well.

"I feel so badly for you; you must have starved," Katya said, shaking her head.

"I honestly did not notice. I was never very full, to begin with; I was bigger than I am now."

Katya stopped pinning and stepped back. "Done."

I spun around. "What do you think?"

"You look beautiful," she said, smiling.

"I have no veil, however, and I am not sure if I will be able to make one." I put my hands on my hips and twirled again. The full skirt swirled around my legs.

"You could always use this quilted square as a veil." Katya suddenly laughed as she placed a square on my head from the quilt that Mrs. Milichkova had just started.

"Yes, that would be quite convincing," I said with a giggle. I then took it off my head and plopped it onto Katya's hair.

She laughed and twirled around the room. "I must say this is quite attractive. I think I would make the prettiest bride in the world with a quilted veil."

"Oh yes," I said as I picked up a quilt from the sofa and placed it on her head.

"My, how lovely," she joked and then gave me a mischievous smile. "What would Alex say to this?

"That you will look beautiful no matter what," Alex's voice came from the doorway. Katya and I swung around to the door entrance. Alex stood there leaning against the door with a big grin on his face. Katya and I quickly threw the quilts on the sofa behind us. Katya's cheeks burned bright red.

"We were just playing, Alex," I said quickly. I wondered how long he had been standing there.

"It's quite all right," Alex said with a smirk. "I thought it was rather funny." Katya and I exchanged embarrassed glances.

"Anyway, Anna, I came to get you. Sima wanted to speak to you. He's in the barn."

"All right, I just have to get out of this dress. Please tell Sima that I will be there in a few minutes."

"No problem." Alex turned and walked out the door. Katya and I looked at each other, and then we burst out laughing.

"Oh, I thought I was going to die," Katya said through her laughter. She wiped her eyes with her hand.

"It was rather awkward. I think it will be all right. Alex did not seem to mind."

"I am still mortified. How awful of Alex to just stand there and not say anything." Katya unpinned my dress and helped me get out of it.

I put on my regular dress and hugged her. "Katya, it is wonderful to have a friend like you." I then said goodbye and ran to the barn. I hoped to avoid Alex. I began to realize more and more that I was relieved that I was not marrying him. I had never learned to be completely comfortable around him.

I ran into the barn breathlessly, and I saw Sima standing by one of the stalls. He only leaned one arm against it. I started to walk toward him, but Sima said, "Wait." I stopped and watched as he very slowly walked towards me. He had a limp in his right leg, but he was walking slowly.

I just stood watching him in amazement as he approached me. He stopped, faltering in his step, but then he kept walking. I put my arms out, and he came over to me and put his arms around me. We did not speak. We just stood in the barn, utterly elated about the fact that our lives were turning in the correct direction.

"I have a gift for you," Sima whispered against my hair.

"A gift? Sima, it is a gift enough that you are walking."

"No, I made something for you." He then reached into his pocket and pulled out a wooden ring. He put it into my hand. I peered at it closely. It was exquisitely detailed with a design of leaves and roses.

"Sima, this is beautiful," I breathed and put it onto my finger.

"Our wedding rings are being purchased by Mr. Milichkov. He went to some neighbors about ten miles from here to have them made. I wanted you to have this ring as a token of my love."

"I could not thank you enough for everything," I said and leaned my head against his chest.

"All I want is for you to marry me," Sima said softly and held my head with his hand. I could feel his hand shaking a bit.

"How about we sit?" I asked. I had a feeling that he had overexerted himself by walking so much. We walked unhurriedly over to the hay bale.

Sima sat down and turned towards me. "I wanted to tell you, though, that the wedding is soon."

"What do you mean?" I asked. I had not even thought about the date for the wedding.

"The priest only comes to these parts every six months, and Mr. Milichkov told me this morning that he is coming in two weeks."

"Two weeks?" My voice almost squeaked as I said those two words. I could feel my heart thudding in my chest.

"Unless you want to wait for another six months, but honestly, I do not want to wait that long."

I looked at him carefully. He had a good point. I did not want to wait either. "I won't have time to make a veil, though," I said sadly. I really wanted a veil, but there was no way I could make one now.

"Do not worry about a veil." Sima smiled and touched my cheek. "I do not care if you marry me in your work dress or even in the pants you wore on our journey. I love you the way you are."

"I will never be as pretty as Katya."

Sima elbowed me in the shoulder. "You are more beautiful than any other girl I have ever seen or kissed."

"You stop that," I said with a laugh. "From now on, there is only one girl you will be kissing."

"That's right." Sima then took me by the shoulders, turned me towards him, and kissed me. I thought it was indeed wrong for me to be as happy as I was at the moment.

Chapter 29

July 13, 1888

Two weeks passed in a flash. Most of the days were spent in the usual fashion. The men worked outside, and the women worked inside and tended to the garden. Our weddings were not going to be fancy affairs. I was a bit disappointed when I had found out that Alex and Katya were getting married on the same day. I wanted to share the day only with Sima. However, due to the necessity of the situation, we needed to get married simultaneously. In a way, I was also relieved. I felt that I needed a friend by my side to share in my experience.

I awoke the day before my wedding with a flutter in my stomach. I had been able to keep it at bay, but after sitting up and talking to Katya, Alex, and Sima the previous night, the flutters and the heart palpitations had started. We had sat deep into the night talking about our plans, laughing about our adventures and the past. Alex had sat with Katya on the sofa opposite Sima and me. Alex had a protective arm around Katya the entire time. Sima held my hand tightly. When I had gone to bed, though, I began to imagine how our future would look. What would it be like to be Sima's wife?

I got out of bed and put on a pretty pink quilted dress that Mrs. Milichkova had sewn for me. It was a perfect dress. I walked out into the kitchen to find Sima standing at the table. My heart stopped in my throat. I swallowed hard as I studied him.

"What's the matter?" he asked. "You look as if you have never seen me before." I just shook my head and smiled at him.

391

"I just wasn't expecting to see you."

"I do live here, you know." He slowly walked over to me. I could tell he was struggling with every step that he took. He took my hand and looked as though he was about to kiss me. It was then that I put my hand on his shoulder.

"How about we wait until tomorrow to kiss?"

He looked at me skeptically. "You mean more than twenty-four hours?"

"Yes, I want to make tomorrow's kiss extra special."

"I think that either way, it would be extra special. Still, I will honor your wishes, ma'am." He winked and grinned at me.

"I love you, Sima."

"I love you too," he said and pulled me into a hug. "I have to go now. I need to help Alex outside."

"Be careful. You still do not seem to be quite yourself." I pulled at his hand as he was about to leave.

He turned with a half-smile, brushed my cheek with his finger, and knelt to look straight into my eyes. "Don't you worry, I will be careful. As always, I make Alex do most of the work. You know how good I am at supervising."

"Of course," I answered. As he was walking out the door, I realized that I was smiling after him. Nothing could compare to how I felt about Sima. Still, I was having difficulty coming to terms with the fact that I would be Sima's wife the next day. I remembered the first time I had seen him when Jason Shubert was briefing us about our journey. The thought of marriage to him had never even crossed my mind.

The rest of the day seemed to drag even with all the last-minute preparations. We put the finishing touches on our dresses. I was excited to wear my dress for Sima, even though there was no veil to go with it. Anyway, I thought it was a bit silly that my dress was a deep blue color. I twirled around in it after Mrs. Milichkova put the final touches on the dress. The soft fabric lifted off the floor and settled around me again. I sighed and smiled to myself.

At lunchtime, I brought food out to the men who were working vigorously in the barn. My only need in completing this chore was to see Sima. He brushed the sweat from his forehead as he picked up the spoon to have a drink of water. It felt strange that he should be out in the barn when we were getting married the next day.

"Thank you," he said and touched my arm as I took the ladle from him. Even that simple gesture caused my heart to beat wildly. I felt my palms break into a sweat. I left the barn quickly with the water bucket. It was only later that I realized I had not even given Mr. Milichkov his lunch or any water. I made Katya carry it back out to the barn. I had no idea how I would go through with the wedding the next day.

After supper that night, I washed the dishes with Katya. She pumped the water into the basin, and I scrubbed the plates with a towel. Alex and Sima fed the animals, and Mr. Milichkov and Mrs. Milichkova sat reading by the fire. I felt as if I had missed out on so much in my entire life. Here was the family that I had been looking for.

"I can hardly believe that we are getting married tomorrow," Katya's whisper interrupted my thoughts.

I looked over at my friend. "I can hardly believe it either." I turned over the dish in my hands and set it on the shelf to dry.

"I am getting nervous," she told me. Her blue eyes burned brightly with excitement.

"Me too," I answered. "I have had this knot in the pit of my stomach since I woke up this morning." As I set the final dish on the shelf, I heard the cabin's back door close. Sima and Alex were back from their chores.

"Are you going to speak to Alex before going to bed?" I asked her. The feeling that I had to see Sima one more time before going to bed was strong.

"No, Alex and I decided that supper would be the last time we talked. Anyway, I want to go to bed and rest. I am tired from all of the preparations."

"Oh, I see," I answered. However, I did not see the reason for preventing myself from seeing Sima. I also did not think that I would get any sleep. My legs were a puddle of jam. I walked slowly to Sima's room and peeked through the doorway.

Sima was leaning back in a chair, his long legs stretched out in front of him, smoking his pipe. He grinned as I entered and took his pipe out of his mouth. He looked so comfortable and relaxed. I, on the other hand, felt as if every nerve in my body had shattered.

"Are you nervous?" I asked him quietly.

He looked up from where he sat and said, "Yes, I only try to smoke now when my nerves are getting the better of me." He stood up then and sat on his bed. He put out his pipe and placed it on the table next to his bed.

I sat on his chair across from him. "I am overwhelmed with emotion. I cannot even think straight," I told Sima as I clasped my hands together.

"I think we just have to take everything one day at a time. It does not help to dwell on how nervous we are." Sima tossed his hair out of his face, and I regarded him with a smile.

I took a deep breath. "I suppose you're right." Whenever I was around Sima lately, it became difficult to breathe. I felt that it was wrong to love him so much. This love seemed to cut into my heart.

"Anna, there is no need to worry." Sima reached over and moved a wisp of hair that had fallen into my eyes. I caught his hand with mine; he held mine tightly in return.

"I do not deserve you, Sima," I said as I focused my gaze on the floor.

He then leaned over to me and lifted my face with his hands. His deep brown eyes looked straight into mine as he said, "I chose you, remember?"

*****

After speaking to Sima, I felt the need for fresh air. My nerves were raw, and I felt short on breath. I headed towards the front door.

I paused on the front step when I noticed Alex leaning against the railing facing the dark night. A circle of smoke rose above his head. I stood holding my breath. His broad shoulders created an oversized silhouette against the night sky. As I was about to tiptoe back into the house, Alex turned his head towards me.

"Isn't it a bit late for you to be out? It is about one o'clock in the morning."

"What about you? You are getting married too, you know." I walked over and stood next to him. I then followed his gaze into the night.

"Are you nervous?" he asked nonchalantly.

"Yes," I answered timidly. I was not sure that I wanted to speak to Alex on the subject.

"Sima's a great man, you know. There is nothing to be nervous about."

"Yes, but you're not marrying him."

"I understand. I am a bundle of nerves myself." I could not believe that Alex would admit to the fact that he was nervous.

"You know Katya is a-" I started.

"Great girl? Yes, I know, I know. You're not marrying her, though." Alex gave a short laugh, turned, and sat on the porch railing. His pipe clung between his teeth.

I also sat on the railing. "I am happy for you, Alex."

"And I for you."

"Alex?" I turned towards him. "Please promise me that you and Katya will always remain close to us. Even if we ever move to Juneau to be close to his parents, you will continue to keep in touch. I feel as if you are both like my family, and I could not bear to lose you." I heard the tears creeping into my voice, and I quickly cleared my throat.

"Listen," Alex said as he turned his face towards me. "You know what I am like and that I would never allow that to happen."

"Thank you."

"I know this is new to all of us. You can be sure it will be an adjustment, but we will never forget the both of you, and you don't forget about us."

"Never," I answered.

Alex cleared his throat uncomfortably. "Anna, I never had a chance to apologize to you."

"About what?" I asked, surprised.

"For kissing you, I should have never done that. I led you on, and I confused you. I was just overcome by everything that was happening at the moment."

"I accept your apology. I began to realize even then that you did not care for me in that way. I just kept lying to myself."

"Does Sima know?"

"Yes, he does. He wasn't worried."

"He probably told you that he kisses better than I do. He always used that line with girls that liked me too." Alex had a smirk on his face as he puffed on his pipe.

"So, who usually won the girl?" I asked.

"I don't know. You are the one with both experiences," Alex grinned as he said this.

My face burned in the dark. "You make me sound like a horrible person."

"Of course, I am only joking. You're one of the best people I know, and if I do kiss better than Sima, don't tell him that."

"Sima won the girl this time." I thought of Sima's words that he had just spoken to me half an hour earlier and a warm feeling started to fill my heart.

"Well, I have Katya. When I saw her again, I realized that she was the person I needed all of my life. It was as if I knew this all the time; everything began to make sense."

"She is sort of your sister." I gave him a teasing glance.

"Hmm, if you don't tell anyone, I won't tell anyone."

"Not many people to talk to around here," I answered, laughing.

"No, anyway, you know that my parents took her in and that we are certainly not blood relatives."

"I know, Alex, it was my turn to pull a joke on you." I stood up and gathered a deep breath. "I better go to sleep, or I will not wake up in time for the wedding."

"Good luck." Alex held out his hand to me. I took it, and then he drew me into a bear hug. I returned it.

"Sima and I would both be gone by now if you had not helped us."

"It was meant to be. Two such wonderful people could not die just yet."

I smiled at his words and marveled at the miracle that life was. I withdrew from his arms. "I better go to bed before Katya and Sima find us like this and get the wrong idea."

"Yes, it would be hard to explain." Alex leaned against the railing.

"Are you going to bed?" I asked.

"Not yet."

I walked towards the door of the cabin and then turned at the door. "Good luck to you too, Alex."

Alex gave me a nervous smile. "Thanks." A funny thought crossed my mind. Wolves, blizzards, and mountains could not scare Alex, but getting married to a girl frightened him. I smiled at that thought as I entered the cabin.

As I lay down to sleep and pulled my quilt up to my chin, a feeling I knew I would never have again settled upon my soul. It was as if I was standing on the edge of an abyss about to teeter over. Everything from the past lay behind me, and my beautiful future lay ahead. However, that future seemed to be almost unreachable. The future seemed as if it would soon engulf me. My eyes were now wide open, and it took me two more hours to fall asleep.

*****

I woke up the following day and sat up right away. I looked in the mirror by my bed and was horrified to see the dark blue circles under my eyes. I quickly began to brush my hair. I was relieved that it had started to grow longer over the past few months. The tips now reached past my chin. I was not sure if it would ever grow again to its former beauty. I only hoped that this would occur; how I wished that Sima could see me with my beautiful hair. I knew it was a vain thought, but I knew I looked better with it long. My hair hung limply around my face. I shrugged my shoulders. I had looked much worse in front of Sima, and he still thought I was attractive. I shook my head in disappointment as I looked down at my reflection in the mirror.

"What's the matter, darling?" Mrs. Milichkova asked as she suddenly entered the room. Katya was traipsing in behind her. Katya's beautiful light brown hair stood piled on top of her head. I wondered how many hairpins she needed to hold up such a large amount of hair. She looked as if she had slept for years, and her face radiated beauty and excitement.

"I just look miserable and tired," I told the both of them as I looked at myself again in the mirror.

"Do not worry so. You truly are a beautiful girl, and Sima will think so too." Katya came up to me and put her arm around my shoulders.

I gave her a weak smile. "All of my hair is gone too. I used to have such beautiful hair, and Sima never saw it."

"It will grow back, my dear." Mrs. Milichkova took both of my hands and pulled me to stand up. "Katya and I have a surprise for you, so close your eyes." I was not sure what was coming, but I closed my eyes obediently. I felt Mrs. Milichkova and Katya put something on top of my head. A soft fabric touched my cheek.

"Can I open my eyes now?" I asked.

"Go ahead," Katya said in a soft voice. I opened my eyes and saw a long lace veil flowing down my shoulders. I fingered the lace and felt the veil on top of my head.

"How did you ever manage this?" I asked. I felt completely overcome with emotion, and tears threatened to break out of my eyes.

"After Katya found out that you had no veil, she sat up the last three nights creating this one for you. It's beautiful, is it not?" Mrs. Milichkova asked as she put an arm around my shoulders. I looked at her and smiled.

"It is more than I could ever ask for." Two large tears started to roll down my cheeks.

"Do not cry. This is our gift to you. You are such a strong person and so selfless. You deserve this after everything you have gone through." Katya also put her arm around me. I buried my head into her shoulder and hugged her tightly. We both stood there paralyzed. Suddenly the enormity of our wedding day struck us, and we stood as though we could not fathom the seriousness of what lay before us.

Mrs. Milichkova was the one who snapped us out of our reverie. "My dears," she said as she stepped away from us. "You cannot stand here all day. The priest is coming to the church at noon, and we need to travel at least two hours still to get there." Then she took both of our hands and said, "I married a wonderful man, and there is nothing to be worried about."

My heart just thudded against my rib cage. I truly hoped that she was right and there was no cause to worry. I just knew that if I had been in Mrs. Milichkova's shoes, I would have been terrified. Mr. Milichkov was somewhat intimidating.

"All right." Katya pulled away and wiped her eyes. "We really must stop crying, or we will truly look horrible for the wedding."

"I will go get the dresses." Mrs. Milichkova said and quickly left the room. I looked after her and wished that one day I would be as kind and energetic as Mrs. Milichkova. Katya and I stood in silence for a few seconds.

"I am so relieved you are marrying on the same day that I am Anna. I think that if you were not there, I would not be able to go through with it."

I turned to Katya. "Yes, you would. I know that you love Alex and that he loves you very much."

"Don't you think he is rather intimidating?" she asked with a laugh, and I chuckled.

"That cannot be a good start to your marriage," I said and then hugged her. I felt as if she were my sister and that we both understood each other. I could not believe that I had not liked her when I first met her.

"Anna, thank you for being here with me."

Chapter **30**   July 14, 1888

The wedding was truly magnificent. I felt as if I was floating on a cloud as I entered the church. Sima stood at the entrance looking at me as if I were the only person in existence. I also could not take my eyes off him. I almost forgot that Alex and Katya were right next to us. As I came up to the door, Sima grinned and kissed me on the cheek. We entered the church together. I felt a sense of wonder as the priest, Father Nikolai, exchanged our rings three times and then led us to the center of the church. I stood rooted to the ground. The candle kept dripping wax on my left hand, but I was too entranced in the beauty and wonder of the day to take much notice. I kept looking over at Sima in awe. I almost could not believe that he would be my husband, my relation, and my family from this day on.

Towards the end of the service, when Father Nikolai wrapped our hands together to lead us around the center of the church three times, he put our right hands together, and Sima grabbed my hand tightly. It seemed as if he wanted reassurance that I was there with him. I held his hand just as firmly. We proceeded around the church slowly, three times. I could feel that Sima was leaning on me for support. I, however, thought that I would faint any second and relied on him as well.

The service ended too quickly—both Katya, Alex, Sima, and I walked to the front of the church. After the blessing, Father Nikolai made us face each other and kiss for the first time as husband and wife. Sima kissed me so tenderly that my heart floated to heaven. After that, we both faced the congregation of people who had come to the service. Several men and women came up to congratulate us. I was surprised by the number of people that had come. I did not know any of them. Mrs. Milichkova later explained that since Father Nikolai came to these parts only several times a year, people of the Orthodox Christian faith would come to all the services they could while he was there. She said that some would travel as far as five hours and stay a few days while Father Nikolai was visiting. I knew that I would be eternally grateful to him for coming and that I would never forget him.

Following the ceremony, and after all the strangers wished us a happy life, we were led outside into the churchyard. Someone had set up a table with cake and cookies and wine. We ate the cake and kissed again and then drank some wine and kissed again. Sima's kisses became more passionate as the afternoon continued. I thought the wine was reacting on us both. Many of the men and women that I did not know made toasts and wished us many years and a happy life, and then we had to drink and kiss again.

"I wonder how long this will go on," Sima whispered in my ear as we drew apart from a kiss. He smiled, though. I could tell he did not mind.

"As long as they want to keep humiliating us," I answered him.

"Since it is our wedding day, we might as well make the most of it." He smiled down at me. I thought that if he smiled at me again in such a way, I would melt from emotion. He held me against him protectively the whole afternoon as if he did not want to let me go. After about two hours, he began to look tired and a bit peaked. I wondered how I looked. I looked over at Katya. She seemed to be radiant, calm, and stunning. I could tell from how she and Alex looked at each other that they truly belonged together. She just could not stop smiling. I regarded my husband, and I suddenly just wanted to be alone with him. An overwhelming feeling of love and emotion poured out of my heart.

"Sima, let's go home," I said as I kissed his cheek.

"But we're having so much fun here, darling," Sima said in a mocking tone under his breath.

"Public humiliation," I answered as I held his hand.

Sima leaned over and kissed the top of my head. "Don't be so shy. You will have to get used to kissing me in public. I hope to kiss you at least ten times a day." His words made my cheeks grow warm.

Sima winked at me. "All right, I will go tell Mr. Milichkov that we will go ahead and take the first wagon home. That way, Alex and Katya will have to go back with Alex's parents."

He stood up and walked over to Mr. Milichkov. I regarded Sima's tall, lanky figure as he walked over to Mr. Milichkov. He and Mr. Milichkov exchanged a few words, and then I saw Sima look at Mr. Milichkov in admiration. Mr. Milichkov then hugged Sima. Sima then turned and nodded his head towards me. I stood up and came over to him. From now on, this is how it would be; I would always be with Sima.

I came over to him, and he put his arm around my shoulders and leaned on me a bit. Mr. Milichkov looked at us proudly. It was thanks to him that I was now married to Sima. His advice had undoubtedly pushed me to be more confident in my decision.

Mrs. Milichkova came over to us as well. She gave us both a hug and said, "May God Bless the both of you."

"Thank you for everything," I said as I hugged her and then hugged Mr. Milichkov. "You have both been so kind. We cannot thank you enough."

"Remember, you are like our family, never forget that," Mr. Milichkov said. "Now you go on." He waved us toward the wagon, and Sima and I both strolled over to it. Sima helped me up into the wagon, and then I gave him my hand to pull him up as well. I could see that he was having a hard time and that his legs were getting tired.

"You're exhausted, Sima," I said as he settled next to me.

"Maybe, but I do not care. I am alive, and I am married to you. Being tired does not bother me." He clicked his tongue so the horses would move forward. I slipped my arm through the crook of his elbow and leaned my head on his shoulder. We did not talk much the whole way home. Silent comforting happiness had settled on both of us. As our wagon reached our small one-room cabin, Sima turned to me and said, "Thank you, Anna, for marrying me."

I looked into his incredible brown eyes and said, "I should be the one thanking you."

"You're wonderful," Sima said. He then pulled me towards him and gave me a kiss that I would never forget.

Chapter 31   November 1, 1888

The next few months of our marriage were the happiest months I had ever known. Sima and I would head over to the Milichkovs' cabin in the mornings, and he would help Mr. Milichkov with the livestock and the outside farm chores. They also worked hard to prepare the cabins and the barn for the winter. As I already knew, the Alaskan winters were brutal.

I would help Mrs. Milichkova with the cooking, the sewing, and the wash. Katya would join us as well. I admired Mrs. Milichkova for the amount of work she was able to do in a day. She also knew so much about the earth and different herbs and medicines. She loved plants and told us that they were the best medicine. She helped me to create poultices and mixtures to relieve the pain in Sima's hip and legs. Also, she gave me a mix of herbs to make a tea for the headaches he sometimes had since he had endured such a severe head injury. Katya, Mrs. Milichkova, and I would spend the day working together and talking about the future.

Katya told us that come spring, she and Alex planned to build a cabin about a half-mile from the Milichkovs' place. I thought how nice it would be if all of us could visit each other and take turns cooking suppers for each other. I knew that I wanted to plant a garden in the spring. However, Mrs. Milichkova said that the climate and the short summer did not allow much to grow. She told me she would help me to make the most of the summer garden.

Sima and I would travel back to our one-room cabin that we had made into a home in the evenings. We always had plenty of food since Mrs. Milichkova was most resourceful and cooked enough food for an entire village. She would always give us food "for the road." Our tiny cabin was only a quarter of a mile away from the Milichkovs' cabin. I enjoyed stoking the fire in our large fireplace that warmed our tiny cabin. After lighting the fire, Sima would lie on the sofa resting his legs, and I would sit on the rocking chair he had built for me with the help of Mr. Milichkov. Alex had made a similar one for Katya.

The nights had gotten colder as the months flew by and winter set in. We would, at times, sit and listen to the wind howl outside. I was relieved that we were not out in a tent on some of these nights. With Mrs. Milichkova's assistance, I had sewn two large quilts for Sima and myself. We would sit in the evenings wrapped in our blankets and talk.

It was on such an evening that I stood preparing supper. I looked over at Sima, who lay on the sofa, his head propped up in a pillow. He looked exhausted, and his eyes were half-closed. We had just returned from the Milichkovs' cabin, and he had helped me light the fire. He took his boots off afterward and lay down. I set the food to warm in our small oven. I came to sit by the fireplace on my rocking chair and wait for our supper to warm up.

"How are you feeling?" I asked.

Sima opened his eyes and looked at me with a smile. "All right," he answered. "I just have a horrible headache, I did not want to complain, but since you asked, I might as well tell you the truth. You would figure it out anyway."

"I know what will help," I told him. I stood up and walked over to our stovetop. I took the bag of herbs Mrs. Milichkova had given to me just that day. The water had finished boiling in a pot on the stove. I took it off and brewed a fresh cup of tea. I wrinkled my nose at the smell. I hoped Sima would not notice. I brought him the cup of tea and set it on the small wooden table next to him. I then knelt next to the sofa that Sima lay on.

Sima looked over at the teacup and made a face. "Please do not tell me that this is another tea that Mrs. Milichkova gave you."

"She said it was supposed to help headaches," I told him.

"Sometimes, I think I would rather have the headache," he said with a chuckle.

"She thinks this will help," I said, offering him the cup of tea.

He carefully took a sip. "It's not so bad. You should try it." He handed me the cup, and I also took a sip. The bitter taste burned my tongue, and I coughed and set the teacup on the table again. "You said it was not so bad." I threw him an accusing look.

Sima raised his eyebrows. "That's what you get for trying to poison your husband. Please tell Mrs. Milichkova that while we appreciate the tea, it might be time to try a different mix of herbs." Sima grinned and leaned back against his pillow.

"I can't tell her that. Anyway, she is just trying to help. I think if you do drink it, it will help you."

"All right, I'll just hold my nose," Sima agreed.

"While you do that, I'll go fix us our supper." I smiled to myself as I went to get our supper out of the oven.

"You make it sound so simple," Sima called after me.

"What? Making the supper or drinking the tea?" I asked as I pulled out the warm bread from the oven, knowing full well what he was referring to.

"Drinking the tea," he said as I saw him take a big gulp from the teacup, although thankfully, he did not hold his nose.

I just shook my head. "Look, I'll make the same tea too, and then we can suffer together." I also poured myself a cup of tea and then brought the tea with two plates of food over to our parlor area, as we liked to call it, and set them on the floor.

"I think we would be more civilized if we had a full-size table where we could eat our supper," Sima said as I finished arranging our plates on the floor.

"Yes, well, this is much better than a tent in Canada," I told him. We then both stood to pray before our supper. There was so much to be thankful for. I had a wonderful husband, friends, and a place to call home. It was more than I had ever dreamed or dared to hope for. I had to go through a lot to get to this point, but I had it now, and I could not be anything but grateful. After we finished our prayer, I sat down on the rug near the sofa, and Sima sat up propped against his pillow. I handed him his plate.

"Would you like to sit on the sofa?" he asked. "I feel bad for taking up this comfortable space while you sit on the floor."

"I am quite comfortable here, thank you," I told him. I would have given him the softest sofa in the world if he would just get well enough to be able to get through a day without feeling pain or stiffness. Sima did not like to complain, but I knew how hard it was for him to bear the pain of his injury.

"You do not have to make such sacrifices for me, Anna," he said softly as he looked at me. His eyes narrowed in the light of the fire.

"It is not a sacrifice if you do something for the one you love. I am selfish in a way. I want you to be the same healthy Sima that I knew back in Maine, the Sima who could talk Jason Shubert off any day." I smiled at the memory.

A sad look entered Sima's eyes as he asked, "You do realize that I probably will never be able to run behind a dogsled?"

I took his hand and said, "Of course. However, I think you are a better man because of it."

He grinned at me mischievously. "I've heard that men who walk with a limp are more attractive to women."

"Perhaps," I answered mysteriously, as I let go of his hand and picked up the acrid-smelling cup of tea that I had brewed for myself. "I will only drink this if you do," I told him.

He picked up his teacup silently and raised it, and then drank it in one gulp. I did the same, and I had to force myself to swallow.

"Oh, it is truly horrible. If this does not cure my headache, you will have to answer to me." Sima lay back against the pillow and closed his eyes. The shadows under his eyes bothered me.

"I drank it too, and I don't even have a headache," I told him and then took a bite of my bread.

"We have Mrs. Milichkova to thank for that," he said as he opened his eyes and smiled at me.

"She's truly a wonderful woman," I observed as I started to gather the dishes while still on my knees.

He raised an eyebrow at me. "Mrs. Milchkova?"

"Yes."

"I suppose I wish my mother were like her."

I looked over at him in surprise. He had not mentioned his mother since I had convinced him to write to her during the summer. He had never received a letter in return.

"I didn't realize that you were still worried about that."

"Of course I am." He gave me a look that told me that I should have known better. I felt bad for assuming he had forgotten about his family. I learned how painful it had been for me to decide not to continue searching for my own family.

I left the dishes on the floor and drew nearer to the sofa. "I'm sorry, Sima." I kneeled near him at the edge of the couch.

"I did not mean to sound so irritated, I'm sorry," he said quickly.

I took his hand, and he held mine tightly. "It's just hard for me because my parents seem to have rejected me. It's not like they do not know where I am. If I had the chance to make amends with them, I would. I do not even know what I could have done to make them not like me."

"I wish I knew the answer," I said as I held his hand. I put my other hand over it. "Perhaps the post has not yet been able to go through. You've said yourself it is a long way to Juneau from here."

He shrugged. "Let's hope that's the case." Then he suddenly put his free hand on top of my head as if he were my father. "Anna, have I told you how much I love the fact that you are my wife?"

I smiled at him as he moved his hand over and fingered the tips of my hair. "Many times," I answered.

"Your hair," he said suddenly.

I looked at his fingers touching the tip of my hair. "What about it?"

"It's gotten so much longer, I hardly noticed." His eyes were smiling.

"What a wonderful thing to say to your wife," I teased. "Anyway, you can thank Mrs. Milichkova for that. She gave me an herb to make my hair grow."

Sima gave me a glance filled with doubt. "How is an herb supposed to make your hair grow?" A touch of humor glittered in his eyes.

"I don't know, but she said to drink it with a glass of water every day and that it would help, and now my hair is growing."

He laughed. "While that is all very interesting, we need to remember that we are not thanking her for this tea."

I smiled back at him and stood up, and kissed the top of his head. "You get some sleep, and I will clean up these dishes."

"All right." He squeezed my hand before letting it go.

By the time I finished cleaning the dishes, Sima was asleep. The light from the fireplace gently reflected off his face. I picked up the second quilt and wrapped it around him. I then took my rocking chair and moved it closer to where he slept on the couch. There were nights when I would just sit and look at him. I could not understand how such a handsome and wonderful man had chosen me to become his wife.

Chapter 32   May 30, 1889

The winter months seemed to go by quickly, even though the snow only started to melt by the end of May. I was glad to see the first blades of grass. Sima and I would also walk down to the river and watch ice break off the riverbank and get pushed down the river by the boiling current. Sima seemed to regain his strength with the coming of spring. He was able to walk to the Milichkovs' cabin, and the limp in his gait was considerably less noticeable. I began to dig out a garden at home, and Sima helped me dig out rocks from the soil.

One day, as I was out in my vegetable garden watering a row of newly planted seeds, I saw Katya coming up the path to our cabin. I was surprised that she had come over. That day I had decided to stay home to finish some housework. I had seen Katya every other day of the week at the Milichkovs' home. Sima was now busy helping Alex build a cabin for Alex and Katya not far from Alex's parents' cabin. I waved to her and wiped my hands on the front of my apron. She saw me and headed towards the garden. I came up to her as she walked towards me. We embraced each other, and I led her into the house.

I set a pot on the stove to boil water for tea, and we both sat at the table that Sima had just finished building. He had told me that we could not possibly use the floor as a table anymore. I had agreed with him and was proud that he could build such a stunning table for me. Katya and I chatted as we waited for the water to boil. The reason why she had come was not apparent. I was sure she had plenty to do at home.

"What brings you here today?" I asked finally, as my curiosity got the better of me. I took the boiling water off the stove and began to brew the tea.

"I wanted to share some news with you," she said quietly.

"What kind of news?" I asked as I brought two teacups to the table and sat down. I looked over at Katya. Her long brown hair hung in a thick braid down her back. I began to get a feeling that I knew what the news was that she wanted to share.

"Well," she cleared her throat and then continued, "Alex and I are going to have a baby." She looked at the table.

"Why Katya, that's wonderful!" I exclaimed as I took both of her hands in mine. "How long have you been expecting?" I asked.

Her voice was quiet. "I think a little over a month," she told me.

"What's wrong, Katya?" I asked, confused by the fact that she did not seem excited.

"I just was not sure how you would react," she told me. "I know that you also wanted a baby. Why, just last week, you told me that you were upset that you were not expecting yet."

"Oh, Katya," I said, waving away her worries with my hand. "That does not mean that I am not happy for you. Actually, I am quite ecstatic. What do you think it will be? A boy or a girl?"

"I have a strong feeling it will be a boy. Although, Alex said he wants a girl that will look like me. Either way, it doesn't matter." She blushed as she said it, and I smiled at the fact that Alex had managed to say something so flattering.

"I wish you all the happiness in the world, Katya. Keep praying that everything will work out for the best."

"My dear friend," Katya said as she looked at me, "I will. I will also pray that you will have your own little one to take care of soon."

"I certainly hope so." I could not help the note of doubt that crept into my voice. "I just hope that I am healthy enough. I am beginning to worry."

Katya smiled at me reassuringly and said, "You know, Anna, that you were weak for a long time. You may need some more time." Easy for her to say, I thought. Then I chided myself for thinking so. I only wanted the best for Katya, and I was truly happy for her.

That evening my mood worsened. I was pleased for Katya, yet I felt frustrated. I wondered why it seemed that everything worked out so well for Katya. I grew jealous of her. She was beautiful and kind, and she had not gone traipsing all over Canada in love with a man who did not love her. She would have never been so silly. As I was contemplating these thoughts, I heard Sima come up to the front door. I furiously pumped the water in our washbasin, pretending not to notice I heard him. I realized that being married did not allow you much time to be alone. I sometimes longed for that privacy. I felt that I had never had it since I left my Maine cabin.

Sima walked in and came up behind me. He then planted a kiss on my cheek. I threw him a look over my shoulder. He stood back and leaned against the table. He seemed to sense that something was bothering me, and he acted as if he would just stand there until I told him. I did not want to tell him the truth. I continued pumping water into the sink.

Sima gave a short laugh. "You know you might just flood the whole cabin if you pump harder."

I let the pump go and turned to look at him. "I apologize. I am not angry at you."

He crossed his arms across his chest. "That's good to know." He looked at me with a question in his expression. "I would appreciate it, however, if when I come to the door, you would at least greet me." I looked down at the floor. I felt embarrassed. He had done nothing to deserve my rude behavior.

"What's the matter?" he asked. I wiped my hands nervously on my apron. I could tell he was not happy with me and that something else weighed on his mind.

"I just need some time to think," I told him. "I need some privacy."

"You were here all day by yourself," he stated, sounding annoyed. It was the first time that I had heard him sound annoyed with me since we got married. Tears stung my eyes. I did not need him to be irritated with me.

"I wasn't," I snapped. I was surprised by how cross I sounded and quickly turned away from him.

"Anna, what's wrong?" Sima asked again with an edge to his voice. I turned back to him, and a tear rolled down my cheek.

His expression softened. "I can leave for twenty minutes and then come back." He pushed away from the table and seemed to be ready to go.

I came over to him and grabbed his hand. "Please don't. I suppose I do need to talk to you."

A smile came to his face, and he wrapped me in his arms and hugged me. I started to cry, and I pressed my face into his shoulder. He just held me and patted my back. He then sat me on the sofa and brewed us some tea. He came over to the sofa, handed me a teacup, and sat next to me.

"Are you better now?" he asked.

I wiped the tears from my eyes. I began to think that Sima thought that I was plain silly.

Sima took my hand in his. "So?"

"It's just that Katya was here today, and she told me," I started saying.

"Oh that," Sima cut me off and pressed my hand tighter with his. "Alex told me that they are expecting a baby. I did not understand why they did not tell us together. Of course, they are a bit strange. Anyway, it's not the end of the world. You still have plenty of time. You are not even twenty years old yet."

"It's not only that," I said. "I started to feel jealous of Katya, and I was angry at her for being so perfect all the time."

Sima gave me a sidelong glance. "Would you stop comparing yourself to her? Katya is very nice. She is also extremely boring. For example, I doubt that Alex would ever come home to her trying to flood the house in a fit of anger."

"Do you really feel that way?" I asked. I was beginning to feel much better already.

He grinned and put his arm around my shoulders. "Why do you think I married you? So that you could flood our cabin?"

"I'm sorry that I took out my anger on you," I apologized again.

"That's all right. I should apologize for being annoyed. It wasn't you either. I want to tell you something. I just do not know how you will react."

I sat up a little in expectation. "Yes?" I questioned.

He cleared his throat. "Well, I got a letter from my mother today."

"Why Sima, that's wonderful!" I exclaimed as I hugged him.

"It may not be so wonderful once you hear what she wrote." He took the letter from his pocket. The paper she wrote it on was pink with roses.

I wrinkled my nose. "Does she think you like roses?" I asked.

"No, but from what I remember, she does." He smiled and then opened up the letter. "Are you ready to listen?"

"Yes." I put my head on his shoulder and waited in expectation. He coughed and began to read.

My Dearest Seraphim,

I was more than relieved to receive your letter. I was glad to find out that you're still alive and that you are getting married. I, however, would have liked to meet your bride before the wedding. I hope she is a suitable young girl with good family ties. I do wonder where you met her, though. I doubt someone suitable would be at Fort Yukon. However, whoever she is, I would be happy to meet her. Your father and I hope that you and your wife will decide to grace us with your presence at some point. I know that you enjoy the Milichkovs' company. However, we are your family, and your father and I would love to help you set up a future here in Juneau. We know that this summer would not be suitable. Hopefully, next summer will be a better time for you to come. Please do come. I want to see what you look like.

Your Loving Mother

I just stared at Sima after he finished reading the letter. He sighed and then shrugged his shoulders. I had not realized that anyone could use the word love in a letter and yet make it sound so distant and unfriendly. I knew that he hoped to rekindle the ties with his family. When I married him, his dreams had to become my own, and no matter how much I would have loved to stay near the Milichkovs, I knew that it would be better for him to see his family again. Nevertheless, I was not sure that I wanted to leave.

"Do you want to go?" I asked him quietly.

"Yes," he answered as he gazed into my eyes. I could see a hidden pain in his expression. "I want them to meet you, whoever you may be," he said with a wry smile and then continued, "I want to see them. No matter how little they seem to care for me, they are my family. Also, I hear that Juneau has great opportunities. Don't you feel as if we take advantage of the Milichkovs' generosity at times? We would be able to be near a town. You could meet more people. What do you think?"

I could not answer Sima right away. I sat silently looking at my hand in his, thinking of what to say. If we left, we would be traveling to an unknown place with people unfamiliar to me.

I took a deep breath and said, "It seems like we just got settled here. It is difficult to think that we would have to travel so far to get there. Also, if we do go, we can't be sure of the circumstances that will be there. Living in Juneau might create more difficulties for us. I wish your parents could come here instead." I looked over at Sima, and he seemed to be disappointed by my answer.

"It would be another year before we leave. That way, you could see Katya's baby. If you have a baby by that time, we could also wait a little longer before we leave." He put his arm around my shoulders, and I leaned back against his arm.

"It's just that I hoped that we would be here for long. The thought of traveling anywhere is too overwhelming." I feared to travel. There was nothing more comforting than having a secure home with people that cared nearby.

"I agree with that," Sima said with a smile. "However, what do you propose we do? Just sit here in the Alaskan wilderness for the rest of our lives? It is Alex's family, not ours." While Sima sounded adamant, I noted a hint of confusion in his voice. His words reverberated through my mind. I realized that his parents were also now related to me, and it would be interesting to meet the people who were now part of my family. Also, I did ponder what Sima said about staying here for the rest of our lives. It was true that there were not many people around here. While I did not mind the secluded quiet, I knew that Sima could not remain without a whole group of friends around him. I thought back to how he had spent so much time talking to the men who had started the journey with us.

"Sima," I said and turned to look at him. "Wherever you go, I go. If you think we should go to Juneau, I will follow. I do think it may be a good idea. I am not sure that I can resign myself to living here in the northern part of Alaska for the rest of my life."

Sima's eyes lit up, and he asked, "Are you sure that you're not just agreeing with me to make me happy? I want us to make this decision together."

"Sima, I would do anything to make you happy. I want to go." Sima grinned and hugged me.

"There's only one thing," I started saying as I pressed my head against his shoulder.

"What?" Sima pulled back and looked at me quizzically.

"How do we tell your mother that I do not have any family ties?"

Sima chuckled and shook his head. "We can tell her you're an Athapaskan princess. Anyway, she can complain all she wants. If she had wanted to have a say in who I married, she should have had a say in the rest of my life. She will have to like you. I will not allow her to think of you badly."

"At least we have an entire year to prepare for our meeting," I said with a smile as I stood. "I have to go get the supper ready. I spent the whole day in the garden."

"I would like to see the progress you have made with your garden first. You are becoming so capable." Sima stood and put his arm around my waist, together we walked out of our cabin towards our newly planted vegetable garden.

*****

The following day, I decided to make myself useful and set out to scrub the floors. Hours in the garden and trekking in and out of the kitchen to the outdoors had created quite the mess. I sat scrubbing away at the dirt-caked floors.

"I don't know that I will ever get used to seeing you inside a house."

I straightened out and sat back against my heels. "How are you, Alex?" I wiped my forehead with the back of my hand. For some unexplained reason, I began to feel self-conscious.

Alex stood as tall as a maple tree, leaning against the door frame. "Where's Sima?"

I stood up from the ground and brushed the hair out of my face. "He's just out back. Would you like me to get him?" My hands shook a bit. I had not spoken to Alex alone since both of us had gotten married.

Alex stepped forward, and I noticed he held something in his hands. "I hope to speak to the both of you, if possible."

I walked towards the back door. "Just make yourself comfortable. I will be right back." I then sped out of the house to the rear garden.

Sima sat on his heels digging up weeds in the garden. He looked up at me as I came near. "What is it?"

I stopped to take a deep breath before speaking. "Alex is at the house. He asked me to come to get you."

Sima eyed me with a curious expression. "What's the urgency?"

"There is no urgency."

Sima shook his head. "Then why are you running like a woman with a wolf at her heels?"

I reached my hand out to him as he tried to stand. "I don't know. For some reason I felt the need to run." Sima leaned against me as he stood. "Sometimes, I really wonder about you." He then leaned down and kissed my forehead. There was a mischievous smile on his lips. "Come on."

Upon entering the cabin, Sima and I found Alex sitting on the couch. He still held the letter in his hands and smiled at both of us as we neared him. "Come sit down."

Sima sat on the couch next to Alex, and I sat on the rocking chair across from him. Sima turned to him. "What brings you out here on such a sunny day?"

Alex's expression turned serious. "You know that I wrote to Joseph Shubert last year before we reached home."

Sima and I both nodded in unison.

Alex shifted on the couch. "I just received this letter from him in return."

"Really?" Sima took the letter from Alex and began to study it. "What does he say? Did he make it back to Maine?"

"Yes," Alex replied in a sad tone. "Although it appears that he has broken all ties with his father who also made it back to Maine."

"What do you mean?" I questioned. "Jason Shubert returned to Maine? Did anyone else return with him?"

"The story seems odd to me. However, Jason Shubert was a man of opportunity. Do you remember that they told us at the fort that Jason had left his supplies there to be sent to Alaska? That is not true. Joseph writes that Mr. Shubert sold the supplies for-profit and then returned to Maine with two men, Steven Lake and Andrew Redlock. Red Fern had traveled as far as the fort and then went in search of Fur Hunter."

Sima studied the letter for a few seconds after Alex stopped speaking. "What Joseph writes appears to be true. We knew it to be odd that Mr. Shubert did not stop by Richard and Ellen's cabin. He knew better than any of us how to find that cabin."

I reached out and held Sima's hand. "Do you think he just left his men or led them into the storm to make a profit?"

Alex shook his head and answered before Sima could speak. "I doubt it. He probably did not intend for his men to become lost. However, as I said before, he was a man of opportunity. He saw his chance for profit without the hassle and took it."

Sima hung his head. "It is sad though that so many men put his trust in him."

I squeezed Sima's hand. "Perhaps it is not as bleak as it sounds. Possibly he had no way out. He might have needed that money for his journey home."

Alex took back the letter from Sima. "We might never know. Still, it seems that Jason Shubert returned to Maine and continues to grow rich."

A tear came to my eye, and I tried to blink it away. "Those poor men, Matthew Davis, Joseph Smith, and Fur Hunter, how could they just be left to die? Selling those supplies and making a profit is a disservice to those men, no matter what the reason."

Alex chuckled a bit. Sima looked over at him with an annoyed expression. "What is it that you find amusing?"

"Oh, Joseph Shubert writes that he is getting married."

"To whom? While I have more respect for him now than I ever did, I cannot imagine who would want to marry him."

"Matthew Davis's widow is engaged to him. He looked her up when he returned to Maine, and they have become friends. It seems he has become a changed man."

Sima smiled. "I hope so, at least for Matthew's sake."

I stood and put my arm around Sima's shoulder. "Perhaps it was meant to be this way. Matthew Davis's wife will find comfort, and Joseph Shubert will become a better man."

Alex stood. "It is strange how all of our paths seemed to pivot around this one event. You and Sima might have never gotten married if we had not gotten lost."

Sima stood as well and pulled me closer to him. "I will forever be grateful that our path led us to safety."

Alex then came over to us and wrapped his arms around us. We stood together, bound by a blanket of comfort and safety. Sima, Alex, and I, the three that made it to Alaska.

I held on to both of them. "You will never know how grateful I am to God that He sent the both of you to me. You are my family."

"I love both of you." Sima pulled us closer to him. "No matter what happens or where we go from here, don't you ever forget that."

Chapter 33

"Are you all set?" Sima asked as he regarded me from the ground. I sat on the wagon seat, waiting for him to join me.

"Yes," I answered with a sigh. I looked back at the Milichkovs' cabin. A year had passed too quickly for me, and we were about ready to start our new journey to Juneau. At least this time, we were traveling by wagon and boat, and it was summer.

Mrs. Milichkova walked out of the cabin at that moment. In her hands, she held a large basket of food for us. "Do not forget this," she told Sima as she came up to him.

He took the basket laden with food from her hands and handed it up to me. "How could we forget?" He embraced her.

She smiled as she returned his embrace. "I will miss both of you so much." I looked down at the small woman who housed so much love and knowledge. My head spun when I thought about how much I would miss her and her husband.

"You will have plenty to take care of without us," Sima said as his gaze shifted over to Alex and Katya, who were standing not far from the wagon. Katya held their son, Joseph, in her hands. She had given birth to him almost four months ago, and he was growing rapidly. My heart hurt when I thought about the fact that I would not see them for several years. Katya and I promised each other that we would write as much as possible. No matter what happened, I knew that I would never forget Katya or Alex.

Mr. Milichkov came around from the other side of the wagon. "The horses seem to be in good condition." Mr. Milichkov had given us two of his best horses as a gift. I did not know how we would ever repay him for his generosity. He stood next to his wife now and put a hand on her shoulder.

Sima glanced back at me and then turned to everyone. "I do think we should be going. We do want to get an early start. We do not want to be late. The wagon train from Fort Yukon will be stopping about five miles south of here around suppertime."

"Yes, we can't delay your departure forever," Alex said. The look on his face told me that he wished we would never leave. Sima nodded in agreement and then turned and climbed into the wagon.

"May God be with you," Mr. Milichkov said as Sima sat down next to me.

"With you too," Sima answered. We both gave the family one last long look. I tried to save the picture of them in my mind so I would never forget how they looked that morning.

"Until a future meeting," Alex said with a hopeful smile.

"Most certainly," Sima told him. He then clicked his tongue, and the horses started to lumber forward.

I turned to look back at the group behind us. Alex and Katya raised their hands in a silent goodbye, and I waved back to them. I could feel tears stinging my eyes. I kept my eyes on the cabin and the people in front of it until we pulled out of sight.

"Are you all right?" Sima asked as he looked over at me. He had not glanced back once.

"It was time for us to go." I let out a long breath. "I just wish that parting was not so difficult."

"We'll see them again. You can count on it." Sima then put his hand on my back and kissed my forehead.

"I will pray every day that we do meet again. Nevertheless, no matter what happens, we're together; that's the most important part."

"Yes, we're together," Sima agreed. He then winked at me. "And I am not going anywhere."

"I certainly hope not," I replied as I wrapped my arm around his waist. We then continued to travel into the unpredictable Alaskan wilderness and towards our new adventure.

Made in United States
North Haven, CT
29 July 2022

21985009R00257